The

WAR

WITHIN

THE WAR WITHIN

Cover composite © Shutterstock.com

Cover and layout design by theBookDesigners

First Edition

Printed in the United States

ISBN 978-0-9838165-3-9

The

WAR
WITHIN

PAULIE P. NICOLL

Eddie Ranch
PUBLICATIONS

DEDICATION

For Russell Palmer, whose documentary provided the genesis for this story but not the plot line, and his wife, Mona, who provided the genesis for my family.

SPECIAL THANKS

*To all the readers who endured all
those readings so patiently: The Sacred Sisters
(Dave included), San Ysidro Writers, as well as
Mona and Tom, Teri, Pat and Pat, Jake and
Kat and special thanks to Chris who encouraged
me to dance like no one was watching and to sing
like no one was listening.*

Prologue

He's said it over and over. Shouted it even—I'm a journalist, an American journalist. If only his hands weren't tied behind his back, he'd show them his papers. They'd never shoot him then. They must have heard him, they had to—he's said it so many times the words were burnt into the back of his throat. He's tired. Confused. His Spanish isn't that good. Maybe the words never escaped his throat. No one has said anything. They haven't even looked at him. Not the man at the back of the truck, not the man with the gun.

An hour ago, maybe two, the numbness in his fingers had spread up his arms. Sometime during the night the ropes binding him stopped burning. The blood running down his wrists and into his cupped hands feels warm. For some reason this comforts him and then the truck brakes to a stop. He's thrown to the floor. Someone yanks the canvas tarp back. Grabs him by the lapels. Throws him to the ground. A bone cracks. He feels no pain, only terror. He fights to control it, he won't give them the satisfaction—he's an American, an American journalist, it will be all right. It has to. He has to get back. To Helen, his wife, the child. Oh God, what have they done—

A soldier jams the butt of a rifle into his back and pushes him toward a wall. The soldier says nothing. He doesn't have to. The moon gives off just enough light—

He sees the other trucks.

The other prisoners.

The pockmarks scarring the wall.

BOOK ONE

1950

ONE

A Sea of Remembrance

"Memory is the diary we all carry with us."

—OSCAR WILDE, *The Importance of Being Earnest*

AN ILLUSION IS defined as an erroneous perception of reality. The summer of 1950 was such a time. America saw the world as an idyllic place. The war was over, signs of prosperity spread across the face of the globe. From its lofty perch the American Eagle looked down on it all. Perhaps a bit nearsighted, it could be said to overlook a few blemishes, small pimples; but Stalin had fallen from favor and the fascists defeated across Central Europe. Even the civil war in Spain had faded from the papers and had, as yet, to make the history books. Almost no one paid it any mind. Certainly not Pru's fellow passengers aboard Cunard's luxury liner as it sailed out of Lisbon bound for Istanbul.

Pru would disembark during a stopover in Málaga. *That's when,* she thought, *it will all come back and I'll have no choice but to face it.* Over the years she'd done her best to forget Spain; but civil war, death and destruction were not easily forgotten, not even after fourteen years. Battles maybe—dates, places of her childhood—who fought and what they fought for, got muddled up in

13

her mind. Even things she saw with her own eyes became subject to the vagaries of memory. Memories were fallible—a thing said on a warm March day could drift in her mind to August or even spill from year to year. Things she heard or read about could find their way into the mix. What was real and what was remembered didn't always stay the same.

But if she were to turn on a radio and hear Joe McCarthy trying to convince the world that communists and anarchists hid under every bed, it could all come flooding back: the crackle of bonfires, the chatter of rifles and the acrid smell of gun powder. And all those other *ists*, the ones no one talked about anymore—Royalists, Loyalists, Falangists—they still troubled her.

As the ship drew closer to Málaga, her apprehension grew. Other passengers might vie for spots on the shuffleboard court, or jostle their way across crowded dance floors, but Pru kept to herself. One day out of Lisbon and already she had her deck chair staked out. She spent her days staring out at a sea so vast, so impersonal, her apprehension found ample room to grow. Even the soft moist breezes coming off the sea failed to give her peace of mind—a peace that had eluded her ever since that day in Rodicio when her father made his way down the steps of the *Casa de Carrillo*, folded his portly frame into his limo, slammed the door and drove off, his secretary at his side. Neither Pru nor her mother had seen him since.

Roland P. Whitley disappeared fourteen years, ten months and twenty-three days ago—there were times it seemed to Pru that all this happened yesterday.

It was but a short time later—one or two days at most—around midnight something heavy had slammed against the door to the *Casa de Carrillo*. Memories of that night always came flooding back in short bursts like grainy flickers of an old black and white film. Maybe it was less painful that way.

Some commotion in the street must have woken her because she was already at the head of the stairs when the soldier banged his gun against the door. A moment later she sensed her mother coming up behind her. Leaning over the rail the two watched as one of the maids struggled to slide back the heavy bolt. With the door opened but the smallest of cracks, the man used the butt of his rifle to shove his way in.

"*Señora* Whitley," he shouted, "Come down at once."

"I will not. You have no right to barge into my house? I shall call the—?"

"*La policia?* Bah! What can they do? I am in charge now. It is not for you to ask about rights. You have none."

Prudence grabbed hold of her mother's robe but her mother brushed her hand away and motioned for her to stay back as she started down. How slowly, how regally she made her way to the bottom of the stairs. How sure of herself she appeared until the man raised the butt of his gun and rushed at her.

Even now, here on the deck of the Caronia II the sound of her mother's screams came to Pru over the waves that rocked the boat. And the soldier, she could remember him right down to the missing button on his dirty brown shirt. How could she forget the way he waved his rifle around the room shouting *¡Càllarse, Càllarse!* Then the soldier grabbed her mother's arm and shook her violently.

Pru could still feel the sting of her own palm as she slapped her hand across her mouth, that little taste of blood when she bit her tongue.

"*No habla español"* the soldier had said with an impatient shrug. "Perhaps you understand better if I say the shut up, no?"

But her mother couldn't or wouldn't stop. One of the maids appeared at her mother's side, "*Por favor Señora,* you must stop the screams, you are only making the more anger."

At last her mother stopped.

"Your husband, *Señora*, he has…we have…that is to say … he is dead." Her mother's face turned as white as her dressing gown and the screaming began again.

"We are not animals," he bellowed. "We will send to you the body; but you, your child, you must leave Spain at once."

"What do you mean? How do you know? Why? Why would—?"

"If I say it is so, it is so." He put his fist right up in her mother's face and shook a crumpled piece of paper at her. From the balcony Pru saw it as yellow with a splash of red across the back. And then again she might not have seen it at all. She was sure, though, of what the man said: "Señor Roland P. Whitley *es morte.*"

Though hindered at every turn, eventually she and her mother had made their way through the Spanish countryside, across the Atlantic, and then to California. No coffin ever followed. Only ugly memories, rumor-laden telegrams, letters and refugees reached that pretentious mansion at the foot of the Sierra Madres with its nine bedrooms, ten bathrooms, private screening room, and a dining room large enough to feed a film crew. *La Casa de la Paloma del Anida*—the house of the nesting dove. Pru, Henri, her mother and Bazil might have messed up the sheets in its various bedrooms, but no one could be said to nest there.

As long as Pru could recall Bazil was the expert on the legend that was her mother even though she wasn't sure when they first met. But that day in 1936, the day they drove to Madrid to see the Prado he already knew her mother. He even called her Marion. Her mother always had, still had many admirers but it wasn't only her movies that held Bazil enthralled. What ever it was he hadn't left Marion's side for long, not willingly.

"You should have seen Marion in her thirties," Pru

remembered him saying. "She made me short of breath. It's no wonder she is admired all over the world." Even in California all those years later Bazil attended every screening of her films, arranged benefits, charity showings and treated her mother with a tenderness Pru envied. He saw to it that Marion stayed on the guest list of most everyone's parties and that her own were well attended. Her popularity with the theatrical crowd, the gossip columns hinted, had more to do with her role as a backer than the parts she played. The fact that the money for this backing came from Bazil escaped almost everyone's notice. Even Marion's. But there was no escaping her mother's beauty.

Now, at twenty-seven, no one referred to Pru as beautiful—striking was the word used. Her features were sharp, her eyes held a gray green cast—little escaped them. And, though she was tall for a woman, she never stooped and wore high heels whenever the mood struck her. Pru didn't have, didn't even want, that feminine beauty, that Alice Faye softness that was so popular. Looking around at the women occupying the other deck chairs, she saw dozens with that look, but still none quite as beautiful as her mother.

Who could blame Bazil? Just when he and her mother became lovers, Pru didn't know. Maybe they never had. Most children avoid picturing their parents in the throes of passion. Pru was no exception. Besides her Mother's Protestant reserve, her subtle aloofness would seem to rule passion out. But then, her mother *was* an actress...? It didn't really matter; this was Hollywood and most of the refugees who arrived in California declared her father already dead. Her friends granted her the right to be passionate. Hollywood gave little credence to the concept of faithfulness, and faithfulness to the supposed dead was nothing short of an absurdity.

Many of the refugees claimed to have heard the whine, the

whistle, of the very bullet that shot him. Others swore he still strutted the streets of Málaga, swinging his pearl-handled cane or that they had seen him at the bullfights, at the cafés. Pru had no trouble believing the strutting part, and her father did love the bulls; but she swore she saw that cane lying on the floor of the *Casa de Carillo,* broken in half. One or two refugees insisted they caught a glimpse of him peering out a window of the *Casa.* There was always something vague about the details, something a little off about their stories. Surely the execution of an American so early in the war would have made the papers. As to his being seen at the Casa, Pru remembered the windows of the ground floor as heavily barred and set a distance from the street.

Even now, as the *Carona* steamed its way towards Málaga rumors were all she had to bring with her. Those cables and letters that arrived daily brought reminders of things best left unremembered—the anarchists had taken Rodicio; the villas of the wealthy were going up in flames; the nationalists had buried the nuns alive; the Moors had arrived and stopped people in the streets to cut out their tongues; and the fascists had stormed Barcelona. Each rumor more vicious than the one before, no side was left unscathed. It puzzled Pru for a long time that each refugee appeared to need shelter from a different "ists." How to make sense of such a war? But perhaps it was hard to make sense of any war. As to her father, could he have survived in such a war?

Her mother ignored the rumors. They were told with such relish she assumed that a bit of Hollywood make-believe infected everyone. But even while denying the veracity of the letters and telegrams, Marion made a habit of dividing them into three stacks. Those answered on the spot, a small number assigned to Bazil, and a more elusive group that disappeared into her desk. A sleight of hand, a click of a key and they vanished.

Her mother seemed to think no one noticed. As a child

surrounded by grownups that for the most part ignored her, what else could she do but watch people, the way they looked, the way they moved, the clothes they wore. It was a habit that died hard. At art school her teachers had praised her eye for detail. But still, if it hadn't been for an off-hand remark of her mother's lover, she might never have learned of a rather large lapse in her powers of observation—the reason for all this secrecy.

One morning, as her mother prepared to work her magic on yet another envelope, Bazil slipped. "Damn it all, Marion that husband of your's and his damn calling cards, he certainly managed to scatter them about." Her mother's face told Pru those calling cards had nothing to do with the engraved ones her mother's friends made such a ritual of passing around.

Later that same day as Marion nodded off over her third martini, Pru pried open the offending drawer and discovered the "calling cards"—a brother here, a sister there, as many siblings as envelopes. *Lies, they must all be lies.* Marion might be good at pretending, or even at ignoring the truth, but hiding something required effort. If something bothered her, she was more likely to get someone else to fix things—Bazil was always at the ready. So why would she take the trouble to hide a lie? A door long closed swung open, something Pru had heard on a beach somewhere—Nanny knocking over their sandcastle in her hurry to get her charge away from a gossiping group of women. Half-hidden under a yellow umbrella, their laughter cut the damp air: "Look at her, poor thing, playing by herself, thinks she's an only child."

Was it the thought of these calling cards or the ever increasing size of the waves buffeting the side of the *Carona II* that made Pru feel a little sick? *How long could a mother keep something like that to herself?*

Some people saw Marion as an actress past her time, many found her helpless without Bazil but Pru saw her more as an enigma—a woman who gave the appearance of needing help; yet a woman who knew where she was going and what she wanted when she got there. She was a woman who liked her gin cold, her nails long and juicy scripts with lead roles to showcase her talent. A woman who went so far as to select her friends— as she did her clothes—for their ability to flatter and further her career. Her closets overflowed with props that helped her be what she was not. They protected her from prying eyes and granted her immunity from the truth.

But, at the same time, if a male came within the periphery of her vision, Marion could wilt like a fragile flower in need of tender care. *But hiding brothers, and sisters? How could she?* That might be carrying the enigma business too far.

Stop! Don't think about that. Pru remembered telling herself to close the drawer. She couldn't. Surely even now she would drown in a wave of nostalgia even as she wondered how she could be nostalgic over something, someone she never knew?

Photographs, there must be photographs, she had thought. *Would their hair be brown?* Like hers? *Their eyes blue?* Would they have her father's strong nose? Her mother's beauty?

"Your mother's beauty is like a Greek statue," her father once said. "Classic, timeless."

As a child, Pru had wondered why anyone would want a Greek statue for a mother, their eyes held no pupils.

"But they can't see," she told her father.

"Women don't want to," he'd said.

"Why?"

"Trust me, they don't."

Was that when she started to question a lot of what he said? After all wasn't she even then a woman? Well, almost. And she wanted to see everything.

But that evening, before Pru had time to wonder what other secrets those drawers held, she had heard footsteps striking the tile floor. Bazil, her mother's most ardent protector, loomed in the doorway. She slammed the drawer shut and looked up into eyes darkened with a dangerous challenge.

"Stamps, I'm looking for stamps, that's all," she mumbled.

"And you found—?"

"Nothing. Nothing at all."

"*Señora*, a cocktail?" The voice of the head steward startled her out of her reverie. In starched white and covered with enough gold braid to rival the captain, he bent over her, a solicitous look on his face. "Madame, I think the ocean is getting a bit rough, perhaps you should go—"

"Thank you no, I'm fine." But she wasn't. So many memories, so close to the surface. Would she never be rid of them? She wouldn't be here on shipboard now, wading through the past, if she hadn't lost yet one more argument with her mother.

The steward retreated, her memories advanced. Had it only been a few weeks earlier, back in California, that Pru came down to breakfast to find a plate of scrambled eggs strewn across the floor and Marion holding a cable out in front of her like a thing contaminated. When she caught sight of Pru she had let it flutter to the ground. Pru bent down and shook off little bits of egg, fragments of china and read: *It is necessary for you to know that he lives, this meddler in—*Marion made a grab for it.

"Money, that's what the bitch wants, it's what they all want."

"Who?" Pru asked.

"The conniving little bitch, it has to be her."

Pru felt a chill as if a window opened and something blew in that sucked the breath from the room. Marion froze in place, her lips stretched in such a tight fierce line no words could escape. Pru looked to Bazil for an answer.

He cleared his throat. "There's nothing to be done for it, Marion you must go back to Spain. Either we find him, or we put a stop to these rumors. I love you, Marion, you know I do; but this not knowing—I can only take so much."

"God knows I loved that man, I never did believe he could be dead, not dead dead, not a man like that; but Bazil darling— my nerves—you don't really expect me to face him?"

"Most likely there's no one to face; but someone —" As one they turned and looked at Pru.

"Oh no, no you don't."

"Really darling, someone must go."

For days that *someone* had hung in the air unclaimed. Marion, the actress, pulled out all the stops. She gave one of her award-winning performances laced with guilt. Not that she needed guilt to lure most people to her bidding. She "cultivated," her word not Pru's, her femininity, her charms. Men and women rushed to do her bidding—more men than women. But when dealing with Pru, who didn't think much of feminine charms, her mother required other tactics: migraine headaches, sulks, spells of weepiness. Dressed in a feathery negligee, cheeks stained with rivulets of mascara, she would declare herself too distraught to join them for a meal. Pru liked to think she was immune to such tricks and often neglected to arm herself against the woman of the fragile negligee. A mistake. To do battle with her mother was to fight whipped cream.

"Be reasonable, darling. You know . . . my migraine . . ."

"Be reasonable, darling, you know I have an interview coming, a chance for a part—"

It might be true, it might not. Living with an actress made it difficult to tell fact from fiction.

Her mother fired off one more *be reasonable* before she left the field of battle to Bazil, "Be reasonable, Pru darling, I am your mother after all."

Bazil took up the *be reasonable* cause. "Pru, saying a husband is dead and proving he is are two different things. We must recover a body or we'll never recover our lives. It's for your own good too, you know. You and Henri, you are married, you shouldn't have to live here, and there's your painting, your studio down—"

"You know about that?"

"Of course. I make it my business to take care of you."

"But, Bazil, I'm twenty-seven, I can—"

"I still think of you as that scared child I helped up onto my yacht all those years ago."

Pru looked closely at him, he had aged a bit. Not much. He still possessed that same dash, that same flare he had when she first saw him. But of course to him she had been a child and apparently, to him, she still was.

"And Mother? " Pru knew her mother did little watching over anyone these days. "Does she know about my studio?"

"No, no sense upsetting her. I followed you one day ... *that* place, the whole scene would horrify Marion. She thinks you're still at your lessons at the college."

"But Bazil, it's you and Mother who aren't being reasonable, it isn't my place—"

"Pru, of course it's your place . . . you're so much more competent than your mother."

"Competent? For God's sake, Bazil, the last thing I want is to be thought competent." Competent meant dull. What artist would want to be thought of as dull?

"Be reasonable, Pru."

"You be reasonable, Bazil."

"Who's not being reasonable, darling?"

Pru whirled around. Her mother stood there. How much had she heard?

"You aren't," she stammered, "Going to Spain could be dangerous. What do any of us know of assassins, firing squads? Do they stop to bury the dead in the middle of a war? Do they even want to?

"Stop it, Pru, we promised we'd never talk of those—"

"No, Mother, you promised. I can't forget and I can't pretend that I have—the shooting, the bodies—"

"Stop! My heart! My heart!"

"You stop it. You're not as good an actress as you think, there's nothing wrong with your heart."

"What do you mean? You know how often the doctor comes."

"Yes, but I'm not blind. He never appears until after five, deposits his bag on the hall table and joins you in the parlor for cocktails."

"You have no right to pry—"

"Into what, mother? The truth?"

TWO

Costly Aftermath

"How alike are the groans of love to those of the dying."

—MALCOLM LOWRY, *Under the Volcano*

THE STEWARD WAS RIGHT, the waves were thumping against the side of the ship, one or two even breached the rail. Most of her fellow deck chair loungers had gone below; but her memories weren't through with Pru yet—the quarrel with her mother still rang in her ears.

She had run from the room, gathered her thoughts, her car keys and fled. When she pulled up in front of her studio, its sagging porch, torn screens and paint-smeared door made her send Bazil a mental thank you. She worked hard at keeping the two sides of her life separate. Her mother would not only find her studio "distasteful"—a favorite but damning word of Marion's—she would ridicule Pru's ambition: "Women are meant to be the muse, not the artist," a role Marion didn't seem to realize she refused for herself.

It was hard enough for Pru to make her way in this enclave of art studios without her fellow painters knowing she was the daughter of a famous actress and the wife of an important film director. In the art world Pru wanted only to be Pru.

She edged her way up the splintered stairs and went inside. *Damn!* A glittery blob of gold paint glared accusingly at her from a corner of her latest canvas. Though she could never remember actually painting it, still somewhere in all her works, a patch of gold could be found. In a quasi landscape, it might appear caught in the fronds of a palm tree or lying on a plate in a cubistic still life. Pru had no interest in painting the world as others saw it; she wanted people to see the world as she did. But why this gold? What drove her to paint such a thing? She didn't know, but she could no more control its appearance than she could control her fights with her mother.

The discovery that once again this splash of gold had found its way into her work sent her reeling down a long, familiar spiral of self-doubt. She spent hours throwing good paint after bad and getting nowhere.

Finally, without even bothering to clean up her palette or soak her brushes, she headed for the bar—that ugly building that squatted along the sidewalk like a tired wino, its padded leather doors cracked and torn, cotton stuffing hanging out. She ignored it all and stepped into a shower of pulsating light raining down from the neon shamrock perched on the roof. She reached out and closed her hand around those little green motes, those elusive promises of warmth. How easy to deceive those who wish to be deceived.

A new freeway severed this area from the no-money-down tracts, their neighborhood schools and Cub Scout packs. On the wrong side of the town, lawns browned, flowers died and families abandoned row after row of 1930's California Bungalows. The Abbey Brothers, grandsons of a silver baron, needing a mother lode of their own, bought up five square blocks of bungalow and erected huge signs: Starving Artist's Studios to let. For a steady income, they converted an old market into a warehouse and filled it with rolls of linen canvas, bins of stretcher bars, boxes of brittle charcoal, tubes of paint and drawers lined with brushes—flat ones to lay down broad swatches of de Kooning color, chiseled ones to carve decisive outlines of thick, chunky, Picasso blacks, or soft wisps of sable to scumble on layers of Kokoschka mystery. None of which, she suspected, the brothers cared one wit about. For the real moneymaker they tore out the lanes of an old bowling alley, enlarged the bar and hung up a dartboard. After hoisting the clover onto the roof, they opened a tab for every tenant. If they didn't get your money one way, they'd get it another.

She might not have cared much for their tactics, but it was only in their bar, her studio, that she came close to shedding the feeling that her life amounted to little more than a cameo in one of Marion's films.

She pushed open the door to a room lit only by the Hamm's bear paddling upstream and the glow from little picture lights that lined the walls. A rich mix of stale whiskey, cheap cigars and unwashed bodies hit her in the same visceral way as rich blobs of impasto. Patsy Cline's *I fall to Pieces* and shouted endorsements for this brand of linseed oil, that kind of turpentine drowned out the clack of pool balls as Pru made her way to the already crowded bar. She passed up the group hurling insults at the ignorance of the art-buying public, their predilection for haggling. She'd heard it all before. She even passed up the coat and tie set of the California Eucalyptus School and their never-ending war against the coverall and blue jeans crowd with their calloused disrespect of the masters. She waved to the crowd at the back of the room, the smattering of black-clad poets spouting their existentialist theories about "the best minds of their generation."

She elbowed her way through the crowd huddled on the

barstools. The odors—Vitalis, Life Boy, the lack of it—wrapped around her. She embraced the camaraderie that rose with the smoke even knowing that it would evaporate when the lights went out and the artists returned to their easels, its transitory nature only heightened its effect.

Bear-like arms grabbed her from behind. She didn't have to turn around, she recognized the sculptor whose studio lay across the alley from hers, by the smell of damp clay that clung to his beard.

"There you are, thought you weren't coming tonight—"

"Precisely what I wanted you to think."

"How about a martini, on me?"

"No thanks."

"Turning me down again? What makes you think you're so special?"

"If I'm not, why waste good gin on me?"

For an answer he raised his glass and waved his arms around the room pointing out the drawings, the watercolors that lined the walls and raised his glass. She blushed.

Too stubborn to owe anybody, her husband, her mother or the Abbey Brothers, she modeled at Rio College. Seven dollars an hour—ten if she took off her clothes—covered a lot of supplies. There was a drawback. Allowed to run tabs, the students who did their drinking here paid up with images of Pru's face, her body. In charcoal, oils or pastels, she appeared in small paper squares taped to the walls, little price stickers dotted the corners— fifteen dollars, twenty dollars. Usually she ignored it, but tonight it bothered her that she came so cheap. So many Prus, each one different, each one the way someone else saw her, or wanted to. Often it amused her that none of them appeared to get it right, at least not in the way she saw herself.

Though there were a few people who said she looked like

her mother—well, almost, she knew she failed to produce the same effect. Her mother was an actress after all. At first Pru had thought Henri Brancusi the exception, but in truth she had little to do with attracting him. Marion had pushed him her way. How better to land a starring role than to have a famous director for a son-in-law.

And so Pru, at twenty-two, in a weak moment—one of those little parentheses of life where one didn't know what direction to take—decided to wed Brancusi, the least macho of the producers and most talented of the directors her mother pushed her way. She had grown tired of her mother's meddling. Marriage would get her out from under the Whitley name and maybe even buy her time to make her own.

The ceremony went well, even with the columnists and their speculations as to why a man with a Michelangelo physique, Botticelli face, and a full staff of cooks, would settle for the daughter. But all went well, no histrionics, no tears marred the ceremony, not Marion's anyway. Pru did detect a drop of moisture in the corner of the Best Man's eye.

That night in the bridal suite of The Beverley Hills Wilshire, as she fidgeted with the appliqué on her negligee and Brancusi filled and refilled his champagne glass until he had poured enough courage to confess: "Forgive me, *mon cheri*, I thought I could do this but, I am *peu dispose.* . .that is you are a lovely woman, but that's the problem, dear heart. You are a girl. Please forgive me, I am so sorry…I should have…it's not too late, we can do something—an annulment…"

Not as shocked as her new husband might have thought she would be, it had only taken Pru a moment or two to digest this before she laughed.

"My motives aren't all that nobler," she admitted. "I was hoping to rid myself… let's just—"

"Give it a try? I could use a pretty woman on my arm—all those rumors, so ugly."

Oddly enough the marriage had worked. Neither one demanded faithfulness, instead they became friends. Pru had always found love difficult to find and impossible to understand. Besides, they both agreed that good friends were harder to come by than lovers.

She was careful to keep all this from her portrayers. Not even the sculptor knew who her husband was, who her mother was. That's the way she wanted it. The two sides of her life were so different. Somehow she preferred the harsh judgments of the art crowd with their sincerity to the cunning flattery of the Hollywood crowd.

The sculptor might be the exception. She elbowed him out of the way and ordered a hamburger. He was a one for the money, two for the show kind of artist. He pummeled and pounded mounds of clay into plump, silky skinned dolphins for the Abbey brothers, and trotted spindly, tortured figures around to the "arty" galleries.

"Tell me," she said as she picked a piece of clay out of his beard, "if someone paid you to fashion your clay into a ball and drop it in the river, how long would it take you to do it? One hour? Two?"

"With a tongue like that who needs wire to cut clay; but hey, it's Friday night. I'm the forgiving kind. Now, how about that drink?"

"Food, I need food."

"One must feed more than the belly, from the look of those," he nodded towards the wall, "you could do with a little less flesh."

"*Touché.*" A truce established, they laughed. One of only three women in the bungalows, most of the men either resented or ignored her. California's pot of gold was not as large as legend would have it, galleries were few, competition fierce. They would have liked her better if she acted a little more like a woman and less like an artist. She didn't want to be liked, only respected. So far she's managed to stay clear of entanglements. They were messy.

The sculptor put a proprietary arm around her, and called to the waitress, "A hamburger for my Georgia O'Keefe wanna-be; and a—"

"Burgundy." She had let his arm stay that night, she needed companionship. And so, when two martinis arrived and no burgundy, she shrugged and stirred the gin with her olive. By the third or fourth sip she settled comfortably into its icy warmth, grateful for the way the gin separated her from her thoughts.

Even here on the ship's deck she could still see the way the sun had streamed in on the sculptor's half finished maquettes, his tables piled high with lumpy clay, their edges scarred by chisels. In the light of morning, what she wanted to forget rushed back—that troublesome gold spot of paint, to say nothing of a troublesome mother, a distraught Bazil. Like a bad cough, her troubles wouldn't go away.

Her skin raw from the weight of the sculptor, damp from his heat, a flush crept across her face, moved down her body. She looked over at the sculptor, his eyes shut, his face puffy with the gin. *Oh shit.* She struggled to slide her arm out from underneath his head, put her feet over the side of bed and stood up. She'd only wanted to let down her guard a bit, soak up a bit of distraction. From the taste in her mouth she got more drink than distraction. Better to leave before he wakes, she thought. Later she'd convince him nothing happened, that he was unsteady on his feet and she helped him home. Anything more he must have imagined.

She took one last look, picked up her clothes and headed for his windowless, dank bathroom, covered with peeling paper and crumbling bits of wallboard. No money wasted on renovation here. She flicked on the light, steeled herself to ignore the scuttle of roaches and opened the cupboard tacked to the wall and rummaged through crumpled tubes of toothpaste, Brylcreem. The only tidy thing in the whole place was a forlorn pile of foil packages stacked in anticipation. Behind that, aspirin. She spotted the encrusted glass perched on the sink and gulped the pills down dry—his place, its dust, its disorganization, a perfect metaphor for her own life.

What did she have? Nothing. She drifted. On some days Brancusi's friendship fulfilled her; on others she ached for more. Things like this were bound to happed. Incapable or stubbornly unwilling to come to terms with her mother, she had yet to break away. Even Henri had grown tired of the constant wrangling between his wife and his mother-in-law.

"It won't be forever," she told him, "but the picture of Mother, crushed and humiliated after her appearance before the House Un-American Activities Commission—I can't forget that." She hadn't gone on to tell him of another picture of her mother that never left her: her mother in Cadiz hurling her own daughter's diary over the ship's rail. Pru could still see the way the book had caught the breeze. For a second it had hung suspended, its little gold lock glinting in the sun. Then like a gull in search of sustenance, it plunged beneath the water, leaving her with nothing but memories. How could she explain to Henri that both of these women were her mother—and she loved the one and had such mixed feelings about the other?

As a child, people often declared her wise beyond her years, yet she knew she could be such a childish adult. At twenty-seven she still floundered. How could she get at the truth of her life, her mother's life, when memory was the great distorter? Despite the adage "out of the mouths of babes," children seldom knew the truth. Grownups went to such lengths to hide it from them.

She used her paintbrush as a weapon to lead her to the truth but lately it seemed that it too might fail her. Or was she failing it? Henri, always supportive of her work, told her "the problem might be that you don't stick to one theme long enough to plumb its depths. It's in those depths that art lies. You act as if you're afraid to get to the bottom of a thought, of life."

She hadn't answered, though she knew what she feared all right—she feared that she might reach that illusive bottom and find nothing there—no talent, no depth, no insight.

She slipped into her things and headed for the door, the fight with her mother fresh in her head. *Damn it anyway*—what does a daughter owe a father? Promises kept? A final resting place? And this daughter, that father? A spider that spun a web so strong, she had yet to escape—did she owe such a father anything? As for her mother, despite the animus that hung over them like a cloud of insects on a summer's night, she knew what she owed; but how much, for how long?

People said doors bang shut, lives change, but life wasn't a series of clean breaks. . It was messy. One period merged into another and another, leaving sticky fingerprints.

Maybe she had lived too much of her life by others' rules—one of those, the most costly had come from her father: "Your mother is not strong, not as strong as you. Promise me you will take care of her when—" He never finished his sentence. She wasn't even sure when she had first heard it. Later, after he left, she couldn't help but wonder—*had he known, even then, that the day would come when he would just drive away?*

At the window of the sculptor's bungalow, she finally admitted to herself what Bazil and Henri had tried to tell her all along—she would never be free of that promise until they all, Marion, Bazil and Pru, learned what had happened or hadn't happened to Roland P. Whitley. The truth seemed as elusive as her father.

By the time she got back to the *Casa de la Paloma,* Bazil was already on the phone booking her flight to New York, a liner to Portugal and finally passage to Málaga.

"But Bazil—"

"No more excuses, Pru. I won't ask where you've been but you're going. It will be all right, I'll have people on tap to help you. The war is over. You have nothing to fear."

"It's not that I'm afraid, Bazil. Not of the soldiers—" *Well, maybe a little.* "It's just—"

"Just what, Pru?"

"Isn't this the wife's job—?"

"You know as well as I do Marion could never do it. And that's that."

"That was that all right!

"That was what, dear?" One brave lady still occupied the neighboring deck chair. She put down her book, pulled her ridiculously large sunglass down to the tip of her nose and peered at Pru. "You do look a bit on the pale side, dearie." With a little pat to Pru's arm, she chided, "We're not a wee bit seasick, are we now?"

Pru was sick all right. But it was memories that sickened her, not the sea.

THREE

Closed Shutters

"To return thence, by the way speediest, where our beginnings are."

—SOPHOCLES, *Oedipus Coloneus*

TWO DAYS LATER, on the top deck of the Caronia II, Pru shielded her eyes against the glare bouncing off the whitewashed houses that clung to the hills behind Málaga. Somewhere hidden behind those shutters her father could be sitting in an easy chair, a son beside him, a daughter bending to light his pipe. *And if he was, what then?*

The ship's whistle let out three short blasts and the loudspeaker clicked on, shaking Pru from her reverie. The Captain announced that the layover would be brief. Those passengers de-boarding would be ferried in. Until then, stewards would serve champagne topside; but before she could develop a sun-and-champagne headache, her launch arrived.

As it neared the dock, her stomach gave a lurch, old fears had her in their grip. Both her mother and Bazil had solemnly promised she would have no trouble, yet rows of soldiers still lined the pier. It didn't take long, however, to notice that their guns were holstered. And this time, instead of cursing, the soldiers smiled benignly at the male passengers and bowed low over the ladies' hands, mouthing polite requests for the proper documents. Apparently peacetime hadn't reduced the moun-tains of paperwork. There were passports, manifests and cus-toms yet to be endured. So preoccupied was she with search-ing her handbag for the required documents, she almost missed the hand extended to help her. No sooner had her feet touched the dock than a man in a gaudily decorated uniform appeared, brushed aside her helper, and saluted.

"*¿Señorita* Whitley, *a su servicio?*"

"*Señora* Henri Brancusi, *Señora* Whitley would be my mother." She wasn't startled, only annoyed that he appeared to know her. Bazil, or maybe even Henri, must have made arrangements for her to be met.

"This way, *por favor, Señorita* Whitley." His second "Whitley" absolved Henri. Though their marriage had its unusual aspects, Henri knew she found the Whitley name a handicap in the art world. She always used her married name.

"*Señora* Brancusi." Either the man didn't hear or didn't care. He whisked her off to the front of the line. Pru allowed her-self the tiniest pleasure in the envious glances of her fellow pas-sengers. This sort of treatment was more the province of her mother. Though noticeably absent from films in recent years, Marion never seemed to lose her appeal. *Oh, why not enjoy it, just for a bit.* Pru would sort out the name later.

She had to lengthen her stride to keep pace but as she man-aged a quick look around, her spirits lifted. There were no signs of the locked and gloomy warehouses of earlier years. In their place stood metal buildings gleaming in their newness, their giant slid-ing doors free of locks and chains, their windows, unbarred.

But before they reached the end of the dock, her wari-ness returned. This man in the gaudy uniform, who was he?

A doorman from her hotel would hardly rate such deference. While a soldier stamped her documents and waved her through, she studied her escort. What about him bothered her so?

She glanced over her shoulder at the luxury liner floating out in the bay. It looked so small, so distant. *No turning back, now.* She would at least allow this self-important man to guide her through customs no matter who hired him. No one stopped them. Even the porters struggling with her luggage sailed right through, Pru's panties and bras spared interrogation.

With a grip perhaps a shade more firm than she thought the situation warranted, the man led her toward a car at the end of the dock—a boxy limousine watched over by two men in rather plain uniforms, their faces as impenetrable as a set of sturdy bookends. Two small red and gold flags mounted on the front fenders caught her eye. In contrast to the starched postures of the doormen, the flags hung listless, dejected captives dependent on the whims of others for life, for that burst of speed, the flow of air that would snap them to life and give them back their dignity. Bazil used the words "suitable," "clean," when he booked her hotel, no mention of "elegance" or "superb service."

That uniform. Those gewgaws on his chest—they were medals. He was no doorman—what had he done to win so many? *Had he—? Could he have been one of— Don't think about that, don't, don't, don't.*

With a click of his heels and a Yes-I-am-polite-but-no-I-am-not-subservient bow, the man took her elbow and eased her into the car. She leaned forward to give the driver directions, but before she could say anything the man motioned for her to scoot over and climbed in, bathing her in a smile as cold and penetrating as an Atlantic mist. The tight lines around his eyes, his mouth, put her in mind of a hunter worried his prey might bolt.

"Who—?"

"General Lemona."

That name. Had she heard it before? She might have. Back in the 1930's the shoes under their dinner table were always filled with the feet of important people—local dignitaries, publishers, authors, anyone her father wanted something from and those who wanted something from him. She couldn't remember ever sitting down to dinner with just her mother and father. Nanny, yes. But never just her parents. And from the look of those medals, this one might be one of the important ones, that or a very good toady. Her father attracted a good many of those. This whole trip was going to be hard enough without her borrowing trouble. And hadn't Henri done his best to disabuse her of the idea that she could travel incognito? Between her mother's fame and the Brancusi's name, no way would she pass unnoticed.

With one hand on the door handle, she tried once again to give the driver instructions. "The Hotel *Caleta Palacio, por favor.*"

Señorita, con permiso, I am to be your escort, no?" Without waiting for her no, the man barked out directions to his driver.

"That hotel, he is old, not much of the monies for repairs." The General reached over, took her hand and brought it to his lips. "*Caleta Palacio,* he is no longer suitable for such an important acquaintance of *el señor.*"

"*El señor?* What e*l señor?*" The general ignored her. The masculine pronoun eliminated her mother. Could e*l señor* be the man in New York Bazil put her in touch with—Von Dulken? He had procured the papers she needed, the letters of introduction as well as letters of credit, visas and such. "He's part of the German delegation to the U.N.," Bazil had said. "He'll take care of you." *Von Dulken had done that all right. That and a lot more.* She smiled, remembering her time in New York.

"I have learned all about you Americans from *el señor,* your need for the latest appointments in *los banos,* your obsession with the need to wash away your sins." A little warmth crept into his voice. "For us it requires only a small dip in the font of holy water."

She answered with a weak imitation of his smile. At least his English was a lot better than her Spanish. He might be useful. But if he offered *el señor's* name, she'd missed it again.

"The *Caleta Palacio* is not for you. *Permite, por favor* I will take you to one of our newer hotels."

Too tired to laugh at his witticism or even much care where or how her bathroom looked, she gave in. "Whatever you wish, but I do need to rest."

"Rest, she comes later. First the sights—the *Alcazaba*, the Archaeological Museum, the bullring. I, General Lemona, I take you to these places." Von Dulken must have gone all out if she rated a General. Obviously a man of distinction, powerful and handsome in a stern sort of way, so like her father. And like her father, he permitted no doubt as to his right to command.

"Thank you but *Señorita* Whitley—" time to set him straight—"who by the way, is *Señora* Brancusi, does not wish it so."

He appeared to acquiesce, said something to the driver and the car picked up speed, though he gave no indication that he noticed or was even surprised at the name change. They moved along the *Calle de Larios*, past streets crammed with people, colorful clothes, freshly patched buildings. A few ruins remained.

"The rebuilding—"

"It goes slow, we have not all the monies we wish . . . your government, the Europeans, they wish to punish us still for *El Generalissimo's* neutrality. Did not enough of our people die to suit your governments?

"Oh, I'm sure—"

"It won't be long now, things are happening. Your United Nations may soon get a little more united."

His seemed distant, his voice a bit bored, yet it held no anger. In his place hers would have. She'd heard enough from the refugees to know he was right. More than enough people had died, most probably her father among them. Was this what she expected? Or what she wanted? *Don't think like that, just get on with it.*

She turned her attention to the streets for signs of the agitation, the confusion of her first trip; but no orators, no soapboxes or fist-waving crowds lined the streets.

"Now the *Señorita* seems puzzled. What troubles send her so far from me?"

Pru decided it was her turn not to answer. "I must do something about this," Lemona went on, "we cannot have this. We will be accused of being poor hosts, something no Spaniard takes lightly. Tonight I take you to *Café de Olvido* to see the flamenco, no?"

"No." After several more no's, each more emphatic than the one before, Pru found herself deposited at the door of a hotel that bore little resemblance to the elegant Peter Cooper—von Dulken's choice for her in New York. She felt a touch of gratitude toward the general. *What must the one Bazil picked have looked like if this is better?"*

Once upstairs in her room, she raised the window to banish the sourness, the taint of failure, the smell of things left undone. So many old hotels possessed these phantom traces of interrupted lives. She unpacked her things, a few of them anyway. Already she felt a sense of urgency, the need to move on. She wouldn't stay in Málaga for long, she must check property records and make a visit to The English Cemetery—a waste of time both Bazil and von Dulken assured her, but still—and then she would need directions to the village, to Rodicio, the *Casa de Carrillo*. There, in that house, she would find some trace of her father, some bit of news that would satisfy her mother.

But to find him? To come face to face with him? *Oh, God… that would be too, too—*

Should she confide in the General? He knew so much about her he must have known her father. *Had known? Did know?* She was at a disadvantage. She knew only that he was a general, most probably sent by von Dulken and his name was Lemona. Though he had done little more than sing the praises of his city, his song had more in common with the predictability of a scale than the soaring of an aria. She would wait.

The city, however, looked anything but flat. Aromas as vivid as ever, lured her back to the window—the tang of incense mixed with the sweetness of oleander, purple jacaranda and roses. A breeze filled the room, and Spain entered her blood with the warmth and excitement of strong wine. Considering everything that had happened, bitter almonds would have been a better analogy for the land's stark beauty, its poverty, its sorrow—a country peppered with laughter, redolent with tragedy and a whisper of hidden terrors. She remembered Helen's ironic assessment of Spain. "If only one would meet Spain half way," she had said, "it would provide a lifetime of emotions, a cleansing, a sweeping away of that tightness that gripped the Anglo soul." That wasn't all Pru remembered of Helen. It had been a dreary November day in late 1935 when Helen first entered their Kensington Gardens House. This exotic redhead had stepped through her bedroom door, hairbrush in hand.

"Are you another new nanny? Have you come to spank me?"

"No and no."

"That's good, I rather like the one I have now and I am too grown up to be spanked."

"You needn't be rude. I am a highly trained secretary. The very highest." Helen liked superlatives. "Your Nanny is unwell and your mother thought we should get acquainted. Lord knows

why, me *mither*—" Helen's brogue thickened with every word—
'didn't pay my fare to London to take care of the likes of you.
'I'll not have you marrying a man like your father,' she says to
me. 'Him and his ways, sneezing coal dust all over me parlor.'"

A look of chagrin crossed Helen's face. She had gotten more
acquainted than she intended. She left the room, hairbrush in
hand, leaving Pru to care for her own hair. But Pru didn't want
to think of Helen, not now. Helen was another one of those trou-
bling bits of history she wasn't ready to face just yet. Helen, her
steno pad, her typewriter and all disappeared into that limo
along with her boss.

Pru pushed the shutters further aside and leaned out. *What if
he's there, on the floor right below?* Málaga appeared to fear dreams
as much as she. People still promenaded up and down the
streets. The glow of lights made frightening silhouettes of the
cranes hovering over the city—giant birds, vultures poised to
swoop down, ready to devour the old before giving birth to the
new growth which seemed to have turned its back on the port.

She gazed off in the direction of the bullring. The General
had talked of the arena as if it had a living presence. Before he
disappeared into the night, he had thrown out one last invita-
tion. They must attend together, he said. The arena lay only
a little way along the *Paseo de Parque.* "I can get us seats close
enough to the action to smell the blood, you'll love it."

No, she told him, she would not.

She spotted the arena off to the right where no cranes were
visible. "The bullring," Lemona said, "the heart and soul of the
city would remain forever unchanged." She felt both drawn to
and repelled by a city with such a gruesome ritual at its heart.
She never understood this passion of her father's. And the
Spaniards—after that ugly war, all they had seen, all they had
done, how could they still take pleasure in tempting death?

But then hadn't her father hunted tigers, ridden elephants, reported on the troubles in Abyssinia, in Mexico? He did what he wanted and he wanted adventure. For Pru adventure took place in her studio, on her canvas. She wasn't sure but she liked to think he would have encouraged her. "Any child of mine should be somebody, someone who wants to do something," he had said often enough. Only after the discovery of the calling cards had Pru thought to question the "any child of mine" part.

There were those times when getting her edification, as he called it, was fun. He took her to palaces, museums, planetariums. Sometimes they climbed the rocks at the shore or studied the stars in the sky. She remembered being very young, sitting on his knee and watching his goatee bob up and down as he counseled her. When she grew too old for his knee, he sat her down on a footstool and delivered lengthy lectures on this and that, most of which she soon forgot. One or two stuck.

"Never surrender the reins. Not to anyone," he had said, "especially not to the horse." But she had. Somewhere along the line she'd surrendered them to her mother. She should have listened. He looked so serious that day—blue-gray eyes locked on hers, his voice with its wintry bite had worked its way under her skin. Odd thing memory, how one thing stuck, another didn't—the place remained vague, the time long gone, but not the voice, she could hear it still. She was eleven, maybe twelve; everything happened so fast, it all sort of melted together. Maybe he tried to tell her the day they sailed for Spain? Perhaps the day he told her to look after her mother. Or that day in front of the *Casa de Carrillo*, the day he left. What did it matter when he told her, it was shortly after that the reins slipped from her hands. Had she ever held them? Somewhere in all those instructions, she sensed the same contradiction. Despite his exhortations for daring, for independence, he hadn't meant then, not while he was in custody of those reins, but later, later after he was gone.

The years had piled up one on top of the other and still she had to separate claps of thunder from the boom of a cannon, the scream of a peacock from that of a woman, her own needs from her mother's. After a while trying to placate her mother and put an end to her needs became as futile as trying to capture the wind in a butterfly net. *It's time to get on with it.* If she were to have any chance at all of getting the reins back she must find her father.

"*Señorita, por favor,*" someone rapped lightly on her door. "*El general,* he has come for you, to take you to *la cena.*"

Pru hadn't thought about food, but when she heard the proprietress, she felt the first stirrings of hunger. No wonder, it must be nine or so. It might come in handy after all, this inability of a general to pay attention to anything anyone said. He was so pompous, what did she have to fear? She would go, she might learn something.

"*Uno momento, por favor,* I'm not quite ready. Tell the general I'll hurry." "*No es una problema.* Our General, he know the ladies."

I'll just bet he does, Pru thought as she headed for the shower.

FOUR

The General and His Men
"It is better to know nothing than to know what ain't so."

—PROVERB, 1874

THE LIMOUSINE moved off down a boulevard lined with palm trees, its tiny flags snapped out salutes to their overgrown cousins draped across the balconies. On the sides of every building huge portraits of *El Generalissimo* reminded the people of the man who ruled them and a war they'd rather forget. She looked over at Lemona. Though he seemed a bit of the buffoon, something about him made her uneasy. She reminded herself that not every one in every army was evil, not every one was good. It had taken ten, twelve days to make their way to Cadiz all those years ago—both she and her mother lost count—and hadn't people on all sides treated them kindly here and there? But there were those others, the ones that—instinctively her hand sought out the scar on her cheek.

Toward the town's center the buildings appeared new. Huge sheets of glass mirrored the dusky light. She could be in the business section of any large city. The ornate buildings, the fine old houses—the ones she remembered from that time her father had driven everyone into Málaga for the bullfights—all gone.

"Have you been to our cathedral? *La Manquita*, the one-armed lady?" Lemona's prattle elbowed aside her memories. He sounded more like a third-rate tour guide than a general. "Sometime I tell you the story," he said. She knew about the unfinished cathedral, the one tower; but, true to character, he didn't wait for her answer.

"Tomorrow I take you there. I go to pray. When I look into the eyes of our Virgin—you are not so Catholic anymore, no?" Once more no pause invited an answer. "You Anglos, in your church you ignore the Virgin. It is only your God who is allowed the eyes to see. Ah, *Señorita*, our Virgin, she sees. And what she sees makes her weep. She weeps for Málaga."

Pru felt a tiny bit of relief. She need hardly have worried about a general who prayed. Or one moved by a Virgin's tears. In another time, another place Pru might even find him interesting. She hadn't prayed since that night in 1936 when she and her mother crouched under the massive wooden table in the dining room of *La Casa de Carrillo*. The crack of the guns, the cackle of the fires set her about her prayers. But God had ignored her—the noises never stopped. She would ignore him. But the General had no way of knowing about that, even though somewhere between the drive to the hotel and this one she'd wondered if perhaps the general didn't wait for answers because he knew them already.

Her relief didn't last long. How was it he knew so much about her, yet she knew nothing of him—other than his name sounded vaguely familiar?

"Our city, she has endured many insults," he said.

By now she wasn't even sure if Lemona even remembered she was there in the limousine. "The troubles of '31—all those factions, all that chaos—"

"But that happened before the war, we were—"

"War, state of war, declared war, the desire for war, they are but words—the plague descended on our country many years ago, even before the anarchists hurled their fire bombs and looted our churches. *El Generalissio*, by the grace of God, he knows the parties that caused the chaos. Did he not fight them? Each and every one?" His voice rose to a frenzied pitch. "And defeated them. As for you, your world, your government, you ignored the suffering, the killing."

"And your government?"

At last he heard her. "We restored order."

"You did no killing?" She had to fight to keep her voice steady.

"Sometimes in war it is necessary to—"As if he realized they had wandered into a dangerous area, he withdrew. "Women, what do they know of such things?"

A lot. Most people were curious enough about her scar to wonder how she got it. He hadn't asked. Was that another one of those things he already knew about? To be fair she was seated on his left and it wasn't all that noticeable anymore.

"I remember —" she stopped. She wouldn't tell him that, not yet anyway. It hardly mattered, his hearing loss had returned.

"*Es suficiente*, enough of this talk." The general shed personalities as others their coats. He turned affable. "It will not aid in the digestion. I shall take you to *El Café de Olvico*. *Señora Delores* she cook for us." The tour guide returned, his voice as smooth as a lover's. "That woman steams the taste of Málaga into mussels, shrimps. She grills the flavor of *Costa del Sol* into sardines. To step inside the café, is to smell Spain. And the pork, Señora is the wizard of *las chuletas*. The chops arrive wrapped in cabbage leaves, fried up with *los tomates, las cebollas*."

Pru suppressed a laugh—was he trying to seduce her with

food? She was hungry enough, if not for those scratchy medals, he might even succeed. "So much food—"

"Only the beginning, *señorita*. Next comes *Ensalada de Langosta*, lobster stuffed with eggs and olives whipped up in a confection of mayonnaise well-laced with garlic." The thought of creamy mayonnaise appeared to do Lemona in. He leaned back into his cushion and let his tongue lap slowly around his lips. He closed his eyes and disappeared into in a haze of gastronomic ecstasy.

Pru entered the *café* on the arm of a general who had regained his martial bearing. He quick-stepped her past walls lined with wine barrels, guided her in and around small tables crowding the floor, their little candles glowing from the safety of brandy snifters. The occupants doffed caps or raised glasses to the general. Pru received only the occasional nod and not so occasional lewd wink. Again, no one appeared to notice the scar. She had applied her makeup carefully. This was not the time, not the place to call attention to it. Sometimes even she could forget about it for months on end. Not so her mother. For Marion the scar served as a constant reminder of something she couldn't or wouldn't talk about. It defied the lotions and creams she lavished on it over the years. Sometimes, though, late at night, Pru traced the scar's path as it wandered across her face and remembered. The child. The soldier. The bayonet. The slight tickle as he drew it across her cheek. Her mother's scream. The soldier's startled look. The blood running down her face, the way it settled in the corner of her mouth. The taste.

Pru and the general headed away from the large stage that occupied the far end of the room and approached several long tables that stood away from the wall, their chairs facing outward like a row of sentries positioned to police the room. Lemona stopped at one of these. He pulled out a chair, motioned for her to sit and introduced five or six men already seated. The beauty of the candle-lit scene, pewter plates, wine bottles, ribbons and medals glinting in their light, even the small beads of sweat on the men's upper lips, distracted her. She missed the names entirely. Lemona snapped his fingers, more wine appeared and then he moved off into the crowd and left her there.

Most of the men at the table wore uniforms, one or two with a sleeve pinned up, canes leaned against several of the chairs. Her apprehension returned. The war remained a presence here. And then it hit her —*could one of these men be that soldier?* She studied them closely. They were about the right age, but she didn't remember her soldier's face. His eyes, she would recognize those eyes, that unexpected sadness that filled them.

A few seats away from her sat the only other woman, striking in a stark black dress, hair pulled back so tightly in a bun that her eyes appear narrowed, her lips stretched into a straight red slash. Pru warranted only one small glance down that well-chiseled, patrician nose before the woman turned to her companion.

"*La norteamericana? ¿Quién está?*"

"*Llamó Señorita* Whitley," a young lieutenant answered. Odd? Lemona hadn't used her name, only theirs. The Lieutenant's next words stunned her. "She comes to look *por su papá muerto.*"

"*¿Muerto?*" The woman's voice rose.

"*Sí*, one of those shot during the war."

Pru jumped.

"*¿El norteamericano? ¿Disparo?*"

Pru glanced down the table toward the woman, but the soldier seated to her left, a captain, leaned in and blocked her view. "You will enjoy later the flamenco," he said, his breath laced with garlic and cigars made her shy away, "here it is very good."

If anyone answered the woman, Pru missed it. Despite the crowded room, the noise, the loudness of his voice jarred. She tried and failed to look interested. He didn't appear to care. Had she said anything to anyone? On shipboard? *Von Dulken, he must have said something, how else—?*

"Perhaps *un communista,*" someone was saying, "*de* Abraham Lincoln Brigade?" The entire table, even her Captain, fell silent, all eyes turned toward her. Just as quickly they turned away. The Captain resumed his prattle "The music, the Moorish wail, it goes back in our history."

"Really?" The sarcasm in her voice blew past him. He turned up the volume on his.

"If he followed the communists," the Lieutenant at the other end of the table spat out the word. She'd heard that hiss before. "If her Papá foolishly made cause with the Republic, it will not be wise for her to remain long in our city."

She did her best to lean away from her chattering neighbor. She needed to hear this and even more reason—the wine had not improved the Captain's breath. "We have taken the dance for ours."

But the voices in Pru's head were from another time, another place—*your father's a fat fascist, a dirty fascist, your father's red, red as a dirty beet, fascist, communist, fascist, communist.* It had gone on that way all through her time in the private high school where her mother had stashed her. One label as hateful as the other. Her mother told her to ignore the taunts. She couldn't. Instead she stole a plot from one of her mother's movies—she wore her raincoat to school belted tightly like any self-respecting spy. She told them she knew things, important things. She didn't. How could she? She didn't even know about her own father. Was he "red?" "Dead?" Her father often quoted someone named William

Bolitho. "Some of Bolitho's words shaped my life," he had said "'We are born free' but in order to live we must cage ourselves in with laws. We are obliged to be thrifty or starve or freeze. We are born to wander but are cursed to stay and dig.'"

She had asked her father what Bolitho meant. His explanation made as little sense as the quote. But he did tell her that his own father had disowned him when he announced that he would never take over Whitley's Button Factory. He would be a writer. Pru doubted if the spurning of a button factory was enough to make a man a communist, but it might have had something to do with why he was so driven to get somewhere, to be somebody. The Captains voice brought her back to the night, the cafe, the conversation flowing around her.

"There is no finer—"

"Do you flamenco, Captain?" She tried to copy her mother's flattering banter. "I would love to see—" She mustn't over do it.

"Holy Mother of God, no." Once more he missed her sarcasm but at least she caught him off guard. It gave him pause and her time to overhear the annoyed voice of the woman.

"Why is Lemona—?"

"I do not know. *El General*, he say to keep her *occupado*."

"*Señores, la Señorita habla español.* She does the listening."

The Lieutenant couldn't be stopped. His eyes appeared to pin the woman in black to her seat. "Your family, they were with the Republic, no?" The woman paled. "Did not your father flee the city when we reclaimed it? Were not his bones found along the highway only last year, no? Even today, it takes only a little digging along the roadside to bring to light old bones, old sins." He pinched the woman's cheek. She tried to turn away. Pru flinched.

"You are privileged to see the real dance," the Captain went on, "not the travesty put on for *los turistos*. The flamenco, she is a dance of control."

"Then the flamenco must be the choice of every man." Lemona, von Dulken, her father, they all appeared to have a need to control. No wonder the poor Captain appeared so tense; he must have been put in charge of controlling her. She strained all the harder to hear the conversation at the other end of the table.

"You worry too much," the Lieutenant continued, "she can not hear, is not *el capitán* busy being charming? I heard her *papá, un reportero*. We did not shoot reporters. We are not animals." She had heard that before, too. And like so many things it was true, it was not true.

"Are there not *norteamericanos* living in the village of Rodicio? I hear tell that in Señor *Carillo's* old *casa* one can still rent rooms." At this, Pru half rose out of her seat, but a cold hand on her shoulder gently eased her back down. The entire table fell silent.

"Gentlemen, Ladies," Lemona cast a look of reproach down the table, "now we dine." As Pru tried to clear her head—an American? Who? Where? She hardly noticed that the Captain had relinquished his seat to Lemona.

A thousand questions died as hunger reasserted itself. Platters of food arrived. The entire room quieted in deference to its quality. When the plates were cleared and the sherry poured the dancers appeared on stage. Somewhere around two in the morning, Pru arrived back in her room exhausted. Her bed rose up to meet her. Too tired to make sense of what she heard, or almost heard, she fell asleep.

Minutes later? Hours? She came awake, wide awake—a soft rustling noise came from near the door. A mouse? A cockroach? Someone in the hall? She reached for the light by her bed, found the switch. Snapped it on. The rustling stopped. No mice, no roaches, just a piece of paper shoved under the door, one corner still tucked beneath it. Her feet felt like iron weights as she swung them over the side of the bed. It took a month of forevers for her to reach the door, lean down and pick it up.

BOOK TWO

SPAIN 1936

FIVE

Prudence Goes to Spain
"There are all those early memories; One cannot get another set."

—WILLA CATHER, *Shadows on the Rocks*

PRUDENCE HURRIED NANNY through the wash-up. With something exciting about to happen—she could smell it in the air, the new country, new adventures—how could she be expected to be patient with something as childish as braids and hair-ribbons? As soon as she could she made her escape topside and dashed across the freighter's deck shouting back at Nanny, "We're here, we're here." She had kept her inquisitiveness in check through the monotony of days at sea, days spent in a stuffy little cabin. Children should be seen and not heard, after all the crew had more important things to do, Nanny admonished. This left Prudence with no chance to eavesdrop on her parents or even the other passengers. Now that they had made port she wasn't going to miss a thing.

She leaned far out over the top rail, one hand held tight to her straw hat, the other fussing with her skirt as it billowed out with every breath of wind. Below her, tugboats belched and sputtered foul clouds of protest as they shouldered their squat little bodies up against the ship. With a cacophony of bells and whistles to warn those foolish enough to get in the way, they pushed and shoved the freighter into position alongside the dock.

"Let's have a grab at that rail, Luv." Nanny hurried up behind Prudence, "We don't want you falling into the brink, now do we?"

Prudence glared down at her skirt. To have a hand free to hang onto the rail she would have to let go of her hat or her dignity. If only she were more like her mother—aloof and calm in moss-green wool that fell softly over her narrow hips. No smocking, no lace; just a deceptively simple cut that made Marion's tiny waist look even smaller. Her mother, standing at her husband's side, appeared oblivious to the wind. The slight flare to her hem permitted only little mincing steps. Prudence never failed to note that men liked to watch her mother walk. They even watched Helen, though with not as much attention as her mother—after all her mother was a star and Helen was only a secretary. But still in her trim suit, she could cause a bit of a stir with that small slit that parted so invitingly over her calf. And here stood the almost-twelve year old Prudence Maria Katarina Abigail Whitley up to her neck in floppy collars, over-worked smocking and hats with streamers that whipped in the wind. Prudence chose dignity over the hat. The offending boater sailed out over the side of the ship, narrowly missing a seagull on its way to the water.

Nanny, enthralled in her Baedeker, saw nothing. Prudence thought Nanny's face might explode with rapture as she recited, " 'And so one arrives at The Jewel of the Mediterranean.' " Ecstasy spent, Nanny sighed the sigh of the romantic denied her romance and closed the book. "Harrumph! The Virgin's crown indeed, such nonsense. Catholics, so overblown, so showy."

Rarely fooled by Nanny's brusqueness, Prudence turned her

attention to the squealing and squawking of the gulls. As the ship gave a lurch and bumped against the tugs, she grabbed on tight and looked down, only to be overtaken by a spell of queasiness. Twenty-one cloudy days without a single trip to the rail, not even during a storm. And now when Nanny, who retched so piteously at sea, appeared unaffected, why did she feel funny?

Nanny put an arm around her, "Hang on love, stop looking up and down so fast, you'll be righto in a mo." Just then, twenty or thirty birds peeled off and dove straight down at a group of soldiers parading across the dock. The men broke formation, shouted "¡Vayase! ¡Vayase!" and waved their rifles in the air. The gulls, intent on the tasty morsels flying out the galley window, ignored them. Pop! Pop! Prudence jumped at the sound. Even the sailor's looked alarmed as they boomeranged shouts down to the men below. One glance at Nanny's pursed lips told Prudence she needn't ask what the shouts meant. Nanny had her limits.

Something shiny distracted her. She forgot Nanny and just about everything else as she spotted a man darting out from behind a huge pile of crates, men in red berets chasing after him. The gold medallion dangling from the chain he wore around his neck, thumped against his chest. Prudence fingered her Saint Christopher's medal—the one her mother gave her years ago on their very first ocean voyage—his medal looked a lot bigger than hers, but from the terror on the man's face it didn't appear to be any guarantee of safety. Not for him anyway. The red berets ran down their prey and threw him to the ground. Prudence looked toward the soldiers, surely now they would help. Instead they shouted encouragement at the captors, who shook the poor man so hard his head bobbed from side to side. The medallion, flashing in the sunlight, threw an indecipherable code across the deck. With each snap of his neck, Prudence felt her stomach move further up her throat. No one else paid any mind.

Holding their captive by the boots, they dragged him off toward the warehouses. Over the clamor on the dock she thought she heard the sound of his head as it banged against the wooden piers. She moved in closer to her father.

The group disappeared behind one of the tall buildings that lined the dock. Prudence tried to keep watch to see if the man would reappear, but row after row of warehouses threw deep shadows across the wharf. They all looked alike. Thick metal rods barred what few windows she could see and rusted chains with giant locks drooped from wooden doors. The buildings hunched over their shadows, giant ogres with secrets to hide, scary ones. She heard a man scream—maybe it was a gull. She searched for her father's hand. Absent-mindedly he brushed her off.

For another hour at least, the group milled about the deck, the buildings appeared to grow more formidable as their shadows crept across the dock. "When, Nanny? When? Why is it taking so long?"

"It is a freighter after all, Luv. Goods come first." But even Nanny couldn't conceal her impatience as carton after carton swung out over the side and made their way to the waiting lorries. "*That man*," she whispered to Helen—a favorite bit of sarcasm, this title she reserved for their employer. "*That man* has a real talent for making things difficult. With his money, traveling by freighter and such a small one at that, indeed!"

When the gangplank finally banged down, more soldiers popped out of the shadows as if shaken loose by the shudder of the pier. The other passengers—a standoffish trio of engineers from Russia—brushed past them and hurried off. After dinner the first night out, her father had pronounced the men "an uncouth lot." The two groups had not mingled.

In their ill-fitting gray suits and colorless ties they looked as if they hoped to pass unnoticed. Apparently it worked. Even on the dock the soldiers ignored the Russians and saved their scorn for this last rather eclectic group of passengers.

Prudence glanced at the object of their derision—this group of overdressed people impatiently waiting their turn to disembark. Her father, shading himself from the Mediterranean sun with an elegantly creased Hamburg, looked out of place on the deck of a freighter. Tall and portly, his camel's hair coat draped casually over his arm, he barked out orders to the bustling women who gathered around him, chickens waiting for the rooster to peck.

Her mother, no less overdressed in a silver fox cape, dabbed at the beads of perspiration forming on her upper lip and rummaged in her handbag for her compact. She flipped it open to layer on fresh coats of Revlon Red to Joan Crawford lips. The ship gave a little lurch, a bump. It didn't matter. Prudence had seen her mother apply lipstick in a moving car, a swaying train and once while riding a camel with nary a smudge, never a smear. Once when she caught Prudence watching her, "You'll learn, dear," she said. "You'll learn."

"The sea, don't you know," she said turning to Helen, "it's so drying." But Helen had problems of her own, ones that made Prudence and Nanny exchange gleeful looks. Helen had allowed several of her boss's notebooks to slip from her grasp and scatter across the deck. An impishly inclined Prudence bent to retrieve the one titled: Spain-1936. "Here you are, Madame Secretary."

"I am not your father's secretary, you little pest, and well you know it. I am his Personal Assistant."

"Better to know your place," Nanny scoffed. Prudence giggled.

But by now even normally staid Nanny looked a fright, hat askew in the breeze, thick ankles overflowing sensible shoes as she tried to keep pace with the younger women. She bubbled over with excitement—as much as an English Nanny could bubble. "Look, Prudence. Look at those warehouses!" she waved an arm in the direction of the scary buildings. "Can't you just smell it all? Those buildings are chuck-a-block full of good things. Olives, huge black olives, succulent and salty. And the oil—think of the sauces you can make with such oil. The fruits, the raisins. And those oranges, those wonderful juicy oranges."

Food being so important to Nanny, Prudence dutifully drew in the pungent aroma of citrus and brine and tried to look interested. With Nanny bent on ignoring the man and all the soldiers, she decided against asking her why warehouses full of fruits and vegetables need locks on the doors, bars at the windows. Fruit maybe. But vegetables, who would steal vegetables? That funny feeling, that queasiness in the pit of her stomach hadn't gone away and somehow it told her that those locks weren't to keep people from getting in, but to keep something, someone, from getting out.

"Over there, child, up on the hill," Nanny, unmindful of her charges discomfort, went on rifling the pages of her guide book. "That's Castillo de Gibralfaro—" she broke off as the Captain came forward to say his farewells. He shook hands with her father, with Helen, then bowed low over her mother's hand, his lips barely brushing her fingertips. Curious as to whether his mustache tickled, Prudence stuck out her hand. The Captain pinched her cheek. Nanny he ignored altogether. Her father moved off in the direction of the gangplank, with the stride of a man confident he would be followed.

Her mother appeared determined to retain both her dignity and balance as her heels caught at the boards of the gangplank. Prudence gave thanks to her Mary Jane's, they may have been ugly but at least they were flat. The soldiers stopped what they were doing—the marching, the peering, the poking into various crates. They ceased their laughter to stare at her mother who looked out over their heads, ignoring them altogether and made her regal way down the gangplank, as if a star between rows of Klieg lights, flashbulbs popping, all eyes on her.

Studied or not, Prudence wished with all her heart that she could copy that cool, unruffled look. Her mother had tried to coach her. "You must learn to keep your head up, Prudence. Reporters live only to catch you with your double chin showing, or your eyes squinched."

Squinched eyes or not, Prudence couldn't take hers off her father's face, that soft expression he wore as he watched the effect his wife had on others. His look of fierceness, his warding-off-all-dangers look—the one that made her feel so safe—dissolved into a cloud of pride. She wanted that look for herself. And so the lightning struck, the thunder roared, envious eyes glanced toward the gangplank. Unmindful of leaving Helen and Nanny to cope with the bouncing and swaying her ignominious descent might cause, she went for the outrageous, the one thing that would guarantee her father's attention. She took off at a run, jumped onto the plank and, giggling at the racket, the clank it made, she raced to the dock.

Her father, preoccupied with disembarking, ignored the laughter of the soldiers. For all that effort, Prudence earned only a small glance, one of his "later" looks. He resumed his strutting and posturing, calling out orders in Spanish to a group of porters gathering around them. He may have been calm, the porters were not. They eyed the soldiers who by now had collected at the far end of the pier, the only exit to the street as if daring *Los Americanos* to pass. Undaunted by brown shirts, holstered pistols and glowering, scowling faces, her father strolled over to them. "The dollar, the good old Yankee dollar, even better than the American passport." He laughed as he slipped some bills into a few outstretched palms. Prudence never understood why people didn't get insulted at this off-handed dispensing of money. Once when she found a pipe her fathers had misplaced, he rewarded her with a dime. She threw it at him.

Two taxis and a donkey cart pulled up. Without a backward glance, her father ushered her mother into the first cab, climbed in, slammed the door and motioned the driver on. The engine coughed and spluttered, smoke belched from a dragging tail pipe. The taxi drove off. "Someday," Nanny said, "*that man* will be the death of me."

"You are such a pathetic worrywart," Helen snapped. "We've only to see to the luggage and we'll join them." How could that be a problem? Each box, each bag or trunk clearly bore the stamp: "Property of R. P. Whitley." Prudence looked from the suitcases to the women and back again—did they all bear that stamp, her mother, Helen and Nanny? She put her fingers to her face and carefully explored its contours.

Stamp or no stamp, Nanny always saw through her. "What a queer little fish you are," she said. "Never quite sure of what we want, are we?" Prudence kept still, though she knew that right then what she wanted was to keep close tabs on that taxi growing smaller and smaller as it disappeared down the road. She urged everyone to hurry, but the words died on her lips. One of the soldiers standing just past Nanny, his eyes narrow and dark, studied the three of them as if suspicious that they would steal something from his precious warehouses. He was holding the medallion. Prudence could see a red smear across its face. The soldier, noticing her stare, raised the medallion to his lips and gave it an exaggerated kiss. His lopsided smile grew even more crooked as he took careful aim at the side of their cab and spit.

SIX

Painted Walls and Angry Slogans
"and found no end, wand'ring mazes lost."

—JOHN MILTON, *Paradise Lost*

THEIR DRIVER ignored the soldier, the medallion and the spitting, saving his scorn for the boy as he loaded the donkey cart with their belongings. "*Ándale. Ándale.*"

"Stop! *Halto*! *Ceaso!*" Pru said. The boy smiled; the driver scowled.

"Excuse me sir—"

"Really Prudence, how rude."

Prudence ignored Helen altogether, but made a great show of mimicking her as she nodded politely at the driver, "I meant the boy, not you."

The laws of gravity appeared to have no hold on the boy. He piled their trunks higher and higher atop his cart. Prudence didn't care if the whole lot toppled, but the donkey looked so sad someone had to speak up for him. She first noticed the downy gray beast while trying not to stare at the vigilantes pawing their luggage. Not that they looked all that vigilant to her. The bags of clothing held little interest for them. They received only a quick shake before they handed them over to the boy. The trunks they examined with a little more care, lifting the top trays and poking around. However they did appear to share her interest in the taxi that held her father, as if what they sought might disappear with him.

The boy went on with his work, strapping suitcases across the back and down the sides of his donkey. From time to time, though more wary of the soldiers than Prudence, he turned to look at her, and she discovered another language as new to her as Spanish—this one spoken with the eyes. She felt all tingly. *Could he? Might he become a friend?*

Though they were Americans and traveled more than they stayed home, England saw the most of them. "If I'd had my druthers," her father liked to say, "I would have been born English." So it was from Southampton they sailed for Spain. Prudence had decided to leave her doll behind. When Nanny wasn't looking Prudence plucked Shirley Temple from her resting place. When Prudence wasn't looking, Nanny put her back.

"You never know, Luv, we just might want her," Nanny had said. Somehow Nanny's "we" made the doll seem less childish. She remembered the first time she introduced Nanny to Shirley, how Nanny had reached out to shake the doll's hand.

Prudence had insisted she wouldn't miss her books. "This trip, I'm to go to school, a real school—with nuns and children and everything." On most of their travels, between the language barrier and her parents need to protect her from odd diseases and unwholesome ideas, tutors became a necessity; playmates, a rarity. Usually barricaded behind a heavy schedule of lessons and well-intentioned governesses, her parents promised that while in Spain the nuns would see to her education. Nuns meant classrooms, classrooms meant other children.

Prudence stole a quick look at the boy and decided she might not need Shirley or the nuns. She caught Nanny looking from her to the boy, and back again.

"What is it, child? You look like the cat with the proverbial canary." Nanny had a way of seeing more than Prudence wanted.

Prudence made a rather weak attempt at looking indifferent, shifting her attention to the donkey. "Can't we do something, the donkey will get hurt." The beast twitched his ears and rolled his solemn brown eyes back in his head as if trying to comprehend the enormity of the load he must carry.

"Try ¡*pare*! Or ¡*parado*!" Helen said. This time the boy paused and smiled a dazzling smile. It happened again—that funny feeling.

"It's too heavy," Prudence explained. "*Largo, largo.*" The boy laughed.

Helen turned up her nose, "*Largo* means long, it's "*pesado.*"

"No. no, *Señorita,* is no too heavy." Prudence gave a little start. She smiled back, taking up the challenge. *Hablar ingles muyo bueno.*" When his smile slid over into a giggle, she wanted to call her words back. He didn't look much older than she but his English put her Spanish to shame.

"It's all right, Luv," Nanny reassured, "time enough your Spanish will improve."

"Not in time to help the donkey. Let's put some luggage in the taxi. Can we, Nanny?"

"Is no *necesario, Señorita,* my burro, she has the strength of many men. She can do the loads no other can."

"Still and all," Nanny muttered, "maybe we should put some inside. What if the rapscallion goes off with the whole lot?"

The boy frowned. "*Mi nombre es Rubio.*"

"Nanny, he understands!" Humiliated, Prudence shuffled her feet, peering expectantly at the marks she made in the dust as if they had the power to erase the pain.

"Pish posh, child, I meant nothing by it. Come along now, get in. Let's go see your new house. Home, I mean your new home." Nanny and her fetish with words had it right the first time. That house, like all the others Prudence had lived in, never did become a home; but though none of them ever caught her out, not her father, not her mother nor even Nanny, Rubio did become her friend.

At last the luggage was loaded and their cab moved slowly away from the dock.

With much straining and creaking the donkey followed close behind. From time to time Prudence craned her neck to make sure Rubio could keep up. The streets were crowded, the going was slow. Reassured at last, she turned her attention to the sights around them.

Before long Prudence noticed the buildings of the city shrinking with each turn of the wheel. "Father said a city, he promised." Trips that ended into the country had a way of ending badly.

"No, dear. Not a city, a village."

"A villa." Helen's laugh had a brassy, unkind sound to it, "We're going to live in a villa."

"*A casa de campo,*" the driver interjected. A house in the country? Prudence felt cheated. Helen, striving to get her chin slightly higher than her nose, ignored the driver. "I, for one, am looking forward to the luxury of the whole thing. A villa, a private villa."

Miffed at Helen's put down, Nanny leaned across her tormentor and opened the window. "We might as well take advantage of the air outside the cab. It's fresher by far."

The road wound its way along the waterfront. Beyond the sea wall Prudence saw small children playing on a narrow strip of sand. She envied them as they ran down to the water to splash through the tide before shrieking their way back up the beach. She could feel the itch of warm sand between her toes, "Will I be able to—?"

The cab stopped abruptly, the driver let out a yelp. Prudence found herself on the floor, Nanny and Helen on top of her.

"What—?"

"The fishmonger, I no can run him down." As they attempted to sort themselves out, the man ran around to the side of the cab and pressed a still wet, still gleaming giant cod in through the window. A horrified Nanny picked herself up and turned just in time to make contact with the cold lips of the fish.

"Ech!"

"*Ve frescura?*" the vendor shouted, "*mi pescado*. He just pulled from the sea, *Señora.*"

"Go away, shoo!" Helen squeaked.

The vendor, not to be discouraged, sang out, "*Compra? Compra ustedes, Señoras?*"

"There is no need to yell. We're not deaf, you know. Furthermore, we do not wish to buy your fish."

"*Compra, Señora. Por favor,*" the man wiggled the tail of the cod back and forth. Helen's nostrils tightened. She shook her head and waved at the driver.

"¡*Vamos*! ¡*Rapidamente!* That obnoxious little man, I wouldn't buy his fish if it was the last fish alive."

Nanny drew herself up. "I suspect," she smirked, "from the smell that the fish is quite dead."

Helen poked the driver in the back. "For heaven sakes, move on. Are we going to be all day at this ride? *Darse prisa, prisa.*"

The man couldn't hurry. His shoulders shook so he could hardly drive. Prudence, in an effort to hide her own laughter, turned and looked out the back window. A little beyond the figure of the irate vendor, she saw Rubio, hands cupped over his mouth, shoulders echoing those of the cabbie.

A few streets more and the driver jerked the wheel left and a truck filled with cane chairs skidded around him, sounding its horn. The cab turned on to a road that led away from the sea and up into the hills. An empty road stretched before them. "The cab, Mother, Father, where can they be?"

"We got delayed back there; we'll catch up to them." Before long the road began to serpentine its way into the hills, the three passengers lurching from side to side. They came around a corner and almost ran into a small shrine at the side of the road, votive candles burned at the feet of the Virgin. A few more hairpin turns and they came on another shrine and yet another.

"On these roads, the need for frequent prayer is obvious," Helen commented. "Can't you drive with more care?"

The cab slowed to a crawl. Prudence fidgeted, they would never catch up to her father's taxi. The hills gave way to mountains, the mountains to ravines, deep gorges crossed by wooden bridges led them towards yet more mountains, long rows of stone fences, prickly pear hedges marking the way. At each horseshoe curve, Prudence peered hopefully through the front windshield. Nothing. If only the road would straighten, they could make a little headway. Whenever it did, herds of sheep and carts piled high with goods for market popped up to thwart any hope she had of finding her father. Their progress so laborious, the twists and turns so numerous. Rubio and his over-laden cart had little trouble keeping the pace. Prudence watched him push and plod his way through clouds of mustard-colored dust. She liked the sound of his name and practiced rolling the "r" the prideful way he had. *Rubio* she said to herself, *Rubio, Rubio, where for art thou, Rubio?*

Finally the ground opened up into terraced vineyards. Helen launched into a monologue on the thickness of the vines, the lush green of their leaves. "That's what it takes to produce the richness of Spanish wines." For once the driver nodded in happy agreement.

"And when have you had the time to sample these wines? We've only just disembarked."

Nanny's joy at getting the first dig disappeared, swallowed up by a grove of olive trees, their trunks gnarled and black like the hides of ancient mummies. The driver appeared as nervous as any of them. He pressed forward ever deeper into the grove and the trees closed over them, rubbing out the sky. Their branches scratched the sides of the cab with the fierceness of crazed eagles trying to claw a way in. Prudence thought it looked rather like the sketches she'd once done of Hansel and Gretel running through the woods. The air of the cab grew heavy with evil spirits, oppressive with the heat of wicked witches. Beads of sweat formed on Helen's forehead. Surreptitiously she removed a handkerchief from her purse and dabbed away. She missed one. Prudence watched it run down her chin, drop to her neck and disappear beneath the frazzled collar of her dress.

Nanny settled into a quiet more ominous than the probing of the ragged branches. "That man," she murmured, "has a habit of moving half-way-round the world at the drop of a hat. All these changes can be so hard on the digestive tract." Prudence smiled, Nanny, with no taste for dirt, disorder or disease, felt put upon. "Oh, I know," she would say, "that that man sees to it that we have our shots, but—" Nanny often found the climate too dry, too damp, too just about anything. Prudence once heard her mother say that Nanny's complaints fit her stocky form with the smugness of a well-pressed uniform.

And now, in the cab, Nanny seemed to take a sudden interest in the contents of her purse, opening and closing the clasp. Snap. Click. Snap. Now and then, she took out their passports, looked them over carefully before tucking them back. With each fresh look she appeared to search out a more secure resting place for the precious leather books. In London, just before they sailed, Prudence had run her fingers over the gilded seal and asked if she might hold on to her own passport.

"No, no child. American passports are magic carpets. They get you into, around and most importantly back out of all sorts of foreign ports. We can't chance losing them, now can we?" Things must be bad if Nanny's thoughts had already turned to leaving. And what good were passports anyway if only one day in Spain, and already Prudence had lost her mother. She spent a little time wondering what life would be like without her father. Not so any rules but she did love him, didn't she? She must, yet she knew what Nanny would say—be careful what you wish for, you just might get it.

She closed her eyes, and put her mind to something nice: the little horse cabs of Hyde park, the beds of gladiolas, the old men bowling on the green in their white shorts and knee high socks, their knobby knees and stringy thighs.

"You weren't scared in the woods, were you Luv?" Prudence opened her eyes to sunshine and blue skies, the offending grove a thing of the past. Something white gleamed off in the distance. How easily fears vanish, the slightest distraction and they are gone. Prudence leaned forward in her seat for a better look. "See it, Nanny, over there against those hills, what is that white thing?"

"A church tower, we're coming to a town. Look how the little houses nestle around her, a mother hen with her chicks."

With the village still some distance away, the cab stopped in front of a small inn and the driver motioned for them to get out.

"Not here, we must go on—"

"El Señor he make the arrangements—"

"Well," Helen squared her shoulders prepared for a fight, "El Señor said nothing to me."

"I think he means we are to spend the night here," Nanny said.

"Mother? Father? Where are they? I don't see—"

"Don't be such a scaredy cat, your father doesn't like that."

"I'm not scared, Helen…I just wondered—"

"Don't worry, child. They must be in the next town, the one with the church tower. This is a very small inn. Perhaps there wasn't room for us all. Right, Helen?"

"I had no idea the villa would be so far from the city."

"*Casa de campo.*" Prudence couldn't help but giggle at the cabby's smirk.

Prudence and Nanny, both tired from their travels, didn't mind sharing a room; but Prudence felt uneasy when she heard a soft sobbing sort of sound coming from the bed across the room.

"Nanny what's wrong."

"Nothing, child. I just was thinking of home."

"Me, too." But for what home? Which house? She had lived in so many houses all over the world. Her nostalgia struck her as hypocritical. Nanny, on the other hand, had earned the right to hers.

"I did my growing up," she often told Prudence, "in a thatched roof house, with my twelve brothers and sisters. The beds and chairs were all taken. To make a place for myself I tagged along with my mother, I set table, wrung out bed-sheets and pinned the shirts and towels to the line. I scrubbed up after my brothers and sisters."

This part of Nanny's story always made Prudence sigh. "You're so lucky. I have no one but me."

"You have me, child. What more could you possibly need?" Prudence managed a quick smile before she fell asleep.

At first light, she woke to the honking of the taxi. The innkeeper urged them to hurry before the driver woke everyone. Prudence saw no "everyone" but was eager to get underway and find her parents, both of them. Helen and Nanny drank a few cups of dark coffee. The innkeeper's wife handed them a basket. *"For the hunger,"* she announced. Helen took possession of the basket and they were underway.

In no time at all, Prudence spotted the tower up ahead, but even before they reached the church she spotted a group of angry looking men. A tall, thin, man stood on a crate facing into the crowd. His hair tumbled across his face as he raged at them, but with each shake of his fist he gave an equally angry toss to his head and his hair whipped out behind him. His gaunt and craggy face so contorted by hate made her stomach lurch. The men surrounding him appeared just as angry. Soldiers stood off to the side. Watching. Waiting.

With each new crowd, the number of soldiers increased. The corners of Nanny's mouth pointed toward the floor. "What are they saying?" she asked Helen. "Can you make it out?"

Helen rolled down the window. *"Las sangres de los pisanos,"* the man screamed. The crowd roared back, *"Viva la España!"* They pumped their arms up and down and shook their fists at the sky as if God himself had committed some sin. *"Esta ensus cabazas!"* Once more the crowd's answer bounced off the walls: *"Viva la España!"*

"Blood?" Helen blanched. "Blood, they're screaming about blood."

Nanny put her fingers to her lips. "The child."

Helen would not be hushed. "It's something about blood, heads and the common man."

"Whose head? Whose blood?" Prudence asked. "Why?" Her face looked as grave as her two companion's and even Helen appeared to take notice of the quaver to her voice.

"Pay them no mind, child," Nanny tried to sound reassuring. "They're nothing but anarchists, every last one of them Anarchists. Believe me, God will see to their sauce." At this the driver let out a snort. Prudence couldn't be sure if it was a snort of laughter or disgust. She couldn't see his face but she could see Nanny's. Both she and Helen looked frightened. That scared Prudence more than anything.

Helen leaned forward to talk to the driver. "*Marcharse de prisa*. Let's get on with it." Helen's voice hadn't quite mustered up as much authority as Prudence would have liked. If only she hadn't left Shirley with the luggage; it would have been nice to have something to hug.

Nanny gave her one of her I-can-read-you-like-a-book looks. "She's here, Luv. Right back there with our things." Prudence looked back at the donkey cart as if willing the doll into her arms. The boy sat hunched over, his chin buried in his neck and his head turned away from the crowds. Prudence could see clearly that he wished himself someplace else.

The cab picked up speed. The two women stared straight in front of them. Prudence couldn't sit still. She squirmed and fidgeted, looking first out this window, then that.

"Those buildings, over there on the right, Nanny, what's wrong with them?" They were passing through several blocks where the fronts were ripped from the buildings. Prudence could see tilted floors, empty rooms, papers and trash blowing up and down stairways going nowhere. In one or two of the buildings, bureaus tipped and leaned across empty beds, drawers open, their contents strewn about. Prudence shivered. Something about the jumbled mess of exposed lives chilled her. She shut her eyes, pressed her hands tight against them and tried to ward off even the memory of those sad rooms. After a bit, her curiosity got the better of her. She opened her eyes.

At last they came to the church. The door stood off its hinges, part of one wall had burned away. In the little cemetery to the side, three or four graves gaped, splintered wood littered little mounds of dirt piled to the side of them. The driver turned to look at his passengers, and for the first time, he smiled—a real one. The only one they were to get.

The driver sped up. They left the village behind and then another and another. Meanwhile three stomachs growled in unison. An hour or so later, the cab entered yet another village, this one larger than the others. Prudence pressed her face against the window, desperate for a glimpse of a park, laughing children. The buildings rose up straight and stiff from the sidewalks, sills barren of flowerpots and their windows held nothing but cold blank stares. The streets were deserted, eerie with quiet. And then splashes of paint scrawled across the fronts, the sides, the backs of all the buildings shouting at them in dripping red letters. And yet, the words were unintelligible, just initials really. Further on, black letters defaced the low walls that ran around the church. The bigger the building, the more room for initials. One set slapped on top of another as if the alphabet warred with itself. She searched Nanny's face, but like the windows of the houses, it held no clue to what lived inside.

Unperturbed, Helen dusted herself off, patted her hair back in place and turned to Nanny. "I need a little something to eat."

"Well you have the basket...but I don't see how can you think of food?

"A cup of tea, that's what I need. There must be people

somewhere. "*Señor*," she called to the driver, "*donde es un café?*" He shrugged.

"Surely we are falling too far behind, perhaps we should—"

"Mr. Whitley left me in charge, Nanny." Helen snapped. "Not you."

"I heard no such—"

"I can't help it if you're deaf."

"Apparently, so is our driver." The cab picked up speed.

"I said stop. *Pare, pare, por favor*," by now Helen was shouting. "Let me out, I'll ask directions." The driver pulled the cab to the side of the road, shut off the engine and twisted himself around to look squarely at Helen, a strange grimace distorted his face and yet Prudence thought he looked quite pleased with himself. She had begun to think she might not like Spain all that much, but she knew for certain she didn't like the driver.

Helen got out, pocket dictionary in hand, walked up a few short steps to a doorway and knocked. No answer. She knocked again, leaned this way and that on either side of the door to peer in the windows. She moved on down the street and tried once more with the same results.

"I can't see anything, the windows are so dirty," she turned and called back to the cab now creeping down the street after her. "I think I hear someone though." She knocked again. "There must be people somewhere, chickens and goats anyway. I can smell them. They just won't come to the door."

"Helen," Nanny called out, "Please, come back to the car. We can try in the next village. I think they've smeared the windows over on purpose so you can't see in. Besides, I doubt that either the goats or chickens that you smell could brew all that good a pot of tea."

"Well aren't we the witty one."

Nanny looked pleased with herself. Prudence giggled.

Helen ignored them both. "And the walls. Why would any one do that to perfectly good homes? Where could the people have got to, the town can't be empty? There's food in the store windows, clothes on the line."

"Something's amiss here." Nanny said.

"Worrywart—Nanny the worrywart, that's what I should call you," Helen almost cackled. "You're nothing but a ground hog afraid to come out of its tunnel in case he should see his shadow."

Nanny's lips settled into a straight line, her eyes misted over. Prudence wondered how a Helen, even one overly preoccupied with her thirst, could fail to notice the paint as it oozed down the walls and into the streets, red and black rivulets of anger. On one building, the words *Salud commrade* overwrote *Viva la España*, on another "*Viva la España*" blocked out "*Arriba*" In the center of town, where the buildings were larger, they spoke in sentences. "*Muerte al Papa.*"

"Death to the father?"

"Really Nanny, did you teach the child nothing?" Helen turned to Prudence. "*Papa* with a capital, means the pope."

"*El Papa,* he deserves the killing. He takes the minds of *sus niños*, twists them, enslaves them with his rubbish. He *est un bastardo.*"

This country was looking less and less like a place to find friends, and now it appeared even the nuns wouldn't be of much help. Prudence craned her neck to look out the rear window. Nothing. No one.

"Rubio. The boy. The donkey. They're gone."

"Hush, child. Hush. He's just fallen a bit behind." But the only signs of life came from the clotheslines strung from window to window. Brown shirts, red and black-checkered scarves, black shawls danced violently in the wind.

"Well," Helen said, "at least they wash their clothes." Prudence looked at the flapping shirts but rather than laundry she saw arms and legs telling them *you don't belong here, go away.*

Nanny reached over and gave Prudence a little hug. "We've seen worse, Luv." At least that's what Prudence thought she said. It could have been: "we'll see worse." A silenced Helen got in the cab. They drove on, the air in the Taxi sharp with tension, except for the driver who muttered contentedly to himself, "*Las Americanas, están estúpida.*" A half-hour, maybe more, the town left far behind, the cab coughed, shuddered, stopped.

"*Su madre es una furcia,*" the cabby screamed.

"Your language! The child?"

The driver ignored Nanny's admonishment. "*Su madre,* she cares no who she sleeps with," he said honking the horn and grinding the starter. "The fascists, the communists. It's all the same to her." When these epithets failed to impress the dead engine, he got out, banged the front fender and kicked the tire. "*Su padre es un hijo de puta.*"

"Surely you can do something." Helen tried to sound reasonable, even friendly as she got out of the cab. "Lift the bonnet. See what's wrong. Maybe it's just petrol, we might be out of—" The cabby threw her a look of such loathing, she paled, took a step back."We must go on, we can't stop here." This time the cabby laughed outright at Helen before letting go a wad of spittle he must have saved up for miles. He turned his back on them and without a word, strode off.

"Come back. Come back," Nanny yelled after him. "You can't leave us here."

SEVEN

Abandoned

> " For, whether the prize be a ribbon or throne,
> the victor is he who can go it alone!"

—J.G. SAXE, The Game of Life

THE SMELL OF FEAR mingled with the staleness of tired seat cushions. In apparent unconcern for the fate of his three passengers, the driver sauntered off down the road. The sun blazed high above him. He cast no shadow.

Prudence latched on tight to Nanny as the two got out of the cab. Nanny grabbed Helen. "Has he gone for help?"

"How would I know?" Helen shook her off.

Nanny's head nodded up and down more to convince herself than anyone else. "Yes that's it. That must be it."

"But," Prudence protested, "we didn't see anyone in the whole town."

"Come child, hop to it. Let's get back in the cab." A subdued Helen followed the two into the back seat.

Once settled Nanny gave a snort, one of her harrumphs. The clasps on her pocket book snapped open, snapped shut. Open. Shut. Helen made a great show of examining her nails and then stacked and re-stacked the notebooks. Prudence nudged her way closer to Nanny's side, peered into the purse, hoping for a reassuring glimpse of the passports.

"He'll be back directly, I'm sure." Nanny made motions to Helen, little flicks of her wrist she hoped Prudence wouldn't see. Helen ignored her. With yet another harrumph, this one louder than the first, Nanny leaned over into the front seat, pushed down on the locks. Then she reached into the travel bag she carried with her and handed Prudence her journal, her little pen clipped to its side. "You might as well do up your day's entries while we wait."

Writing in her journal could sometimes be a bit of a chore. Nanny could be bossy and keep Prudence to her work more than she liked. Writing should be a delight, not a chore. Still Nanny was Nanny and a good person to have on your side. Prudence remembered that day at Charing Cross when her parents had climbed aboard a train, and no one—not her mother, not her father—had reached around to help her on. She was left standing there on the platform. Even her cross, old French Governess was nowhere in sight. Something was very wrong. Her mother looked nervous, though dry-eyed. Prudence wanted to cry, but when she saw the steely cold look on her father's face, she choked it back. They were going someplace and they weren't taking her. Then she felt a hand on her shoulder and Nanny slipped quietly into her life. And ever since, no matter where her parents were or how busy they might be, Nanny was always there when Prudence reached out.

To make her thoughts come out a little quicker, Prudence began to chew on the cap of her pen.

"That's enough child, what do you think your father would have to say about that?" Prudence stopped her nibbling and began to draw a picture of the soldiers on the dock, the medallion. Pictures were better than words—words were slippery things, they could have so many different meanings. She tried to imagine a scene: her father pacing angrily, her mother wringing her hands; maybe she could put some tears streaming down her face. She couldn't quite get a handle on it, her mother didn't cry very often. Her father never did. If they wouldn't cry, she wouldn't. She went to work on a portrait of the donkey. She gave it big brown eyes, sort of Rubio eyes.

An hour, perhaps two, passed before any of them realized just how alone they were. Prudence put aside her sketches, glanced up and down the road and saw only the little dust devils that came and went, coating the car, the windshield, their faces and hands. No one had seen Rubio or his donkey since before they entered that empty village. It would take a miracle or, short of that, a long time for help to come.

"Now, now, Luv, your father, he'll send someone when we fail to show up." This was a little more hopeful than Nanny's usual bromide: "The Lord helps those who help themselves." Her father put more faith in his own solutions than he did the Lord's, but then he wasn't here. He didn't even know where they were. Her mother in answer to most problems buffed her nails. "People fret too much." Buff. Buff. "Problems solve themselves." Buff. Buff. "If one only has the patience to wait them out." Nanny and Helen weren't exactly brimming over with suggestions. She'd better try to come up with something. If she couldn't, they'd be here forever. She giggled at the thought of an eternity glued to the back seat of a cab. She decided on another drawing: Prudence getting old and fat, a wrinkled witch bursting the seams of her blue-smocked dress, veined legs growing out of Mary Jane's. Her eyes grew heavy. She fell asleep.

When she awoke Helen and Nanny were examining some of the parcels in the basket. "Peppers, hot peppers, some kind of meat." Nanny said. "It's hardly edible."

"Nothing would suit you, you old dullard."

"I don't notice you indulging your palate." And the two were off —Prudence decided it best to fake sleep.

"The Mrs., she acts as if she's the greatest," Helen said, setting aside the basket. "I mean how hard can it be to memorize a few days' lines at a time? Oh, she might have been a great stage actress, but on film she just stumbles and stammers. And those close-ups, what makes her think she can still play an ingénue?"

"That's no way to talk about your employer's wife."

"Wife, ha! She only married him because she flopped as an actress and she's not all that better playing the wife."

"And you, you red-headed floozy, you'd be better?"

"Don't talk about Mother that way, I'll tell."

"So you're awake after all, you little pest—you tell and I'll remind your father of a thing or two."

"Now, now," Nanny said, "It might be a good idea if we started walking."

"And just where to?" Helen retorted.

Anywhere but where you are, Prudence thought. "Maybe Father forgot us, he does that sometimes. We move so much he forgets where we are." Often, when one move fell too quickly on top of another, her mother would wonder why he couldn't just sit patiently and wait for stories to come to him. "Unlike you, Marion, I cannot waste my time waiting around for someone to hand me a script. I make things happen." And he did. He went out, found the place, the politics, the people and either he wrote about them himself or found someone who would. He published five or six books a year, a biography or two, maybe a treatise on some boring historical subject—some he wrote himself, others he hired out. He never published a novel. "People make fiction enough out of history," he would say, "no need to add to the store." In his pursuit of a reality worth writing about, he often left his little group stewing in some airless hotel, while he climbed a pyramid or wandered into a jungle. He might not reappear for hours, days even.

"Don't be silly, Prudence. Stop acting like a child, you know he doesn't like it."

Nanny shot Helen a fierce look. "Not to worry, Prudence your mother will remind him."

Helen ignored them, tore open the paper on a fresh pack of Marlboros, fished around for a matchbook. "One of these days, I'm going to buy one of those little silver lighters. Smaller but like your father's. Maybe I'll even have my initials engraved on it."

"Copycat, copycat," Prudence muttered, picturing her father's lighter, the elegantly scrolled RPW. "Your tongue will be split and every little doggie in town will have a little bit."

Nanny smiled. Helen, preoccupied with forming smoke rings, ignored her. "I could have found a café, we might have tasted wild rabbit stew, lamb and chickpeas or if we were lucky, calamari boiled en *su tinta*."

"Only someone as depraved as you, Helen, could find something inviting about octopus boiled in its own ink."

"We should be sampling local wines, stretching our legs right now if only you hadn't been so fearful and pulled us away."

"What we really could use is some water—"

"I want a taste of the real Spain, that's what I'd like to find."

"Trouble is what you'll find," Nanny said. "It's what you do best."

Both Prudence and Nanny resented Helen a little bit, and then a little bit more. Right from the very start, in a Scottish accent, thick enough to give Prudence trouble, she had growled, "Stay clear of my coattails, child. It's not to take care of the likes of you that I shook off the dust of the coalmines, studied dictation and earned my Certificate of Excellence. I intend to be indispensable to your father." She must be, Prudence thought, she and her father spend a lot of time together.

All this bickering only made the cab seem hotter. Nanny produced a handkerchief, dabbed at the perspiration on her cheeks. "Without you, Helen, your demands, your distractions, the driver might have paid some attention to his motor, spotted the trouble. At the very least, he might have found food, if—"

"And just what did you do to help?"

Nanny's mouth drew down into a small tight line. The moisture that collected in the corners of her eyes had nothing to do with sweat. Prudence could do little to blunt its sting but lean over and nestle her head in Nanny's lap. It was enough. "It's just the dust, child, the dirt. I must have gotten something in my eye. I'll be fine."

Nanny's life had not been easy an easy one. Before she could make a run at it, first her father and then an older brother needed nursing. Lung diseases in Storth appeared with the frequency of houseflies. By the time her farther and, a year later, her brother "found their way into the church yard," there was little money left for her dowry. Governess to others' children was the best of the meager options left her. Nanny, always good at the stiff-upper-lip, would smile at Prudence and pronounce her gray and silent life at an end when she saw her charge looking so woe-be-gone, so much in need of love.

Helen retreated behind yet another cigarette. With a great show of worldly expertise, she tapped it out against the pack, the match flared, her lips pursed around the ivory-colored tip. Cigarette after cigarette burned down, Nanny's patience dwindling with them. "In this heat," she coughed, "do you have to?"

"Someone better come along by the time I smoke the last of these. I'm destined for bigger things than dying in the back of a stuffy taxi cab in the middle of nowhere."

Prudence squiggled out of Nanny's grasp, reached over, unlocked the door and stepped down into the dirt. The air had crisped. She shivered. "Do you hear that?"

"What?" Nanny got out and stood next to her. Distracted by the need to get her circulation going, Nanny shook first one leg and then the other. "I don't hear a thing."

"Someone's singing. Lots of someones."

"For once the child has it right." Helen joined them. "Down that way, it's coming from the direction of the village."

In the distance, a group of figures separated themselves from the dust. At the head of the procession some men carried colorful banners on long poles, ribbons streamed out behind them. Then came men grunting and gasping as they strained under the weight of a huge platform covered with velvet. In its center, dressed in glossy black satin and trimmed with gold lace, a huge statue of the Virgin gazed demurely out at the world. Mounds of fresh flowers surrounded her. Then came the women wearing black dresses made of "good serviceable cloth," Nanny said. She had a coat just like it.

The solemn group, heads covered with shawls, worried their beads and chanted their *"Aves."* Some of the women cradled burning candles in hands cupped against the breeze. At the rear, men in dusty gray suits hurried the others along. Prudence blanched at the sight of the shiny gold medallions that dangled from their necks. Could soldiers be there hiding behind them in all the dust churned up by the little parade? Prudence turned, headed back to the car.

Nanny stopped her. "It's all right, Luv. Probably some Saint's Day."

"In Spain, everyday is a saint's day," Helen snapped and stepped out into the crowd. "Our driver," she asked, "have you seen the man?" As if the three were no more than ghosts, the wary group looked straight through them and hurried off down the road.

Before long Prudence realized the people in the procession weren't afraid of soldiers or even Helen, but rather the ragged group that came chasing after them. No shawls, no lace veils, no singing. Shouts of *Viva La Republica* alternated with chants about *Los papistas*. The ruddier looking ones made derisive popping noises with their hands as they stumbled along the road, carrying wine bottles and sticks in place of crosses and candles. They laughed and shouted insults at the worshipers. Little boys picked up what rocks they could find. Now and then they paused to improve their aim before hurling their missiles; but for all that they missed a time or two. Some hit the side of the cab and one grazed Helen's cheek.

Nanny grabbed Prudence, "Over we go Luv," she said as she shoved her charge over the low stone wall that lined the road. "Oh, good God!" Nanny started to get up.

"Stay down," Helen ordered.

"But my purse, the passports, I left them—"

"They aren't bothering with the car." The three of them stayed crouched behind the barricade, their petty quarrels forgotten until the shouting grew faint. The dust settled and a new sound filled the air.

"Turtle doves," Nanny said, "they're cooing. It's all right now."

Back in the cab, they tried to steal a little comfort from the lumpy seats. An hour, perhaps more passed. The newness and novelty of Spain already tarnished, a troubled Prudence gave up searching the road when Helen called out: "Look who's here, it's his highness, and—"

"Father?"

"Don't be ridiculous, Prudence. The cabby. He's got petrol."

Helen had been right all along—they had run out of fuel. Nanny looked mortified. "Now where did he get that?" she said.

"Who cares?" Helen in victory could afford to be gracious. "Good Lord, what now? He's pouring the petrol under the bonnet." She jumped from the cab. "The gas tank, *Señor*, it's in the back."

Nanny made a grab for her. "You're doing it again, you're telling that man his business."

"*El carburador*, he needs the priming."

Nanny threw Helen a triumphant I-told-you-so look. "Unlike some people, there are those of us who know our jobs."

"Hush," Prudence said. The two of them spun to look at her, even the driver. "I mean, I hear something. Don't you hear it: clip-clop, clip-clop?" Twisting around, she saw an overburdened burro coming down the road.

The nets tied to either side of the donkey held cans of petrol. No luggage. No doll. Prudence had a momentary vision of a lost Shirley Temple propped up against one of those smeary windows back in that deserted villa, ringlets sagging down on either side of dusty cheeks, the once scorned doll taking on added importance with each passing minute. At least she had Nanny, serviceable black coat, lisle stockings and all.

The old man pulled the donkey to a stop and proceeded to pour the gas into the tank. "*Cincuenta centavos, por favor, Señora*," he said. "Fifty-five for each."

Helen turned to the driver, "I rather think that's your responsibility."

"Don't argue," Nanny said. "It's getting dark. Let's get on with it."

"Robbery. Highway robbery. Roland, I mean, Mr. Whitley will hear of this. You can depend on that." Helen counted out the coins. The cabby climbed in, turned the key and attempted to start the engine. It sputtered. On the third try, it wheezed back to life. The collective sigh of relief from those in the back gave the first breeze, the first stirring of air the inside of that cab had felt for hours. None of the hungry passengers made reference to the odor of wine and garlic that climbed in with the driver.

Prudence settled her head on Nanny's lap. She would ask her father to offer a ransom for Shirley. It hadn't worked for the Lindbergh baby, but maybe . . . anyway they were on their way, passports in hand and they had only to find her father. He would be so glad to see them and wouldn't even notice the missing luggage. Would he?

EIGHT

It's Just Jesus

". . . nightly pitch my moving tent a day's march nearer home."

—JAMES MONTGOMERY, *At Home in Heaven*

·PRUDENCE FELT HOT, stiff, something poked at her side. She did her best to ignore it, she didn't want to wake up; but when the cab clattered to a stop, she sat up, scrubbed at the sleep in her eyes and looked around the cab for Shirley. Then she remembered.

On her right a hill sloped away, the few houses that perched precariously on its side looked like rocks tumbling down the bluff, while below the village swam in shadows. On the far side of the cab, a large stone building, back lit by the moon, blotted out the rest of the world. She and Nanny shuddered.

"Where are—?"

"*La Casa de Carrillo*. This is it, Luv, your new. . .this is where we will live." Nanny wiggled her purse out from behind Prudence.

Prudence thought she might still be asleep, but no she couldn't be—she'd even heard the word that didn't get said: home. The three-story house for all its size looked chunky as it squatted by the road, a disgruntled *dueña* who would brook no frivolity, no sliding down the banister, no short sheeting of beds.

"Now look at you," Nanny started fussing at her hair. "We should have done you up in braids." Nanny thought braids such a practical solution to the natural untidiness of little girls.

Nanny brushed at her charge's clothes, trying to press them out with her hands. "That will have to do," she said as she reached down and gave the wandering socks a yank back into place.

"You could do with a touch of an iron, yourself," Helen said, a little smile playing around her mouth. "You look a fright. But then you'll probably be on your way back to England when I tell Mr. Whitley how you lost the luggage."

"I? I lost the luggage?"

Helen's indifferent shrug infuriated Nanny. "Listen here, you Scottish sl——. You're not so young as to ignore good advice. You best be careful where you toss the Bread of Affliction. It may end up on your plate."

"What do you mean by that?"

"You know full well what I mean." The barb must have hit its mark. Helen had no comeback.

Prudence took advantage of the truce and opened the car door, swung one leg out, then hesitated. The cab had become the known; the world outside, the unknown. How could she leave its safety? She would dare herself—if her foot touched ground, if she felt actual rock, gravel through her shoes, she would know this was no dream—she would spend her days in a glassy-eyed fortress that even moonlight refused to gentle.

She reached back for Nanny's hand, climbed out of the cab pulling Nanny with her and headed towards an iron gate, the only opening in the whitewashed wall that surrounded the house. More grille work, spiked and dangerous, sprouted along the top. Once on the other side, she faced yet another obstacle. How to get in? There were doors, two of them, side-by-side, huge, with carvings of angels and demons worked into the panels. The windows on the ground floor were set high in the walls and, like the warehouses, they too had bars—though these were shiny enough to look very new. Prudence half expected to see a black-robed monk or a *conquistador* stare out from behind them. At the very least, she expected her father. But the windows remained blank; the doors, shut.

She gave the cast iron handle a twist. The door resisted.

"The bell, pull the bell," Helen scolded. Prudence hesitated, this place had an aura. Something about its spirit didn't like her. It wouldn't let her in and, even more worrisome, it might not let her out.

"Child, will you get on with it, I'm famished." Helen reached around her and gave the bell cord a yank. The door opened and Prudence stumbled into a woman who motioned for them to enter.

It took a moment for Prudence's eyes to adjust to the flickering light of candles housed in wrought iron sconces. When at last she could see, she wanted to turn, to run, to find her way back to the boat, back to England. A huge wooden cross, five, six feet tall towered over her. It hung suspended, high over her head. In the dim light she made out the figure of a man, his arm stretched along the crosspiece. Her arms echoed with his pain—the tear of muscle, the wrench of bone from socket. His head slumped in anguish, weighed down by its crown of thorns. Huge drops of pearl oozed from the corner of each eye. She thought his pale skin might tear so tightly did it seem to stretch over his fragile bones. His feet twisted one over the other, pierced by a thick nail while translucent beads of blood ran down and oozed between the toes. Any second the whole thing must fall on her or she would slip and fall into the puddles of blood that surely must be gathering at her feet. But the tiles were clean, cold, barren. Still she couldn't move.

"Don't gawk so, child," Nanny gave her a nudge, "it's just Jesus. He won't bother you."

But he did. He bothered her a lot.

NINE

The Errant Raisin

"As the last taste of sweets . . .
Writ in remembrance more than things long past."

—SHAKESPEARE, *King Richard The Second*

THE GIANT CRUCIFIX was not the only one in the *Casa*, but it was the scariest. Prudence passed two more before Nanny led her through a large room to the right of the entry, past ornate pieces, dark heavy furnishings. Intricately carved figures scrambled up and down the arms, the legs of every table, every chair. Even the tiles surrounding the fireplace were decorated with religious fervor. No surface escaped embellishment by tortured saints and Moorish arabesques. With everything so massive, so huge, Prudence felt she had turned into Alice after the mushroom.

"In the library, dear," Nanny prodded her forward, past a maid snapping a dust rag at the shadows. "Go on in, give them a kiss, shall we?"

Prudence looked down at her feet, gave her dusty Mary Jane's a quick swipe against the back of her socks and stepped toward the door. She heard the voices, but the thickness of the walls made it hard to sort out what they said. She looked back at Nanny. Should she go in, should she stay?

"It's late. Maybe I shouldn't—"

"Get a wiggle on."

She opened the door a crack. They took no notice of her. "But Roland, we shouldn't have gone on so far ahead. They didn't know the way."

"The cabby did."

"My poor baby, my little pigeon—a new country, a new home—it must have frightened her. Why couldn't she have ridden—?"

"For God sake, Marion, the child's almost thirteen—'

"Almost twelve, Roland, almost twelve."

"Whatever. Children tire me, you know that Marion."

Prudence clamped her jaw tight, *I didn't want to ride with you anyway, you and your silly old rules.* It wasn't as if her mother never stood up for Prudence but there were times and there were times. This wasn't one of them. "We females," her mother would sometimes say in a conspiratorial whisper, "we know it's best to avoid such contretemps. What does one gain? A momentary victory and a month's worth of a glum curmudgeon? With a change of subject, an interesting problem posed—one could ask what wine to serve with cheese, what dress to wear to the concert—and men, who naturally consider themselves too busy for such trivial matters move off, you and your momentary lapse forgotten."

Prudence knew better than to ask what contretemps meant, her mother would only remind her that she had her very own dictionary.

But this time her mother did persist. "She's a sensitive child, she frightens easily— "

"And she always will, my dear, if you continue to pamper her. Fear has its uses, you know."

Prudence often wondered how it was that her parents knew so little about her. She had her fears all right; but they weren't the kind they thought. Night-light or no night-light Prudence would willingly take on a bogeyman. She worried more about the disappearance of people she loved. The family moved so much, so quickly, that people always seemed to disappear. And if it turned out to be someone like Nanny it would send her reeling backwards into the revolving door of ever changing nurse-maids, to the way life used to be. And she worried about her mother—her last line of defense, her Maginot Line—that she might break under the strain of so demanding a man.

With her father her fears were a little different. After all how could such a big man, a man everybody knew, disappear? With him she feared she might not measure up to his mandates: to be bright, witty, beautiful, to bring fame to his name and, above all, never to show weakness or fear. Some days he'd quiz her; it could be about manners or the books he demanded she read. Sometimes she had to write a report, particularly if it was a book he'd published, or worse—one he had written. She dreaded that most of all. She never understood them. Why didn't he write interesting books like *Heidi* or *Jane Eyre*? What he did, or didn't do or even what he wanted her to do, turned her childhood into one long breathless race—always running, always trying to catch up, to be what he wanted. Somehow she always fell short.

Her palms sweaty, Prudence lost her grip on the door handle. It rattled. They didn't see or hear her. "This country, Roland, it's possible this country may not be as stable as you led me—"

"Marion—"

"Yes, but perhaps we, that is the child and I, we should have stayed—"

"Don't go borrowing trouble. You take care of the house. I'll handle this sort of thing."

The talking stopped. "Go on," Nanny said. "They're waiting." She gave Prudence a reassuring pat and pushed her into the room.

Barricaded behind a desk at the far end of the room, her father looked her up and down as if to make sure she wasn't broken. But even as she made her way toward him, his demeanor changed. "And what, may I ask, have you done with my things?" His voice, his question, a slap in the face.

Those suitcases, those clumsy boxes, the overstuffed bags, the battered old trunks, that's all he cared about! You didn't win very often, not with her father.

Her mother smiled at her from the depths of a large leather chair and threw open her arms. Prudence rushed forward, tumbled into them. "What happened, darling? We—I mean I, worried so."

"The cab ran out of gas." She peeked out from under her mother's protection to see what her father thought of this. Sometimes she could wrangle a little sympathy by acting childish. It worked much better with her mother than her father.

"Marion, have you no pride? The child is much too old to hang on you like that. She's disheveled, dirty. Prudence, you should know better than come in like that, I'll have a word with Nanny about this. Now go wash up."

Her mother didn't win all that often either and now it looked as if even Nanny was in trouble. Prudence got to her feet, smoothed out her dress and turned towards the door, forcing herself to walk slowly, shoulders straight, letting her posture betray her anger.

"One moment," he called after her, "you may give me a kiss." Prudence felt a flash of triumph—so he had missed her, had worried. Good. She didn't pause, didn't turn. He called out again. "Child, I said—" She didn't stop. She closed the door behind her. Sometimes she won.

Once Nanny retrieved Prudence from outside the library, the maid pulled at Nanny's sleeve, "*La niña, el señor dice que está dormer.*" She pointed upstairs and to the right.

Nanny, not one to take being told her business with grace, glared at the girl, "I don't need you to tell me my job, I know where the child's room is." She led Prudence up the tall, spiral staircase. They paused at each landing to examine the small niches, each holding a statue, each somehow the same, yet different from the one before—the Virgin Mary, her dress blue, her halo golden, a bleeding heart in the middle of her chest; the Virgin Mary, her dress blue, her halo golden, kneeling at the foot of the cross; the Virgin Mary, same dress, same halo, hands together in desperate supplication. Prudence rolled her eyes heavenward in imitation of the Virgin's worshipful gaze. At the top, the stairs opened into a narrow hallway. A balustrade on one side looked down into the entry; on the other, arched windows let in the night. The house formed a giant U. Nanny headed for the right leg and through a door into a sitting room, then down a dark hall, past two rooms, all the way to the back of the house.

"This is it, Luv, your room." Moonlight, streaming in on three sides and slim candles in iron sconces competed for her attention. Neither one appeared capable of victory. On the wall across from her bed, caught in the crossfire, yet one more crucifix shrieked out in pain. Prudence looked from it to the bed, back again. It would be the first thing she saw in the morning; the last thing, at night.

To one side of her bed a set of double doors opened onto a balcony. Through the large window on the back wall she could see silhouettes of mountains, the dark chasms of valleys, villages, each with their own bell tower guarding the night.

Despite the haunted Christ there was something about the room she liked, its sparseness—the only furniture was a rather small bed, one bureau and a desk with a straight-back chair. It would be a good place to write in her diary. Nanny said clutter set one's nerves on edge. Prudence wasn't exactly sure what nerves were except that her mother had them. She would learn, though. This house would teach her.

No screens obstructed the view. At the window, she leaned out and the world fell away. The back of the house hung out over a black abyss. She grabbed for the sill, took a deep breath, surprised to feel not the fear she anticipated, but a strange exhilaration, a feeling of freedom, an exemption from the laws of gravity, those conventions that bound so many to earth. Doom, gloom, worry and fear dashed against the rock of the ravine. She thought she could see into forever, to Málaga, the sea and safety.

Nanny made a lunge for her, "Careful, child. That would be a drop." Nanny always found the passage to adventure threatening, dangerous.

Nanny moved off. "Out here, Luv," she called, "have a go at this." Prudence followed her onto the balcony. Nanny pointed below to a huge fishpond shaped like an elongated Maltese Cross that took up most of the patio. The soft light pouring out of the rooms that surrounded it, gave it an air of mystery.

"Can we go down, have a closer look?

"All in good time, child. Now we clean up."

Prudence looked around. "Where, I don't see any—"

"The lavatory for this side of the house is off the front room. This is Spain and villa or no villa" Nanny looked smug, "even Helen will have to share a bathroom. Come on now, we must hurry down to supper."

"It's so late. Cook will be in bed. She'll never fix us supper now."

"We all have adjustments to make. Cook, too. Here people dine at ten."

Downstairs in a room between the dining room and the

kitchen—the pantry, Nanny called it—Prudence saw a small table set for two. Two bowls, two forks, two spoons. She looked around at the glass-fronted cabinets lining the walls on one side. Stacks of dishes, heavy pottery bowls, hammered silver plates and platters overflowed the shelves. She'd never seen so many dishes, Damask cloths, linen napkins and fine china. Rows of spices. The open shelves on the side held boxes, crocks, sacks of beans and rice. And on the end wall, a crucifix, as tortured looking as all the rest. Prudence shuddered. *What kind of people wanted so many dead bodies hanging around, even when they ate?*

She and Nanny pulled out their chairs. Nanny unfolded her napkin with a flourish and began telling of the delicious variety of meals they would eat, the elegant service they could expect, even if tonight it appeared they would dine alone. Then Cook called from the kitchen, "You best come serve yourselves, the others are busy setting up the main room."

Nanny's face took on a sour look as she eyed the scrambled eggs, pickled beets and squares of toast set out for them, a far cry from the soups and sauces she so dearly loved. They carried their plates back into the pantry. Scarcely giving them time to finish, Cook barged in carrying bowls of bread pudding. "Be sure and leave the pantry by the side door. No need to disturb them that's eating."

"What is it she thinks we're about?" Nanny hid her disappointment behind a close examination of her bread pudding. Prudence followed suit, counting her raisins. Fourteen. She looked across to Nanny's bowl. Twelve. She scooped up the fattest, juiciest raisin she had and plopped it right in the center of Nanny's bowl. Fair's fair. As she picked up the pitcher to let the cream make puddles around the cubes of bread, she stole a glance at Nanny. Nanny had spooned up the offending raisin, reached across the table and dropped it back in its original resting place.

"Why?"

"Child, child. What is the matter with you? Thirteen is bad luck."

Prudence didn't have much use for superstitions. "The building blocks of ignorant minds," her father called them. Once he teased Nanny about booking her into a room on the thirteenth floor of a hotel in Tahiti. When they got there, Nanny discovered that all the rooms were little huts built up on stilts only a few feet off the ground. Chagrined at having revealed her ignorance of such things, she tried to make light of it, though she did grumble about the unfairness of life. Full as it was of unexpected twists it hardly seemed fair for "that man" to do it deliberately.

Nothing to be done for it though, Nanny found it more comfortable, more natural to be denied than satisfied. She often wore the look of someone who bit into a crab apple and was surprised to see she liked it.

Prudence plodded her way through her own pudding. From where she sat she had a perfect view down the long table of the main room to the throne-like seat at the far end where her father would reign, untroubled by such matters as thirteen raisins. Two young women in long black dresses and dazzling white aprons bustled around the table, careful to place three crystal goblets at each place. Nanny twisted about for a better look.

"One for water, two for wine," she said as she sipped distractedly at her own glass of a "rather ordinary, serviceable burgundy," and eyed the bottles lined up on the sideboard. "Well, it's not as if they don't have plenty of the good wines. The white wines of Verdejo, the reds of Rioja. At least I learned a thing or two from Helen. And speaking of Helen, why isn't she eating with us?"

In the next room, the hammered silver plates rang out as they were placed on the table. A butler hurried past, carrying a platter piled high with fruits. Before he returned to the kitchen, he went to the sideboard, picked up the giant candlesticks, and placed them on the table. As he walked around he touched a lighted taper to each wick and the candles sprang to life.

Darting in and out and all around him, the maids laid down the knives and forks, several of each. They inspected the spoons, vigorously rubbing away any imperfection with a corner of their aprons. Prudence heard a soft hiss. She didn't have to turn to know that Nanny had leaked the first sigh of what would probably be an evening of sighs.

"You may have been born with a silver spoon in your mouth," Nanny fidgeted with her second-best flatware, "but don't expect life to serve your happiness up on a platter such as those," sigh, "that you have to earn for yourself." Sigh. Sigh.

Her father entered the dining room, a plump matron on his arm. Behind him, a mustached man in black, a red and gold banner across his chest, escorted her mother.

"The mayor of the village, I do believe," a slight smugness to Nanny's voice betrayed her pride in being just a room away from such important people. "And that man, that's the Bishop."

Prudence put down her spoon, leaned forward to get a better look. "Rodicio has a bishop?"

"You should know by now that men willingly travel a long way to see your father. Now finish up your pudding, there's a good girl."

Several more couples—generals and their ladies—took their places at the table. At least she knew now why her father had been so upset about the luggage; he needn't have been. True, her parents in traveling clothes could have looked out of place next to the beribboned Mayor, his lace-encrusted wife, the generals and their colorful ribbons. They didn't. The two sat tall and straight in their chairs, their faces said we have no need of fancy clothes to impress the likes of you.

And there came Helen prancing in on the arm of a young man, plainly dressed, but definitely the handsomest of the lot. Prudence glanced back at Nanny, expecting to see her on fire with jealousy. Instead Nanny chortled, "Ha, Helen drew the village teacher. He wouldn't even be here excepting he is the Mayor's son-in-law."

"Where's his wife?"

"It hardly matters." Nanny turned her attention back to her pudding, turning over spoonful after spoonful in search of raisins. She savored each and every one. Poor Nanny, so careful with the pleasures of her life, she would wrap them in tissue, save them up, dole them out one at a time. Once spent, they could not be induced to return. And now, the raisins were gone. Prudence knew the sighs were not.

Another maid staggered through the pantry with a tureen decorated with the same swirls and patterns Prudence saw on some of the floor tiles.

"Gazpacho." Nanny picked around for another raisin.

"Gazpacho?"

"Soup. Icy tomato soup. Cook does it up so beautifully, those little fluted slices of cucumber floating on top."

In the next room Helen maneuvered as close to her seat-mate as the giant chairs allowed, smiling at his every utterance. Prudence looked toward her mother, watching the way her mother's lacquered fingernails flashed red in the candlelight mesmerizing the mayor with her charm. Prudence knew from past experience that halfway through dinner her mother would switch her attention to the diner on her other side.

In a few minutes that very thing happened and the mayor, freed from her mother's spell, looked toward the head of the table.

"You were lucky, *Señor*, to get this place." He glanced around the room as though the *Casa* was his. "H*err* Schiller has had his eye on this place for quite awhile. What with the troubles and all, he thought he—"

"The troubles?" The rouge on her mother's cheeks stood out in little circles against the freshly paled skin.

"The peasants, some minor labor trouble. *Señor* Carrillo has experienced *un problema pequeño* renting the villa. *Herr* Schiller made an offer—"

Her father waved a hand in the direction of the mayor, as if to rid himself of some bothersome insect foolish enough to invade his dining room. "Suffice to say, I make my own luck. Carrillo extended a favorable lease to me, so that's that." Her father's wave metamorphosed into a motion to the butler. "Some more Madera for the Mayor, his glass appears to be empty . . . again." The pause, his emphasis on the "again," was loud enough to make even a petulant Nanny smile.

The pace of the parade quickened with platters of fish, slices of peppered steak, and bowls of vegetables sautéed in olive oil. As the food warmed up, so did the conversation. The generals, the mayor, spurred on by the young teacher began arguing loudly, talking each on top of the other. They spoke of wars, of embassies, of generals and kings until even the bishop entered the fray. Nanny and Prudence, caught up in it all, sat absolutely still, their jaws slack, their pudding temporarily forgotten.

"You can't govern the people without the church. Look what happened in `33."

Prudence sat up, now maybe she would learn what the cabbie meant by the troubles of `33. She didn't, the conversation swerved yet again.

"What we need," the village teacher insisted, "is democracy, tolerance, lots of tolerance."

"That you'll never get," the mayor replied. "The villages have more need of bread, schools. Your republic is not providing them."

"It was promised."

"Is it not always promised, this good life? How often is it delivered?"

"And you, General, is that what you plan to deliver?" The teacher's voice made it clear he expected nothing but evil from the general.

"You fools, you wish to vote in the *inteligencia*. One never gets anything done with those people holding sway. We, on the other hand—"

Prudence leaned toward Nanny. "Who are they, the *intel*—?

"Hush, child."

"You are here for the lining of the pockets," the young man interrupted. The talk flew around, words she'd never heard caromed off the walls. She could hardly keep up with it, much less grasp what it all meant.

The bishop cleared his throat, "Have patience," he counseled, "our schools—"

"Your schools teach," the village teacher could barely disguise his scorn for the church schools, "you teach the children very little and from the pulpit you tell us it's a sin to vote liberal. It will take revolution."

"The world will not let it happen; they will put a stop to it." Her mother's voice quavered like the tremolo stop on an organ.

"Don't be so sure. Half the world is terrified of communism," the teacher paused as if savoring his own observations, "the other half fears fascism. Each will bite off the head of the other. Brother will kill brother; friend, friend. The propaganda machines will gloat over the horrors, magnifying them for their own purposes. For most of the world this will be a war of words. For us Spaniards it will be the letting of blood."

"But surely someone will come." Her mother looked hopeful.

"Ah—a handful of idealists will come, they will die. In the

end, so will Spain."

"Here's to the passions of the young." Her father raised his glass.

The oldest of the generals, silent until now—that ominous quiet of those who listen to what others say, the kind that take notes, file them away and then remember where they put them—spoke up. "You Americans, you think youth is everything. In your country, always the tomorrows, the new. Here we remember our yesterdays. That which endures is best. We do not easily do the letting go.

"All movements start out as brave new systems," the general cleared his throat, sipped his wine, "systems full of ideals, nobility and then—"

"Ah General, you are wise even beyond your years." Prudence was startled by the unexpected sadness, the rarely heard resignation in her father's voice, but it was Nanny's eyes that held her riveted to her seat. They had widened until they reached the size of the saucer that held the now neglected pudding.

"Gentlemen, gentlemen," her father tapped his spoon against the glass. "Later, in the library, with our cigars," he bowed in the direction of his wife, "we mustn't bore the ladies."

Prudence glanced from Helen to the mayor's wife, she couldn't quite tell what they felt about all this; but she understood her mother's look. Had her father mistaken terror for boredom?

Nanny's sighs grew so pitiful, so loud, Prudence feared discovery. They might be sent to bed. Yet something about the tightness around Nanny's mouth, the fingers drumming on the table, told Prudence that her supply of sighs had yet to be exhausted.

What could she do? Poor Nanny, she worked so hard. "I try to cause as little trouble as possible," she had told Prudence over and over, "I always place a saucer under my cup."

Quickly, before Nanny could face round again, Prudence

returned the errant raisin, the plumpest one of all, a surprise, a treat, a sweet to wipe away the hurt. Nanny's bowl now picked clean of fruit, what could be the harm? Nanny turned back to her bowl, and then Prudence heard it, felt it, that little rush of air, that sigh—the missing one, released at last.

TEN

A House is Not a Home

> *". . . a fair house built*
> *On another man's land."*
>
> —SHAKESPEARE, *The Merry Wives of Windsor*

PRUDENCE WOKE to a quiet so bewildering, she found herself straining to hear it: no street noises, no foghorns. Her head rang with the silence of the world. She heard only the clatter of her mind. At last even the clatter quieted and she heard the chatter of the birds as each tried to outdo the other as they bragged of their morning finds. She opened her eyes, it took a moment to adjust to the pinkish light that washed the walls and settled on the crucifix, melting its harsh edges into shadows. Her arms ached to the sag of its arms, the droop of its head, the face etched in sorrow and eyes that seemed to accuse her of some sin. Mortal? Venial? Were there any other kinds she could be guilty of? Last night? Nanny, the raisin?

With a God at the helm, the number thirteen should hold no power. But she had moments she doubted God could keep it all together—then witches and goblins and thirteenth raisins would matter. They'd matter a lot.

A complicated, slippery thing this God business—if he existed why did mean things happen? And even if he didn't, people either blamed him or gave him the credit anyway. Her mother said "Thank God" whenever they dodged a danger. Nanny God Blessed every sneeze.

Around the time Prudence turned six she decided to put God to the test.

"I'll say my prayers, and I'll even mean it if you will let two whole days pass without my father scolding me." That hadn't worked out too well, so she decided to give God another chance. "Okay, how about this: the next time I'm given brussels sprouts, make them disappear right off the plate, then I'll believe."

But the sprouts sat there on the plate until they turned brown. And as far as she could recall, she'd never gone two days without a scolding, not when her father was at home anyway. She behaved better when he was gone. She tried the God game a few times more and then she got caught.

"With God," Nanny cried, "with the Almighty, you play games?" To Nanny God was the only plausible explanation for the world's suffering, which made no sense to Prudence— if you wanted people to love you, to adore you, why scare them half to death with earthquakes and pestilence? Unless of course that was the same as hellfire and brimstone. Why didn't God just say: Yes, I exist, now say your prayers and we'll be done with it? Instead he spied on you, judged your every thought. Good ones, bad ones, you couldn't stop them; but did he care? No, you were going to go to hell anyway.

One time, a few years earlier, Prudence thought some really bad thoughts and hell took on a whole new reality. They were living in France, a small house in the Dordogne and her mother, all puffy in the face, had taken refuge in her bedroom. She lay in bed surrounded with pillows, stacks of magazines, her hair loose from its pins, the polish on her nails chipped. The entire household seemed smothered in a black stillness. Women tiptoed in and out with trays and hushed Prudence if she laughed, scolded her if she ran. Other than that they pretty much ignored her. She resorted to eavesdropping and gleaned little snippets here and there. "The Madame, she is too old for—" though the gossip stopped whenever anyone saw her. What could her mother be too old for—jump rope? Yes, but what else? Then early one morning she heard people running in the hall outside her door. Her father came in and told her to stay in her room. He would be back later to read to her. Prudence waited and waited, thinking all kinds of evil thoughts when she heard her mother scream, "Do something, damn it! It hurts."

Her Governess at the time—a no-lap lady who Prudence couldn't decide what she liked least about her: the lap business or the bad breath—came in with a tray, hot chocolate and oatmeal with cinnamon. "You're a lucky little girl, your Mother has given you a baby brother." Her voice overflowed with the forced cheerfulness grownups use when trying to convince a child of something they aren't that sure of themselves. Right after Prudence saw her brother, that blotchy red-faced bundle bound up in a blue blanket, she understood No-lap's hesitancy. Hardly a brother to play games with, he looked more like a squalling kitten whose mother forgot to lick clean. Brothers must belong to that class of things grownups gave you without asking. Now a pony, that would be luck.

She retreated to her own room, but paid close attention to the comings and goings out in the hall. One day, maybe two later, her door opened and a dour-faced priest came in and pinched her cheek. If that wasn't bad enough, he took her by the hand and led her into her mother's room. The curtains drawn, the lights dimmed, the room reeked of incense. He pushed her up next to a small wooden crate. She looked down. The kitten's cheeks looked bleached, its lips turned a dirty gray. The bundle lay very still.

From the shadows she heard the priest's voice. "Kiss your brother." Prudence leaned over, her lips brushed something cold. She ran out of the room, down the hall rubbing her mouth with the back of her hand. In her bathroom, she turned on the tap, grabbed her washcloth and scrubbed and scrubbed. The feeling wouldn't go away, she ran out into the garden, pulled up a daisy and ripped its petals off two or three at a time. God exists, he doesn't. He exists, he doesn't. He doesn't. He doesn't.

That night, she and the governess, deep into bedtime prayers, her father threw open the door to her room: "Damn it, woman, stop all that praying! Don't stuff the child's head with that nonsense."

He walked over to the bed, took her chin in his hands and whispered in a hoarse and scratchy voice: "This God everyone fusses so much about, he didn't exactly answer your mother's prayers, now did he?"

No one told Nanny about the prayers, and after she arrived the nighttime ritual began again. Try as Prudence would not to think about the women at the church who bent down to plant wet kisses on her cheek, she couldn't forget them. "Don't worry," they had said, "your brother never suffered, God called him home while he slept." She could take the now-I-lay-me-down-to-sleep-part; but the If-I-should-die-before-I-wake part—.

A year, maybe two, later her father took her with him to pick up the head of a tiger he had shot. The taxidermist popped a shiny glass eye into a tiger. Somehow it made Prudence think of her brother, the dullness to his eyes that day. "Why," she asked her father, "do people, things have to die?"

"If no one ever died," he said, "the world would be crowded. You'd never get a seat on the bus." She thought it odd, the part about the bus—how would he know? He never rode one.

Left to ponder the similarities, the differences between God, luck and an overcrowded bus, she noticed that as she prayed she never saw the picture-book face of God—the face she saw looked a lot more like Roland P. Whitley.

Here, in Spain, in this house with all its gruesome reminders, how tempting for Jesus to jump down off his cross and make off with her soul. Who could stop him?

Enough of that, the dawn had given way to a blue that lacked the transparency, the wetness of an English sky. This harsh, flat color formed a sturdy, immovable lid to the world. One could depend on a sky like that. Prudence jumped out of bed, made her way to the window just as the sun scaled the distant mountains, the faint chime of church bells offered up a reward for its promptness. Time to go exploring.

She tiptoed down the hall and toward the front of the house. At Nanny's door, a symphony of snorts and snores assured her she wouldn't be missed for a while. She made her way to the next room. She could tell it was a small one, it was the last one before the day room. She put her ear to the door—not a sound. So small a room, it couldn't be her mother's, definitely not her father's—he always took the biggest bedroom of all. Cautiously she peeked in and saw a bookcase crammed with books—some she recognized as hers—a blackboard, one large desk and one, only one little desk. There would be no school friends. Her mother had lied but please, please God make it that she hadn't lied about the nuns. Don't let her father be her tutor. Not again.

She once endured ten long, miserable days of his tutoring. He set her to memorizing multiplication tables, dates and capitals in the liquid heat of Jaipur. He lectured her on self-discipline. "Force yourself to do that which you do not wish to do."

Two weeks later, tired of facing that which he did not wish to do, he retreated to the cooler highlands and hired a sweet soft-spoken woman, Dahara of the beautiful eyes and the mysterious deep brown sooty mark right in the middle of her forehead. From the folds of a brilliant blue sari threaded with gold, from its mysterious folds she produced two small books. "Can you keep a secret?" she asked. Prudence could. "Then we shall read together." The words were almost poetry, the ideas, new and challenging. They spent hours locked in those pages until her father slammed into the room. "Damn socialist." He snatched the books from Dahara, ripped pages out by the fistfuls. "Get out, before I have you arrested." Dahara and the pages of *Brave New World* and *All Quiet on the Western Front* went out with the trash. Her next tutor could barely read.

From then on, the people who taught her had only one thing in common—no matter if they were men, women, nuns or angry spinsters—they never taught her the things she wanted to know. Not a one. Things like: what makes your heart ache? Can you die from it? Why do you feel the most alone in a room full of people? Does rain fall up as well as down? But surely the nuns could answer the God question. What if they were old and crotchety? They might not even like children. What would she do then?

The longer she looked at that blank slate the bigger, the emptier it looked. She searched for a piece of chalk, took down her copy of Dante's *For The Young Reader* and scribbled across all that blankness. *Abandon all hope, ye that enter.* She closed the door behind her and went on down the hall.

The day room faced the front of the house and looked as if it had been moved lock, stock and barrel from the morning room in the London house. Overstuffed couches and chairs covered in floral prints invited a good sit. Yet hidden in a corner, hanging above a tasseled lamp, there it was, a crucifix, small but still . . .. From these windows, she could see that the house stood alone on a crest; yet here the slope gentled its way down to Rodicio. The rumble of a cart separated from the clucking and cackling of the chickens at their chores, but the twist in the road and the occasional roof top that stair-stepped its way down to the partially hidden village kept her from seeing who it might be.

She ran down to investigate and struggled with the heavy door. It opened at last onto a tiny garden where two fountains, little more than birdbaths, gurgled in conversation with the bougainvillea. At the gate, she rattled the latch. When it wouldn't give way, she hiked up her nightshirt, climbed over, and dropped to the ground. She turned around just in time to see Rubio, his donkey and cart stop right in front of the house. Next to him, high on the seat, sat Shirley Temple.

"*Señorita*, she is yours, no?"

"No." Why had she said that? She was glad to see Shirley, wasn't she? She blushed and rushed on. "Are you all right? Where were . . . what happened—?"

"*El vieje mucho largo.*" A long trip? Her confusion must have showed. "I go the long way." Still she didn't understand. "Round Regalado—"

"Regalado?"

"The village, I no go there. *No me y mi familia*, we no welcome there."

Little wonder she thought. That town didn't appear to like anyone. "But all that distance, your poor donkey—"

"Pepe, always Pepe you worry about. Pepe and Rubio, we

like this work better than *los limpiabotass*—"

"Limpia what—?"

"The shining of the shoes. I did that for a while but now only the soldiers, the police have moneys for the shoes. I no work for them."

"Oh, I see," at least she thought she did but something about his hair bothered her. "Why are you called Rubio, that means blonde doesn't it?"

"So, you have some of the Spanish, no?"

"No, but I heard Helen say—"

"The cab driver, he tell me that woman—that a funny name, Helen— she talk a lot." Rubio smiled. Prudence laughed and then she heard a noise, no need to turn she knew who it would be. The front door—"Quick, you must unload. My father, he'll be angry." But he wasn't, he sent for men to help with the luggage and tipped Rubio generously.

During breakfast, she puzzled over her father's behavior. Why wasn't he mad at Rubio about the luggage? She decided to follow Nanny's advice and "count her blessings." Her father, busy laughing over the misplaced luggage and complaining to her mother about Cook, had nothing to say on the subject of her street-side appearance in her nightdress. Even now he didn't seem to notice the way she pushed her kippers around, avoiding the rich dollop of sour cream Nanny spooned over the fish. Even the English muffin, spread thick with quince jelly, lay neglected on her plate.

"Marion, you simply have to do something," he complained. "The way this one cooks we might just as well have stayed in London."

"But Roland, she is English after all, what can you expect?"

"In Spain I expect things Spanish. Work it out, Marion. And damn quickly."

Prudence tuned them out, they could go on like this for hours, her father issuing instructions; her mother, explanations. She had her puzzles to deal with—why did she love some things about her father and hate others? Her mother too? And even Shirley? To love someone, did you have to like everything about them? Something about the mental picture of Shirley on a wooden cart, deep in the Spanish countryside kept her pushing and poking at the little fish dotting her plate until Nanny's voice brought her up short.

"Stop fussing, if you didn't want them, you shouldn't have taken them."

Prudence knew Nanny would like to lean over, spoon up the kippers and pop them into her own mouth but her father's presence put a damper on any high jinx. Prudence took up the biggest kipper and made a great show of smacked lips as she grinned at Nanny. The salty taste bit her tongue and sent her back to her musings about Shirley and her silly, wishy-washy, bleached out skin, the light brown hair; and now, the scratches on her cheeks, the chip near her mouth—hardly the look of someone strong enough, sturdy enough for steep hills, tall cliffs, harsh skies and bottomless ravines. Angry men, splashed paint and a silly pasted on smile didn't go together and yet . . . .

After breakfast, she'd take Shirley upstairs, wrap her carefully, maybe in an old sweater, and put her in a drawer. She couldn't throw her out. You didn't do that to old friends, particularly ones who let you cling to them when you were scared, hug them when you were lonely.

"Prudence? Prudence Maria Katarina Whitley, do you hear me? The Sisters will be here in an hour."

"Abigail, you forgot Abigail, Nanny." Her father insisted on honoring not only his mother but every last one of his aunts as well.

"Ah, my sweet Abigail. The Sisters of Charity are coming to school you."

Prudence wouldn't let the disapproval in Nanny's Church-of-England voice spoil her relief at not having to do lessons with her father. She could handle nuns, she'd done it in Mexico. Skittish, scaredy-cats who bunched up together like spider bites. You never saw just one. They talked in whispers and fingered their beads; and she couldn't help but wonder what they looked like underneath all that black cloth.

She'd had her talk with Nanny, she knew what women were supposed to look like. Her own body was changing. Every day something about it looked different, hair popped out under her arms and between her legs. Her chest, that flat expanse, had started rising up in—"women things" Nanny called them. Prudence checked their progress every morning. How could she be expected to concentrate on schoolwork with all that going on?

Through the French doors of the dining room, she looked longingly at the pond—there just might be time before the nuns came and her lessons started. Testing the waters to see if she could ask to be excused, she looked around. Her father, hidden behind the London dailies, sat at the far end of the table while her mother mumbled over the pile of papers Helen had dropped in front of her—lists for the servants, rooms to be opened and aired, silver to be polished, menus to plan, groceries to purchase for a dinner, a fancy dinner, "Our coming-out party," her mother called it. Helen sent the invitations from England but the really important questions still needed answers: where each guest would sit, who to place next to whom. A person's position in society, the regard in which the host and hostess held them, could be told by one's position at table—above the salt shaker meant favored, important. Reputations could rise and fall on just such details, the hostess as well as the guests. The two argued the pros and cons of the various arrangements. Last night's dinner took care of the locals; now the foreign dignitaries, friends of her father's, the authors, the producers, would come. The freighter's speed, or lack of it, had put them behind schedule. The banquet would take place that very night.

"By the way, Marion," her father spoke through a barricade of papers, "Take Helen with you when you go to the village for supplies."

"It isn't necessary, dear. I can handle—"

The papers went down. He peered over the top of his reading spectacles. "Helen will go—"

"I'm sure she has other things to do. Your office to set up, etcetera, etcetera."

Nanny's intake of breath deafened as her father folded the financial section. Slowly, carefully he ran his thumb down the crease, once, twice. The air went out of the room. Rooted to her seat, fork poised halfway to her mouth, Prudence watched him shuffle through the entire paper, placing each section in its proper order. As the last piece topped the pile, he cleared his throat. "Helen will go with you at all times. Do I make myself clear?"

The fishpond would have to wait. Now might not be a good time to ask—not even why her mother mustn't venture out alone. Could Rodicio be as scary a place as Regalado? So much uneasiness, so many scary feelings. Prudence couldn't help but wonder if all of Spain might not turn out to be a frightening place.

Upstairs, Nanny selected a pleated skirt, plain blue with a crisp white blouse topped by one of those dreaded Peter Pan collars. No lace. "We don't want the sisters thinking we're heathens, do we now? Nanny pulled and tugged on the braids, Prudence squirmed. "We know how to comport ourselves, right?" Without waiting for an answer, she went on with her catechism. "Sit up straight, answer the questions, don't smear your papers. Nuns won't tolerate that." The word "nuns" produced a chorus of hissing sounds. "The Church," Nanny's church, "managed quite well without nuns. Women married to Christ, it's hardly decent."

"But Nanny, maybe the nuns can answer the God question."

"Oh, they'll answer it all right. Just don't you go paying any attention to what they say. Your father's given strict orders about that sort of thing.

"Go along with you, now."

Prudence tried out her desk, it was comfortable enough. But where were the sisters? This tiny room stifled her. The window was useless, so high in the wall all she could see was a patch of the room across the way. The only thing that told her there was a world out there was the footsteps coming from the floor above. She had heard them last night as Nanny put her to bed.

"What's all that," she had asked.

"The maids, they live up there," Nanny added with a chuckle, "Helen's room, it's up there too. Now let's get some sleep, tomorrow is an important day for you."

From the way Nanny had acted, these nuns must have come straight from the office of the Grand Inquisitor. The quotation she'd written on the blackboard no longer seemed funny. She jumped up to erase it, knocking over the glass inkstand on the corner of her desk. An ugly dark blue blotch spread across the floor. She grabbed some paper, blotting furiously. The door opened, two pairs of eyes glared down at her. To Prudence, down on her knees, the women looked ten feet tall, hollow cheeked and cross. Their headdresses, with acres of trailing veils, tangled as they tried to get through the door.

The taller one stepped aside, motioned to a third nun, plump and friendly looking. "Sister Sabatini, help the child, she's making a botch of it." The nun paused, as if to gather more ammunition. "The quotation, you've botched that as well." Eyes, blacker than her habit, pinned Prudence in place: a miserable specimen, an ink-stained bug. "*Lasciate ogni speranza*: Leave all hope, not abandon. A common enough mistake for the uneducated, though you appear to possess a passing familiarity with Dante. None, of course with Latin, but we'll fix that." A bony hand shot out from beneath a floppy sleeve, gestured at her chair, "Over there, behind the leg, you've missed a spot." Prudence and Sister Sabatini worked on the spill. As the last crumpled paper hit the wastebasket, the tall nun motioned to the others. The nuns retreated, the door closed. Before Prudence could rejoice, it opened again.

"I am Mother Mary Thaddeus. I teach mathematics, geography," with a grand gesture she waved her hand waved around the room, "and anything else I deem necessary." Mother Thaddeus looked as if she could turn useless dolls and paint splattered villages into minor problems.

The pale, other worldly looking nun rambled on in Spanish. Prudence caught only her name, Sister Agatha. Throughout the morning Agatha dispensed fact while Sister Sabatini nodded and bobbed agreeably, fetching papers, pencils and wiping off the blackboard. Charts and tables, lists of Spanish verbs and provincial capitals appeared and disappeared. Scolded and shamed over this infraction, that misplaced preposition or incorrectly conjugated verb, her performance declined steadily until the lunch bell rang in the middle of one of Sister Agatha's lessons. It wouldn't be the last of Sister Agatha's facts that Prudence would question. Her father had told her that bone was bloods factory and Nanny said "you can't get blood out of a turnip" so how could Sister Agatha's God get Eve out of Adams rib? The bell saved her from having to argue. Prudence let out a Nanny sized sigh and closed her books.

As she stood up to go, "*Uno momento.*" Mother Thaddeus said.

What now? The nuns, propelled by some invisible hand, turned toward the crucifix and genuflected in unison. Still no one left, Mary Thaddeus impaled Prudence with her glance. She wasn't about to drop a curtsey to that ugly thing.

"God wants your devotion."

Prudence said nothing but those eyes went on prodding, pushing at her to say something. The Sister had that kind of manner, the pauses, the silences, the dagger eyes that forced a sinner to say more than they meant to, and sure enough before Prudence could stop it, a Nannyism popped into her head:

"Wanting isn't getting."

The nun stretched herself up taller and taller until Prudence thought her wimple would scrape the ceiling, but just before it could she heard Sister Sabatini's stomach give a mournful groan. Prudence got up, gave a little bob in the general direction of the cross. Sister Sabatini looked grateful; Mother Thaddeus, triumphant.

A dismayed Prudence found herself in bed right after lunch. Nanny laughed as she finished putting away her clothes, "not a nap, a *siesta*. Here everyone does, even your mother. You'll see, it's best to sit out the heat of the day." Nanny hurried off without mentioning her father. Prudence lay as still as she could. Five minutes. Ten. A century and a half passed and still she couldn't sleep. Her mind played back the morning's events and stopped at the sight of the boy and his cart. Why had she pretended the doll wasn't hers? Why the blush?

Maybe it had something to do with everything that went on inside and outside of her. Not only the way she looked, but the way she felt about things changed every five minutes. Most days she loved her mother; yet no way did she want to be like her. Even her body wouldn't hold still: the swellings, the ache to her bones, the jumble to her thoughts and then things like that blush. Nothing seemed as sure as it used to. Why anything could happen—a thought slammed against the front of her head, like a lightning bolt. She sat up. She must get rid of it. Somewhere in the very deepest part of her, a little voice shouted: *Don't think thoughts like that, you'll tempt the fates.* But the thought hung in there waiting for her to put words to it. If her own body could not be counted on to stay the same, then nothing could. The old Prudence could disappear, poof. If she could, then so could—

She jumped out of bed, ran over to the window, to dash the thought on the rocks below, but the damage had been done. She'd thought the unthinkable. Her mother— Nanny—they could disappear. Even her father. No, not her father, there was nothing powerful enough to make him disappear.

At the window, with the sun now overhead, the land below looked flat, uninteresting. No shadows, no bells, no birds. Prudence turned to the statue, it hung limp and mute in the mid-day heat. Even Jesus appeared to nap. Then it hit her—it must be then, during his naps that disasters slip in, that floods and plagues descend. Reason enough to skip her nap and go exploring.

Out on the balcony, she peered down at the pond. The air settled against her skin softly, like a silk dress. It wasn't hot at all. She tiptoed through her room, down the stairs and out the dining room doors.

She knelt down, peered into the murky surface of the pond. Something flickered. Goldfish—huge ones, a kaleidoscope of reds and oranges, fish speckled with blacks and purples. Bunched up in little groups, they milled about unconcerned with the world and its doings as they skirted clumps of reeds, tangles of lily pads. At every corner, guided by some unseen hand, they averted disaster, shifted direction. Their need for constant motion echoed an impatience in Prudence and she felt a connection, a kinship with these creatures. Huddled together, they appeared fated to follow the largest one. Like her, they, too, had no control of their destiny.

She heard voices in the library. Her father? Helen? She went in. "You mustn't disturb your father," Helen snapped. Prudence smirked, Helen would get hers. Her father liked it when she asked questions. While her father's back was turned, she stuck out her tongue at Helen.

"Father, how do they know what to do?"

"How does who know what?"

"The fish, the way they follow each other, turn all at once. Can they talk to each other? Are they looking for a place to live? A home?"

"Let's not be overdramatic, that's your mother's forte. Fish don't have a home. And they swim because they are fish and, that's what fish do."

Helen didn't miss her chance to return the smirk. But then her father redeemed himself. "Come with me," he said, "I'll show you something." He walked out to the pond, leaving Helen to mutter about Nanny not doing her job.

At the edge of the pond, he turned into the father she liked, the one that talked to her as if she were more than just a speck on the wall. He produced a small packet from the pocket of his smoking jacket, opened it, stamped his feet and sprinkled a yellowish powder into the water. He took her hand and pointed to the bubbles exploding everywhere. Together they laughed at the fish shouldering each other aside to get to the cornmeal, the sucking sounds, the wrinkling and puckering of lips as small bits of bread and grain disappeared down their gullets.

"Are they trying to eat each other?"

At first her father appeared startled by her question, then he laughed. "They're not that different from people." Though he went on, the laughter had gone out of his voice. "When there is too little food, even people will fight over it." A new expression, one she hadn't seen before, crowded his face. Fear? Uncertainty?

"Never mind, you'll learn soon enough," the old father bounced back, "see to it that they have enough to keep them from their quarrels, but not so much they swell up and die. It's quite a responsibility, you know, having other's lives in your hands." He turned, walked back toward the library.

Prudence sat down on the edge of the pond, took off her shoes, her socks, put her feet over the side and let them dangle in the water.

Several fish swam up to her, nuzzled her toes. One so gold it looked orange, one so orange it looked red. Another so red it dazzled. Others swam over for a look, a huge black one, a speckled one and one the creamy color of fine stationery; but the three that nuzzled against her feet would become her friends. *Ora Aureo, Jaspeadora and Dorado Rojo*, she named them. They're tails—at least twice their size—trailed behind them like giant filmy sails, wispy veils of gauze wafting in their wake. When they surfaced, pursing their lips, whispering of their hunger, she told them stories of her travels and asked about theirs. At last her new friends swam off. Where to? She pulled her feet from the water, turned around, knelt down and ducked her head under. Something grabbed her from behind. She came up, coughing and spluttering. Nanny had a death grip on her dress.

"You could have fallen in, drowned."

She shook loose of Nanny. "Do I look all wavy and broken up to them? Do they see colors? Do they know how beautiful they are? What does water feel like to them?"

"Wet. Wet and cold."

But it hadn't felt that way to her. Warm. Safe. And quiet, a nice quiet. She didn't know how to tell Nanny that, she didn't want to hurt her feelings. "Have you ever seen the bottom of a lily pad? It's a little map of the pond, the good places to swim."

"Nonsense." Nanny brushed the mossy tendrils from Prudence's face. "You're getting too old for this sort of stunt. If you want to see the bottom of a lily pad, you should check an encyclopedia. Or ask someone."

"I did."

"Who?"

"Father."

"And, what did he say?"

"Nothing." As Prudence had known it would, it pleased Nanny to learn that her father lacked some answers. "But I have to know, can fish talk?"

Nanny paused, Prudence could see her thinking, the lines in her forehead deep with puzzlements as she thought of a polite way to best her employer. She smiled, "Child, when I scowl at you, do you know what am I about to do?"

"Punish me for something I've done wrong?"

"How did you know that? Did I say anything, out loud I mean?"

Prudence had her answer.

ELEVEN

The War of the Bulls
> *"make thick my blood,*
> *stop up the access and passage to remorse"*

—SHAKESPEARE, *Macbeth*

PRUDENCE HAD LITTLE TIME left for exploring. Shortly after the banquet the *Casa* began filling up with guests. Prudence and her mother were expected to entertain them.

"But Roland, what should I do with them?"

"Marion, you know Helen and I have work to do, you and the child must come up with something."

"The bullfights, that might do it. I'll arrange a trip back to Málaga, we can stay the night and you'll have plenty of time for work." With that suggestion her father's workload magically lightened. Not only did Prudence and Nanny motor back to Málaga and the hotel *Caleta Palacio*, but they found their cab dutifully trailing her father's limousine and the taxis he hired to transport the authors, the publishers, the dignitaries who needed entertaining.

After seeing their baggage settled in their rooms, the grown-ups went off in search of anchovies and sherry while Nanny tucked Prudence into bed. There would be a fiesta the next day, they would be up half the night with the dancing, the singing. Nanny insisted that Prudence needed her sleep. This didn't fool her one bit. Nanny liked her sleep almost as much as her sauces, but as usual the choice was not hers. Dutifully Prudence climbed into bed.

After what seemed like hours, she woke to a room shrouded in darkness and felt the warmth of a strong presence. She tried to force her eyelids open but they refused until the sound of her father's voice unsealed them.

"Shh, don't wake Nanny. Get up, I have something to show you. You *can* dress yourself can't you?" Prudence flew into her clothes, ashamed that, even for a moment, he thought her childish enough to need help with that chore.

Whisked down the back stairs, through the streets and out to the port, she felt somewhat reassured. He couldn't think her too much a baby, else why spirit her off like this through the late night streets of Málaga with no Nanny to keep her in her place, no Mother, no guests, not even Helen and her notebooks to come between them. But his long-legged stride and her struggle to keep up left her without breath enough to ask questions. They didn't stop until they reached a wharf, smaller and darker than the one where they had docked. The eerie glow of flaming torches strapped to the pilings bounced off the sides of an old boat. Nothing else. No warehouses, no soldiers. Were the two of them the only ones awake in the entire city?

He settled his arm across her shoulders. The touch startled her but she liked the feel of it. "Keep your eye on that hatchway. No, no, not up there. Down here," he pointed to a place almost level with the dock where a short wide gangplank jutted out from the ship, like the tongue of a naughty child. She laughed. His smile said he understood how she felt. "Look sharp and the bulls will dance in the streets for you."

Bulls? Dance? Her eyes hurt from the strain of staring at the hatchway and then her heart sank with disappointment. Two slow, dull-witted animals ambled down the plank. "But, they're oxes. Ordinary, everyday oxes."

"Oxen, Prudence. Oxen. But beware *Los cabestros*, the tame ones, are there to lead the others."

"But if they are tame—"

"Don't be fooled. Many far stronger, wiser, than you have deceived themselves into thinking they had nothing to fear from such docile, weak creatures." He paused for a moment, cocked his head at her, as if he questioned whether or not she understood. "The strong often weary under the burden of decision making, and when they see someone else taking charge, a sense of relief makes them drop their guard and follow." He bent down, eyes level with hers and, in a tone that sounded like a minister delivering a prophecy, he said, "Prudence, remember this: no one, not even . . . " He paused, reaching out for her hand, "no one is invulnerable to the lure of the Judas Goat."

She wanted to cry. This whole magical night would come to nothing more than another one of his tiresome lessons. She turned her head away and kept her eyes on the ship, refusing even to blink. She would not let him see her disappointment. And then it happened, the glint of a horn, curved and dangerous, caught the light. In the gaping black of the hatchway, the first of the bulls stood poised, ready to descend. The dull beasts moved off and the first bull stepped into the light, then another and another. The beauty of the huge beasts drove everything from her mind. The clatter of hooves, the snorting, the stomping deafened her to anything else. Beads of moisture glinted off mahogany hides as they lumbered down the gangplank. Great streams of spittle fell from their mouths and the smell of wet earth and the heat of savage breath brushed against her skin as they passed. They shook their heads, moisture sprinkled across her face like holy water from a priest's censer. Beneath her feet, the dock trembled from their weight and her heart slammed against the sides of her chest. She felt her father tug at her hand. She didn't move. If only the moment could last forever.

"Enough," he said, his voice gentler than she remembered ever hearing it. "We'll see more of them tomorrow." Prudence looked at him with amazement. Had he sensed how she felt? Had he wanted her to absorb the power of the bulls? She forgave him everything—his preaching, his lessons. She stood twelve feet tall, free and independent of him and yet never had she felt so close to this man who held such power over her. Never had she loved him more.

She woke to a Nanny in "high dudgeon," Nanny's favorite state. "Imagine, the nerve of *that man*, keeping the child out half the night. Why she might have been kidnapped, carried off by white slavers—"

Prudence perked up at that. "White what?"

"Never mind. At the very least you might have caught a chill." Prudence had slept so late that Nanny had come to wake her. "Hurry along now, we're to see the cathedral and then we're off to the *fiesta*."

Prudence had forgotten to ask her father about the *fiesta*, but now that she knew the bulls would be there, nothing else mattered. Not even Nanny and all her complaints could darken the day.

As the cabs gathered at the door of the *Caleta Palacio*, Prudence marched up to her father. Surely after what they had shared the night before, she would be allowed to ride in the front car. But he looked down at her distractedly, as if unaware of who she might be. He waved her off and disappeared into the first cab. Nanny guided her gently back to her place, the place where children are seen and not heard.

Not the first time he pushed her away. Probably not the last. But this one hurt more than most. All her soft and woolly feelings for him vanished. She needed revenge. Maybe he had the power to banish her, but she could deny him the power to hurt, or at least from knowing he had. Once, accidentally on purpose, when she forgot to kiss him good night she overheard him complain, "Why is it, Marion, that the child kisses you goodnight, and not me?" She felt the thrill of discovery—that she, small and unimportant as she was, had the power to hurt him. She would do her best to never again let him see that he could hurt her. To let someone know that they could hurt you was to surrender some of your power. Her store seemed too meager to waste. She kept still.

The cabs entered the *Paseo del Parque*, and fell in line behind the cabriolets and barouches, each vying with the next in a lustrous display of hammered-silver and colorful blankets. Women in shawls and lace *mantillas*, men in broad-brimmed black hats rode at their sides, waving grandly to the less fortunate who moved about on foot. Even the *guardia civil*—despite the sheen to their black hats and well-polished pistol belts— appeared less frightening in the dapples of light that flickered through the leafy plane trees. Music—guitars, tambourines, and castanets—spilled from every doorway.

At the cathedral, she looked dutifully at the statues, the paintings, but instead of saints and virgins, every dark and vibrant swatch of earth tones formed itself into a bull, every flicker of light taking on the glint of a horn. By the time they pulled up in front of the arena, she had recovered from her pique. Up ahead, her father directed his guests. "Follow me, follow me." A huge gaggle of people did just that as they entered the arena and dutifully aligned themselves along the row he'd indicated.

Prudence found herself wedged in between Nanny and Helen in a tier only three or four rows above the arena floor. "We'll miss nothing from here," Helen glowed with pleasure.

Immersed in the spirit of the day, Nanny addressed Helen in more or less friendly terms, "*That man* has done himself proud with these seats." Though their seats were on the shady side of the arena, Prudence squiggled and fidgeted. What happened to the food, the music? And the bulls, where were they? A trumpet blared. Across the ring another trilled an answer. Behind her someone shouted.

"*El paseo*, he is about to begin."

On the far side, a gate opened making way for a procession of men on horseback to enter. They passed in front of Prudence, their proud, haughty looks echoed their stiff, straight posture as they sat their mounts. The horses wore blindfolds. She felt the first twinge of uneasiness. "Why are they blindfolded."

"So the sun won't bother their eyes, that's all," Helen said. Helen couldn't have seen what she saw: bones that poked through skin, knees that buckled under the rider's weight, burdened down as they were by gilded, bespangled costumes and ornate silver trappings. No one seemed to care. The crowd cheered, handkerchiefs fluttered around the arena as the parade passed in front of them.

Behind them came three men whose suits twinkled and glittered like the jewels stitched into her mother's ball gowns. The crowd hushed, their attention shifted. Another roar and a lone man walked out into the light and took up a rather bored looking stance to one side, as if all this excitement needn't concern him. But Prudence felt the tension that spread its way through the crowd as the horses disappeared behind the wooden barricades scattered about and three men holding capes the deep color of the bougainvillea reappeared. Again, the trumpets.

"Jerico," Nanny giggled. Once more, the gates opened. Prudence drew in her breath. At last, there they were—no, just one, a solitary, hump-backed beast who appeared lost without his Judas goat. Prudence watched the bull run around and around, sniffing at the air as if in search of his guide. He raised his head, the crowd roared. He lowered it, they roared. He snorted and pawed at the earth. She wanted to believe this might be an altogether different bull. This one appeared so lost in all this vastness, so much less powerful than the bulls of the night before. The arena trembled beneath her, not from the might of the bull, but from the excitement of the crowd. Caught up in the frenzy, she started to yell and cheer. She clapped her hands over her mouth. What was she doing? How could she cheer at this? Someone, something was going to get hurt.

Below them the men's capes rippled like water across a pond. For a moment the bull stared, then inched his way forward as if curious to see what they would do, these foolish men who would ignore his horns. The men stood on their toes, twisted their slim bodies first this way, then that in some private ballet meant only to lure him ever nearer.

"The picadors," Nanny whispered self-importantly.

"*Banderilleros*," Helen hissed.

Prudence ignored them both. The closer the bull came, the more grace and strength they seemed to gain. How could these men be so calm? If she knew the bull studied them, surely they must know. On the dock the beasts concentrated so on the oxen she hadn't been afraid, but this one's horns appeared to grow with every step he took. At last a hush came over the crowd and she thought she could hear a sound like the whisper of silk as the beast's horns brushed against the legs of one of the men.

She tried to look everywhere at once, all over the whole arena people moved about. A flash of light caught her eye and she turned back to the bull in time to see one man and then another drive beribboned metal spikes into his shoulders. She jumped up. Helen tugged on her skirt, "Sit down, you make a better door than a window, people in back can't see."

As the spikes slipped into the bull, Prudence felt a pain stab at her side. Why would anyone want to see that? Yet she couldn't look away. The bull shook his head back and forth in a valiant attempt to dislodge the spikes that quivered like the quills of a terrified porcupine. But before a single spike came loose, the firecrackers attached to their tips exploded and the men, looking quite satisfied with themselves, walked away.

In the harsh light of the open arena, against the white of the sand, the bull's power appeared to drain away, the sound of his snorts grew weak. Prudence leaned forward trying to catch her father's eye. Surely this couldn't be the dance he talked of. He would put a stop to this. The look on his face told her he would not. Once before in India, riding on the back of an elephant, clinging to her mother's waist, someone had yelled "Tiger!" The tall grass parted, her father raised his gun, his face dressed in the very same look. The sound of the shot still echoed through her mind.

He liked it. This is what he wanted to happen. She couldn't be sure which hurt the most, the look of joy in his eyes or the look of defeat in the bull's.

The horses re-entered. Back and forth she glanced, from the men to the bull, from the bull to the men. She settled on the bull. She no longer cared about the men. She pressed her hands tight to her eyes, but that did nothing to block out her father's voice. Like the gunshot, it held the power to shatter her ears.

132

He leaned forward, calling down the row to her, "Come now child, don't hide, you'll miss the best part."

"It's the sun, it hurts my eyes."

"Poppycock, you and your mother. Watch Helen, see how she relishes it."

Prudence looked down the row at her mother instead. Her mother's body may have been in the same row but her mind focused somewhere far away, out across the arena, above the top tier of seats, on some unseen object in the sky.

"Not your mother—Helen."

Prudence turned toward Helen. With the smile of a cat squatting by the unlatched cage of a cannery, Helen matched her father cheer for cheer. As if the sun had fallen from the sky, Prudence shivered

The bull ceased pawing the ground. He looked more con- fused than anything—the way she felt when grown-ups asked too much of her. The bull looked up at the men, shook his horns and, mustering some dignity, he moved off to the shadowed side of the ring. A man, done up in silks and armor like Wilford, Knight of Ivanhoe, entered the ring on a horse even more decrepit than all the rest. At first she thought he'd come to save the bull. How could he? His mount barely managed a waddle, his gait hampered by the thick pads he wore. The horse caught the scent of the bull and tried to shy away. Ivanhoe urged him on.

The crowd began to taunt the bull in his retreat. "*Toro, toro, está valiente.* We permit no cowards here." The bull shook his head at the men around him, more in protest than in warn- ing. "Your snorts are but the grumpy complaints of tired old men," the people yelled. And how brave might you be Prudence wanted to shout if someone stuck those things in you?

And then, something did go wrong, terribly wrong. Ivanhoe,

having closed the distance to the bull, raised his arm and plunged a lance deep into the animal's flesh. A spurt of blood burst from his neck. The bull ran out into the sunlight, looked around at all the people and shook his head as if in disbelief. Rivers of blood cascaded down his side, mingled with the deep brown tones of his legs, crossing the bone color of his hooves and seeped across the sand.

The crowd's bravos shook the stadium—her father's loudest of all. Helen echoed his every cheer while her mother still found that object in the sky in need of her attention. Down in the ring, the man turned his back on his victim and rode off. The bull cast a morose look after him and waited, as if unsure what to do. After an eternity of despair, Prudence saw his head come up, the muscles on his flanks tighten. He moved toward the horse, slowly at first and then he dug his hooves into the sand. Like lightning he was on the horse. He brushed aside the pads as if they were no more than paper and plunged his horns deep into the horse's belly. Prudence threw her hands in front of her eyes. A new roar lured her into spreading her fingers in time to see the terrified horse gallop crazily around the ring, dragging his entrails behind him.

She looked up, down, everywhere but at the bull. The lone man stood at the far side of the ring and Helen gushed something about his aura being more golden than a saint's halo. "Fool's gold," Nanny shot back." Prudence appeared to be the only one who heard her. Everyone fixed their attention on the matador who moved silently to the center of the ring, his back to the bull, his pose of aloofness fallen away.

Once more Prudence allowed herself to look at the bull. Behind the matador, the tired bull lowered his head, lower and lower until his horns struck little crosses in the sand, and just when she thought he might give up, lie down, he charged.

Once more, the stomping crowd shook the arena. Surely the man could tell that something was about to happen, but still he ignored the bull. With a slight narrowing of his eyes, a twitch to his cheek, he drank in the cheers of the crowd. The pit of her stomach told her that whatever was about to happen, she would never forget. No one would help the bull—no one was supposed to help the bull. Prudence hated her smallness, her weakness. She would have no part in the animal's shame. She covered her eyes.

Time stopped. Trumpets sounded from the far sides of the earth, the shouts of the crowd, like a nest of hornets, buzzed in her ears. The world ended. Helpless to do anything, her hands dropped to her lap. The bull lay in the sand, his head at a strange angle. The man with the cloak stood right in front, the sand at his feet stained a deep burnt color, his suit wet and sticky. The look in those eyes cut right through her as he gazed into the crowd, arms raised high over his head. In one hand he clutched a bloody ear, in the other, a tail.

Shouts of "*Olé, bravo*," rocked the stadium, the crowd rose to its feet. The men threw kerchiefs; the women, flowers. Prudence threw up.

For the rest of the afternoon, a banished child and her Nanny huddled forlornly in a hot taxi. From time to time clouds of dust rose from the arena and great cheers filled the air. Prudence might still doubt whether she loved or hated her father, but there was no doubt in her mind: she hated the Judas Goat.

Later, much later, the crowd streamed from the arena, her father's group the last to head for their cars. A breeze had come up and her mother cupped her hands around her hair to protect her set for the party that night. Behind her, Helen matched her steps to those of her father. The wind caught a long strand of her hair and blew it back across her father's face. You're in for it now, Prudence thought, serves you right. But her father took the offending wisp between his hands, caressed it like Prudence might stroke her mother's furs.

Back in the hotel, a tear worked its way down Nanny's cheek, paused momentarily on her chin, and dropped to the floor. "I didn't know, Luv. Helen should have told me, she just said we were going to *La fiesta bravas*. How could I know?"

Prudence fished about her suitcase for a clean handkerchief and handed it to Nanny. "Don't cry, we still have the music, the dancing, the famous café." A slightly shamed Nanny snuffed back her tears and, hurried off to see about some toast to settle her charge's stomach.

Prudence heard voices in the hall and put her ear to the door. "She's just child. Such a spectacle. . .Sir, no one should expect—"

She has disgraced me with her childish stupidity."

"She is not stupid, Mr. Whitley. Far from it, but for all that she's still a child." Her father remained unmoved. Prudence jumped away from the door as the handle began to turn and Nanny returned, her face long and dour. "We won't be going—"

"So, who wants to see those stupid old dancers anyway?"

"You don't fool me, child. I know who it is you don't want to see."

"I hate him. Hate him! Hate him!" Prudence ran into the bathroom to hide her tears.

Nanny called after her, "Poor little thing, the only one you fool is you. I see the way you fasten on him as if he were a piece of candy you fear someone will steal away."

Furious that Nanny should know things she wouldn't admit to herself, she ignored all pleas to come out. But, when she heard a knock on the outer door and a waiter announce their dinner trays, she gave in—her hunger stronger than her will.

Boiled fish and cabbage balls not much of a salve to her wounds, she pushed the food around her plate and thought instead on the bulls and their Judas goat.

When the waiter came to clear the dishes, she and Nanny settled in by the open window. From all over the city the music floated up to them. The streets filled with women promenading one way, men the other. In various corners of the park people danced, some in couples, most alone. Nanny grabbed Prudence by the hand and the two of them pirouetted around the room, exhausting themselves until Prudence fell gratefully into bed.

Prudence woke to the whomp, whomp of explosions. The walls of her room danced with blue and red lights. She ran to the window. Fireworks! The sky lit up from one end of the city to the other, and smoke, alive with the colors of the rainbow, rose in the air. A heaviness came over her and settled in around her heart. At first she mistook it for fear but as she watched open-mouthed, the smoke twisted into the shape of a huge beast, a huge bloodied beast, and she knew what caused the heaviness. Betrayal. Her father had betrayed her and punished Nanny just to get back at her. That wasn't the worst. He had betrayed their time together. He showed her the bulls and she thought he loved them as she did. He didn't. He let them die. And while they died he cheered.

She looked toward the bed where Nanny slept, a frown on her face and a leftover tear on her cheek. It wasn't fair. Prudence tiptoed over to the door and opened it. A little way down the darkened hall she stopped, ear to the door of her father's room.

She heard nothing. She went over to the stairs, walked down one flight, then two, then one more. At last, she heard voices coming from a barroom off to the side of the lobby. And above all those other voices, there was no mistaking her father's. From the doorway, she saw him, his back to her, his friends around him, their glasses raised in some sort of toast.

She felt the anger, it started in her toes, ran up her legs. They trembled. The pit of her stomach churned with bile. When it reached her throat, she yelled, "You're mean! You were mean to Nanny, mean to me and mean to the bulls."

One or two men turned around, looked at her. Before turning back they laughed at her. Had he heard? He must have, the distance between them seemed no further than the short distance traveled from love to hate. She walked over to him, tugged at his elbow. He looked down. She took a deep breath, shook her fists at him and yelled as loud as she could, "I hate you! I hate you and I probably always will." Then she turned and ran from the room.

Upstairs, back in bed, angered by her own stupidity, timidity—why had she said *probably*? Before she figured it out, the door opened and even in the dark she knew who it was—the faint smell of violets, the Yardley's shaving lotion, she had given it to him for his birthday. She shut her eyes, pretended sleep. After a moment she felt his breath on her cheek, his aura as strong as that of the bulls. But he didn't speak. He got up and called to Nanny.

"The child will have to be punished. I will send her to the convent in the morning."

"I will pack our things."

"She will be going alone."

"Sent to Coventry," Nanny said, but softly, very softly. Only Prudence heard.

Banished to the convent, she was marched into the chapel, one nun on each side of her. She wondered if that's how the poor man had felt that day on the dock when the soldiers marched him off. Once inside, the sisters pointed out the confessional, the wooden box. It put Prudence in mind of a coffin standing on end, at least it had two doors. The flame of a small candle flickered over one.

Sister Agatha pushed her in that direction. "The priest is ready, go in and tell him how you have sinned."

"But I haven't."

"We all sin, child. We all sin," she chanted and pushed Prudence through the door. So dark, so hot inside, she might have stumbled into hell. She jumped when a little door slid open and a man spoke to her.

"Come, come. Let's hear them."

"English, you speak—"

"Of course child, now let's get on with it. Have you honored your mother, your father?"

"Honored? Why should—?"

"God commands it." She tried to work out a plan of escape as the box closed in on her. "Come, come, we can't be spending all day at this."

"Out there, in the chapel . . . can the nuns hear what I say?"

"No, no, your sins are safe with me, only God will hear of your sins."

"Good." She got up off her knees and left.

TWELVE

Tea With a Dash of Anarchy
> *"Dost sometimes counsel take*
> *—and sometimes tea."*

> —POPE, *The Rape of the Lock*

MOTHER THADDEUS unlocked the library cases, removed some leather bound volumes—the lives of the saints, some Andalusian poetry— and read to Prudence in a voice not quite as soothing as Nanny's. Still it held Prudence enthralled. To her father, poetry was the mark of the educated and he "would make damn sure" she was one of them. Sometimes he had a way of making it difficult for her to admit she liked the things that she actually did. But sentences with the prophet's eyebrow and the rising sun on the same line were startlingly beautiful if only for their strangeness.

Most beautiful of all were the lives of the saints—not that she read them. It was their hand-painted illustrations, the elaborate letters, the rich colors, the golden halos that she loved.

"But," she told Mother Thaddeus, "not all that torture stuff."

"Stuff is not the sort of word a lady would use."

"Sorry. But why is it God is so generous with death and

140

torture and so stingy with his rewards?"

"Heaven is the reward for a good death." That didn't seem quite enough for Prudence—what could be rewarding about death? She had other questions, but she decided to keep them to herself. Not because Mary Thaddeus didn't have answers, she had them all right, long convoluted ones that made no sense. The other nuns appeared content—Sister Agatha prayed a lot but looked happy doing it and Sister Sabatini had a laugh that would brighten anyone's day.

"Can I try?"

"To be a martyr?" Though Mother Thaddeus remained composed Sister Agatha's hands flew to her mouth. Prudence thought she had shocked her, but then she heard the sound of muffled laughter.

"No, no. I just want to make pictures like that."

Mother Thaddeus handed Prudence one of the rare editions of the gospels, the kind with the magical illuminations that danced around the capital letters—"to look, but not touch." She gave Prudence pen and paper and told her to copy the designs. When she thought Prudence had progressed far enough, Sister Agatha handed her a quill and several bottles of colored ink. Prudence soon made up designs of her own.

She walked the cloistered halls lined with paintings while Mother Thaddeus instructed her on the fine points of linseed oil and circular composition. Out in the garden, Prudence examined the statues. Allowed to clamber up the pedestals, she ran her hands over the cool marble curves and imagined the beautiful curved lines they would make on her drawings. Mother Thaddeus supplied her with paper and soft charcoal sticks, as well as lessons in the anatomy of the draped figure. "Forget your paper, study the model and your drawing will draw itself. Meanwhile be careful not to neglect your convent duties."

Sister Agatha first had her running upstairs to help inspect the row of small, dark cells where the nuns slept, then back down to dust the chapel. The gentle beauty, the soft light and those thin sweet voices floating their song on the morning air, cast the sisters in a friendlier light, turned them into women she knew, women she liked. Maybe it took a bit longer to warm up to Mary Thaddeus, but in the kitchen with Sister Sabatini who taught her to make little sugared pastries in the shape of angels—how could she not like a woman so generous with hugs and packets of powdered sugar?

But exciting as she found her drawing, her reading, her walks, nothing could take the place of Nanny. And then one morning several weeks later Mother Thaddeus stopped her on the way to chapel, "Your governess," the nuns didn't approve of Nanny any more than Nanny approved of them, "will be here tomorrow to take you home."

"That's not my home, it's just a house."

"Now child, let's not be so willful, shall we?" Prudence dutifully, if somewhat reluctantly, agreed. After all hadn't Nanny said, "Discretion is the better part of valor."

And she did so want to see Nanny again.

Back at the *Casa*, the guests still in need of entertainment, her Mother had planned a tea for that very day. Prudence wanted no part of it.

"Do I have to, Nanny?"

"Your mother wants you to help."

"But I'll drop something, I'll—"

"Just be grateful, you goose, without the tea you might still be at the convent. Now get on in there."

"Aren't you coming in with me?" Who would nudge her

142

when the time came to drop a curtsey? Or tap her on the shoulder when a yes ma'am or no ma'am needed saying?

"Now Prudence, it's you that's been telling me you're too grown up for my help."

"But—"

"No ifs, ands, or buts about it, you get on in there. Lord knows we've practiced often enough. You pass the little tray, sugar on the left, creamer handle toward the guest. And don't forget to hold it level as you bend over."

"What will I talk about?"

"Just smile, let the ladies do the talking." It sounded like the same old "children should be seen and not heard," song and dance. If she was grown up enough to pour tea, why wasn't she grown up enough to talk?

"Don't forget to curtsy, but not too deeply. You're not meeting the king, you know." Once Nanny had done that very thing, a curtsy she never let Prudence forget.

At the living room door, Prudence peeked in, peered around the huge room. At least a dozen women sat as stiff and straight as the furniture in their struggle with the tea things.

Her mother beckoned to her.

"Ladies," her mother tapped her spoon against her china cup, "this is my daughter, Prudence—Prudence Maria Katarina Abigail Whitley." Prudence did a quick up and down bob, enough to pass as a curtsy and hoped no one noticed that her name was almost as long as she was tall. What next? Oh, yes. The walkabout—one quick turn about the room, trying to remember the names.

By the third woman she had forgotten everything in the boring sameness of their questions. She tried to make her answers interesting, but how fascinating could her life be to these women whose fingers were weighted down with stones of every size and color, their shoulders draped in furs the heat of the day hardly required?

A woman with a turban twisted around her head, held on to Prudence's hand and in a voice loud enough to stop conversation, called out to her mother, "Your daughter's a real charmer, Marion. How old is she."

"Twelve going on thirty." Everyone laughed. Prudence tucked that answer away for future teas. Her father said the world turned on interesting conversation; but how many different ways could she say, "twelve" and "Yes, she was tall for her age?" By the fifth woman, Prudence realized it didn't matter, no one paid any attention to her answers.

One question, though, gave her more trouble than most: "Aren't we missing our home just a mite?" Though the question came in as many varieties as places she had lived, it always had the word *home* tucked neatly into it somewhere. How to explain that she couldn't miss something she had yet to find? The word deserved its very own place, a personal Valhalla. She never stayed in any one spot long enough to sort out the night noises, separate the groaning stair from someone coming, the creaking floorboard from a ghost at the door. Surely in a *home* one could do all that.

As she met the last of the guests, her mother motioned toward the tray. Prudence raised the glass platter by its silver handles, balancing it carefully and made her second pass. "One lump, or two?" "Lemon?" "Cream?"

Somewhere between a proffered lemon or a dropped sugar cube she noticed a shift in the air as the women's voices took on an edge, a shrillness that made her feel all goose-bumpy. One voice separated itself from the others. It came from the round face of the lady wearing a gold cross around her neck. "What's to become of this country? The way the people treat the clergy, it's a disgrace. Dirty peasants breaking up services, parodying the worshipers, poking fun at the Saint's Day observances."

Another voice chimed in. "Ever since the Popular Front—"

The woman with the turban twisted round her head, slapped her teacup against its saucer. "Our government, a duly elected one, may I remind you, has every right to curtail the church."

"Curtail and encouraging ridicule—surely they're different things? I went to buy a new rosary, the clerk snickered at me, and he . . . he spit, in my direction."

"Perhaps," Turban lady said, her voice sharp, unkind, "perhaps you chose the wrong shop. You are not the best of—"

"But I have gone there often."

"There you are then, that's the trouble. Now, as I was saying, you're not the best judge of either character or quality."

Another woman, pretty in a fussy taffeta sort of way, broke in. "The people, they might be angry. Someone told me about some monks that poisoned a well?" The room erupted in to a clamor that approached panic.

"My God, Clare, don't drag that old bone out again. That took place a hundred years ago." Turban lady laughed. "I mean it, really. A hundred years ago."

"No. The butcher he told me. They did it, I know it," Fussy Taffeta screeched, as terrified as if she herself had just sipped the waters of that well.

"And the government has closed the schools—the Catholic ones anyway."

"They will start shooting the nuns, I just know it."

A short, stocky woman, with silvery hair bobbed short like a boy's, intervened. "I'm sure, Mrs. Silverton—"

"Clare, call me Clare."

"All right, Clare, there was some mistake." Prudence struggled to remember the speaker's name. Lupin something or other. "If you are still in need of a new set of beads, I'm at your service. I know a shop." Oh yes, Lupinek, that was it. Mrs. Lupinek smiled pleasantly at the distraught woman who had a few more gasps left in her before she settled into a mollified silence.

"*Le Democrate*." It was the woman wearing a hat that hid half her face. Prudence watched as she sipped her tea, cherry lips pursed and pinkie poking straight out, amazed that she could do it all without lifting her veil.

"*Demokratie und Spanien*," said a woman with braids tightly wrapped around her head, "two words as out of step as oil and cream—"

"Oil and water, Frau Lifschin." Madam Turban turned to her seatmate, "Mrs. Malaprop in the flesh." Her mother searching frantically about for some way to turn her tea talk back to safe, innocuous topics, or her favorite—her films—motioned to her daughter. "Be a dear and ask Cook for the tea cakes." By the time she returned, the women were nearing hysteria—Madam of the Gold Cross wept as Turban Lady shook her finger in her quivering face.

"They'll come after us, I know they will," the woman dabbed at her eyes. Braided Hair, seated next to her, kept crossing and uncrossing her legs, "Discipline, the people need discipline." Her teacup chattered against her saucer.

"But the *Guardia civil*, they are there to protect us."

Mrs. Morgana—that was it, that was the turban lady's name—huffed haughtily. "In some of the small places, perhaps but in Málaga now we have the—"

"The Shock Police my husband calls them."

"There's anarchy everywhere you look, they're burning houses again, "Clare jumped to her feet, "and don't tell me they're not. Just last night I smelled smoke."

"Scones? Jelly?" Her mother fought valiantly to bring some order. "Prudence, see if Mrs. Morgana won't have some." But Mrs. Morgana was not to be distracted. By now, most of the women were on their feet, falling first into this cluster and then that, insisting they be heard. But not the woman with the cropped hair, she smiled invitingly at Prudence and patted the couch at her side.

"I see you're a listener, too," she said. Prudence hesitated a moment before nodding her agreement, unsure whether or not she might have just confessed to some sin. "Good, keep it up you won't get sucked under that way." Prudence wanted to ask what it was she was going to get sucked under but Mrs. Lupinek didn't give her time. She asked about her studies and appeared surprised to hear about the nuns.

"I would have thought, your father—he dislikes the church so—" She stopped mid-sentence. "Never mind, it is of no consequence. By the by, my name is Dorothy Lupinek, my friends call me Dordo. Will you be going to Madrid with us this week?" Her mother had planned yet another outing to get the guests out of her father's hair after his mysterious workload returned. Pru didn't pass this part on, but nodded that she would be there.

"I'm so glad," Mrs. Lupinek said, "the Prado is well worth seeing. We can do it together."

Prudence searched her mind for something appropriate, grownup sounding to say, but the best she could come up with was, "I want so much to see the Goya's, the Velázquez's." And at that she knew she hadn't pronounced the names right, particularly that last one, but Mrs. Lupinek just smiled kindly, a new experience, an adult talking to her, not at her. No "dearie," no "sweetie" or "there's a good girl," not even a question about *home*.

"Your mother's a film star, is she not?" Prudence nodded. "Poor soul," she added kindly, "right now she looks as if she could use a director." Prudence tried not to giggle. She wanted so to be like the woman, no pretenses. No postures. Dordo— Even her name was no-nonsense. Dordo didn't seem to feel the need to push herself on others or impress them with her clever-ness even as the rest of the guests darted here and there, vying for the privilege of basking in the group's attention.

The arguments, the discussions, flew about the room; her mother scurried after them trying to pour oil on troubled waters when all she had at her disposal was tea. Yet Mrs. Lupinek sat, patiently, listening intently, waiting for those rare moments of silence. When the teacups danced and the little silver knives dove in and out of the jelly, she slipped in her summations, her refutations.

"I don't care what you say," a woman with a very Russian name, declared defiantly, "the people will have their say, they will prevail. They must." The room fell silent.

Mrs. Lupinek stirred. "Unfortunately, they will not—I do not say, that they should not prevail—but merely that they *will* not. The people so rarely ever do." A storm of voices crashed around the room with such force Prudence thought the books might tumble from their cases. Dordo gave a little shrug and waited. One by one, the women quieted and turned to look at her once more. With a catch in her voice, she continued. "Not for long, anyway. Money, power, armies, those things prevail. And yet, there are times when the people even knowing all this refuse to go quietly. This is one of those times."

"But I am for the Republic," the Russian persisted, "I will be safe in Málaga."

"For now perhaps you will, but for others there is no other way for it. There will be violence on both sides no matter who or what you support."

Prudence felt her jaw drop. A few women seemed perplexed, unsure of how to take this; others appeared determined to over-look Mrs. Lupinek's speech as they would some breech of good manners; the rest were too busy formulating their next salvo, their brilliant *bon mots*, to give heed. The conversation flowed on as if Mrs. Lupinek had never spoken.

Prudence remembered she'd heard the name Lupinek just the night before at dinner. Someone had said that in the hierarchy of embassies, the Dutch counted for little; the English wife of the Dutch attaché should by all rights count for even less; but Mrs. Lupinek always sat well above the salt. It was said she actually ran the consulate in Málaga and ran it well. The rest of the room might be overlooking the woman, but not her mother. Prudence took note of the strange look on her face as she stared at Mrs. Lupinek.

"Prudence, the lemon. Frau Lifschen needs . . ." Impatient to get back to Mrs. Lupinek, she passed quickly around the room proffering little wedges of lemon. As Mrs. Morgana muttered, "Poppycock, the woman talks poppycock," Prudence saw her mother cross the room and draw Mrs. Lupinek aside. She strained to hear.

"But why violence? Why must it always be violence?"

"It's all the people have, Mrs. Whitley—"

"Marion, please."

"How else, Marion, can the powerless respond to their impotence but to use the same methods the strong use to terrify them?"

Her mother caught her listening. "Prudence," she exclaimed, "it's time to ask the cook for the hors d'oeuvres and perhaps— well, Cook will know. Now run along."

Cook seemed prepared when Prudence delivered her message. Plates of olives, chickpeas and fritters—a Moroccan touch—made their way to the sitting room. The tea things disappeared. The women were served Barley water. Small dollops of Scotch were made available.

Mrs. Lupinek laughed. "A good idea, Marion. The smoothness of a well-aged Scotch can temper the edges of most nerves.

The ladies will be easier to deal with now."

As Prudence returned with a tray of glasses, she heard Mrs. Lupinek warning her mother of the dangers ahead. "This war will be brutal—"

Prudence caught her mother's look of displeasure, she hadn't intended for her daughter to return and she interrupted Mrs. Lupinek. "That's hardly fit conversation for the child's ears."

"Remain in Spain, Marion, and your daughter will not remain a child for long."

THIRTEEN

Perfume at The Prado
> *"To wake the soul by tender strokes of art . . .*
> *. . . For this the Tragic Muse first trod the stage.*

> —POPE, *"Prologue to Mr. Addison's Cato"*

MRS. LUPINEK'S TALES of love and duplicity flowed effort-lessly as she and Prudence paused before each portrait—this king regal in silks and satins, that one old and ugly, all barri-caded behind swirls of cloth. The young, the beautiful, a Duke, his Duchess, his mistress. She matched each portrait to its tale and Spain and its history came alive in a way the nuns, for all their lectures, hadn't managed.

The cavernous halls glowed with a light that seemed to ema-nate from the paintings themselves—flesh tones, a speck of high-light in an eye. The glimmer and shimmer of the women's satiny gowns, luminous blues, frothy pinks, vanilla-ice whites, issued from backgrounds that plunged from murky browns to deep blacks. Outside on the streets, the flower stalls and fruit vendors painted the color, the women's clothes supplied the blacks, the browns. The harsh light fell equally, unflatteringly on all, the tiredness to their skin exposed the harshness of their life.

"The paintings of royalty," Dordo told her, "may speak of beauty. They don't always speak the truth. A bit like the times, not everything is what it seems."

That sounded a little ominous to Prudence but the day was pleasant and uneventful until she glanced down a side hall and saw *him*. Mrs. Lupinek's anecdotes paled in comparison to the tall slim man in a camel's-hair-coat that brushed his ankles. His silk scarf tossed about his neck gave a little whisper as he turned his head to study a painting. He stood, feet wide apart in a confident stance, hands clasped behind his back. He looked as regal as any nobleman in the paintings—a Duke, an Earl at the least. His chin appeared chiseled from marble and his eyes sparkled like the jewels in the paintings. He had a full head of thick wavy hair. One shimmery, silver lock carelessly caressed his forehead. From time to time he unclasped his hands and gestured gracefully toward a painting. He appeared to be talking to someone leaning against a pillar; Prudence couldn't quite make out who it was. His voice drifted down the corridor like the sound of water washing softly over pebbles, a little raspy, a little rough but musical as he explained that the woman in the painting had run all the way to France to escape a revolution. His accent was new. Prudence liked it but then she liked everything about him.

"Prudence, what's holding you up? … Ah, there you are." Mrs. Lupinek had doubled back to find her. "Let's go, I want to get another look-see at *The Garden of Earthly Delights*." Prudence thought she was looking at it.

"Why Count Zavokov, I haven't seen you since Paris in `26. Prudence, this is Count Bazil Zavokov." Mrs. Lupinek turned to the count, "May I present the Whitleys' daughter."

"Charmed, of course." The Count appeared distracted. He glance around, spoke quickly, like one who had something to be nervous about.

Mrs. Lupinek seemed to sense it, too. "Come Prudence, let's be off, the Count wishes to be alone with Zurbarán's St. Casilda." Though she had no idea where it came from, Prudence had the feeling that it wasn't Zurbarán's saint making the Count nervous. The clack of high heels retreating across the marble floor made her look towards the pillar, a swish of a skirt caught her eye and faint hint of perfume drifted across the room. She thought she could put a name to the scent. Almost but not quite.

She had no nose for perfumes. A great drawback for a young lady. Her mother claimed that a woman should pick a fragrance early, stick to it and make it her signature. Her mother's had something to do with flowers, though Prudence never saw her mother out in a garden. Besides, flowers changed their scent with the weather, smelling one way on a warm day, another on a cold one. Her mother pronounced her daughter a failure at all the feminine arts. "Her father's fault naturally, the education he is giving her." She claimed to exhaust herself trying to "make up the deficit." Prudence, for her part, had tried to look grateful or as if she cared, but those were the very arts she found silly, boring at best.

Mrs. Lupinek gave her a little nudge, shattering the spell. With a knowing smile, she led Prudence away to a large room hung with paintings to match its grandeur. "This is what you wanted to see, what most people come here to see, a whole room filled with Velázquez." Prudence despaired of ever letting that name slip off her tongue as easily as it did Mrs. Lupinek's.

Their party had already gathered in front of portrait of a young boy, Prince, Baltazar Carlos, the women cooed over the boy, how handsome he looked, so much nicer than those skinny stretched-out people of El Greco's. What could they be thinking of? The boy was covered with baby fat and didn't hold a candle to the Count Zavokov whose entrance she caught out of the corner of her eye. She dug around in her mind for something witty, clever, grown up to say to him if he came her way; but his glance skittered its way around the room right over her head, as if looking for a painting, perhaps his favorite, one he had come specifically to see. From the disappointed look on his face, she could tell he hadn't found it.

Mrs. Lupinek took her elbow and hurried Prudence off to see a painting of a naked woman running through the woods, a dog nipping at her behind. Ordinarily such a sight would elicit a giggle or two but Prudence barely looked at the work, her preoccupation with Count Zavokov was complete. Where had he come from, he seemed to know everyone in their group. Mrs. Lupinek had said something about seeing him in Paris.

She was trying to get up the nerve to ask when Mrs. Lupinek noticed her interest. "The Count is from Budapest," she said, "he's an art connoisseur and a film buff," as well as a connoisseur of—never mind."

Prudence, intent on Mrs. Lupinek's account hadn't noticed a raised platform, a bit like steps leading up to an altar with an icon-like painting resting a top it. She tripped and started down. Somehow he was there to catch her before she fell. Her skin burned where he touched her. She felt short of breath. Why was this happening to her? First Rubio, now this. She wasn't sure she liked the way it just happened: the burning skin, the funny feeling in the pit of her stomach. The feelings didn't bother her—they left her tingly and alive, ready for something, even if she didn't know why. What bothered her was that she had no control over when they came, when they left or even how strong they were.

"Are you all right, Prudence Maria Katarina Abigail Whitley?" How was it he knew her name down to the very last aunt? She smiled and thanked him, and felt disappointed when he released her. They moved on, he to the right, she and Dordo to the left. But not quickly enough, not before she fell in love.

More galleries, a hundred more paintings, at least it began to seem that way, and even the adult's eyes were glazing over. The group retreated to a nearby restaurant. Count Zavokov barely looked at his food, he couldn't take his eyes off her mother who picked contentiously at the shrimp, the herring, the deviled eggs, as if the food had done something to offend her. She barely touched the *cocido Madrileño*, yet her appetite for smiling and laughing at the Count and his stories, appeared undiminished.

Prudence sat at the far end of the table, doing a bit of picking on her own. The blister forming on her heel had begun to throb. These shoes, these ridiculous Mary-Jane's, why did she have to wear such silly shoes? Why couldn't she wear sling pumps like her mother?

Everyone talked at once of what they had seen, the latest gossip. Heavy with food the diners began to discuss who could be counted on to remain loyal to the government, who couldn't. The conversation appeared to annoy her mother even more than the shrimp. Prudence had tired of it herself. Mrs. Lupinek worked on this guest and that until the conversation drifted back to art. Her mother's smile returned with it.

After what seemed an eternity of Goya's and Murillo's, Carlists and Monarchist, they finally rose to leave. Prudence stepped into the bright sun, her eyes blinked shut but a voice behind her, Mrs. Lemfeste's she thought, made her open her ears. "What is that perfume you're wearing, Marion? You smell like a bouquet of gardenias."

Prudence might not have learned the womanly arts that day but she did learn her very first lesson on love—one could find a love, and lose a love, all in the same day.

The group assembled by the limousines for the long ride home. Dordo, her mother and Prudence may have ridden up together, but for the return trip, Dordo and Prudence were shown to the second car, Nanny hustled in after them. Prudence looked up in time to see Count Zavokov hand her mother into their Cadillac and climb in after her.

The caravan drove slowly down the treacherous roads toward Málaga—they were to spend the night in Méderina, to see the Roman bridge, the huge arches and the gypsies who lived beneath it, and the basilica where a young girl spit in the eye of a high official, rather than renounce her faith. Nanny's feelings, hurt by her charge's obvious preference for Mrs. Lupinek's conversation, gave her a there's-a-lesson-in-here look as she related how the poor girl had ended up tied to a stake and set on fire for her perversity.

Just outside Méderina, a mob of laborers waved hammers and shook pitchforks as they ran up to surround the cars. Some shouted slogans, others pelted then with oranges and onions and the occasional rock. Prudence jumped when a rock cracked the rear window of her mother's car. She wanted to open the door, go to her mother, "She'll be frightened," she told Mrs. Lupinek who held her back. Just then a ripe tomato splattered against her window, juicy rivulets dripped ever so sluggishly down the glass. Prudence prayed her stomach wouldn't betray her again.

"I should do something—?" Her father wasn't here and hadn't she promised to take care of her mother when he wasn't there?

"Stay inside the cab, dear. The Count is with her, he can do more to help than either of us, we better just let the driver get us out of here as fast as he can."

At last the crowd ran low on missiles and settled for hurling insults, the worst of which seemed to be "foreigners," "capital-ists," and "fascists."

"Why, Dordo? We haven't done anything to them, have

we?"

"No, Prudence, not you, not your Mother, but they're agitators spreading out across the country, whipping everybody up. I
warned your father before we started out that this sort of thing is
getting quite common of late. He said not to worry, he had made
arrangements, the *Guardia Civil*, they would watch over us.

Mrs. Lupinek appeared to stare a while at the group surrounding the cars and then she glanced back at Prudence and
added. "But in this part of the country we're better off without the *Guardia's* help. Besides, the people's complaints are reasonable enough, the Republic is moving slowly on the reforms.
Change comes hard. The agitators are in a hurry. They just
want to scare us a bit, they won't do anything. Your father is
right, there are so many cars, so many of us. We'll be fine. It's
going on dinnertime. You'll see, they'll stop soon."

It didn't take long, the road cleared; the cars picked up speed,
turned onto the main street and kept right on going straight
through to the other end of town. Though Méderina appeared
calm, the cars didn't stop.

The roads were bad, the trip, long. It was late the next day
when they arrived back at the Casa, tired and dirty. When they
pulled up in front, Prudence realized that while she'd slept her
car must have moved to the front of the caravan. When her
mother's car finally arrived, she peered inside, Mrs. Borgiona
and Frau Lipschin were seated on either side of her mother.
There was no sign of the handsome Bazil Zavokov. Some
instinct made her hide both her surprise and pleasure when he
appeared at dinner that night.

Her father expressed no joy and only a little surprise at seeing him. "Ah, Count Zavokov—"

"Bazil."

"I enjoyed your art collection, Count Zavokov, while Marion

and I were in Budapest. And your Mother, she still lives with you?"

Her father might well have enjoyed the paintings; but, to Prudence, it appeared obvious he didn't like the man. For the next few days he spoke to him rarely and used his you-don't-know-what-you-are-talking-about voice and never once called him Bazil.

Alone of all the guests, Bazil never laughed at her father's jokes or rose to the bait at his insults. And something else—where the others ignored her except for the occasional pat on the head, the Count talked to her. At times he even whispered funny stories in her ear. She didn't remember any of them. It didn't matter, it was nice not to be ignored.

One night, seated to her left, he appeared to notice her growing confusion as the butler made his way down the table with a platter of fish, carefully boned and sectioned and put back together. As soon as she saw it, she started wondering how she would get this gruesome thing onto her plate. A wilted tail hung off one side, its head the other—probably all that would be left by the time it got to her she'd just as soon it all landed on the floor. But when the Count Zavokov served himself, he worked the silver spatula under a second piece, a very tiny piece and deposited it gently on her plate. She smiled her thanks and, losing herself in his smile, she almost missed Mrs. Borgiono's remarks. "Marion, I admire you, your spirit, but the drive up from Malága, it has become *muy peligroso.*"

"Dangerous, how?"

"I know these things don't bother you. Well, in any case, I will go home to *Italia* but, and as your friend, I must tell you that you should consider this yourself."

"Why should we leave?" Her mother sounded alarmed and Mrs. Borgiono looked confused, as if she thought she had gone too far.

"Forget what I said. It's just that I am a woman alone, and of course you have," she gave a nod towards the head of the table where her host sat, "I mean . . .no one would dare interfere with the two of you." Prudence glanced down the table at her mother who, in turn, was looking at the Count.

"Still, you and your daughter," Mrs. Borgiono continued, "are *molto coraggio*."

Thrilled to be called brave, Prudence decided to ignore the look on her mother's face, besides she couldn't quite decipher its meaning. She glanced back at her father, surely it would please him to hear his wife and daughter called brave. The scowl on his face took her by surprise; but it was her mother's next words that brought her up short.

"Perhaps dear, we really should think of—I mean I could take the girl, we could—"

"No need to concern yourself, Marion. I have everything under control."

Her mother wasn't convinced. The slight tremor to her hand as she raised her glass in the general direction of the butler, gave her away.

"Marion?" It was her father's turn to raise a brow.

"But Roland, this Madera is quite classical, don't you think?"

"It must be, Marion. That's your third glass."

FOURTEEN

Rabbit Hunting

> *"I hear a sudden cry of pain!*
> *There is a rabbit in a snare."*
>
> —JAMES STEPHENS *The Snare*

PRUDENCE KNEW what was coming next. Guests or no guests, she would be sent to bed. At the slightest hint of a quarrel—one of many things she wasn't supposed to hear—and off she'd go.

"Prudence, I think it's time—"

"Yes, Mother, may I be excused?" Why was it, she would wonder, that the adults never seemed to know how much she knew? Eavesdropping was, after all, her best way of learning anything useful. She climbed the stairs half-way and started to settle down on her favorite stair to have a listen, but then she remembered that this was to be a special night—Rubio had promised to take her rabbit hunting.

She got up, continued her climb, opting not to listen and not to look at the walls with their painful crucifixes and bloody paintings, the ones the sisters told her Don Carrillo had commissioned for his "wayward son's edification. Such paintings—all those bleeding hearts, Christ on his knees on the way

160

to Calvary, blood seeping from wounds all over his body, his tongue hanging from his mouth. Ugh! That one made her think of some tortured dog too long without water.

At least she didn't have to come up with a plan to get Nanny into her own bed early. Nanny had appeared pale and tired ever since their long drive back from Madrid. She would be glad enough for an early to bed.

After Nanny closed the door behind her, Prudence forced herself to count to one hundred as slowly as she could—one thousand and one, one thousand and two, just like she measured out the time between lightning and thunder. When she reached the magic number she jumped up put her clothes on and lay back down to wait for Rubio's signal.

It got dark, very dark, but still no signal. To make the time pass faster she practiced her signal, but softly, very softly, no need to wake anyone.

She and Rubio often slipped away late at night to go walking in the upper part of the ravine, just enough below the rim so as not to be seen. What she had taken to be a sheer drop-off from her upstairs window turned out to be an overhang that obscured a small trail carving out a path down the cliff.

Rubio would parcel out his knowledge and name the plants, the animals, their habitat and habits. Once, below and far off to the left, he had pointed out a very small village. "Its soil, she is only fit for the growing of revolution." His tone, his look when he said such things, sent an eerie scratching up and down her spine. She hated it when he reminded her of the soapbox men on the streets of Málaga, the ones she had seen that first day. She worried that Rubio might turn out to be one of Nanny's anarchists that "God would see to."

Rubio's preaching never lasted for long, soon enough his voice would soften and before she knew it he would walk right up to some small creature, a lizard perhaps. With a solemn tender air about him, he would cup it in his hands and tell her to close her eyes and run her fingers down its silky back. But Rubio was full of contradictions. Once, in broad daylight, he caught a rabbit. In his hands it lay frozen with fear, ears laid back. In a second—half a second—before she could even draw breath, he had wrung its neck. That he could do such a thing to something he had held in his hand shocked her. "For the stew pot." She hadn't looked convinced. "Death, she is necessary for life," he added.

Prudence was growing tired and still no signal. She fought off sleep and had almost lost her battle when she heard the hoot of an owl. She sat up, let out an eerie shriek, the best nighthawk screech she could come up with and hurried out on to the balcony, down the outside staircase, shoes in hand. At the bottom of the stairs, she saw Rubio bent over the pond. She hoped to startle him. She hadn't.

"*Buenos noches, señorita.'*

"What are you doing?"

"Watching the fish. They don't sleep, you know."

Grateful to possess some knowledge, she smirked, "I know. From the balcony I can see their shadows slipping through the water, even in the middle of the night."

"It is strange, no? Nowadays no one, she sleep. Not fish, not my countrymen and not the *señorita*?" He put out his hand, took hers and led her through the pantry and out the side door of the kitchen, like one who knew the layout of the house.

It was when they reached the edge of the precipice, but before they began their descent, that he spoke of Don Carrillo, the hatred in his voice cutting cleanly through the night air.

"Don Carillo he is *un hacendado grande,* all this land you see above, below and around, it all belongs to *el patron.*" The way he twisted his tongue around the words made them sound like a mortal sin. "Our families, they have worked this land as long as his, longer." His voice swelled with anger. She thought she might tell him of yesterdays scare and the angry mobs but now she was ready for an adventure, a fun one.

"Not tonight, please, Rubio."

"Someday," he went on, "with the help of the Republic, all this will be ours again. All over *la españa* the people are taking back what is theirs—"

"Rubio, please—" She didn't like it when he ignored her. He was her friend, not one of those boring men that hung on her father.

"Don Carrillo is not one to do the giving up easily."

"Neither are you."

"*Es necessario*, we fight." He lowered his voice, uncurled his fists. Rubio had come back.

He had chosen the night carefully. They needed to make their escape before the moon rose, and then the reverse—they would need its light to guide their descent; but, at just the right moment, the moon must slide behind the escarpment and allow the dark to cover their final approach.

His timing perfect, a few moments after they reached the ledge, the moon popped up. They walked on for what seemed like hours until it disappeared once more behind the precipice and the dark became a presence, a weight on her skin. Not trusting her feet to find the ground, she hesitated but he hurried her on. "We must get there ahead of the rabbits; they have the sensitive ears, the knowing eyes."

She felt his hand on her arm, his head bent close to hers and his lips brushed her cheeks. A tremor ran through her body. "Don't be afraid," he said as she drew back, scorched by an unfamiliar feeling that had nothing to do with fear.

"What she is wrong?"

"Nothing . . . nothing." She let him guide her down the path until she drew up short at the sound of an awful scream.

"The first of the night's victims," he whispered.

"A rabbit?"

"No, the rabbits come after the black of the sky turns the color of the sea. When the edges lighten, the blue of the Virgin's robe dresses up the sky, then the breeze comes and sweeps the stars away and—" Perhaps the Virgin and Mother Nature might be one and the same to the Spanish, but Prudence decided not to ask. Rubio made it all sound like the poetry books in the nun's library; but she must keep her mind on the hunt.

"Then the rabbits come?"

"No, first the vultures circle, they search out the remains of the night's kill. The rabbits are the wariest, you must have the patience. The first sliver of light will deliver them to us but hurry now, we must get to the bottom before the sun she rises. If we are there long enough in the dark without touching them *los conejos* will grow used to us."

Clumps of cactus and prickly pear gave way to sage. She became aware of the smell of wet earth, rotted leaves. They were nearing the bottom. Once there, Rubio said that they must sit quietly and wait until the animals accepted their presence, their smell. Animals, he explained, find smell of man reason enough for fear.

"Men maybe, but I don't smell."

"We all do. Some good, some not so good, but you . . . I know you are coming before you are there, the clean smell, the smell of good soap." She thought of her mother's perfume and wished he'd picked something a little more . . . well, a little fancier.

At first she saw nothing, heard nothing, but a moment's quiet brought her the sounds of scuttling lizards, scurrying mice. The floor of the ravine began to vibrate with the comings and goings of small creatures. Rubio found a rock for her to sit on, it would be all right, he said, they didn't have long to wait. As the dark weakened, she saw the slingshot in his hand.

He studied his weapon as if unsure of its value, "Soon I will have my gun."

"But you said the rabbits are for your family to eat, you didn't want them filled with buck shot."

"Yes, for now my hands, the rocks, they are enough. The gun she is for later."

"Later?"

"The war."

"You, too? Why does everybody think there is going to be a war?"

"Do you know what *española* means?" She shrugged. "*Mi Pàpa*, he say that long, long ago, somewhere hidden in that part of our language that swam over from Africa, it meant 'land of rabbits.'"

"Are there more rabbits even than donkeys?"

Rubio's smile slipped quickly into a sneer. "*Sì*, but this name, she does something to our people. Always we fly in all directions, our ears aquiver, alert to every rumor. We never learn to move as one. *Pàpa* tell me that long ago we could not put our shields together, to make the phalanx. That is why it is so easy to defeat us—" He drew in his breath, gathering strength for his next words. "But we learn, some of us, we learn."

She tried to tell him the talk she overheard, but she talked too fast and her words pinged like little pebbles against the rock. He put his fingers to his lips to silence her.

"The rabbits, we must listen for the rustle of leaves."

In the stillness she felt the cold, the hardness of the rock, but she stayed as motionless as she could until she saw a sliver of light, a halo crest the hill.

"Rubio—"

"Shh! There, over there, *Señorita*, look." He picked up a rock, loaded it into the slingshot. She heard the rush of air, a thud and then few yards off, a moan. Her eyes picked up the outline of a rabbit lying still a few feet away. Rubio went to it, picked it up and held it toward her as an offering, a gift. She took hold of it and hugged its softness to her chest. The faint flutter of its heart beat against her. How fragile life must be, she thought. How sad to have it end so mysteriously, brought down by something it never saw. With one hand she reached out, touched Rubio's chest. The beat of his heart reassured her. He smiled.

FIFTEEN

Eavesdropping

". . .if you be afeard to hear the worst
Then let the worst fall on your head."

—SHAKESPEARE, *King John*

EVERY DAY THINGS happened, the death of rabbits began to seem unimportant. Prudence didn't understand half of what she saw and little of what she heard, but that didn't stop her from worrying about it all. She even worried about whether or not she should worry. The way the grownups acted—the way they tried to keep things from her—she thought probably she should. But about what? Who? Hurried conversations trailed off at her approach. Not always soon enough, not before she caught snatches, bits of conversation that bristled with words like "guns," "allies," and "non-intervention treaties." She had no idea what some of those things were, but they must be important, the men never tired of discussing them.

Whenever she could she crouched behind the newel post and watched men she had never seen before, some clutching over-stuffed briefcases to their chests, others with tucked rolls of maps under their arms. All scurried about in badly pressed suits. Men in uniforms covered in ribbons genuflected and traced the sign of the cross on their chest as they rushed passed the crucifixes. Each time the library door opened, the smell of burnt paper wafted up the stairs and Prudence saw Helen on her knees, poking long, thin, curls of paper into the fireplace. No matter how fast she poked, she couldn't keep pace with the Teletype. A group of men stood around the chattering machine ready to catch whatever fresh rumor it spit out.

The nightly dinner parties grew more contentious. The men, oblivious to the bits of oregano bread spewing from their mouths, shouted insults across the table. The amusing stories, the anecdotes of Spanish myths and customs disappeared underneath a barrage of angry quarrels.

Ever since the night the German monopolized the conversation with his lecture on "the joys of war, the thrill of battle," she and Nanny had been consigned to the pantry. The man made a point of belittling everyone's fears. He told them to put their faith as well as their money "on the guns." "War," he had said the last night she dined with her parents, "can be profitable."

Bazil, who usually had little to say had pushed his plate away. It had nothing to do with the fish, he loved lemon-pepper sole. "You damn fool, did you, your country learn nothing in the Great War? All those cannon balls—the ones you shaped so lovingly—do you know what happens to them when they leave your factory?"

The German just picked his teeth and stared at the ceiling, as if Bazil and his look of loathing were of no more importance than the piece of gristle caught in his molar.

"They plow into mother earth, churn her up, expose the muck, the mire." Bazil's pent up anger gave his voice the timbre of corroded metal. "Do you know what they find in all that? Do you?"

Prudence held her breath. The German pulled out his toothpick, examined it carefully, then shifted it to the other side of his mouth.

"They find the soul, the poor miserable human soul and flay it open, warts and all."

Her father's lips pursed in disapproval. The room fell silent. Her mother stared down the table, her search over when her glance locked on her daughter's. Prudence tried to muster the courage to smile, but before she could, her mother looked away, her hands fluttered about her hair as if in fixing it she could fix the world. She turned to her husband, whispered in his ear. Prudence and Nanny were sent from the table.

For at least a week now Prudence and Nanny had dined in the pantry on tiresome soups. As the maid cleared the bowls, Nanny pointed out little flecks of meat, chunks of vegetables that looked suspiciously like bits she had left on her plate from the day before, or the day before that. Stomachs a-rumble in protest, the two rose from the table and headed upstairs, Nanny mourning the loss of the English cook and her penchant for thick slabs of beef.

Prudence much preferred the young Spanish woman who had taken her place. Unlike her tight-lipped predecessor, she often coaxed Prudence into the warmth of her kitchen, let her add a little cumin, a touch of saffron to the kettle and showed her how to lay sprigs of bay leaf, slices of wild mushroom, as decorations around the platter. This Cook would ladle out tidbits from the *suquet* pot, chunks of eel and bits of shrimp afloat in garlic sauce for her to taste. But all that had stopped. Prudence wasn't sure just why but now the kitchen door remained closed to her.

That night, as she and Nanny crossed the hall on their way to the stairs and boredom, Prudence glared at yet one more closed door and thought she could smell some oregano. Surely the food being ladled on to those plates must be better than she and Nanny were getting. "Despite the *Unsettled times*,"—everyone appeared to find this a less frightening way of referring to what was going on all around them—her father would have no patience with soup and gruel. Prudence decided enough was enough. If no one would tell her what was so unsettling, she would find out for herself.

After dinner the men would gather in the library to light up their cigars, cigarillos and pipes. The air would fill with perfumed smoke and conversations too controversial for the women's ears—those telling sentences that sealed the pantry door. Prudence formed a plan. After the first of Nanny's gentle snores, she would creep back down the stairs, into the dining room and out onto the patio. She would have no trouble hearing. The warm night air guaranteed that the doors would be open.

Crouching behind a pot of bougainvillea, she chanced her first peek into the library and saw the mayor, the schoolteacher, the aide to the Governor of Málaga , some generals, one or two of the genuflectors and several men she had never seen. The authors, the artists, had disappeared days earlier—not Bazil, though he rarely joined the men in their after dinner rituals. Tobacco made him sneeze, he said. Though Prudence noticed he didn't seem bothered by her mother's Marlboros.

Prudence sat patiently while the talk worked circles around the food, the wine, the merits of various cigars. She had eavesdropped often enough to know how her father's guests, how they behaved. Soon enough the voices would rise in anger and the arguments begin. Then she would learn why doors were slamming shut and why everybody ignored her. Though Bazil and Nanny didn't exactly ignore her, they tended to talk on and on about nothing, as if to keep from saying something.

"Some of these men, Lozaño and his ill-clothed Republicans, they hate the church, the Royalists." She felt little pinpricks creep along her arms. This *ist* business, she'd noticed that whenever the men got together, every other word ended in *ist*. So many *ists*, how was she supposed to tell one from another? She would keep track of them, save them for a time when she could ask Rubio. She began to count—Royalists, number one.

"Surely you, as an aide to the Governor, will not support the Falangists?" Number two.

"No, I—"

"And the Carlists—?"

Three.

The teacher stood up, raised his fist. "*Una varicela*, a pox on you with your money, *tus negocios*. When it comes to the people, there is nothing to negotiate."

"Ha! You altruists," *number four*, "you profess to love the little people, to spurn talk of practicalities, of money. Yet I never hear any of you turning back your salaries, or even passing on some of your riches to the little people; and yet you have the gall to begrudge us businessmen our profit."

A well-tailored man, until now seemingly content with eyeing his smoke rings, spoke up. "Surely you don't support the communists, those dirty rabble."

Five.

"*Los comunistas, los socialistas*—" *Six? Seven?* Socialists were six. She'd heard communists so often she may have counted it twice? Three times? "*—comerán este país arriba.*"

"Take care sir," the mayor spoke up, "do not speak of communists eating the people, the country up. At least do not do so in Spanish—the walls, the servants, they have—"

"My servants are loyal." Until now her father had said little.

"Begging your pardon, *señor*, in such times, no one's servants

171

are loyal."

Cook? The maids? What about the gardener who thinned the lily pads in the pond? Must she fear them all? Nanny wasn't a servant, not really, and she certainly couldn't be mistaken for a Spaniard. Nanny could never be disloyal.

The teacher moved back into the shadows and the mayor drew himself up, puffed out his chest, as if he wished to command the room. But without his uniform or his medals he seemed so insignificant. I myself will remain loyal to the Republic, however there are rumors—"

"You with your rumors. There are more rumors making the rounds than I have students."

"The talk is that the army in Morocco will revolt, Franco—"

"That damn fascist!"

Nine? Ten? The mayor lost control. Prudence lost count.

The men spoke one on top of the other. "More than likely you got that bit of news from *Señor* Gomez, he's just come from that hotbed of spies."

"Biarritz?"

"Where else?"

"Franco enjoys his exile in the Canary Islands, he will not bestir himself. The army will remain loyal to the Republic."

"How do you know?" The general's voice mustered such power, such authority, it stilled the hubbub; and, though she crouched a distance away, his smile chilled her. "Some of us are Carlists, some Monarchists, some Falangists and some—" Prudence felt helpless in the presence of so many *ists*. What would happen if *ists* had more power than her father?

"Most of you are damn fools." The German's face tightened, he looked so stiff and somber, he might just have climbed out of a vat of starch. "The army will go with the generals. Only today, Sotelo has called for military action."

"Surely," the mayor appeared shaken, "you misspeak. No fool when it comes to politics, that canny lawyer would not stir—"

"This very day he spoke in the Chamber of Deputies."

Her father moved across the room, just out of sight but she recognized the voice. "War does not have to come. The Republic, despite its showing in the February elections—"

"Elections, too much time is wasted on elections." It was the German again. "I told you, it's the guns—"

"Shut up about your guns."

"He can't. After all, it takes more than oil to grease his machines."

Her father ignored the interruption. "The Republic is still shaky. It must reject the communists firmly. And equally it must reject the CEDA—"

"That far right bunch of goons—"

"Give the government time. They have released some of their political prisoners. I made front page of *The Times* with my story on that."

"A grave error, *Señor*, this release of prisoners. They will live to regret it."

A crude laugh shook the beribboned chest of a general, his voice stronger, his posture stiffer than the others. "You misspeak; these men will not live to regret it, at least not for long."

Her father didn't appear to enjoy the general's joke. "Now, now Lemona." Her turned to the others. "Once again, I counsel you gentlemen . . . time is needed."

"But the strikes, the disruptions," the older businessman tapped out his pipe, "even you generals can not agree among yourselves."

"Spain produces a variety of generals, as many as she does wines, each with their own smell. *Perdóneme*, bouquet. I should have said bouquet."

"Ah yes, but when speaking of generals that word does not tumble easily from the lips."

Prudence held her breath; a giggle would give her away. She looked up in time to see her father move back into sight, the tension drained from his face. This time he had liked the joke. The maelstrom of conversation resumed. "Hell, most of this damn country looks as if it's already under siege, has been for years. You can spit out any window and water a hard-scrabble life."

"That, my dear sir, is precisely why the masses are flocking to the P.O.U.M."

There it came again, that creepy feeling that made Prudence shiver—something about initials, the way they stood for faceless people. Initials tended not to have families, ties to anything but their cause. Initials might do anything. But it grew late, so many initials, so many *ists*, and despite her best intentions to learn everything, she grew bored. Her legs ached. She sat down, rubbed her eyes as her father spoke, even the passion in his voice failed to rouse her. "Mark my words, gentlemen, there are those—private citizens, armies—who will see that they do not."

"At any cost?"

"A way of life must be preserved."

"*Gut Gott*, you and your damn words, you think words alone can save this country?"

The German barely registered the glare her father sent in his direction, a look that should have opened the floor, swallowed him up but he never flinched. "You, your country," he said, "you don't even figure in this. Mind your own business."

Someone Prudence didn't know turned hastily to her father and asked, "You expect war then?"

"I did not say that, the Republic—"

"The German, he is right about one thing. You will not help.

The Englishers either. You will sail away, take your family and seek safety." The schoolteacher sneered.

"No." Her father's voice came out strong, steady. "I will stay and see to it that Spain remains Spain."

"But your wife, your child?" At this Prudence came awake.

"They will be safe. This place is small, out of the way."

"Those are the very places civil wars start. The people are armed. They are angry."

"Well, if there is fighting, they can always go to Málaga, cable from there." They? Her father had said *they*, not we. No trace of her sleepiness was left now.

"*El bufónes*, all of you. Do not wait, cable your countries now."

Is that what he said? *They*? They not we?

The aide to the governor jumped up. "Málaga teems with socialists, anarchists, they are everywhere, who can tell one from another and, at that, who will you trust to put your cable through?"

They. They. Why had he said *they*?

"Perhaps all of you should listen to the man, he has the Governor's ear." The mayor spoke. "It is time to demand that your countries send ships to evacuate their nationals. And perhaps, *Señor,*" he stood on his toes, attempting to place his arm on her father's shoulder, "you put in the good word for me? Yes?"

Her father shrugged him off.

"You exaggerate," it was one of the English businessmen, "you have done this before, why should we listen to you?"

"Yes, you little wormy weasel, afraid of your own shadow." It was the schoolteacher again. The mayor stood close to the window, Prudence could see right into his troubled eyes. He appeared to collapse inward, as if his chest, without the support of his medals and ribbons, could not handle the strain. The men looked embarrassed for him, for his show of fear. It's a good thing no one could see her face. She was glad when her father spoke up.

"That's hardly necessary. He is not alone, we all want to survive."

"You foreigners," it was the young man, the one who had spoken so of revolution on that first night, "I doubt you are willing to pay the price."

"The price? Of survival?"

"Yes," now the young man had everyone's attention, most especially hers. "Survival does not come cheap, each man's survival is bought with the death of some other poor fool." The men looked from one to another, as if to ask who among us is to be killed, who will do the killing?

The young man waved his arms contemptuously, taking in everyone. "You stuff yourselves with food and drink, but you will not be satiated until Spain, she bleeds to death."

No one spoke. Prudence shivered. Why had she ever told Nanny she was grown up? She felt so lost, so alone as she crouched in the bushes. Though she knew no children, like children everywhere she looked at the universe as if she stood at its center, as if everything revolved around her. How could anything bad happen without taking her into account? True, her father had left them before, but not in a place ready to jump headfirst into chaos, where people spoke in initials, talked of cannon balls, battleships and the cost of survival as coming too dear. Her father, after all that's what he was, *her* father—how could *her* father do such a thing?

The men in the library drew apart from each other as if they too felt a chill. She saw her father pale, watched him fight for control of his emotions until at last he spoke into the silence. "Be honest, *señor*, look to yourself. Tonight at table, you too stuffed yourself . . . with the duck, did you not?"

The room erupted in laughter, conversation resumed, the *ists* and initials caromed off the walls, bouncing into each other. After awhile the voices blended together, her eyes refused to obey. She couldn't stop herself, she fell asleep, one voice, one word ringing in her ear—*they*. He had said *they*.

SIXTEEN

Defenders of the Faith

"Who can believe what varies every day
nor ever was, nor will be a stay?"

—DRYDEN *"The Hind and the Panther"*

LATE IN JUNE her world began to fall apart.

For three nights now, Prudence had tried to be good, to go to sleep, and ignore her fear the way her father taught her: "Don't rationalize it, don't try to understand it, just slough it off; fear is as unimportant as parsley on fish."

It was only the last instruction that she really understood. Not that it mattered; she hadn't believed him then and she certainly didn't now that her world had filled with new sounds that ate away at her resolve—the echoes made by distant rifle fire, the harsh crackle that came from the bonfires fueled by the anger of the villagers as well the contents of the church library. She'd overheard her father say, "Those heathens have no sense of history, burning books, indeed!" On top of all this, for the last few days an even stranger sound had appeared, one that could not be ignored like parsley. A loudspeaker boomed out across the village and stole up the hill, spitting out static filled predictions of dire happenings. Lately Nanny used that word a lot. Lately Nanny found lots of things to be dire.

Prudence might tug at the shutters on her windows, but she could never close them tight enough to blot out the howling of initials, the mindless slogans, the rumors calculated to terrorize. How could she just fall asleep, how could anyone? Even the crucifix, as it rattled against the wall, appeared to be issuing constant reminders of death.

She had trouble making out the voices, whose they were or what they said, but her curiosity only made her strain all the more to hear. Once she thought she recognized the voice of the baker, the one who did up the long loaves of crusty bread with the bitter seeds, the one whose cheeks turned red as he yelled *prisa, prisa* at the little boy who helped him. Another time the voice sounded like the bleating of the old butcher who wallpapered his shop with the carcasses of goats.

When the bells began to clang and clunk out the hours—the big bell needed repair the nuns said—she found herself counting them like she would sheep. *Nine, ten.* By the twelfth chime she appeared to be the only one in the house awake, but she knew she wasn't the only one aware of the dangers. The morning after the first bonfire, some of the guests had called for cabs and sped off into the dust. Every day more left. A few maids disappeared as well though no cabs for them, they just vanished. Her mother and father acted as if they hardly noticed. But the dust begin to gather on the furniture, even the crucifixes appeared to lose a little of their luster. The butler removed a leaf from the big dining room table.

During the day, those that were left moved from room to room locked away in their own concerns. Her mother appeared absorbed with the daily menus, the housekeeping schedules, Nanny starched and re-starched, pressed and re-pressed clothes fast wearing out from her ministrations. She warded off every question Prudence posed with "we'll just leave that to the authorities," or "have you finished your lessons yet?" as if she didn't know the nuns were nowhere to be found. The few grownups left wandered aimlessly around, doing their best to follow her mother into her land of make-believe where all went well. No mere child could be expected to notice that things were amiss, that her lessons had stopped, that people had vanished. Did they think she wouldn't notice that the villagers left their fields untended by day and danced crazily around bonfires at night?

No one paid any attention to her. She took to pinching herself every now to make sure she hadn't eaten too much of Alice's mushroom and disappeared all together. She played tag or hide-and-go-seek among the lily pads with the fish and fed them, and fed them, and fed them, and tried to remember not to feed them too much. When her games took her to the library side of the pond, she couldn't resist a peek inside where Helen kept up a constant assault on the typewriter and her father paced from the Teletype to the desk and back again. Sometimes, as he passed the globe, he would stop, reach out and give it a whomp that set it to wobbling dangerously on its axis.

Even before her banishment from the table she had begun to worry about her father; he had begun to skip meals. Her worry had nothing to do with his food—Nanny said, with his build, *that man* could afford to miss a few meals—but she worried because he usually treated mealtimes as occasions for ceremony, ritual celebrations of his wit and wisdom. He looked forward to holding court in the dining room and without him conversation fell flat and dull against the plates. The few remaining guests, unsure of what to say, looked expectantly from one to another, then looked away.

At night the house entered into a conspiracy of silence. Along with another day's layer of dust, an uneasy quiet settled over the Càsa, a sullen disinterest in all that lay beyond its walls, as if the village and its troubles could be kept at bay if no one gave them any notice. The electricity winked on and off without warning during the day and by nightfall it rarely put in an appearance. Most nights her mother sent her to bed early. Without a nightlight she couldn't read, couldn't keep up with her journal. With nothing to do but lie there and squirm and fidget, her legs twitching along with her curiosity, she grew restless.

One night, she got out of bed, gathered up her nightdress and crossed to the inside windows. No lights, no murmured conversations. Nothing. Through the hall, past Nanny's room, reassured by the soft purring snore that came from behind the door, Prudence made her way to the front sitting room. At the window she looked down. A soft red glow lit the sky above the village. It fascinated her that something as ugly, as evil as a bonfire could turn the underside of clouds into such spectacles of light, such changeable glimpses of beauty. Not the smoke though, its lurid red-tinged blackness twisted into the air like the tail of a rattler. She knew what fueled those fires. The nuns had told her.

A few days earlier, it seemed more like a week—time moved at the pace of a garden snail—she had passed the door to the wine cellar and noticed it open. Her father would be angry. He wanted the door kept closed so as not to "wake" the wine. Once she heard Mrs. Lemfeste make a joke. "Mr. Whitley takes better care of his wine than he does his family." Somehow it no longer seemed funny.

Just before she clicked it shut, she heard a squeak, a rustle. A mouse? A tired hinge? A little bored and with nothing better to do, she decided to investigate. Halfway down the stairs the sound turned into a whimper, she paused to let her eyes adjust and there below her, glowing out of the semi-darkness, she saw the white of Sister Sabatini's wimple. It shook with her sobs. Over in the corner, Mother Mary Thaddeus knelt on the stone floor, her rosary sliding through agitated fingers, the click of the beads as loud as claps of thunder. In between her Aves, she tossed angry glances at the weeping figure. Sister Agatha, seemed bent on imitating the carved saints, hands clasped in front of her, eyes rolled heavenward, as if asking for guidance— should she cry, should she pray?

The sight of the three nuns surrounded by crates and spider webs left Prudence with questions of her own. Whether to creep away, pretend she'd never seen them or go for help? A little shift of her weight and choice vanished. The stair creaked, the three looked up. They all began to talk at once. What little English they possessed had gone up with the smoke of the bonfires. Prudence strained to sort out what she could. Perhaps if she were closer she could understand.

"Paintings. Books. The heathen are stealing everything they can get their hands on. They steal from the church, from the convent." Mother Thaddeus seemed calmer than the other two, more in control, yet angrier. It showed in the tightness of her lips, the blotched cheeks. "The mob," she spit out the word, "they warm their backsides just as easily with Thirteenth Century masterpieces as with old trees."

Had Prudence let out a gasp? Looked shocked? As suddenly as the cacophony began, it died. Mother Thaddeus wrapped herself round in all her old authority. "Child, you are not permitted the cellar. What possessed you to come?"

"I heard—"

"You heard nothing. You must leave at once. Forget what you saw, what you heard."

Prudence looked at the crying Sister Sabatini, there must be some way to help. "Prudence, the best you can do," Mother

Thaddeus said, her voice now gentle and kind, "is to pretend you never saw us. It will go easier on everyone if no one knows we are here."

Turning toward the stairs, Prudence tripped over one of the crates. The label pasted neatly to its side read, "Manuscripts-RPW." *His note books? The ones he brought. The ones Helen guarded so carefully. What are they doing here?* A sharp hiss followed her up the stairs, "*Cierre la puerta, por favor.*" She pushed the door closed behind her. Did "no one" include her father? Probably not. Words like "no," "never," or even "not," rarely did. Had he offered them the safety of the cellar? She would keep their secret. If prayers didn't help what good could she be? Perhaps the bonfires wouldn't matter that much, the convent held so many paintings, so many books, a few here or there—what would it matter?

But the fires had gone on for three nights and she began to fret about one painting, a little one, an unimportant one, but one she hoped they might overlook—the baby Jesus on Joseph's lap. Different from all the rest, it had no angels, cherubs or virgins in flowing robes resting on billowy thunderheads, no saints with bodies pierced by arrows—how could it offend? Arouse anyone to anger? It didn't even seem religious. Simple, strong faces in clean, friendly light. A man, his son. That's all, but she liked the way a bit of swaddling kept its secret, it could well have been a man holding his daughter. Apparently, even the nuns busy with their prayers for others, thought little of the piece, it hung in the morning room, behind the door, hardly important enough to burn.

And that special book of *Andulician* poetry, if she were to pray she would ask God to make them overlook it too. A verse popped into her head, she repeated it over and over, a mantra to save the sisters, their books, their paintings.

PAULIE P. NICOLL

Is there no way I might
Open my heart with a knife
I could slip you in
And close the cut again.[1]

She thought of those gloomy halls, the picture lights, the paintings hung wooden-frame to wooden-frame and the manuscripts piled high to the ceiling in glass cases, preserved for centuries, everything crisp with age. How quickly they would burn.

She made her way to the sitting room, somehow needing the comfort of overstuffed furniture, but soon her eyes itched from the smoke. She closed them for a moment. When she opened them again she thought she saw the outline of someone on the roof of a garage just below the road. Rubio? Had he come for her? Did he want to go hunting in the ravine again?

Her throat felt dry and scratchy but she did her best to imitate the hoot of an owl. No nighthawk shrieked in answer. Catlike, Rubio climbed down off the roof, came over to the wall below her window and scrambled up onto the capstone, cradling something long and skinny in his arms. A rifle.

"What are you doing? You can't be hunting from the roof."

"*Si, Señorita.* I am."

Prudence shook her head, "There are no animals on the roof."

"It is the fascists, the socialists, I hunt."

"But the maids, even the cook, sometimes they call us those names."

"It is the time for the calling of names. I am called anarchist." His voice so full of pride, she shuddered." I must protect the villagers from the Moors. "

"The Moors, why would they want to come here...?"

---

1 Ibn Hazm

184

"Maybe they remember the beauty of my town from before."

"From before?"

"Yes, a long, long time ago, the Moors came. And stayed and stayed and stayed."

"The poetry, the words about the prophet. . . so that's why the nuns were the custodians of all those books of poetry."

"You must be very special. The sisters, they never show those books to the people. But you no need to worry, I will protect you or they will cut out your tongue, roast it on a spit and eat it for the breakfast."

Prudence felt her stomach turn over. "How do you know?"

"My father orders me to watch from the rooftops. They will come, he says, marching out of Africa, that Judas Franco at the head. I will hear the shrill sound of their pipes, see the white of their robes, the flash of their swords and I must defend my family, my homeland."

"But the sisters say you should defend the faith."

"The sisters were good to me. They taught me my letters but I am a man now." He drew himself up to his full height and raised his fist, shook it at the red sky. He looked like one of those posters in Málaga, the ones with the harsh colors, the huge block letters screaming words she didn't understand.

"Death to the Monarchists, the Royalists, the Falangists," he shouted in a hoarse whisper. His hatred had a squeaky sound to it, his voice lacked the anger of those at the crossroads. Surely he didn't mean death—real-cold-dead-never-get-up-again, nothing-to-do-with-the-movies death. And yet he held himself so straight, trying to look grown up and his eyes had such a sober cast to them that her throat got lumpy and she dug her nails into her sides so she wouldn't cry.

He held out his open palm, showing her the bullets. She felt better, he had so few, he couldn't possibly kill that many people.

How many people, she wondered, would it be all right to kill? Would she still like him if he killed two? Six? There were so many *ists* to kill, more than fish in her pond.

"Do not worry, *señorita*, I no waste them."

She remembered those *ists* she'd saved up to ask him about. "Rubio, how do you know who is a Royalist? A Loyalist? How can you tell them apart?"

Before he answered, the loud speakers coughed to life again. "*Atención, Atención*. A new regime, a new government, *Sánchez Román, el jefe.*"

Rubio spit on the ground. "*Román* can no lead, the man is a traitor. *Mi Papa*, he tell me if he is the government, then we must prepare to die."

"You, your father? Aren't you afraid?" Rubio frightened her with all his talk, every word he said took him further and further from the boy she knew, the boy with the gentle donkey.

"No, he tell me life she no everything."

Now she had him, she had a way to talk him out of playing soldier. "If you're an anarchist, Rubio, you don't believe in God. And if you don't believe in God, then life *is* everything."

"You talk with cleverness, like your *Papa*, it no matter. We die. Many peoples must die so that the people will win."

"But Mrs. Lupinek, she says the people never win." She felt cold, terribly cold. She wished she'd put her robe on. "Can't anything be done to stop it?"

"No. We start with *el calde*."

"The mayor?"

"He must go first. He is in the bed with the generals."

"What bed? What generals?" A burst of gunfire scattered her words to nothingness. The sudden spurt of flame that followed licked at her conscience. How could she even have picked a number that would be right for him to kill? How many deaths would it take to banish that the funny feelings she got when she was with him? She turned to ask him, "How could I ... would I even like you if—"

The roof tops were bare, the capstone empty. Rudio had vanished.

SEVENTEEN

The Book of Knowledge
> *"Then I, and you and all of us fell down*
> *Whilst bloody treason flourish'd over us."*
>
> —SHAKESPEARE, *Julius Caesar, Act III*

RUBIO HAD DISAPPEARED into the night, bullets and rifle in hand. She needed to do something, tell someone. What if the Moors caught them in their sleep? She took the stairs several at a time and raced down the hall to her father's room, the static from her heart drowning out the speeches and slogans pouring from the loud speakers. No matter how her heart rattled against her chest she must wake him, warn him.

A small light leaked out onto the hall carpet. She put her ear to the door but heard nothing. She hesitated, the fear of his anger at being wakened at war with her fear of the Moors. Rubio crept through the night, jumping from roof to roof, risking his life, the least she could do—she'd done it often enough for fun—was risk her father's anger.

She took a deep breath, knocked, once, twice, then hard enough to hurt her knuckles. No answer. She turned the iron handle pushed open the door. The bedcovers, though turned down, looked smooth, unused.

Where could he be? She went to the head of the stairs, strained to listen. Did she hear them—voices drifting up from the library? Downstairs, she paused at the door ready to knock, but some uncharacteristic flush of caution stopped her hand mid-air—one of those pauses that would puzzle her for years to come. She went out through the dining room and around to the French doors and listened. The screech of night birds and the chirp of insects replaced the usual clink of glasses, the shouts of anger. Night had cleansed the air of tobacco. Dark. Quiet. So what had she heard? She drew closer to the house, cupped her hands to the glass as if to peer in, yet, at the same time, she squeezed her eyes shut. Something told her she wouldn't like what she found. She forced them open to see a dim light,—a reading light cast a small circle on the desk and the chair. The chair was empty. Somewhere near the back of the room she heard a soft murmur, like the cooing of morning doves. Before she could place the sound it changed into the frightful panting, gasping of animals chasing down their prey. Then silence. The nothing, scared her more than the panting. She strained forward, heard a soft moan and put her hand to her chest to quiet her heart, her pulse pounded so she could barely hear over its racket. Voices? Soft, consoling. One heavy, thick and slurred—a man's. The second, lighter, more feminine, the purr of a well-fed cat.

Another table lamp snapped on, a man stood up, moved into the circle of light, one hand tugged at his vest, the other smoothed back his hair. The light fell short of the couch but as he moved toward the desk, she saw him. The only thing that surprised her was that she felt no surprise. But the woman? She strained her eyes, squinted trying to take in the figure on the couch. The sound of a bell distracted her. The Teletype clacked into life. Her eyes swung back to her father. He walked over to the machine, glanced at the thin strip of white paper and stood there for what seemed a long time, time enough to study his ruffled appearance, to think about the look on his face. She'd seen that look before, that first morning, the morning of the goldfish when he had appeared so troubled, so sad. The papers slipped from his hand and he cleared his throat, not once but twice, as if too upset to talk.

"We'll leave in the morning. It appears we have the excuse we need."

The woman spoke up, her voice sounded almost sleepy, asking only out of politeness, as if she didn't care. "Why, what's happened?"

"There's been an assassination."

The voice now sharp, harsh, "My God, who?"

"Calvo Sotelo. It will start any day now." Prudence wanted to cry out, to get them to slow down. She needed time to catch up, to think about what was happening. She had a new word to puzzle over, to hate. First the "they" and now the "we."

"Tickets, I'll have to get tickets."

For where? For what?

"I would have thought you'd have them by now. Never mind, we can pick them up at the station. It's going to be worse, much worse than we thought," he shook the tape in the woman's direction, as if he couldn't quite believe what it said, needed to convince himself more than her. "It claims the body may have been desicrated or at the very least he was beaten and then shot. There is no telling where this will end, who will die next."

"And the bank, I need time to get to the bank." Who was this woman, how could she talk of banks and tickets? Why didn't she step into the light, make herself known, it was almost as if she knew she should hide, as if she knew Prudence was out there.

Prudence tried to reason out who shot who. What had happened in that room? And who was *we*? The world wasn't about to stop spinning to give her enough time to think about it; yet a thought she didn't want to face, was fighting to make it through the fog. Then her father opened a desk drawer, took out a packet of bills and tossed them on the top. "I've kept this handy. And film, I've been stocking up, I knew—" his voice broke. What had he known?

"We have enough?"

"Yes, we could make a full-length feature, if we wanted. As for stills, we can flood the world's newspapers. They'll be enough tragedy to go around."

"Oh, Roland, I hope it doesn't get that bad."

"It will." How could he, how could she, talk about money, photographs. How could they just talk and talk and talk?

"It's just a circle—"

"They killed Calvo in retaliation." He read the tape over and over again as if familiarity would alter it, "to avenge some of the work of the *pistoleros*. The damn fools. You can't run around a country shooting union leaders and not expect trouble. But what a man to pick."

"Well, it's worked out for us. We'll need to pack."

Shut up. Shut up. Just step in the light, that's all. Why doesn't she? Prudence needed to know. She didn't want to know.

"The rightists will have to avenge his death. No random victim, Calvo. His death is a declaration of war." Her father's voice had a different sound to it, a sadness, something like the moan of a cello.

The woman went on talking. "Shoes, I'll need sensible shoes—"

Ignoring her, her father went on, "By the prickling of my thumbs, something bloody this way—"[1]

"Notebooks, typewriter—" Prudence put her hands over her ears, as if that could keep her heart from knowing what her head had figured out. She could be mistaken. The woman could be anyone, couldn't she? But not her mother. No not her mother.

Her father made a dismissive, impatient gesture with his hands. We've discussed this enough all ready. You knew it would come to this eventually. I pay you to be prepared."

Helen stepped into the circle of light, her clothes wrinkled, her red hair tangled and disheveled. "Sometimes, Roland, I think you're more interested in the war than—"

Prudence wanted to rush in, hit Helen, hit her hard. She wanted to run away, to have Helen run away, to pretend it never happened, to tell her mother, not to tell her mother. She hated Helen, hated her mother—it was her mother's fault, she'd let this happen. Prudence stepped back a step or two and bumped into one of the gardenia bushes that lined the patio and for some reason she remembered the *Prado*, that painting, Zurbarán's St. Casilda and—

"Don't pull a Marion on me, don't go all soft and rabbity."

Prudence shivered and shook, yet she didn't move. She tried to pick up one foot, to put it in front of the other, to push herself off toward the dining room but her feet wouldn't obey. She watched as her father reached into the center drawer and took out the passports. He selected two from the pack, they made a slapping sound as he set them down beside the money. The others he returned to the drawer, twisted the lock.

Two? Only two? And like fireworks it all exploded around her and she knew, knew for sure, for awful sure, what he meant. Now she knew who she hated the most, him, his "we." It never

---

1 Macbeth, Act IV, Shakespeare

had included her. Her passport, her mother's would be the ones lying in the dark recesses of that drawer.

That time he told her she must take care of her mother, she hadn't really understood from what. But now she knew. It was her father, the things he did, that she had to protect her mother from. She would do it, she would. Anger melted the ice on her feet, she turned and fled, not caring if they heard her. No one stopped her. No one called after her.

EIGHTEEN

Left Behind

"When little fears grow great..."

—SHAKESPEARE, *Hamlet Act 3, Sc. 2*

PRUDENCE DIDN'T REMEMBER how she got upstairs to bed, but she would never forget what she heard. What did it mean? How could she tell her mother? She should have taken care of her before now. But what if she was wrong about the things she saw, the things she heard?

She must sort everything out. Right then the if-I-die-before-I-wake part of her prayers began to seem a terrifying possibility. Prudence had to survive, if she didn't how could she take care of her mother? She'd failed her mother once; she mustn't do it again.

She jumped out of bed. Where were those matches, the scented ones Sister Sabatini gave her? Crossing the room, she searched the drawers until she found them. One by one the votive candles under the crucifix sprang to life, but their tiny glow offered no comfort, no warmth. Back in bed, covers up to her chin, she stared at the crucifix. Perhaps somewhere in those phantom shadows, the answer danced before her.

After a while the first rooster came on duty; the night must be almost done with her. She hadn't heard the church bells in quite a while. She sat up, looked at her clock. The hands, planted in a stern, irrevocable right angle, condemned her to navigate two more hours of darkness. Could she have forgotten to wind it? No, the sky told her night was still firmly at the helm and, for all her thinking, she was no closer to knowing what she should do.

"Four in the morning until five is a good time for prayer," Mother Thaddeus had said. "The world quiets down then. God can hear you better." She could get out of bed, kneel on the floor but the hard floor would hurt her knees. Pain didn't appear to stop the nuns. They didn't mind all that self-sacrifice—they couldn't even have their marmalade or toast before they said mass and gave thanks for their food. Despite Mother Thaddeus's patient instruction, Prudence had never made peace with praying. She wasn't very good at it. Every time she bowed her head or closed her eyes, she heard her father's voice, "Better to use your brains than your knees."

Once she asked Sister Agatha what she found to pray about in her cell—the word was enough to make Prudence shiver. To give to you *la inteligencia, la cultura de su Papa,*" Sister had replied. Proof positive that praying got you nowhere, for if she had her father's intelligence, she would know what to do now.

A gust of wind crossed the room and found the candles. They danced and bowed, faded and sputtered. "Don't go out, please. Not now," she called out. She looked up into the face of Jesus. He didn't appear particularly interested in her problem. Tired, maybe even a little bit bored. What if God, weary of the endless stream of requests directed his way, had simply stopped listening? The picture of the nuns, crouched in the dark and damp of the cellar, made it look that way. The sisters could end up like the saints, the ones pictured with arrows piercing their bodies or "tongues of flame" searing their flesh. She had come to like the sisters; even Mother Thaddeus softened over a good verse of poetry; and what kind of a God would let Sister Sabatini burn like a roast of pork twisting on a spit?

A busy God, perhaps. A distracted one. So much was happening, even He might not know where they were. Sister Agatha said He knew everything. Prudence didn't take to the idea of a nosy God. She had tried to picture him leaning over the edge of heaven, peering down to watch her crouch outside the library. It made her laugh. God was no more real than those statues.

"Plaster and paint, that's all they are," Nanny had maintained. "They coat them in gilt and pearls to make up for their inadequacies in the miracle department. Catholic mumbo-jumbo, that's all—the incense, the sacrificing, the moaning and crying and carrying on in the streets." The God of the nuns was too unstable. You couldn't depend on a deity that required so much fussing. People couldn't get on with their work. Nanny's God was a different matter. He remained behind in England where all sensible souls stayed. Prudence couldn't exactly pinpoint the moment, but somewhere along the way, her more-often-right-than-wrong Nanny had given up on Spain.

So how many Gods were there? The English one. The Spanish one. The Indian one. It seemed simpler to go along with her father's dictum. "When I see him, I'll believe in him."

All that thinking must surely have used up two hours, but outside the window the sky refused to surrender its dark. She needed more light, more candles. Once out of bed something moving caught her eye. A spider, a rather large one, scurried nervously back and forth across the outstretched arms of Jesus in its search for a hiding place. It looked as harried as she felt. Her thoughts did as much scurrying as its tiny legs. She too, wove a web. Instead of food, her web held fast to thoughts that dwelled on bad things, sacrilegious things the nuns called them. Sister Agatha told her that she must guard her thoughts. "God can seek them out," she warned. "He can look into *los ojos* and see everything, absolutely everything." Sometimes when she listened to the nuns—they were so convincing—she doubted everyone, even her father. At other times, she mixed God up with her father. Which one had the power? Did they share it?

Sister Sabatini had tried to calm her. "You are as the smallest bird, the most fragile flower—an innocent, you will be safe in the eyes of God." Prudence repeated the phrase over and over as she got back in bed. It would be all right. She concentrated on opening her heart to let the first worry slide away, but before she could push the next one out, she remembered that she hadn't told anyone about the Moors, the tongues, not even about Rubio and his plans for the Mayor. Worst of all, she should have gone straight to her mother. She hadn't. She'd run away. What sort of a protector would do that?

The spider, as if to prove the nun's point, scurried up the neck and over the cheekbone, wiggling into a crevice just below the right eye of Jesus. He had found his safe spot. Prudence slid back down under her covers. In the morning she would look for her safe spot. Surely by then she'd have her answers.

She slept quietly, no dreams. Dawn slipped into the room, dimmed the candles and drove out the shadows.

By eight o'clock Nanny had not come to wake her, but hunger had. Still unsure of what to do, she dawdled on her way downstairs and amused herself by catching the dust motes that circled in the air below the windows.

From the hall, she spotted her mother's empty chair. A

reprieve, a little breathing space. Her father was there, though. Just in case the nuns were right about man being made in God's image, she hurried to her seat, head down. Better not let him get a look into her eyes, read her thoughts, at least not until she'd made up her mind what she would do.

"Prudence, have you forgotten something?" He tilted his head up, proffered his cheek for his morning kiss.

Time had run out. She had to decide, and quickly, which sort of person to be—one like her mother, willing to make peace at any price? The one she wanted to be, the one who would do what she knew to be right? And being right meant keeping her promises, and hadn't she promised to protect her mother?

A rabbit frozen in fear, time held its breath. The sound of a distant quarrel drifted in from the kitchen. The candle under the coffee urn sputtered and spit. A fly buzzed over the bread. Head tucked down, eyes carefully hidden from him, she shook her head. There would be no kiss. Not today. Not tomorrow. Not ever again.

She heard his coffee cup crash against its saucer, his chair scrap back.

"Good morning, Sir." It was Nanny. "I found this in the front hall." She handed him a paper. "What's the matter with you, child, all scrunched over? Sit up, you'll turn yourself into a gnome." Prudence straightened her back, but to keep her eyes averted she pretended to study the silverware and discovered something odd. The silverware, its pattern was familiar but its surroundings weren't. This wasn't the tableware that belonged to her grandmother, this belonged to the pantry.

She looked up and smiled. The world wasn't such an awful mess after all. Last night—the whole thing had been a mistake. Maybe she dreamt it. Maybe her father and Helen were talking about making a movie or describing a plot for a book. That was it. How foolish of her. And the passports in the drawer? That was a mistake too. They were all going. Here was the proof— the silver. Her mother must have already begun the packing, that's why the good silver had disappeared.

Distracted by Nanny's arrival and the newspaper, her father had forgotten the undelivered kiss. She had only to worry over Rubio and his nonsense about killing the Mayor.

"Roland," her mother came through the pantry door, "if you're still planning that dinner for tonight, we need to send someone to the village. There is no reasoning with Cook. She refuses to go."

"Sit down, Marion. There will be no dinner."

"No dinner? Don't be silly Roland. I don't understand cook she's always in a temper nowadays. And the staff, maids disappear, new ones pop up. I can't keep up with it. Cook keeps the whole place stirred up. The way that woman raves on, you'd think the devil himself inhabited the village of late."

"Perhaps he has, Marion." His voice hid no smile.

"Roland, don't talk that way, you're frightening me."

"Stop nattering on, Marion. Sit down. Stop your whining and listen to me. I have something important to say to you." Her mother, her father, they were going to fight. Not now, not when things seemed about to be right again, they were all going away, back to London. What could possibly happen to them in London?

"I'll go with you, Mother. I can help you." On the way to the village she could ask about the silver and check on Rubio. If he had shot the mayor, surely Cook and the maids would know by now and they would tell her mother.

"Prudence, hold your tongue. You will remain at home. And Marion, I told you to stop your whining. Get hold of yourself."

"You need some more of that *Manzanilla* Sherry." Her mother paused, her voice shifted. "Helen is more familiar with the local *bodegas* than I. Much more."

Her father looked up. Prudence kept still. Her father had it wrong. She knew her mother's whine, it didn't sound anything like that. Her angry voice—that's what it sounded like.

"I have more important things to worry about than sherry." Now it was her father's voice that changed. A flat you-must-pay-attention-to-me tone and yet a tone that sounded far away, as if the speaker no longer cared about her mother, what she did.

"And for that matter Helen, too, has enough to worry about." He pushed his chair back and started to leave, then turned back, scooped up the newspaper and left.

Through the steam that rose from the teapot, Prudence saw the round rouge spot on her mother's cheek, It stood out sharp and hard against her pale skin.

"Nanny?" she asked, proffering the pot with a hand that shook as badly as her voice.

Nanny raised her cup, then busied herself with the cream, the sugar. Her mother's eyes widened as she stared at the spoon Nanny tapped so tidily against the rim of her cup.

"What's this?"

"What's what Ma'am?"

"The pantry silver. What's it doing in here?"

Nanny looked down at her spoon, seeing it for the first time. "Why, I don't know." Prudence held her breath.

Marion jumped up, pushed her way through the pantry. From the kitchen came the sounds of a fresh argument. The voices grew louder. Her mother, Cook each trying to out talk the other. Prudence pushed her eggs to the side of her plate, even the honey-dipped biscuit lost its power to tempt.

"Here child, try some preserves." Nanny tried to divert her attention. The screaming stopped. Her mother reappeared, took her place at the table, picked up her napkin, and shook it out as if trying to banish something unpleasant, a sticky crumb, a persistent fly. The grim line of her mouth, the jut of her chin said something quite different.

Nanny looked at her quizzically.

"Can you believe that woman? She had the nerve to tell me we've been robbed. If anyone has robbed us, it's that sly fox." She looked at Nanny for confirmation. Getting none, she added, "Should I ring the police?"

"Perhaps you should speak—"

"Don't tell me to ask Mr. Whitley. He's always busy. There is no one to ask, most everybody's gone. And as for going into the village—"

"Ma'am?"

"What?"

"I don't think this is a good time to call the police. I don't even think it's a good time to go into the village. It would be better to stay away from all things Spanish just now."

Prudence watched the fight go out of her mother, not slowly, not like a leak, but all of a rush, gathering speed as it went until her mother appeared almost calm.

"You are right of course, Nanny. I haven't wanted to go there even with Roland the past few weeks. And when I'm alone, it's even worse. People press around and ask questions about the *Señor*. They want to know what he writes about them. I try to walk on but they stare so, it frightens me. I can feel their eyes on my back."

"That's odd, Madam. How do they know he writes about them? I haven't seen any copies of *The Times* in the village. Come to think of it, when was the last time you saw one here at the house?"

"What was that Mr. Whitely was reading just now?"

"The local paper, at least I assumed it so, seeing as it was all in Spanish." Nanny looked sick. Oh, no. Could he? Would he be doing a column—"

"Don't even think such things." Her mother's calm evaporated. "Bazil warned him, I warned him, everyone warned him not to get mixed up in local politics."

"It's more than politics, Mrs. Whitley, if you don't mind my saying. It's war."

Prudence heard someone—Dordo at a tea? Bazil, before he left? Anyway, someone had said, "War is politics with swords not words."

"And this business about Helen," there was no mistaking it, her mother's voice rose with every word and her anger matched its pitch, "why can't he send her when I want him to; at the beginning he'd insisted on it, made such a fuss about it. I bet Helen knows the answers to the villager's questions. He won't send her though. Those two are always holed up in that library working on that damn book."

Prudence choked on her biscuit. Nanny managed a distracted, half-hearted pat on her back.

"All you hear nowadays is Popular Front this, Royalist that, Nationalist something or other," her mother went on. She paid no notice of Prudence, her choking, spluttering. "Even Cook, I try to ask her about the menus, about silverware and all I hear is slogans, propaganda. And she shouts it at me."

"I know. She whips that knife of hers up and down over the meat, shrieking about *los bastardos, los generales.*" Nanny looked up quickly to see if she had presumed too much.

"Ah, but which generals are the bastards?" Her mother didn't sound mad any more. Just tired.

Prudence cleared her throat, she had to speak up, tell what she knew. "Mother?"

Her mother looked over at her, startled to see her. "Don't bother me now, Prudence. I've—"

"There's something I need to tell you." She wouldn't tell her everything, but shouldn't she warn her?

"Later."

"But it's important, I need to talk—" behind her, the pantry door opened. She didn't have to turn around. His aftershave, it's sweetness—she wondered if she'd ever forget that smell.

"By the way, that list you have—" Her father put out his hand for it. "It won't do, won't do at all. You'll need to make a complete one, a week's worth, maybe two. Enough to keep you, Nanny and the child fed until—"

It was coming. Everything would come undone. Prudence reached for the jar of preserves, knocking it over. The purple stain oozed across the cloth.

"Roland, leave this sort of thing to me, produce won't stay fresh that long. Besides, what about you? Helen? Have you two lost your appetites?" Prudence had.

"I . . . I'm off to Madrid."

"Madrid? Don't be silly, Roland, Bazil said it's much too dangerous."

"I suppose that's why he's high-tailed it back to France—"

"He didn't high-tail anything. He went to see to his yacht incase we needed it—"

"Never could see what you saw in that man, Marion. No *cajones*."

"Roland! The child. And what about Helen, where's she off to?"

Prudence pulled the spoon out of the jar, ran her tongue

down one side, then the other. She inspected it carefully to make sure she had left no telltale traces of jelly and then she cast about for something else to do, anything so as not to appear as if she listened.

"Helen will be coming with me, I need someone to take notes. The book, you know, the newspaper."

"You can't be serious. You have a wife, a child—"

Prudence heard Nanny's sharp gasp. She looked over at her. Nanny had pressed her lips back against her teeth, a thin blue line of disapproval. For the first time, Prudence noticed her eyes. Dark rings, purple blotches almost hid them from view.

"*The Times* expects some up to the minute reports from me, Marion. I can't take their money and stay in this backwater."

"Not now. Dordo says that in —"

"I do not govern my moves by what that woman says" he looked over the top of his glasses at her, "for that matter, what any woman has to say, is that clear, Marion?" Her mother appeared to have lost faith in the power of her own tongue. Her anger transformed into acceptance. The director handed her a role. She would play it.

Her father's voice went cold, "I will be departing for Madrid some time tomorrow morning, right after the mayor arrives. I have some instructions to leave with him."

"Instructions? About what?"

"You needn't concern yourself, Marion."

"Concern? Concern? Of course it concerns me, us." For the first time, Marion turned and looked directly at her daughter.

Now she sees me, how much does she know?

Prudence began to shake, it was her teaspoon's turn to betray her, it crashed against her saucer, skittered to the floor. She jumped from her chair. There was no book, no movie. He was leaving.

NINETEEN

The Judas Kiss
"He saved others, himself he cannot save."

—MATTHEW, *XXVII*

UPSTAIRS, SHE SAT at her little desk. The hard slats to the back of the chair made her sit up straight. "Slouching keeps one from thinking," Nanny would say and Prudence needed to think if she was going to get everything down in her day book— the library, the passports, the breakfast table. How awful her father had been. How much she hated Helen. She checked the number of empty pages. Did she have enough room to write how much she hated Helen? Her father? And what about her mother, did she hate her too? If she was going to protect her why hadn't she rushed into the library last night and told her father he couldn't do that, couldn't go off and leave them. She'd just sat there on the cold patio and done nothing. This morning, still nothing. *Why?*

Now she couldn't even write any of it down—the pages were all ruled, ready for her to use her best penmanship, but the pen never moved. Her thoughts were so tangled up in her anger, they wouldn't cut loose, travel down her arm and out her fingers, no matter how straight backed the chair. The rest of the day slipped by in a blur. She was awake. She was asleep. It had happened. It hadn't happened. It was a dream, a bad, bad, dream. It couldn't have happened. Her father had done a lot of things. He'd left a lot of times. But not this way, not while everything seemed so dangerous. Could she have dreamt it? That's it, she dreamt it. Slowly the room darkened, her eyes closed.

The next morning Nanny came into her room, her face strained. She sounded breathless, as if she had spent the night running from a nightmare. "The Mister is ready to leave. He wants you downstairs." Prudence wasn't the only one having problems with words, Nanny's old stand bys—"your father" or "that man"—had deserted her.

Prudence pulled the covers over her head. This was no dream. He was going and he was taking Helen with him. Not her, not her mother. Just Helen.

Nanny held out her robe, Prudence shook it off and dressed slowly, Nanny prodding her the whole time. At the head of the stairs, she refused to look down, no need. She sensed him there below, waiting, and took the stairs one deliberate step at a time, grabbing at dust motes as if desperate to stop their downward spiral, saving them from the accusatory stream of light that poured in through the east windows. Had she fooled him, did he think she didn't care? She hadn't fooled herself. Out of the corner of her eye, she took it all in, the boxes, the bags, the crates that held his camera, his rolls of film. He had gone off and left them before, but right down to the buckles of her Mary Jane's, she knew this time would be different. Life would change the minute he walked out that door. It had already started. The couch, the rumors of war, the Moors, the mayor, the nuns in the basement—nothing could be made to stay in its place.

"Prudence," her father called up the stairs. "Hurry now, I

have to be off." Mistress Mary quite contrary, she thought, and slowed all the more.

"Now dear," worry made her mother's voice quiver, as if she knew there would be no retakes. "Your father wants his kiss."

"No."

Her mother rushed to cover the echoes of that no, to offer up a placating compromise, "A h-hug dear, your father wants a, a hug."

"Prudence, a kiss. I said, give me—"

"No." She was almost to the bottom step.

"Perhaps you didn't hear me. I said now. Right now."

"No. No. No."

"Prudence—."

She had one "no" left. To say this one she stood as tall as she could and looked him right in the face. "No."

She wouldn't. She couldn't. Not this time, not next, not ever again. She fixed her gaze on the foreboding crucifix, the one that scared her so the day she arrived, and thought she saw it smile, enough anyway to stiffen her resolve. She gave her father her most hateful look, turned toward the stairs. She heard the front door open and Rubio's voice announce that the cab stood waiting. How could he betray her so, and help her father? She turned, cleared her throat, a small *a-hem*. In the stillness, she knew Rubio heard but he didn't look at her. The morning light, slanting through the doorway caught the beads of moisture running down his cheeks—sweat? So early in the day, the air still cool, the luggage not yet loaded and Rubio was sweating, why? And then it hit her, the mayor hadn't come to the house as her father had asked, could it be? Had Rubio already—?

She rushed past her mother, a smell, different—not flowers, not perfume— made her hesitate. She couldn't place it at first.

On her way up the stairs, she realized she had forgotten to warn her father of the Moors. She took one step, "Too bad for him." Another step, " I don't care." And another. "I don't" "I don't." One more step. "Why should I?" And yet another. "How could he?" And then she remembered her mother. She must tell her. She'd do it at lunch, how else could she protect her. Her mother had to listen. She just had to.

Upstairs Prudence hurried to the sitting room, opened the shutters and looked out in time to see Helen hefting her type-writer into the cab and her father leaning over her mother, but her mother turned her face aside. His lips barely brushed her cheek as he delivered his Judas kiss. When it was over, when he had gone, Prudence would wonder what made her mother turn away. Did she know? The daisy game again—her mother knew. Her mother didn't. Prudence would tell. Prudence wouldn't.

Later, as she waited for the sound of a lunch bell that never rang, she remembered something else: her father, in the eve-ning, with his gin and tonic beside his chair, she would bend to bestow a goodnight kiss and she would smell that smell. This morning. Her mother. That same smell.

But now her stomach growled out its hunger. Enough time had passed. She went to the stairs, sniffed once or twice but smelled nothing, not even garlic. She ran downstairs and into the dining room. No plates, no table service laid out. No one sorted linen in the pantry. The kitchen quiet, the stove cold.

She could tell by the light that it was late in the day. Where was everybody? She hadn't seen Nanny since morning. No sign of her mother either. The village? Maybe the two of them had gone after the supplies her father talked about, but why hadn't they taken her with them? Nanny anyway. Nanny hardly ever left her alone, even when she'd wanted to be left alone. She was always telling Nanny she was a grown up, had Nanny at long last decided to believe her? She better act like one. Maybe they needed her help. Or maybe they'd just forgotten her. There had been a lot of forgetting lately.

She hurried to the front door, opened it wide and glanced up and down the road. No one. She unhooked the gate and started down the hill. Halfway down, she stopped to get her bearings, where should she look, the vegetable market? The butcher's? She heard a shot. Her legs went out from under her, she sat down in the road. A second shot, then a third, all coming from the same direction.

Fireworks, it could be fireworks—a Saint's day? It must be that. It has to be that. The thought helped her legs to work. By the time the ground leveled out and the village opened up, she was running. In front of her, behind her, all around, the streets were empty. No women gossiped from balcony to balcony, no children kicked balls in the streets. She stopped to listen for some sound, something that would tell her what was going on. From somewhere above her she heard static, a voice floated out over the street: *"Calma, calma."* Calm, the voice told her to be calm. *"No tienes necesita temer."* Their advice had come too late, she already had the fear. Lots of it.

Still no sign of Nanny or her mother but even as she heard the announcer's reassurances that the government had everything in hand, the ominous murmur of a crowd reached her. She followed the voices to the central plaza. There backed up against the fountain, hair disheveled, their eyes as large as a pair of night owls trying their best to penetrate the darkness, she saw her mother and Nanny, their meager packages spilling at their feet, their arms raised not in greeting but in trying to ward off the crowd of shouting women.

"Las americanas, son las fabricantes del problema, espías." Nanny, a spy? Her mother, a troublemaker? They couldn't mean that.

Prudence regretted fidgeting away her Spanish lessons. If she had paid attention, maybe she wouldn't feel so helpless now.

Then the tone of the yelling changed—this time she recognized some of the words: "Fascist!" "Communist!" "Anarchist!" She'd meant to ask exactly what those *ists* meant. How could such little words cause so much trouble? But now she didn't care. The crowd had begun to separate into little groups, each calling out for the downfall of the others. One side wanted death for the Fascists; another demanded to know what they had done with *sor hermanas del Christo*. The nuns—did they want to kill them too? Was that why the sisters were down in the basement? No comic opera this, no Punch and Judy show. She could see her mother's fear, and yet something seemed different about her.

Just then a pathway opened up between the two groups. "Mother," Prudence called out. Her mother's head jerked from left to right, searching for the familiar voice.

"Prudence, are you all right? Where are you?"

"Over here, by the church." The crowd, distracted by their anger at each other, forgot *las americanas*, and the two scrabbled to collect their packages and ducked down, as if by crouching they might become invisible. They made their way across the plaza to her. The three pushed against the big wooden doors and hurried inside.

"There must be a back door, a way out of here," Nanny urged, but as the front doors slammed against their backs, Prudence and her mother stopped, huge slabs of black paint ran down the marble columns across the floor and up to the naked altar. The gold candlesticks, the laced altar cloth—everything gone.

"There is a door, a little one," Prudence said, "I'll show you." She took her mother's hand and slowly they made their way down the aisle through the nave. Her mother pointed to the communion wafers scattered about the chancel. Prudence, eyes to the floor, watched where she put her feet—Mother Thaddeus said the wafers were the body of Christ. Prudence thought this was asking a lot of something as small as a wafers but still—and then there, right where she was about to step—the baby Jesus, a sliver of wood pierced his eye. She tried to stifle her scream.

"It's plaster, it's only plaster," her mother pointed to the Madonna. Every statue in every niche smashed beyond recognition, only the blue-robed Madonna appeared to have escaped the carnage. And yet the infant she had rocked so lovingly in her arms, now lay on the floor. In her arms she cradled the head of the dead Christ. Her mother pointed to the crucifix over the altar, the head of Christ neatly severed.

Nanny's face was all red and blotchy, she sounded out of breath, "They won't be happy until they have killed us all." Caught up with the phrase kill-us-all, she repeated it endlessly until Prudence found the door to the room behind the sacristy. She remembered it from the days the nuns had tried to teach her to sew. Once a week they saw to the church. For a while she helped Mother Thaddeus with the altar cloths. When confronted with the loose and loopy stitches of her protégé, Mary Thaddeus brought the lessons to a close before Prudence could ruin any more of the elegant cloths.

Once outside, the three of them—her mother struggling to keep up in open-toed pumps and stocky Nanny's breath coming in huge gasps—barely made it to the foot of the hill before Prudence heard the crowd behind them. Once more her legs tried to betray her, but from down a side street, she heard the clip-clop of hooves. They would be all right. She sent Rubio a mental forgiveness, forgetting that he didn't know he needed any.

Rubio pulled up beside them "Get in, all of you. We must hurry," his tone so authoritative, her mother didn't question him. They tossed their packages into the cart and tried to follow them up and over the side. After a few scraped knees, Prudence and Nanny got behind her mother and gave her a boost. Next, Prudence pushed and her mother pulled, as they slid Nanny over the side. The two women, one to each arm, yanked Prudence to safety; during the whole operation the cart barely slowed.

The sound of the crowd faded into the distance. At the top of the hill, they moved around to the kitchen side of the house. Only then, nearing safety, did Prudence remember that in the crowd around her mother and Nanny, she had seen only women. Where were the men? And Rubio, where had he come from? The sound of the shots came back to her. She looked at Rubio, really looked. The stain on his pant leg, was it blood—? Could you see it on someone's face? Would you know by the sound of a voice? Did someone change after they, if they—how could she be sure of what she knew, really knew about anyone after this?

In the chorus of *Gracias* that greeted Rubio, hers was noticeably missing. Her mother, using the same tone she would have when talking to any grownup, perhaps not her husband, but anyone else, asked Rubio, "What are we to do now?" As if he had given advice to adults all his life, Rubio answered in a voice that betrayed no signs of anxiety, "Stay indoors for a few days, I'll see to your provisions. The peoples, they will calm down, forget. I will send Cook and the maids back."

"No." Her mother and Nanny turned toward Prudence, their mouths open. She hesitated a bit as she tried to find a voice as commanding as Rubio's, one that would deflect their questions. "We can take care of ourselves." She had seen the statues, their raw wounds, the axe marks on the pews, and she thought of Mother Thaddeus, Sister Agatha, Sister Sabatini in the basement.

Rubio helped unload the packages and left. The women looked after him but Prudence ran for the house. "Where are you going, child? Come back here. You're the one that said we could take care of ourselves, now help with the supplies." Prudence didn't stop, she ran to the basement, rushed down the stairs, she would tell the sisters they must stay where they were, she would tell them about the church, about the statues.

She saw the crates, the wine racks, the spider webs drooping from the ceiling. She didn't see Mary Thaddeus, Sister Agatha, not even Sister Sabatini.

TWENTY

The Man at the Door

"Heaven knows its time; the bullet has its billet"

—SIR WALTER SCOTT, *Count Robert of Paris*

PRUDENCE HAD RUN upstairs, straight to her room and slammed the door. It seemed to her that everyone had deserted her. Her father had driven away, her mother and Nanny ran off to town without her, and the nuns had just plain disappeared. She'd show them all she didn't need them. For the next few days, she hid out. She saw little of Nanny, and her mother hardly at all.

They spent their time in the little upstairs English sitting room at the front of the house, as if its very Englishness would protect them. She could hear her mother crying and Nanny offering what comfort she could. They worried more about supplies than anything else. Prudence spent her days sulking in her room.

But one day when hunger loomed larger than pride, she ventured downstairs, pushed open the kitchen door, hoping to find a little piece of sugared toast. Instead she saw Cook, her back to the door, stuffing things into an old pillowcase. Cook hefted

214

the sack over her back and hurried out the back door before Prudence could even guess at what had disappeared into this sack. The silver was already gone.

She didn't follow, what was the use? She hadn't been able to get her mother to sit still and listen to what she had to say about the Moors, not that she'd tried very hard. And she saw no sense at all in trying to tell her about the other, her mother seemed unhappy enough. Anyway, now that she was here in the kitchen she might as well try to find something to eat. She found some rolls in one of the cupboards. Then she lifted the lid on the giant crock—midnight raids taught her that Cook liked to keep salted meats and cheeses cool in this thick-walled jar. She reached as far in as she could and groped about until her hand closed around a piece of salted cod. She would share it with the *Aura Oreo, Jaspeadora* and *Dorado Rojo*.

The fish, at least, appeared eager to see her. By the pond, she could think things through. Most nights she had lain wide-awake, anxious-eyed with worry while outside the village erupted in strange sounds. Reflections from the fires lit up her walls—what could be fueling them now? Surely all the books had long since gone up in smoke. As for the shooting, it seemed to take shots fired into the air to get people riled up enough for the speeches. Sometimes the popping and crackling came from firecrackers the children tossed on the pyres. The sound of their laughter, their squeals at the miniature explosions, often made her forget what had caused all this, sometimes. The oddest thing of all—at times she caught herself wishing she were out there playing with them.

But there were times when she knew it wasn't harmless fire-crackers. Those shots came from further away, she could hear them echoing through the ravine. The eerie stillness that fol-lowed frightened her more than the noise. If only she could talk to Rubio again. But she hadn't seen him since the day her father left, after he helped with the groceries. And then she'd been too mad at him.

But this day, after she finished with the salted fish, she went back into the kitchen and took a sack of meal from its hiding place behind what little there was left of the English China—a spot she picked because, with her father gone and the guests with him, the china didn't get much use. Carefully she unwound the twine tied securely around it. She used a secret knot Nanny taught her, that way she would know if anyone else had been at her supply. These days even fish food was scarce. She must be careful not to waste it.

As she leaned out over the pond and tossed a handful across its mossy green surface, she heard a noise, a rat-a-tat-tat, rat-a-tat. Not far away. Not fireworks. It was still daylight. Cook told her daylight was for farming, it shouldn't be wasted on politics.

Please, please, she prayed, don't let this be one of the eerie, quiet, times. No shouts, only one burst of gunfire following another and then another until a deep, thunderous boom shook her world. Nothing had prepared for such a monstrous sound. Her knees trembled. She sat back down, forgetting about the fish until a splash of water crossed her hand. She had dropped the sack, the meal sunk slowly into the murk. *Ora Aureo, Jaspeadura* and *Dorado Rojo* swam frantically about, their fan-like tails making waves in the water as they dashed headlong from corner to corner seemingly bent on suicide. All their rhythm, their uncanny sense of when to turn gone, they crashed headlong against the sides of the pond. She tried stamping her feet to get their attention, but they ignored her. They would kill themselves. "Help, somebody, help." She thought about her father, he would know what to do. What could she be thinking? Even if he did appear, she wouldn't ask him for anything. Not after what he did.

She ran into the library and bumped into Nanny who grabbed hold of her. The look on Nanny's face seemed to ask, who are you? What are you doing here? Where were the reassuring pats, the there-theres, the it-will-be-all-rights? Nanny just dropped her arms and gave Prudence a little push as if to send her away.

"Nanny, my fish, the explosion, what—?" No help to be had from that frozen face, Prudence backed off. The explosion, it must be something very terrible. Nanny, a speechless Nanny, how could that be? Prudence headed for the stairs, the safety of her room. Halfway up, Nanny called after her in a voice as placid as butter.

"The power is off again." At least that was something familiar. The power went out almost every day now. "Your mother has decided we will dine early." Down below, Nanny's face tried for a smile. "Go and clean up. I'll be there directly. We'll read a bit, how's that?"

Once in her room, Prudence rushed out on to the balcony and looked down at her fish. The water in the pond still churned but she could see them. They seemed to have quieted down somewhat.

Nanny hadn't come, not directly, not at all. Prudence didn't see her again until dinner. When the three of them entered the dining room, neither Nanny nor her mother seemed aware that they really hadn't seen her for a couple of days. Her mother gestured at her father's chair, "Sit there." Prudence hesitated. "Go ahead, do as I say." Her mother's voice, the voice of a stranger, held no hesitation, no apology, no diffidence. "Go on now," she said, "I'm tired of looking at the damn thing."

Prudence pulled out the chair and sat down gingerly, as if the furniture might somehow take revenge at her audacity. "It's all right," Nanny said, "it's only temporary, your father will be back directly the fighting stops. Someone must write the reports." Prudence could tell that Nanny meant her little speech more to reassure her mother than anything. Her mother looked so limp, worn out and pale, like the towels the maids took down to the riverbank to beat against the stones.

"It'll be all right, Mother. He'll be back. He might leave us in a jungle, or a hotel but not now, not here, not in the middle of all this, this . . .." Prudence didn't know just what they were in the middle of but she did know she had to do something to change that look on her mother's face. She thought about going to her, sitting on her lap. What would happen? What would her mother think if she just hugged her without being asked, without it being time to say good night?

The moment passed, she became distracted by the sound of heavy boots running on the road. So loud, so purposeful, they must be right outside the villa wall. The others heard it too. Their mouths opened, their spoons paused halfway there. Shouts of *Arriba España, Arriba España* crashed through the open windows.

Her mother looked stricken but Prudence felt a giggle rise to her throat. She jumped up and went to the window. "A country: How can a country 'get up?'" she said. No one laughed at her joke. Not even the maid who cleared away the soup. Despite her protests, Rubio had sent most of the help back. At least she thought it was his doing, they had drifted back a few at a time, sheepish looks on their faces as they scurried around the house, never really looking anyone in the eye.

"Close the shutters. Come away from there, it's no concern of ours."

"But, Nanny, who else could the footsteps be for? No one lives this far up but us." The gate rattled, they froze to their seats. The lock held. After a forever or perhaps two, the footsteps died away.

After dinner, the three settled into the large leather chairs in the library and listened to the English translation of that evening's news. Nanny brought out her darning basket. Her mother worked at a needlepoint—a monarch butterfly, wings spread wide beat its way against a blue background. Prudence hadn't seen the pattern since the days her mother sat self-consciously at her father's bedside after his skiing accident. She'd had as little patience with her husband's foolishness as he had of the time his leg was taking to mend. "Honestly, dear, who but you would insist on skiing down a steep slope and taking pictures at the same time."

Prudence had no needlework to do. She could only fidget until something on the radio caught her mother's attention. "Turn the volume up a bit, will you dear? I want to catch the translation. There's a good girl."

"The Government has the situation well in hand.
It is not true that the army in Morocco has revolted.
There is no uprising of the military. Rumors, all
rumors. They must be stamped out. The Government
has the situation—"

For several nights now, that same phrase dominated the news, repeated first in English, then in French. After the German translation, the whole cycle would start again, but that night a voice announced that music would be played. How could anything be wrong if there was time for music? Suddenly the staccato sounds of poorly played Mozart—her mother said Mozart did too much pussyfooting—were interrupted by the strains of the *Internationale*. Before her mother could reach the radio to turn it off, the anthem exploded into a burst of static.

"That noise, it's shooting. The maids say there is shooting in the streets of Madrid, we must do something, Madame. We can't just sit here, we'll all be killed!"

"Get hold of yourself, Nanny. They're not shooting at

anybody." Prudence looked about the room, unsure that it was her mother who just spoke. The voice was so strong, so sure. But no one else had come in the room. "It's the transmission, something got garbled. See, it's all over." It wasn't.

"*Señores, Señoras*, there is no need for alarm. *El Gobierno tiene la situación pues en mano.*" If the government truly had everything under control, Nanny asked, why the need to keep saying it over and over, each repetition only weakened their case.

"Enough of that," her mother snapped the radio off. "Let's get a little reading in before we go to bed." She turned to Prudence, "Look what I found for you, one of Nanny's favorites, *The Adventures of Sherlock Holmes.*"

The rustle of unread pages filled the vacuum left by the radio. Prudence kept her head down, though she did raise her eyes now and then to peek first at Nanny, then at her mother. From time to time two pairs of eyes chanced to meet only to retreat into their books, each ashamed to have been caught out by the other.

Shutters fruitlessly closed against the noises from the village, the room grew uncomfortably warm. The fat candles her mother lit for them to read by didn't help and, through the cracks in the shutters, the glare of the bonfires set fire to their nerves.

The noise grew louder. She squirmed. Her mother, her voice as steady as before, assured her that it must be fireworks, some feast day. "You know, dear, they always have them."

"The bonfires seem larger tonight."

"No, Nanny. The air, perhaps it's clearer."

The steady thump of marching feet grew louder. "It's the *Guardia Civil*," her mother said. "They're trying to restore order,"

"No, Madam, it's the workers. They want to frighten us." And, her mother's voice to the contrary, they were doing a good job of it.

220

"You can't tell, Nanny. Maybe it's the *Generalissimo* himself."

Prudence hadn't forgotten what Rubio had said of the general and his soldiers. Here was her chance. "The Moors, mother. They're coming, they'll cut out our tongues."

Nanny paled. "Tongues? What are you saying child?"

"We better hide, down in the basement like the Sisters did."

"The Sisters? In the basement?" Nanny wasn't frightened anymore, she was terrified. Her mother, puzzled. Too late, Prudence realized they didn't know.

"Surely Mrs. Whitley, you are not hiding the nuns? Don't you know that if the workers catch us with Papists, they'll kill us all?" Nanny looked so small, her face so white, her lips were little more than a dull blue slash across her face.

"Pay her no mind, Nanny, the child is confused."

A burst of gunfire sounded close by. There was nothing confusing about that. "Mother, they're shooting at us."

"No. I tell you, they won't bother us. Your father has promised."

"Madam, what do bullets know of his promises? At the very least, we should get away from the windows." No one seemed capable of making a move. "Listen to them, all that shouting. How can anyone make out what they say? They all talk at once, Popular Front this, Royalist that, Nationalist something or other. We can't get away from it, not even here in the house."

"I know, I know."

"But what shall we do?"

"I don't know. I'll work on it. We have to do something, go somewhere; but the problem is they are all angry. They all hate and most of all they seem to; some for one reason, some for another. And I don't know how to tell them apart."

"Mrs. Lupinek might know what to do," Prudence whispered

No one paid any attention. Nanny got up, "Come along

now, let's off to bed. The back of the house should be safer."

The next day passed slowly. No one ventured out. Prudence helped her mother and Nanny take inventory of the pantry. "We'll have to do something about this first, too much is disappearing." Prudence knew her mother had a lot more to worry about than the meat and cheese. She still hadn't told her everything.

As it grew dark they again took up their posts in front of the radio.

Señores, Señoras, there has been an insurrection in the provinces. But let me assure you, *Señores,*

Señoras, that Morocco may have fallen to Franco, nevertheless the government has the situation well in hand. It is but a rumor that the Moors and the Foreign Legion are disembarking at Seville. There is no battle raging in Barcelona. A small one perhaps, that is all. A few general strikes have been declared. One or two may have gotten out of hand but the navy is not under rebel control. We are looking into the stories that the officers have been thrown to the fishes.

The wish-I-were-English accent signed off; there would be no further translations. Clearly something very startling had happened, even if they wouldn't say what. For the next hour a voice droned on and on in Spanish, at times he sounded firm and authoritative, at times not. Her mother and Nanny looked strained and uncomfortable as they tried to follow the broadcast. Prudence understood the occasional *guerra* or *insurrección*. And then *eliminar todo los traidores*, those words she understood. So did Nanny who wailed, "See, I told you they would start shooting people."

"Get hold of yourself, Nanny. We are not traitors, why would they hurt us?"

But by the third or fourth repetition of the phrase, Prudence wasn't so sure. "What does it mean exactly. I mean who are the traitors and how do they intend to *eliminar* them?"

"Please Prudence," her mother sighed, "go to bed. I'm tired, so are you." She put her arms out, gathered her daughter up and dropped a kiss on the top of her head. Prudence had tried to stay brave during the pounding boots, the gunfire, the power outages; but her mother—this unexpected intimacy—terrified her.

She did as she was told but the shrieks and howls of cannon and mortar soon replaced the pop and crackle of side arms and rifles. She shut her eyes, squeezing them as tight as she could to block out the flashes of light. She hugged her pillow to her ears hoping to drown out the noise. After a few hours, she could stand it no longer. She went to the window and looked down on the fishpond. Red and gold reflections burst across its surface. She thought she saw the thrashing shadows of the fish. Acrid smells drifted in through the window. Something cold and dead weighed on her. She ran out into the front hall, bypassing Nanny's door. She must find her mother. It would be all right. It had to be all right. Just as she reached the head of the stairs she heard a banging on the front door. Someone shouted, "*Abierto, abierto.*" Should she go down? Open the door? She started for the stairs, but a sleepy maid padded her way to the front of the house.

As the maid struggled with the heavy door, a man pushed past her and rushed over to the bottom of the stairs. And then there was her mother, standing right beside her. They both leaned out over the railing for a better look. Her mother clutched a candle in her hand. Prudence followed her gaze down to the man standing in the front hall but the béret pressed low across his forehead kept her from seeing into his eyes, even when he raised his head and called up, "*Señora*, come down at once. I must speak with you." His English sounded too practiced, the accent not exactly that of a Spaniard. Blurred over, smoothed out, his voice didn't want you to know where he came from. At first, her mother had refused, but there was more shouting.

"Don't go, don't go," she tried to tell her mother, but her mother had already started down. The man waved his gun at her. Her mother screamed; she screamed for a long time. The man said things Prudence didn't want to hear, tried not to hear. It seemed that time stopped until the door slammed shut behind him.

Prudence ran down the stairs, "Go to bed," her mother yelled at her and then began shouting out orders. Servants appeared from all corners of the house and stood stolidly, waiting with expectant looks on their faces. Where had they all come from? So many had already left and yet here they were; and what struck her even more, most of them, despite the late hour, appeared fully dressed. Whatever it was they were expecting, it wasn't her mother's orders.

"Get the trunks," her mother shouted. No one moved. "Don't stand there, do something. *Darse prisa. Darse prisa.*"

Cook spoke up. "We must speak to *el Señor.*"

"My husband will not be coming back."

"Our wages? What of our wages?"

"You'll get your money." The quaver in her mother's voice reached the top of the stairs. "There's been a mistake, a terrible mistake. The *Señor* is . . .."

"*El Señor,* he promised me the monies." Cook glared at her mother. "He told me he would have the monies for me." Prudence tried to get between her mother and the excited maid who crowded around her, but still Prudence didn't really want to hear. She put her hands to her ears. It all leaked through. She heard every last bit— about the wall, the men with kerchiefs over their faces, about the volley of bullets that echoed through the streets of Madrid. How much had her mother said? How much had the maids said, it all ran together. And the maids didn't care about the fact that something had happened to her father, they just wanted to know who did it.

"A spy, they think he is a spy."

"Who? Who shot him *Señora*?"

"I don't know. Who was that man? Why should I think he's telling the truth?"

The maids were not to be deterred. "The Loyalists? The Republicans? Who?"

"I don't know, I tell you. I don't know."

"For which side was he doing the spying?"

"He wasn't . . . Oh God, I don't know."

"But the monies, *Señora*, he promised me. I must have it." Cook seemed more disturbed about the money than the shooting. Hadn't Cook liked her father? Her father liked Cook, they often talked together. "For which side," louder now, more insistent, "tell us, *Señora*. Tell us, we must know."

"I'm telling you, I know nothing." Prudence thought her mother should be more upset, more scared, but she seemed tired, resigned—perhaps even detached as the maids crowded around her.

"You *Americanos*, you know nothing, there will be trouble for us all if he was a spy. We must know which way to do the running."

"It's a mistake, a horrible mistake," her mother's composure appeared to ebb. Anger took over. "They wouldn't shoot him. I don't believe it. He couldn't have been a spy. He was a journalist I tell you, a writer . . . a nobody." Her mother pushed the maids out of the way and looked up at Prudence. "Don't be frightened, child. It isn't true. It can't be true. The man has no proof. He is just trying to frighten us, he wants us out by morning. Go. Get dressed. Get Nanny."

Prudence reached the top stair, the candle her mother held

sputtered out but the hall still burned with the eerie light of bon-fires. Prudence ran to the window. Though the sky appeared alive with flames, gloomy shadows crept along the white walls. Clouds of smoke hid everything.

She made her way down the hall to Nanny's room, over to Nanny's bed. How still, how calm she looked. Perhaps she hadn't heard. Maybe she hadn't wanted to. Who could blame her? Besides, the nightcap pulled tightly down over her ears could have blocked the sounds. She shouldn't wake her, Nanny worked hard, needed her sleep but Prudence needed Nanny, her smiles, her pats, her hugs. She leaned in closer, put her hand out to give Nanny a little shake. Her hand hung there mid-air. Nanny's eyes were open. Prudence could look deep into them, as deep as she wanted to, but she saw nothing, no light. No love. No nothing. Nanny hadn't even blinked. Not once.

TWENTY-ONE

We are not Beasts
"What art can wash her guilt away?"

—OLIVER GOLDSMITH, *Vicar of Wakefield.*

DESPITE THE MAN'S orders, they didn't go. "Where to?" her mother asked. Prudence had no answer, she was too busy trying hard not to think of Nanny. Nanny lying in that bed. Nanny dead. If she did, she would cry and her mother had begged her not to. "Prudence, I can't think if you cry. And I have to. Your father would want you to be brave, you know that don't you?"

What did being brave have to do with it? Didn't her mother know she wasn't crying because she was afraid? Her tears were for Nanny. No, that wasn't quite it. Her tears were for herself because she had no hand to hold. Or maybe she was crying because she couldn't stop. She would have to try for her mother. She would really try hard.

And she did. But how? And then she thought of a way. She had walked ever so slowly into her own room, opened her bottom bureau drawer and rescued Shirley from her hiding place. At the window, she sat with Shirley in her arms, rocking back and forth, back and forth until Shirley rescued her.

For the next few days, the crackle of bonfires, the chatter of the guns and the dull thud of small artillery continued to rattle the walls as well as their nerves and yet they didn't leave. Some shells landed terrifyingly close to the *Casa de Carrillo*. A few actually broached the walls. Still they didn't go. Prudence hadn't seen Cook for a while. One day? Two? Time was acting up again. One by one the gardeners, the maids disappeared after making sure Prudence and her mother heard every rumor. They were not spared a one. Each village between Rodicio and Málaga had apparently fallen to one *ist* or another. The tales of the atrocities raining down on the people grew in proportion to the relish lavished on the telling. The upstairs maid approached her mother and whispered that Málaga had erupted in violence. There was shooting in the city, her family lived there.

"Go, of course," her mother fished through her purse, handed her some pesos, though I am sure they wouldn't shoot unarmed men." How could her mother be so sure? They couldn't even tell who or what was being shot right down the hill from them.

Prudence could keep still no longer. "Mother, shouldn't we go?"

Her mother hardly looked at her. And then another maid— her smile that of a cat who had just pounced on a helpless mouse—let them know that the communists, the ones *el Señor* hated so, held Málaga. How did they know who the *Señor* hated? She didn't. Her mother didn't. A few maids, even the butler swore the Republicans held the town. The Militiamen? Anarchists? Everyone had a different opinion, grounded in a different rumor. Prudence remembered Mrs. Borgiono and her rosary. Mrs. Borgiono thought every thing must be the fault of the Reds, the ones the nuns called "infidels." Bridges were being mined to keep the Moors from crossing into the country-side. But the rumor they heard the most, the one told with the greatest relish—offered up as if a gift, its wrappings torn away slowly so as to embellish the details—the homes of the wealthy were going up in flames every night, some nights with the owners still inside.

Her mother hadn't flinched but she sent Prudence in search of buckets. Prudence suspected "busy work," the sort of thing Nanny had thought up to keep her from underfoot. As to the rumors, "Common sense should tell you, child, the rumors are just that, rumors."

Prudence exhausted her search for buckets—she found only two—her mother didn't seem to know where to put them. They wandered the empty rooms of the villa inspecting the damage. That night they went into the seldom-used formal living room and hoisted the heavy cushions from the sofas and carried them into the dining room. They placed them on the floor under the heavy oak table. That's the sort of thing done for protection in an earthquake. Her mother reasoned it would serve them just as well in war. Didn't the earth shake as much in the one as the other?

They made a great pretense of getting comfortable—plumping the cushions, smoothing out the blankets and faking a yawn or two. They tried to sleep. To no avail. They could no more stop their minds from overflowing with awful thoughts than they could hold back the war.

"Mother?"

"What now, Prudence."

"Daddy, Helen . . . what did the man say? Tell me everything."

"You don't want to know—"

"Yes, I do. Everything."

"He said, your father had been taken prisoner—"

"Why?"

"Prudence, if you keep interrupting with questions, I won't

be able to—"

"All right, go ahead. I won't say anything." For once her mother talked to her like a grown-up. Maybe now all those overheard bits and pieces would fall into place.

"They held him there—"

"And Helen?"

"—in a prison in Madrid," her mother ignored the interruption and went on in voice stretched as taut as the guy wires that kept the palms from going over in a storm.

"They questioned him for days and then one night, they came for him . . .." a catch in her voice made her stop. She stopped to clear her throat. Coughed again.

"Go on Mother . . . they came for him and what?"

"Somewhere in Madrid, in some dirty little courtyard . . . they said—"

"What, please, please tell me what….?"

"They stood your father up against a wall and . . .. "

"And?"

A bitterness, an edge, the roughness of a person filled with hate resonated in her mother's voice.

"And, they shot him." Her mother lay back against the cushions. "He is dead," she said with the finality of a slammed door. Prudence wouldn't leave it at that.

"But you said the man lied. You said he just wanted us to leave—"

"Go to sleep. We need our rest."

"But Mother, maybe we should leave? "

"He might come back. He might, he—" Her mother fell silent. Prudence studied the underside of the table. She didn't see sturdy legs sculpted on a lathe, the dark wood sanded and polished, not even the well-mitered joints that held it all together. She saw stone walls, heard bullets, whimpers, screams.

Her father falling, falling and yet somehow he never hit the ground. There's been a mistake, she thought, if he were dead, she would see him on the ground. In the morning, she would tell her mother this, she would make her see that they might yet get out of all this. Prudence shivered. She rolled over, turned her face away and prayed for daylight. Whenever she shut her eyes she saw more walls. Walls so pitted, their roughness grated on her eyes. Stains, purple-brown stains, trailed to the ground.

Had her father been a brave man, blindfolded, bearded chin jutting out in defiance? Or a slightly overweight man in a rumpled suit, crying, begging for his life as he squirmed behind the black rag across his face? She heard the zing of bullets, the thump of punctured flesh, the scream—the gored horse galloping around the ring.

Prudence turned over, looked toward her Mother. How could she lie so still? There must be a zillion things going through her mind. She wasn't asleep. Prudence could see the white of her eyes, startling against the cold dark, her shoulders shaking with silent sobs. Prudence wanted to sob, too—huge sobs, floods of tears. She couldn't. She let her breath out slowly, very slowly. After a bit, the crying stopped. Her mother crawled out from under the table, stood up, went to the window, put her hand to the glass and peered out as if searching for her husband. Almost confident that he would appear, perhaps even worried that he might scold the two of them for sleeping on the floor.

Prudence had spent so much time thinking about her father, the way he towered over everything, her mother paled in comparison. Not anymore, not the way she slammed a clenched fist into the palm of her other hand. "God damn him, God damn him to hell."

Prudence tried not to take another breath. If she did, something would crack. Break. Over in the corner she saw a

movement—a mouse, solemn in its grayness, its nose twitching as it tasted the air, up, down, back and forth. It made cau-
tious headway across the room, pausing at each spilled crumb to
nibble and then set on its path again, determined to do what it
took to survive. It paid no attention to the flashes that now and
then lit up the room.

Prudence watched its resolve and thought of the fable of
Robert The Bruce, the Scottish King and the spider. When the
mouse reached the edge of the table, she would tell her mother
what she had seen, what she had heard. She would tell her everything— how she loved her father, why she hated him, what she
saw. But a sudden loud boom, closer than all the rest, scattered
her thoughts among the little flakes of the plaster that filtered
down from the ceiling. When it cleared, she couldn't find the
mouse.

She must have slept, it was light; she didn't remember falling
asleep. Had she imagined it? Had the man really come? Had
her mother told her about the wall? And had she told her mother
anything, anything at all? All those pictures of her father—she
couldn't bring them back to mind, another larger one blocked
them out: her father straightening his clothes, picking at strands
of long red hair.

She looked over at her mother's makeshift bed. Empty.
Prudence got up, wandered into the hall. A small envelope, the
paper so cheap so white, it jumped out from its place on the hall
table. It hadn't been there the night before. She took it into the
kitchen where her mother set her hand to burning the toast.

"I'm sorry, hon. I don't seem to able to get the hang of this."

"But where are the—?"

"They're all gone, it's just us."

"Let me do it Mother, I watched Cook."

"I can't get the fire going."

"You need a match."

"You always were the watcher, the listener. You think I didn't see you on the stairs, all those nights? Nanny didn't call you "Little Pitcher" for nothing." At the reminder of Nanny they both fell silent. Prudence had listened in on the grownups all her life. That's how she learned. No one told her things, not the things she wanted to know. But now that she had things of her own to tell, she must be grown up.

"What's that in your hand, Prudence?"

"I found it."

"Where?"

"On the table in the hall . . . it's got your name on it."

"Some one was here, while we slept?" Her mother took the paper, unfolded it slowly. Her hands shook.

"Helen's alive. She's being held down in the village. They want me to go there."

"And what about . . .? She couldn't bring herself to say father, she didn't want to hear her mother's answer. "Maybe it's a trick?"

"A trick?"

"What if they want to get you down there so they can shoot you too? Don't go."

"The note says I have to . . .."

Prudence rushed over, grabbed the paper, tore it in little pieces and threw it in the stove after the toast. "First Father, then Nanny . . . now you. You can't, you can't, you can't go off and leave me here alone."

"All right, Prudence. No one's going to shoot anyone—"

"What about the man, father—?"

"We don't know that, we just have his side—"

"But why would he lie?"

"I don't know Prudence, but if Helen is alive, he might…he must be too—" For a moment the enormity of the idea silenced them both.

"I must go, I have to know. "

"Don't leave me. "

"I must — "

"Take me with you. I won't stay here. I won't. "

"Prudence you're being unreasonable."

"I'm scared, mother. I'll run away. I'll find you."

"If it will make you feel better we'll go together. Now go upstairs and put on your warmest clothing."

"But it's not cold."

"Prudence, if you question everything I tell you, I won't take you. You must do as I say. I've got to think this through and I need your help. You're grown up now."

She must be grownup after all she had all these secrets. Adults always had secrets, still "I'm only eleven—"

"You're always telling me how grownup you are. It may not seem it right now; but if you are going to come with me, I need you to be grown up, so you are grown up."

"You're scaring me."

"It's all right to be scared, Prudence. We all are—" Her mother stopped as if she realized that 'all' was only the two of them. It wasn't so much what her mother said that frightened Prudence; it was that her mother wasn't her mother anymore. Some mystical window had opened up and the old, indecisive mother had drifted out. Prudence did want her mother to be strong, it just that it took a bit of getting used to.

"I meant to scare you, it's important that you do what I say, when I say it. Now go upstairs, dress like I told you . . . and your coat, don't forget your coat. I want you to find a pin, no two—"

"What?"

"Prudence!"

When she came back down her mother, already in coat, hat and gloves, waited. Gone the tottery heels, the open toes. Her museum shoes, her sightseeing shoes, that's what her mother had on.

"The pins? Did you find—?" Prudence held them out, her mother took them, opened her coat, reached up under her sweater and carefully pinned some money to her blouse. She did the same with her own. Then she opened her purse and took out a hairbrush. "Sit down over here, I want to do your hair." Her mother brushed and yanked and began plaiting her hair.

"Stop, you're hurting me." And then the final indignity— her mother tied a wide, floppy ribbon to the end of each braid. "If you want me to be grown up why are making me look like a little girl?"

"Trust me," and for a little while, Prudence did. What else could she do? Her mother didn't seem completely blinded to the dangers by hopes of seeing *him*. Prudence had no way of knowing that this was but the first of the many times they would play the daisy game—was he? Wasn't he?

Her mother took her hand as they walked to the village. "Whatever happens, Prudence, no matter what, be quiet, don't sass . . . don't look at me that way, you do too sass. Now, let me do the talking and, whatever you do, do nothing to anger anyone. An angry enemy is more dangerous. Promise?" She promised. "Promise me again. I can do this, but you must help. Come on, promise me one more time, I need to be sure."

"I promise. I promise."

"What do you promise?"

"I promise I won't say anything."

"Or do anything."

"Or do anything. Cross my heart and hope to die."

"Oh, Prudence, don't hope for that. Not even in jest."

To everyone they met along the way her mother asked, "*Dónde está el carcel?*" Open mouthed, hands tossed high in the air, they stared at her; no one answered. At last an old man appeared to listen, his head shook more in sadness than anything.

"No. No, *Señora,* you no wish to go to the prison."

"*Sí, por favor.*"

"*No es la carcel.* They are using the stable. It is no place for a woman. They have put the prisoners in with—"

"With the horses?" Her mother giggled, a nervous high whinny, a lopsided, ugly grin. The man backed off.

"Helen, the little . . . they're holding her in a stable." In the time it took to reach the stable, worry lines had replaced the smirk.

Soldiers milled around in front of the stable, guns everywhere. Stacks of them by the door. Each man wore a holster and carried yet another rifle. Prudence grabbed her mother's hand. Her mother shook her off and hissed.

"Don't let them see your fear. You know what happens if you let a dog know you're scared, don't you?" Prudence nodded, "All right then, heads up, ignore the dogs." Prudence blinked, something about the sunlight, the way it bounced off the bayonets, she looked right into the mouths of the dogs and saw the sharpness of their teeth.

"*¿Dónde está su jefe?*"

A man, his sweat-stained uniform wrinkled and torn, twisted his face into a lewd grin as they approached the

236

entrance. Prudence had seen that look before, on the Germans, the older ones, just before they chucked her under the chin, or pinched her backside. She felt herself go all queasy inside; but her mother, with all the bravado of a Roland P. Whitley looked right over his head. "Step aside," she demanded, "you're not the Captain. I will speak only with the Captain."

"*No es un Capitan—*"

"Well then the Lieutenant, the General . . . I don't care what you call him as long as he's the head man." A tall man detached himself from the ones stacking the guns. He gave her mother an appreciative look. That was more like it. That's the way most men looked at her mother. Maybe it would be all right after all.

"Captain Morilla, *a su servicio.* You have come to see your husband's secretary? His p-r-i-v-a-t-e secretary." The word slid out slowly from behind his mustache like something dirty, bad. His English sounded English, his Spanish—one more of those accents that slipped around in disguise.

"You are English, American perhaps, Captain?" Though Prudence could tell nothing of the captain's mood, she caught the hope in her mother's voice.

"I ask the questions here." He waved them in front of him through the stable door. After the bright sunlight, the gloom inside appeared impenetrable. Prudence stumbled. The Captain reached out, steadied her. She pulled away.

Her mother's eyebrows raised in warning. Prudence tried out a smile, she felt it stretch weak and sickly across her face. Her eyes adjusted to the darkness. Between the slats of the stalls she saw dirty, unshaven men who scarcely looked up as they passed. And when they did it was with dark and hollow eyes, eyes that asked no questions, they reflected only a dull acceptance of their fate.

In another stall, women clung to each other, weeping. From

the rear of the stable a group of men moved toward them, their laughter, the babble of their language as mismatched as their uniforms.

The stench was unbearable—the order of human sweat, urine and dung. Prudence gagged. She heard a ringing, a buzz that grew into a roar. Her head, it was all in her head. She felt faint, dizzy and fought to keep her eyes open. If she shut them, even for a moment, her mother might disappear into the gloom, maybe forever.

The men stopped before an open stall. She and her mother could go no further, they blocked the way. Her mother's chin appeared to quiver. Now Prudence was really afraid. Inside the stall she noticed a pile of straw and on it, all spread out . . . hair, red hair. Helen, clothes stained, cheeks smeared, looked up at them.

The first soldier grabbed her mother's purse, then pushed the two of them into the stall with Helen. The place came alive with men, uniformed men, men in peasant boots. Everyone pushing, shoving, tearing at their clothes. Over all the confusion, Prudence heard a voice, "The Señor's women, they must be taught a lesson." The voice spoke English, the accent wasn't Spanish. Someone shoved her mother to the ground, grabbed Prudence by the shoulder, "No. Not the child, we are not beasts." Someone else caught her by the arm, dragged her away and threw her into the stall next door.

Through the slats she saw her mother, Helen . . . they twisted this way, that. They spun. Swirled. Struggled. It did no good—leaves caught in a river, they rushed to the edge of the falls.

And then, an eerie quiet. It was over. The soldiers left. Prudence tested the door to her stall, it opened. She crawled through the muck, the straw, to where her mother was and stood up, slid back the bolt and went in. Her mother, Helen and Prudence, they all three of them cast careful, quick little glances around the stall, looking anywhere but at each other. Each ashamed in their own way. Her mother because, at the very moment it ended, when all struggle ceased to matter, she saw Prudence peering through the slats.

Helen because she had dragged the other two into this. And Prudence? Prudence felt shame because she had done what her mother said, nothing to anger the men, nothing to help her mother. But what about her promise to her father? She hadn't protected her mother. She had sat there. Watched. And done nothing.

Now the dim light of the stalls seemed too bright. They saw clearly what they didn't want to see, not yet. And what they didn't say rang louder than any noise Prudence had ever heard. Once again the world had changed. There would be no going back. Helen lay with her skirt up, her blouse ripped. Her face stripped of pride, of ambition. Her shield, her look-at-me-aura of superiority, lay shattered in the straw around her. Perhaps she wanted only to be back at that plank table, in the heart of Wales. The dirt, the soot of coal must seem infinitely better than this.

Prudence heard a cough. "Helen," her mother hissed. "Where is he?"

"I don't know—"

"You weren't together then?"

"Clare Singleton showed up in Madrid, she needed some help. Roland, I mean Mr. Whitley, sent me to get some papers for her. When I got back to our . . . to his hotel room. He was gone. The soldiers were there, they took me to—"

"Then you didn't see it, you didn't see them shoot him?"

"Please, not so loud. I was told . . . they said I must tell you—"

"Tell me what? Hurry, before someone comes."

"I was to tell you they shot him, they said if I didn't they would—"

"What, they would what—?"

Helen moaned. "They already have, many times. It makes no difference now. The truth is I don't know . . . that night at the prison they separated the men from the women, they said he was there, they said he wouldn't come to help me, to help any-one. I don't know what happened to Mrs. Singleton." Prudence thought of the woman at her mother's tea, the woman of the fussy taffeta. "Then they came for me. I thought I was going to die; instead they put me in a truck and brought me here. There were lots of others, Spaniards mostly. I didn't see Roland, I mean Mr.—" her voice faltered. Over the dung, Prudence smelled fear. Pity, she should have felt pity. She didn't. She felt noth-ing—no that wasn't true—something stirred somewhere inside her, something that didn't belong. Revenge? Justice? Prudence thought of Nanny, the pain Helen caused, the spitefulness, the petty barbs, the creaking sofa, the honeyed voice. Prudence flushed with shame at the seed of gladness that sprouted inside her. What would the nuns think? She looked at Helen again, the dirt smears, the terror in her eyes and did her best to push the feeling down.

"It's his papers, his manuscript, they want." Helen spit out the words. "They think he's a fascist, they think his book will hurt their cause."

"Then these people, they must be the communists—"

"Who knows, I think it was the JC's that first arrested us, they were young, boys really. But then there were arguments, the Socialists came and wanted to take us back to Madrid. They spoke of a trial. The others laughed. Men shouted 'hurry, load everyone on the trucks, the POUM were coming.' They thought they would steal the prisoners, then I heard—" Helen stopped.

"Heard what," her mother said. "What? Damn it, what did you hear?"

"Shots, that's when I heard the shots. Hours later they put me on a truck, there were many, row after row. In the dark I could see long lines of people shuffling along, some towards the truck, some towards a wall . . . after that I don't know what, I don't know who. These men, the peasant boots—they're, they're—it doesn't seem to matter who they are, they all appeared to know Rola . . . Mr. Whitley."

Prudence listened to her quiet sobbing and looked away. She studied the dirty straw that separated her from her mother, she should crawl to the back, to the darkest corner where her mother lay. She wouldn't look at her yet but she would go there, do something, comfort her. What could she say? What could she do? No bread pudding, no raisin could make this hurt go away. She waited. At last her mother got up and straightened her clothes. Her eyes looked so blank, so cold, Prudence winced. Gone that prideful, far away look, the over-the-heads-of-the-people one she taught Prudence. The way to ignore rude crowds, the way she ignored the goring of the bulls, the way she ignored anything and everything, all gone. Instead this was a don't-come-near, don't-try-to-get-inside-me look, a there-are-things-no-mother-wants-a-daughter-to-know look. Don't-ask-me, I-won't-answer, look. It all seemed so clear her mother might well have said it all out loud.

But when her mother stood up and came over to her it was as if nothing more than a trip to the market was on her mind, though the smile she smiled seemed all tooth, it looked pasted on; and then slowly and deliberately she brushed the dirt and hay from Prudence's hair, took hold of her hand and led her to the door of the stall. She hesitated, not wanting to step out, did she think the soldiers in the corridor might shoot?

"I demand to see your chief," she shouted. "Now. I want him now. We are Americans. We have American passports." Her mother's voice rang out as if she were the general, as if she was the one with the army behind her. But the hand that held hers squeezed so tight, Prudence bit her lip so as not to cry out. All her mother's softness, willingness to please—gone. An angry, very angry woman had her by the hand. And Prudence knew their safety lay in that anger.

The man came to the door held it open and motioned for them to come out. "Stop your yelling, *Señora,* we are done with you, you meddling foreigners. Do you have any more doubts about who is in control here?"

Her mother turned to Helen. Helen jumped up, "My clothes, I'll need—"

"Shut up, bitch! You'll need nothing."

The man let Prudence and her mother pass, then his hand shot out, blocked Helen's way. "You," the soldier turned toward her mother, "you may go *Señora.* And the child. But she stays, there is much yet for her to tell us."

"She knows nothing . . . you think my husband would tell important things to her? She is . . . she was . . ." her mother hesitated, "my husband's . . . *puta.* I wish to deal with her myself."

The Captain laughed.

Her mother stared straight ahead, "It may be amusing to you *Señor.* I do not find it so." The soldier looked hard at her, as if to assess his enemy's strength, "Do you need another reminder, Señora? He smiled am awful smile, pulled Prudence to his side, placed the edge of his bayonet along her cheek—her mother screamed, Prudence flinched. The blade cut.

"Go home, *Señora.* Save the life of your little girl."

TWENTY-TWO

Passport to Chaos
"...and I carry it in the inside pocket of my mind."

—ELIOT PAUL, *The Life and Death of a Spanish Town*

ON THE WALK back to the *Casa de Carillo* they didn't hold hands, they didn't touch. No one said a word. To Prudence, it seemed as if they had walked for miles, but at last, her mother turned to her, pulled out a handkerchief and tried to dab away the blood running down Prudence's cheek.

"Alcohol, I have some rubbing alcohol, somewhere."

"It'll sting."

Her mother kept trying to wipe away the blood, "You always were an odd one." Dab. Dab. "It will be all right, Prudence. It will be all right."

Somewhere inside her, deep, deep down, Prudence held onto one small thread of hope; though she had broken her promise, she hoped her mother's promises might be one grownup's promise she could believe. She crossed her fingers. She would have crossed her toes, but she couldn't figure out a way to do it and keep walking.

"I know one thing—they never meant to let Helen go," her

mother muttered more to herself that to Prudence. "It was a trick, they wanted us to leave the house, but why?"

From as far away as the gate, she had her answer. The giant wooden door stood open. Inside the house was a shambles. Cupboards open, their contents strewn across the floor, drawers empty. Ripped and torn cushions scattered every which way, the grayness of their stuffing floated in the light from the window, covering the room like an ugly rash. Something about those wads of cotton that oozed out of every slit, made Prudence think of her mother, Helen, the straw, the floor of the stable. And she knew crossed fingers weren't going to be enough to help, not ever again.

Her mother came up behind her. "Why is it," she said, "that man is so brutish." Prudence wondered why her mother had said man, not men. Surely it had taken more than one to do all this.

"Everything in their path, everything—they think they must to destroy it." And then Prudence understood her mother was talking about more than ripped and torn cushions. She turned, faced her mother expecting anger. She saw resignation.

Whoever did this was thorough. The china, the crystal, all gone. Family photos torn, silver frames missing. Everything destroyed. In the library, it was worse. Every book thrown to the floor, drawers pulled out, papers scattered everywhere. She almost tripped over her father's cane. She bent to pick it up, it was only the crook. The rest of the cane lay over by the desk.

"Maybe Helen was right. Maybe they came for his papers and the tiresome manuscripts those two spent all their time over. But why? Who would want them? As for his reports, all they had to do was buy The London Times and they could read those …."

"But, Mother, the frames, the china—?"

"Payment for their trouble."

Prudence felt too confused to think it out clearly. She didn't care very much about the frames or the china but surely he would have taken the manuscripts with him. Her mother must be right yet Prudence remembered seeing the manuscript some-place odd, a place the soldiers wouldn't normally look for some-thing as precious as his writing—the boxes, the ones in the base-ment. They wouldn't know they were there unless —?

She tried to ask her mother but she wasn't listening. She had gone to the desk. Prudence stopped talking and watched her pry open the little top drawer—the lock popped so easily with the tip of her father's cane, it seemed odd that the men had spared it. "Thank God," her mother let out a sigh as she pulled out the envelope. The passports—they were there safe in her mother's hand. It would be all right. Passports mattered; china, picture frames or even manuscripts didn't. All they needed was their passports and right now that seemed to Prudence like a very good idea. And her mother had them.

But then something went awfully wrong with her mother's face, it sort of collapsed. "My God, what have they done?"

"Done what?" Her mother handed her a passport, she could hardly tell whose it was. Someone had taken a greasy, black pencil and slashed an ugly, jagged x across each and every page.

"I will never understand this damn place . . . I don't know who wanted your father dead, Prudence. He would have showed them his papers, he was a reporter, a legitimate reporter. People don't kill reporters. But he's—" her mother's voice broke, "someone wants us to think he's dead and someone else wants us out, another wants us trapped here in this, this . . . .." Her hand went limp, the passports slid from it, fell to the floor. "I don't understand. I just don't."

The sound of her mother's heels on the bare tiles as she ran from the room echoed the clack of the bolt on the stable door as it closed on Helen.

There was much Prudence wanted to ask her mother, but on the way home her mother said nothing. Now, before her mother went upstairs, before she could become another person, she'd done it once, it could happen again—she had to have some answers. "Mother—" she called after her. Her voice faltered, she stopped, cleared her throat. She had lost the battle to hold back her tears.

"Prudence, you mustn't—" Her mother came back, patted the pockets of her coat. "I can't seem to find—"

"I should have done something, Mother."

"Prudence, sometimes things happen, terrible things—"

"I should have—"

"No, you shouldn't. I told you not to anger the soldiers and you didn't. You did the right thing and now I need you to do something else for me."

She would do anything to shake this feeling of guilt, anything at all. "What is it?"

"I want you to forget that it happened."

"All of it, the whole—"

"Yes. It's over. We must both forget it. We have more important things to do. We must leave, now. Promise me—we won't speak of this again."

"But Mother, how—?"

"Please, Prudence. Please. I simply can't."

To Prudence it seemed impossible not to and yet if that was all her mother asked, she would do it, but how? Maybe her mother could manage—she was an actress, an actress could pretend. All Prudence could do was promise never to speak of it. It seemed as if promises were piling up on top of promises. Almost as if one promise worked against another promise. But she would never forget a moment of that day—not the look in her mother's eyes, the smell of the stalls, or the sound of Helen's whimpering, the feel of cold steel against her cheek. And the shame of what she had done, the broken promise. She had done nothing to protect her mother. How could she forget that? She took a deep breath.

"I'll . . . I'll try."

"Good girl. I knew I could count on you."

Prudence wasn't so sure. She stayed behind to poke around on the floor, found a picture of her father, slipped it in her pocket and went on sorting through photographs until she found the passports. The smears across the pictures, the marks on their faces, made her feel dirty, uncomfortable, the way she felt in the stable. She shook her head back and forth, until the room blurred enough to force that picture out of her mind. She'd promised. She had to try.

As the room spun, she heard Nanny's voice, scolding, "American passports. They are precious documents, never let them out of your sight." It couldn't be. Not Nanny. She'd left Nanny upstairs, lying on her bed, dead. Very, very dead. *Don't think about Nanny, not now. Later. You can think about her later.*

The only sound from upstairs was that of her mother moving about. Prudence went to the kitchen to find some rags and did her best to wipe the passports clean. The more she rubbed, the more she smeared, even her tears failed to wash anything away.

She started for the stairs, the house so quiet she heard her heart bang against her chest as if it wanted out. She tried to quiet it and then, at the top of the stairs, she heard water splashing. And singing? At the open door to her mother's room, she realized her mistake. A high reedy wail, and words, the same ones, over and over again came from the bathroom.

"No. No. No. It didn't happen, it couldn't happen. No. No. No."

Prudence tiptoed over, bent down and peered through the keyhole. Her mother stood in the tub, one of the maids cleaning brushes in her hand, rubbing her arms, her legs, her breasts, scrubbing them so hard her skin looked raw and red. Prudence didn't want to see this. She hadn't seen it. Like her mother, she would pretend she hadn't seen anything at all. Her mother in the stable, her mother in the tub. None of it. She hadn't. She wouldn't. She couldn't. She had.

She backed out of the bedroom, pulled the door closed behind her, but not before she noticed her mother's clothes, or what was left of them, on the floor, her empty jewelry box, upside down on top of them. Everything gone. Even that necklace, her favorite, the one her father had especially made up for her.

Out in the hall, an awful smell permeated the air, it came from the other wing. She crossed the hall and entered the sitting room, that warm, safe comfortable place where she and Nanny nestled down into the cushions to do their reading—cotton batting, stuffing floated everywhere, the air thick with it. Prudence put her hand over her nose and rushed through into the hall and down to the schoolroom. Here the smell seemed worse, it mingled with torn maps, the books on the floor, and then she saw the words on the blackboard. "*Muerte a esos que nos negarían Libertad.*" Like the ones that dripped down the village walls, the letters forming the words looked dangerous—huge, chunky blocks screaming in their silence. She recognized *Muerte*, death and *Libertad*, liberty. She better tell her mother about this; but first she would check her room. Suddenly more than anything, she needed to hold that once spurned doll.

She started down the hall, but the door to Nanny's room stopped her. Unlike every other door, this one remained shut. *That smell, that's why they didn't—*.

She opened the door, she had to make sure. By the door she

tripped on something, a leather case, one of her father's cameras inside. They must have come in, but they didn't stay long, the rest of the room stood as neat and clean as if Nanny had just put everything to rights, everything but that the leather case on the floor. What was it doing in here?

She could stand here, holding her breath, her hand covering her nose and puzzle it out all she wanted to but she knew that eventually she would have to look toward the bed, toward that small lump under the covers. In death, just as in life, Nanny took up so little room—that small lump all she had been, all she ever would be.

Prudence clenched her teeth, swallowed hard, closed the door behind her and moved on down the hall to her room. One or two drawers were open but that was all. Nothing else seemed touched. Not quite, over on the bed, against her pillows where she had left Shirley propped up...nothing. Shirley was gone. Prudence felt an ache in her arms, right in the places that stuffed body, stiff curls and china head would have nested. Her throat tightened, she couldn't get her breath, a huge lump blocked the way. Only crying could make a lump that big go away. She sat down on the floor ready to cry, she wanted to get rid of every last tear. She tried crying. She tried screaming. Her eyes burned dry, the tears wouldn't come, the screams stayed in her throat, and the lump that settled there grew and grew. She felt different all over, something in her body changed, tightened. She thought she might never cry again. And the lump in her throat, it might never go away.

She got up and walked back down the hall to where her mother picked through the clothing on the floor, a coat hanger in one hand an old purse in the other. She looked up when Prudence entered.

"The furs, my jewelry, all gone."

"That's not all—"

"It's a good thing," her mother went on as if she hadn't heard, "I put the money in our clothes. They would have found it all for sure. And that soldier, he's in for a surprise."

"What soldier?" What was her mother thinking? She was treading on dangerous ground.

"The one that took my purse—" as if she remembered, her mother stopped. "Never mind I have others; our money is safe. We'll go to the American Consulate for new passports."

"But the fires, the shooting—"

"Rumors. They're just trying to scare us." Her mother seemed preoccupied, excited even, almost as if she anticipated some event, a tea, a dinner as she examined her clothes. She settled on a plain black dress and some sensible shoes.

"Perhaps if I put my hair in a bun, I can pass for a *Señora*?" She swept her hair back from her face. "What do you think?"

"Mother?"

"What?"

"They did."

"Who? Did what?"

"The rumors, they scared me."

TWENTY-THREE

A Time To Go

"Leave the substance for the shadow.
Leave your easy life . . .."

—ANDRE BRETON, *Set off on the roads*

LATE AFTERNOON, they started for Málaga. Her mother drove. They had looked for Rubio earlier, but no one in the village would admit to seeing him.

Prudence never told her mother about the words on the blackboard or the doll; she only managed to stay awake long enough to warn her about the village where Helen had tried to get lunch that first day.

"There's a road around, Rubio took it. It would be better —"

Her mother thought it would take too long, but as they neared the village and saw the bonfires, she turned off.

"So this is where you lost Rubio?" It all seemed so long ago, a different country, a different place. In the middle of that awful olive grove of scary trees, her eyelids drooped, she fell asleep. In the short time, since her father left so much happened, she had so many new things to fear. Twisted limbs and gnarled trunks had lost their power to terrorize.

"You awake, Sleeping Beauty?"

"I smell the ocean—"

"It won't be long now, a few more ups and downs and we'll be on the coast road."

Prudence noticed movement at the side of the road, an almost endless stream of shadowy figures hurrying along, all scrunched over, as if hoping no one would notice them in the growing darkness.

"Who—?"

"I don't know. I started seeing them a few miles back and the closer we get to the city the more—"

"Mother?"

"Another question?"

"If everything is all right in Málaga, why are they leaving the city? And why do they turn their faces as we pass?"

"The Cadillac," her mother said. "We haven't seen another car for … well, not since we left Rodicio. They must think we're some sort of officials. They won't bother us."

They passed the next few miles in silence. Prudence felt almost safe in the closeness, the two of them in the car alone. No more crying. No more wailing. And then she broke the silence. "Look," she shouted.

"Hush, not so loud."

"But that lady, over there . . . it's that Mrs. Morgana! The lady with the turbans."

"Certainly not, that woman's dressed in tatters."

"But mother, I think—"

"Keep a sharp look out on the road. The rocks, the stones, they're not good for the tires." Her mother seemed oddly determined to distract her.

"But—"

"No more buts. How can I concentrate on the road and answer your questions too?"

As they started down the last grade, heading towards a curve in the road, they saw the beam of headlights, Her mother reached down, shut hers off. A car came round the curve, moving quickly towards them, the lights grew larger, brighter. Her mother spotted a little dirt path leading off to the right and swerved into it, pulling the car deep into the bushes with such a bumping and jostling, Prudence fell to the floor.

"Quick, get out."

"But why——" Her mother reached across, opened the door, gave Prudence a shove and slid out right behind her.

"Keep going," she whispered and pushed Prudence further and further into the bushes. Prudence started to speak. Her mother put a finger to her lips. By now the car was close enough to hear it's motor, see the suitcases and trunks strapped to the top. From a ways down the hill another set of lights approached, they moved even quicker than the first. The second car came abreast of the first, swerved around it and forced it to a stop. A group of men jumped out and surrounded it. Shots. Some laughter. More shots.

"Get down," her mother hissed. Prudence peering through the bushes, saw the terror on the faces of the people inside before her mother could push her head down. She held it there until the shooting stopped. Her mother loosened her grip. "Be still." They heard more laughter, then the sound of glass shattering. They watched as the men pulled the passengers from the car. Only then did Prudence notice that the people walking along the road had melted back into the bushes.

She could barely make out the ones lying in the road, they weren't moving. The men kicked at the bodies, pushed them aside before they jumped into their own car, turned it around and headed back the way they came.

The two remained crouching in the bushes for hours. At last a little crack of light threw the mountains behind them into silhouettes. "Before the phantom of false morning died,"[1] Prudence took some comfort in reciting those lines from her favorite poem. Her mother shivered.

Prudence, legs aching, started to stand but her mother pulled her back. "Wait!" She glanced up the road in the directions her mother pointed. Figures emerged from the bushes and ran down to the car. They gathered around the bodies, some cried, others turned the dead men's pockets inside out.

"They're stealing their money!"

"I think they're looking for papers. You know, to see who they are."

"Those poor people, why?"

"There must be a reason why they were shot, I mean people just don't shoot people for no reason." Her mother's words were confident, her tone wasn't.

As they waited the sun worked its way higher and higher. They crawled even deeper into the brush to escape the heat, every muscle cramped, their arms and legs itched from the stickers that covered them.

"Mother, I think I'm bleeding, these bushes are—?"

"Prudence, listen to me. We'll get out of here. I don't know how, I don't know when. But we are Americans, we'll be all right. They have no reason to hurt us. But there is something else you must promise me."

Was this another one of those things she must forget?

"Never, ever again ask why."

"Why?"

Her mother's smile widened, she even laughed.

---

1 Rubáiyát of Omar Khayyám Edward Fitzgerald

"Prudence, if we are to make it, you must learn to do what I say, when I say it and without asking questions. There just isn't time for questions." Prudence felt better. If she could make her mother laugh, things might soon be all right.

"Mother, I'm thirsty."

"All right, it's been long enough, we'll go now."

Prudence stood up, her legs barely supported her but she headed off in the direction of the car.

"No, this way," her mother grabbed her arm. "It will be safer without the car." Prudence started to ask, and then remembered. "That's a good girl," her mother smiled, "we'll look more like refugees if we walk."

They walked for miles until Prudence could hardly put one foot in front of the other. She sat down by the side of the road. "I can't—"

"Yes, Prudence, you can."

They heard it coming long before they saw it. Clip-clop. Clip-clop. They both wanted it to be Rubio come to rescue them; but of course it couldn't be, he had no way of knowing they even needed rescuing. As the cart approached, her mother said, "It's only an old man, I must chance it." She stepped out into the road and put up her hand.

"*¿Agua, por favor?*"

The driver stopped reached around behind him and handed down a goatskin bag. Her mother encouraged Prudence to have the first sip. She tipped it back, gulping greedily. The wine burned its way down the back of her throat. The man motioned for them to climb up.

By late afternoon, they arrived in the outskirts of Málaga, every bone aching from the jostling. Along the way the driver had peppered them with questions most of the way. Had they seen his family? Did they know any of the people in the photographs he showed them? Had they seen any soldiers on the road? What was happening in the rest of the country?

They told him about the soldiers, about the people. "But not these people, not the ones in the photographs." The driver was thrilled to find out they were Americans. "I have a cousin, he bends the steel in the Pittsburgh. He tell me America is a great place, I should go there. Do you know Pittsburgh?"

"I have been—"

"Then my brother, you might know him?"

"I'm so sorry, I don't; but," her mother hastened to add, "I will look him up as soon as we get home." So home was America. Prudence had never been but the word home had a comforting sound to it. She repeated to herself. *Home. Home.*

"The last few weeks," the driver went on, "she bad. There have been killings—"

"Who is doing the killing?"

"I mind my own business, it's safer that way. Everyone she have the guns, old women, young boys."

Prudence wanted to ask if he knew Rubio, she didn't. Somehow she knew Rubio had moved on from the killing of rabbits . . . she wouldn't think about that.

In the hills overlooking the bay, they could clearly make out the ships in the harbor. "Where are the British, the American ships? I can't see any flags." The disappointment in her mother's voice made Prudence uneasy.

"Those ships, they hold the prisoners. The planes come and drop some papers, some bombs. Then people come for the prisoners and every time they take some away and shoot them." Her mother winced.

"Sorry *Señora*, but that is what the rumors they say."

"Any Americans on those ships?"

"Oh no, *Señora*, who would shoot *Americanos*?"

"See Mother, maybe he isn't—?"

"Hush, child. *Señor*?"

"*Sí*."

"Who is it? Who is this *they*, the *they* that does everything."

"I do not know. People disappear at night. So many die, so many different peoples—a man of much importance, the city councilor, they shoot him. A socialist leader, bang he is dead. Then a priest. Next a labor unionist—"

"I thought you said the Republic held the city, why—?"

"That is what I tell you, *Señora*. Everyone is this *they*, everyone she kill. Shopkeepers, butchers. Houses burn, churches are robbed. The rich, the religious they flee and yet you two, you come here?"

"But does no one stop them?"

"I am but a poor driver, what would you have me do?"

"Mother, can't we stop?" No matter how hard she tried, Prudence couldn't keep the whine out of her voice. She couldn't help it, not with the ache in her bones, the bruises on her backside; besides her mother wasn't listening, her eyes darted everywhere, as if afraid she might miss some vital landmark.

Just when Prudence thought she could stand it no longer, her mother called to the driver, "Here *Señor, por favor*, you may turn here along the boulevard, I think this is the way to—"

"Excuse, please." The driver pulled his cart to a stop. "You must get out here. I go no further into the city, she is too dangerous."

"But we must go to the consulate."

"I can do no more, I wish it otherwise, *Señora*. It is not to be."

Gingerly the two climbed down, their legs too cramped to support them at first. The driver looked away politely as they wobbled their way to the side of the road. *"Buena suerte,"* he called out as he turned his cart around, "don't forget my cousin in the steel. Tell him you saw me."

"Wait, *señor*, the American consulate—?" The man didn't answer. "The embassy, I mean *¿Dónde está la embajada—?*"she shouted, "He must be deaf, he doesn't seem to hear me."

Prudence put her fingers to her lips. "Shh! People are look-ing." That wasn't true, there was no one around; but last night, that car, the men, the guns, they had appeared out of nowhere and, she knew, even if her mother didn't, that the man hadn't wanted to hear. As if to attract even more attention, her mother stopped, opened her purse, took out her compact and began to powder her nose with the deliberate motions of a knight don-ning armor.

"Mother, please—"

"Give me a minute, Prudence. Let me get my bearings. Your father took me there once, a reception. I think. The problem is I'm not sure where we are right now. " Her mother walked over to the street sign. *Calle de Artimo.* "That goes to the *Alameda Principal*, does it not?" Before Prudence could inquire as to how she could be expected to know, her mother pulled a book from her purse." Nanny's guidebook? *"Las ciudades de España.* Maps, that's what we need."

"All right, here we are," she pointed to a spot at the edge of the map before she tucked the book away, "Let's just keep it between us that we are strangers too. It looks peaceful enough"

Prudence looked around. They were in the middle of some homes, not very grand ones; but flowers bloomed in window pots, bougainvillea climbed the walls and lemon trees marched along the streets in innocent oblivion of danger. What was worrisome, though, was that her mother appeared to be just as innocent. She didn't have a good sense about danger and never saw it coming. "Danger is your father's department," she had said often enough. But with him gone and with no one left to cling too there was nothing else for Prudence to do but be brave. Maybe never seeing danger coming left her mother ready to be brave when it was right there, on top of them *like that time in the*—she mustn't think of that. But still, if her mother would worry a little ahead of time they might stay out of trouble.

Her mother worked her hair back in place with one hand and smoothed her dress with the other. "Do something with your clothes, dear. You're a sight." Prudence gave her skirt a few swipes and tugged at her socks. "That's better. We're going to be all right. All that talk, that's all it was, talk. People, the way they love rumors, exaggerations. Chin up now, all we have to do is pretend that we know what we're doing."

There she was again, this new woman—would this woman stay or change back? *No, no, please don't let her change back.* Maybe that brave determined woman was there all along and Prudence, in that self-absorbed way of children, just hadn't noticed.

But then it happened again, not needy mother but the not-seeing-signs-of-danger mother. She hadn't noticed the little wisps of joyless gray that dulled the sky, the ominous scent of burnt wood and stale ashes that all but erased the perfume of the flowers. Prudence needed only to glance up and down the side streets to find more than enough reasons for the smell. At the sight of each charred door, she quickened her pace.

After they passed the third gutted house Prudence, about to point out one where a doll leaned against a cracked sill, noticed the doorjamb held no door and that the flowerbeds bloomed with broken glass. Maybe her mother didn't want to see. Prudence walked on and soon, too tired, too hungry to keep it up for long, she plunked down on the curb.

"Come on Prudence, don't give up on me now." She got up. Closer in to the center of the city, the streets began to fill with people. "Don't make eye contact," her mother hissed as she tugged her first to the left, then to the right, following some invisible map in her head, "we don't want anyone asking questions." That didn't turn out to be so easy. A few blocks further on, a man leaned against a building, trying hard, too hard, to look as if he wasn't looking. When she spotted the pistol strapped to his hip, the rifle nearby —the cut on her face began to throb. His scraggily beard and the hastily put together, wish-I-were-a uniform didn't help. Her mother grabbed her hand. "Chin up, eyes straight ahead."

At their approach, the man straightened, held out his hand and demanded, "*Señora, señorita*, your papers." Prudence noticed there was no *por favor*, not even in his tone of voice. She felt all shivery.

Her mother slid her purse further up under her arm and stared right through him. "You are in my way, *Señor*."

"English?"

"Americans, let us pass. We are on our way to the embassy."

"Your accent says English. Why you lie, say you are American?"

"The embassy, which way to the American Embassy?"

"Papers first, then we'll give thought to directions."

"*Señor*, I shall report you to the authorities. You are blocking my path." Whether the threat of authorities or the new-found firmness to her mother's chin deserved the credit, Prudence couldn't be sure, but the man stepped aside. Her cheek cooled as the new-found respect for her mother grew larger by the minute.

A few blocks further on, another slouching man fastened his glance on them; but her mother went on the attack. She marched right up to him and in a loud Roland-P-Whitley voice made her own demands. Caught off guard the man pointed straight ahead. "A mile or two more, no further."

Instead of looking up and down the streets for the next few blocks, Prudence vacillated between hunger and fear. Hunger won. She shook her hand loose from her mother's. "Can we stop for something to eat?"

"*May*, Prudence. *May* we." But they didn't stop and the few chunks of bread the cart driver shared with them had done nothing to quiet her hunger. Now that the streets were dotted with little stalls, their counters stocked with pastries and fruit, Prudence couldn't hold back any longer. The smell of bread and cheeses, the heady aroma of garlic only made her legs tremble and her stomach growl.

"Mother? Did you hear—?"

"Oh Lord, of course. What was I thinking. I'm starving, myself." At the next stand, as her mother counted out the pesos and centavos, Prudence spotted a familiar figure hurrying down the boulevard.

"Look, Mother, Mrs. Lupinek."

"Who?"

"Dordo, the lady from the Dutch Embassy. She was there at your tea. You must remember—"

Before Prudence could finish her sentence and forgetting any thought of not calling attention to the two of them, her mother hurried across the street, shouting as she went.

"Dordo, Dordo, stop a moment. It's us," which wasn't quite accurate. Prudence had stayed behind, electing to wait for the food, but she kept her eyes and ears open.

"Marion, what are you doing here? Didn't the carrier deliver my message?"

"Message?"

"Well, it doesn't matter you're here now, safe." Though as

Prudence caught up with them, Dordo paused and looked closely at her. "It looks as if you've had a bit of trouble, Prudence. Your cheek, how did you get that cut?

"It's nothing, I just—"

Her mother broke in, "I'll tell you everything when were rested up, but its good to see you're safe too, we saw lots of damage as we entered town." Her mother had noticed.

Later, settled in Mrs. Lupinek's office, nibbling pastries, sipping tea—Marion nibbled and sipped, Prudence gobbled and gulped—they poured out their story. Her mother did a little script editing. The stable, the stall, her mother glossed over the details. The blame for the cut on Prudence's face was transferred to some broken glass in the *Casa*. Prudence tensed as they neared the part about the passports. As a sort of official, Mrs. Lupinek might have to turn them in. Prudence held her breath. Her mother stopped just short of the ruined passports.

"Then you don't know, I mean—not for sure—what's happened to Roland." Mrs. Lupinek looked solemn and sympathetic but her voice seemed to pry.

"No, I have no way of getting any real news . . . rumors, you get lots of those."

Mrs. Lupinek smiled. As she sat forward in her chair, leaned in closer, her voice took on more of an edge, a sharpness. "What are you going to do now?" Marion appeared flustered. Mrs. Lupinek waited, no signs of curiosity, only a touch of impatience on her face.

"I don't mean to scare you, but you must do something. You have already waited too long." Mrs. Lupinek paused to refill their cups. Prudence watched her mother's face darken, her tea-party-bright voice fade. The decision to confide in Mrs. Lupinek was made.

"Passports, we have no passports, Dordo." It all tumbled out—almost all. There was no mention of the scene in the straw, but her mother spoke of the ripped furniture, the torn clothing and the ruined passports. "We were on our way to the American consulate for new ones when we spotted you."

"Thank God, you did." Dordo's voice turned firm, authoritative, "Whatever you do, don't go there."

"But why? Who else—? What can I do—?"

"I thought perhaps you had already done something, obtained some false papers and that is why you hadn't mentioned your passports to me."

"I don't understand?"

"You see, Marion, I already knew—"

"About Roland?" Prudence winced at the hope in her mother's voice.

"No, no. About the passports."

"How could you?"

"It's not as if you and your husband are ordinary tourists. Roland is not unknown, you know that of course and then . . . well he was not always . . . how shall I put this . . . not always overly polite to the Vice-consul. I told your husband he made a mistake not inviting the Vice-consul to join his party that day at the bull ring."

"Roland never liked being told—"

"I know, but that man is a vengeful petty bureaucrat. Only yesterday, he called me. He said I should come to the consulate he had a message for me. I was shown into his office, he didn't look up or stop his paper shuffling; but, before excusing himself and leaving the room, he pulled a paper out, dropped it casually on top of the pile. I think, no I'm sure, he wanted me to see it. When he returned he looked awfully pleased with himself. Silly, spiteful man. The paper he pushed under my nose concerned you, your family—"

"What did it say?"

"I only got a quick glance, something about Mr. Whitley serving the fascists with his column. You were not to be allowed to leave until you paid for—"

"Pay? For what?"

"Any damage his columns may have done."

"Done to what?"

"The Cause."

"The Cause? I know nothing about a Cause, surely, if I explain—"

"Listen to me, Marion. That man will not help you. He even warned me not to interfere. He is young, inexperienced and probably hopes to be Consul someday. The other consulates are working hard to get their citizens on boats and out of here. As for your American, I don't know who he is more afraid of offending—his superiors in Washington, or the Reds in the streets. He is refusing to help anyone whose papers are not in— how do you Americans say it—apple pie order?"

"But he is the Vice consul, he has to help."

"Let me finish, Marion. From where I sat it was perfectly clear that he took great delight in the fact that your papers are not in order. Even if they were, this one is trouble."

"But the *London Times*, they'll—I'll write."

"Marion, think about it, how is it he knows your papers are not in order?"

Prudence watched as her mother paled.

"Besides, I'm not sure you have all that much time and, if they were to answer you, the French are reading mail headed for Spain and reporting sympathizers of Franco to the communists. And if you are for the Republic, the workers, there are those all too eager to turn any unionists over to the fascists. Casual letters from well meaning friends can send people to their deaths no matter what side they're on.

"There is a lot of sympathy these days in London for the reds. You lived in London long before you came here. Roland— anyway very few people are willing to upset the communists and like it or not, Málaga is effectively in their hands."

"The rumors, we were told the Republic held the town."

"Right now the anarchists appear to be in charge, but one can't be sure. It changes almost hourly, even block by block."

"But how?"

"If you are surprised, you are the only one. Even your husband—" Mrs. Lupinek smiled sympathetically and once more changed tack. "Everyone knew there would be trouble." Prudence thought of the library, the aide to the Governor, how agitated he had become. If he knew, her father must have.

"I was never sure why Roland brought you here. The troubles have been going on for years; and then in February, after the elections . . . surely Roland told you how they were rigged."

"Rigged? How would Roland know, he never told—"

"He was, I mean, is a reporter. I read his essay in *The Guardian*—he wrote about the early voters being turned away and told to come back at nine and when they did, the glass jars they used for the ballots were already filled and the unionists, the reds were pretty well positioned. He knew it—we all knew. It was only a matter of time."

"But when did the communists take over?"

"On the seventeenth of July, General Paxtot—"

"Well he couldn't have known—"

"Yes, Marion. He could have. He did. Even you met the General at the bull fights. He moved his troops into the center of the city, and then he thought better of it. Not wanting to provoke shooting, he sent his men back to the barracks. The next

day someone began to hand out guns, rifles, and the incendiar-
ies—the agitators had begun stockpiling them right after the`32
strikes. Everyone knew of these hoards, even Roland."

"He couldn't have—"

"You didn't read much that he wrote, did you?"

"I had, I was—no. I'm sorry. Go on, Dordo, what happened
then?"

On the nineteenth they surrounded the barracks, threatened to dynamite the buildings, the men surrendered. Who can
blame them? Then the real trouble—the looting, the burning
began. The agitators opened the prison doors."

Prudence could tell by the tired, flat voice Mrs. Lupinek
used that this was a story she had had to repeat many times.

"Didn't anyone try to stop them?"

"Who, Marion? The Chief of Police tried, but the anarchists
told him to go home to bed and wanting to see another sunrise,
he did. Then the house-to-house searches began. The Republic
is trying to maintain some order but they have yet to gain complete control, anarchist bands still roam the city."

"But surely the consulates cabled for help."

"Yes, but what few ships answered the call have come and
gone. More appear to be hanging off shore, waiting. But it isn't
safe for you here. I tried to get word to Rodicio, to tell you to stay
put until I could send help. But I guess things weren't getting
through, though it's a little better now that we have . . .."

"Have what, Mrs. Lupinek?"

"Dordo, I told you, call me Dordo. As to 'what,' it's best you
don't know, Prudence."

Prudence turned away from Mrs. Lupinek and watched her
mother's gaze drift to the window. The bay looked empty, even
the tide had gone out. Dordo put her hand on her mother's shoulder, her voice gentled. "Marion, with Roland being Roland and

making more enemies than friends, they'll be no ships here for you I'm afraid." The color drained from her mother's face, her shoulders slumped.

"But if Roland did all that writing for the papers then everyone must know he is a reporter . . . and they don't shoot reporters, do they?"

"It wasn't his reporting that got him into trouble, it was his essays, his opinion pieces. And that book he was writing was not exactly a secret. Look, you two need more to eat than just pastries. Come home with me, stay the night. You'll be safe enough there."

"Safe enough? But we're Americans." Her mother's face was open, guileless.

"You Americans, you are such innocents—the world is not what you think, nor is it what you want it to be. The fact that your husband was political nullifies any cachet your citizenship might entitle you to."

"Roland wasn't political."

"Oh, Marion, really."

Still her mother struggled against the truth. "But Dordo, if we had our passports, we—"

"But you don't, Marion. You don't." Prudence watched her mother's hopes and illusions drain away like the waters of the bay.

"You two need a plan, a way to fool the authorities, the soldiers and the peasants if you're to get to Cadiz."

"Why there?"

"The British, if they send more ships, they'll most likely opt for Cadiz. It's in Nationalist hands. They have the force to control the populace."

Her mother went on with her questions. How could she know there would be ships at Cadiz? Whose ships? When?

"Well, Marion, the Dutch embassy is still fairly neutral. Leave the worrying to me. Let's go home now and get a little solid food in you."

On the way back to Mrs. Lupinek's they stopped at the street stalls to buy garbanzo beans and spinach. "With a little onion, a little tomato, they will do up into a nice soup. The farmer's wives are selling what they can, they're not sure how long they'll have a product to sell. Their husbands, the conscription, there's no telling what's around the corner."

Back at the house, Mrs. Lupinek moved about her kitchen, concocting a plan along with supper. Prudence and her mother, too tired and hungry, couldn't seem to muster up the energy to do much about either.

"Never you mind, Marion," Mrs. Lupinek peppered the soup. "I'll think of something. Here you go, Prudence, be a good girl and lend a hand." She set Prudence to chopping the onions. "We might as well eat fresh food while we can, already the prices are so outrageous that I started a little garden out in the back."

Prudence had noticed patches of freshly turned earth, but with the burned and smashed front doors on either side and the red slashes on the curbs on front of them, the digging could have meant anything. Something as innocent, as ordinary as a vegetable garden helped shed a little of the weight of fear she had carried with her all the way from Rodicio. She chopped with vigor. The warmth of the room, the rich smells of the soup combined with Mrs. Lupinek's chatter made the world seem almost normal.

"The rioters were considerate," Mrs. Lupinek laughed when Prudence asked about the paint on the curbs, "they marked the houses the night before they looted them."

"Why were you spared?"

"I saw them, marched out there bold as brass and told them that this was the Ambassador's residence, of course Hans is not a full ambassador, but still, they didn't know that and they left us alone. Sometimes it helps to be forceful, to pretend you know more than the next fellow."

"Where is your husband now?" It was Marion's turn for questions.

"In Madrid, he left me in charge. He often does that you know, and like Roland, I'm not unknown. Hans, of course, never made fun of . . . well never mind. Anyway, you'll be safe with me while I work out the details." Her mother's attention drifted away with the mention of Madrid.

"Dordo, your husband he might be able to inquire about Roland."

"He already has, dear. I cabled him after I saw the letter in your consul's office. He hadn't any news. Though we both worried about the two of you being alone, he heard that there was fighting in your village. He promised to let me know if he learned anything else."

Later that night, over custard, Mrs. Lupinek laid out her handiwork. "I've got it."

"Got what, Mrs. Lupinek?" Prudence was growing tired and her understanding had grown as thick as the soup.

"Dordo, Prudence, Dordo. Friends call each other by their first name. And another thing, friends trust each other, right? And what I've got is a plan."

"A plan for what?"

"I know what we must do to get you and your mother safely out of Spain. Forget the hurt feelings of the American Consulate, forget papers. Did Roland leave any of his cameras behind, any that the marauders didn't steal that is?

"I don't think so."

Prudence jumped up—Nanny's room. The canvas bag. "His Leica, mother. He didn't take it, and they—"

"How—?"

"I saw it on Nanny's floor. The soldiers must have dropped it when they saw, when they smelled—"

"Smelled?"

"Nanny's dead."

Mrs. Lupinek pulled Prudence to her, put her arms around her. "I'm so sorry, dear, what happened? I didn't know the soldiers—"

Marion seemed almost agitated as she drew Prudence back to her side. "Her heart, it just gave out. Now, the camera. I don't understand, how will a camera help?"

"Hear me out. We have to get you to Cadiz, they're still some important people that need plucking from shore. If you're there they can hardly refuse to take you too."

"But how will we get—?"

"On the way, you and Prudence, you'll pass yourselves off as reporters. The Fascists, the Loyalists, the Royalists, all soldiers, no matter their side, want their story told. You yourself said they don't shoot reporters. They'll ask few questions, they might even wine and dine you. String your husband's camera around Prudence's neck and even the *Guardi Civile* will be so eager to get their picture taken they won't look too closely at the child and preclude them from questioning your motives. The male ego is so malleable you can use it to your advantage. And if soldiers have anything, they have the male ego."

"That's the trouble, Dordo. If they think she's an adult they might—" Her mother clamped her lips shut, but Dordo looked from one to another and her eyes went soft and knowing. Prudence realized she knew or at the very least guessed.

"Marion, trust me. If they think Prudence is a child, they

might shoot you both as spies. What reporter, in the middle of a war, a bloody civil war, ever brought a child along?" The enormity of what her father had done hit Prudence with the force of a bullet. It didn't matter that he bought her books, taught her about the stars, took her to see the bulls. None of that mattered. She would never, ever forgive him.

TWENTY-FOUR

To Tell One From Another

"Leave-takings are but wasted sadness"

—J.K. JEROME *The Passing of the Third Floor*

"PRUDENCE," Mrs. Lupinek said, "I need you to pay attention now. All right?"

"I am."

"You're half asleep, but you must—"

"I mean, I will."

"Good. I need you to think up a name for your paper. We mustn't use a real one, we don't want to compromises anyone else's credentials."

"The Washington Newsday."

"Why that"

"Everybody's heard of Washington."

"It will do. I've never heard of a Newsday in that city." Dordo assured them that the openness of their American faces and the slight British twist to their speech, "to say nothing of your beauty, Marion, will make any journalists you might meet pause long enough to allow the two of you to tell your story, garner sympathy and perhaps even assistance." As to their names,

"Better not make too radical a change," Dordo told them, "When you're frightened it's easy to forget."

Frightened? The very word scared Prudence.

"Try to stick to Miss Smith and Miss Jones for the most part, save Marion and Prudence for private times. It will help you stay in character." Turning to Prudence she added, "Your mother can teach you the way to walk without skipping, the way to modulate your voice so you don't sound childlike. Not that you ever have."

Her Mother had been quiet through all this but at last she spoke up, "Dordo, we will go to Madrid first, then Cadiz," she said. "I must look for Roland."

"Don't be such a horse's patoot, Marion." Mrs. Lupinek winked, Prudence laughed. "Now that's a sound I like to hear."

"Marion, Madrid is too far out of your way and definitely too dangerous. Take a look at this map." Her fingers traced the path of a blue line that ran along the coast, "This road runs straight to Cadiz." Prudence studied the squiggle that would carry them to safety, it didn't look very straight. She tried to memorize its twists, its turns, the names of towns. Her mother wouldn't bother, not while she was wearing her I'm-only-half-listening face. She often told Prudence, "Half an ear is more than most deserve and fooling people is easy once you master the art of acting." Getting out of Spain would require fooling a lot of people, though Dordo was not to be deceived so easily.

"Marion, now it's you who are not listening."

"But I . . . we need Roland. As for abandoning him, what would people think?"

"Would it matter? Isn't that what he—?" For a heartbeat no one spoke.

"I'm sorry Marion, forgive me. But I *am* trying to help. If there is any news, any at all, I'll get word to you somehow. And if we find him, we'll let him know that you got safely away. That is, after all, what he would want . . . isn't it?" The length of the pause, Dordo's hesitation, set Helen's face flickering to the front of Prudence's mind. And then the tone of Dordo's voice, that faint rise at the end of a sentence, that invisible question mark echoed her own thoughts. Had Helen and her father plotted not just to go away for a bit, but to not come back, to leave them behind? How did the soldiers know where they lived, where to look for the remaining passports? Her heart plummeted and then bobbed right back up again. Helen's face, there in the stable—how could she even think such a thing? Still, if her mother could teach *her* to act, then Helen could—?

Mrs. Lupinek touched Prudence gently on the shoulder, "Look at me dear, it's important that you both remember where you are."

"Where we are?"

"In whose territory. You'll be in Republican hands till somewhere between Marbella and Estipona."

"You see, Dordo, that's the sort of thing Roland would know."

"You'll just have to learn, Marion. Now where was I—oh yes? After that you are likely to run into Nationalists, Fascists. The rebels—"

"The Rebels? "

"We did have, albeit only a short time, a republic. So the fascists, Franco, the Nationalists are actually rebels no matter what they call themselves."

"Oh, Dordo, I'll never understand any of this."

"That's why it's better for you to avoid politics all together, admire their uniforms if they're wearing any, natter on about their bravery, and if you have to say anything mention the justness of their cause. Just don't mention what their cause is. Try to stick to declaring you have come to let the world know their side of the story, let them tell you which it is. Their machismo will kick in and they will be so intent on getting their pictures in American papers, they'll likely not question you at all. Marion try to do most of the talking. Prudence, try to look wise and impressed—no, impressed, that will go over the best.

"Like all things Spanish, the game is complicated. The lines between here and there are not clear. Who knows? My news may be out of date. Don't let your guard down even in the small villages; a lot of them are in the hands of anarchists." Poor Nanny, it seems God had not seen to their sauce. "And even in the Nationalist strongholds there are pockets of communists. Franco's swift march inland has stirred up the Royalists and infuriated the Leftists. The Rebel forces already hold Granada, at least that's what the radio says. But who knows"

There they were again, *ist* after *ist*, after *ist*. Somehow the *ists* had gotten control of her life. It wasn't fair, Prudence had no idea what they were all about and couldn't even tell one from another. And to make things even worse, her mother seemed determined to drag her right through the middle of every last *ist*. She didn't care that Mrs. Lupinek insisted she drop "this nonsense about Madrid."

"But Roland could help us, Prudence wouldn't have to act the adult if he were here to protect us."

"He isn't though, is he?"

"But—"

"Madrid is out of the question. There are daily skirmishes in the streets, homemade bombs," Marion's eyebrows shot up. "Wine bottles filled with petrol. It's the ammunition of the poor. And that's not all, Hans tells me he wakes to the noise of snipers and falls asleep to the sounds of the executioner's squad."

Her mother winced.

"Oh Marion, I'm sorry. My blunt talk gets me into trouble so often. Roland is probably all right. You know as well as I that he can talk his way out of anything. Cruel men enjoy staging executions, there are those they need to frighten into talking, or troublemakers they want to scare off—Roland's category most likely. They march them out, tie them to a stake and then shoot a couple of rounds just over their heads. Hans told me that was a favorite with the Germans during the last war."

"But Helen said—"

"Helen could only repeat what she knew, and she was in no position to know anything they didn't want her to know. Whatever has happened or has not happened, there is little you can do. Someone here has it in for you, and you better listen to what the *Jefe* said and get Prudence to safety. If Roland's alive he'll turn up."

Prudence hoped her mother hadn't paid too much attention to the alive part, she would want to go to Madrid for sure. Could she stop her? Would her mother go looking for him if she knew he had gone off with Helen to do whatever a man and a woman do when they go off together? Prudence hadn't told though. Perhaps it had something to do with watching her beautiful mother turn into a tired, ashen-faced, trying-to-be-brave mother. She thought of the passports, those smeary photos; that's what her mother looked like now. How could a daughter add to such a mother's sorrow? Prudence had no way of dealing with these kinds of decisions, they had been the parents, she the child, nothing she said or thought had ever been important before.

Mrs. Lupinek gathered up the dishes. "All right Marion, that's enough. We can talk again in the morning. Ramon, one of our assistants still has his *salvo conducto*, he can get you back safely to Rodicio. Pack lightly, but wisely. From there you are on your own."

"But why can't he—?"

"There are other things he must do."

"What could be more—?"

"Marion, I can't tell you everything. Please trust me."

It was her mother's turn to be sorry. "Oh, Dordo, I'm just not thinking straight." Attempting to atone for her self-absorption, she added, "He need only take us to our car."

"Better abandon the Cadillac all together, a little rich for reporters, don't you think? Even American ones," a slight smile crossed her face. "Come on, you two. No need to be so grim, you'll be all right."

"But the car, it would be so much faster."

"Think about it, Marion. Roland had to get an import permit for the car, they would have the license by now. You'll leave just after dark. There'll be a moon, but still fewer patrols move about at night."

On the drive back to Rodicio, Marion made Ramon stop at the crossroads where she drove the Cadillac off the road. They followed the tire tracks into the bushes, but the car was gone. Prudence, worried by Marion's stubbornness, breathed a sigh of relief. Ramon dropped them off at the edge of Rodicio with a flurry of last minute warnings to be careful, though the village appeared peaceful enough.

Their time at the Casa almost done, Prudence expected to feel nervous about the trek to Cadiz, but not this sadness, this feeling of things left unfinished, as if a part of her would stay here, the part that held the hand of the woman behind the closed door. Knowing what her mother thought about *feelings*, she kept hers to herself.

Loading the film took a lot longer than they allowed for—just finding some took up most of it; and then, once they found a roll they had no idea where to put it. Neither one ever dared touch his cameras before. Her father ranked cameras only slightly lower than books in the hierarchy of sacred objects. As they fumbled with this button and that knob Prudence wondered about wives and children, where had they ranked?

The few remaining hours they spent rehearsing their roles. No longer mother and daughter, they were now Marion Smith from the *New York World Daily* and Prudence Jones of *Washington Newsday*. It took a few tries before Prudence could say Marion without stumbling.

After a few rehearsals her mother called her a natural, though she did "over-act a bit." The dead giveaway of an amateur, she said. Prudence wanted to tell her mother that it shouldn't be hard for her to pass herself off as a grownup. She knew more about how grownups acted than she did children. Hadn't she spent all her time around them? Her only child friends were ones she made up. And maybe her fish, it was hard to know how old fish were. It was children who were the alien beings.

They went over the Spanish phrases Dordo suggested: the world—*el mundo entero* —must know of your cause. Our paper, our pictures, will tell them.

Next Prudence strode back and forth the length of the living room until she could traverse the entire distance in a pair of her mother's heels without once bending an ankle or making a grab for the furniture. She even began to take pleasure in the silky softness of the stockings against her legs, the way they whispered to her as she walked: *you're a grownup, you're a grownup.* Getting them to stay in place was another matter; they appeared as bent on sagging as her socks once had. Though the garters pinched they were better than that frightening gadget her mother had fastened about her hips. Its dangling straps, little metal buttons and rubber knobs put her in mind of the torture devices the nuns told her the inquisition reserved for unbelievers. Nanny's brassiere was pressed into service. Her mother's were too big.

Late in the afternoon, her mother suggested they pack up what clothes they could, they would leave in the morning. Cadiz would be their final destination, but her Mother clung stubbornly to her plan for Madrid. "We must find Roland and then the three of us can make our way to the coast."

Prudence would deal with Madrid later. Nanny had taught her patience, and a lot more besides. From time to time she had bowed to her father's order's, "You are not here to coddle my child, you're here to instruct her."

Prudence decided to go out, say her goodbyes and feed her fish one last time. *Ora Aureo, Jaspeadora* and *Dorado Rojo* were glad to see her. She chanted their names over and over, first to herself and then out loud. Her voice rose and fell to the music buried in their names. It distracted her from some of her pain, the pain she felt at leaving her friends, the pain she felt at leaving Nanny alone upstairs.

She had found a bit of stale bread in the pantry and tearing it in strips she dropped them into the water. The fish leaped up, snapped them out of her hand, too hungry to wait for the chunks to moisten and sink. What would they do with her gone?

Before she finished, she heard the first shots. Her mother came to the library door. "You better come in. I am heating up the leftover soup Dordo sent with us."

"Goodbye. *Ora Aureo*. Goodbye *Jaspead*—" More gunfire, louder, closer.

"Now, Prudence. Right now."

The two of them ate in silence, lost in thoughts of the next day, how it would go. Prudence tried once more to convince her mother to abandon Madrid.

"Mrs. Lupinek was right. Daddy did leave us, he's done it lots. This time he—"

"Prudence, don't talk about things you don't understand."

She almost said it then. "No Mother, there are things *you* don't understand" lay waiting to jump off the very tip of her tongue. "Children should be seen and not heard," her father had said that time and time again. She clamped her teeth down on to her tongue to remind it to hold its peace.

"Come on Hon, let's go to bed. You can sleep with me if you want."

"I think I'll say goodbye to my room." She had listened to her mother's sobs the night before and knew she couldn't keep her promise not to talk about the soldiers, what they had done, if she heard her mother cry again. There was another reason, her mother had told her to leave her diary behind, to "burn it" she said. Nanny taught her the importance of keeping a promise, sometimes that seemed harder than it looked. Hadn't Nanny made her promise not to play with matches?

She didn't go to her own room though, she didn't want to pass Nanny's door. Even with the sheets her mother stuffed round the cracks, the smell leaked out and painted everything. Her mother tried to call the convent, hoping the nuns had gone back, that they might know what she could do. The phones weren't working. She couldn't go to the authorities to ask them to come and get the body. There were no authorities. Rubio might have helped but "the damned boy, seems to have fallen off the ends of the earth."

Prudence tried not to think of Rubio, the ends of the earth or why the Mayor had never shown up that morning. She settled down in the sitting room. After doing her best to cram some stuffing back into the sofa cushions, she curled up under her coat and watched the reflections from the bonfires cross the ceiling.

An eerie sort of dance, fed by books, paintings, and maybe, maybe even Shirley. She pictured that blond hair curling in little brown crisps, that smile melting right off Shirley's face.

More shooting, rifle shots. She'd never sleep. She made her way back to her room. The house muffled the noise somewhat, and then, for some perverse reason, she strained to hear, as if she needed to know, needed to feel every shot, to think about where it might be going, whose flesh it might be plunging into. In the brief periods between the shots, she held her breath and waited for them to start again.

After a few hours, the sounds seemed heavier, more booms than rat-a-tats. The bottles of gasoline Dordo had talked about? The fires had grown so large that even here at the back of the house she could see the glow in the sky. She untangled herself from her sheets, went to the window and looked down on the pond. Red and gold reflections burst across its surface, silhouetting the thrashing shadows of the fish. Acrid smells drifted in through the window. A cold, dead weight grabbed her by the heart. She felt her skin crawl, as if a thousand spiders ran across the back of her neck. Someone was in her room, watching her. She knew it. Though her legs felt like sticks of lead, she had to look. Ever so slowly she turned. There, over there—it stared at her, that face, that scary face glowing in that hateful light—the dying Jesus. A vague uneasiness grabbed at her, she remembered seeing, no she remembered not seeing, something. She started for the stairs—the crucifix, the huge one that hung in the downstairs hall, the one that frightened her so that first day. She ran all the way down and looked up at the wall where it should be. Three holes, three gaping mouths stared at her. Someone had ripped the cross from the wall. It was there when they left for Málaga.

Once again someone had come into the house and they hadn't even noticed. Any doubts about taking to the road vanished. Someone wanted them gone all right, no telling how far they would go to scare them. They might even be in the house now. Prudence stamped her feet and shouted. "All right, all right, we're going."

Just then an explosion sounded right outside the house. Prudence ran back upstairs and just before she jumped into bed, she grabbed her diary off the nightstand and slipped it into her suitcase. She'd worry about what to do with it later. Then she lay down and pulled the covers over her head. She couldn't help it, the tears started. She cried for Nanny, she cried for Shirley; mostly she cried for Prudence.

The fires danced higher; the explosions boomed, each one louder that the one before; she would never sleep. And yet, the next time she opened her eyes, daylight had driven out the flames. Her mother stood over her, smiling. "Up! Up! I'm fixing us some oatmeal for breakfast, whoever stripped the cupboards missed it." To Prudence, that was logical, who liked oatmeal anyway?

After breakfast, Prudence and her mother wandered list-lessly about the villa, alone in a jumble of overturned furniture, open drawers, and bare cupboards. Nothing left to keep them here. Well one thing, her fish. She went outside to say one more good-bye. Debris littered the patio, jagged holes pocked the walls. Cracked and splintered tiles tilted drunkenly across the ground. Whole sections of the pond lay shattered, water oozed across the ground. The fish lay strewn about, one eye to the sky, all color drained from their flesh. *Ora Aureo, Jaspeadura* and *Dorado Rojo* could not be told, one from another.

TWENTY-FIVE

Wandering Across Spain
> ". . . *the voices of the wandering wind*
> *. . . A moan, a sigh, a sob, a storm, a strife.*"

—SIR EDWIN ARNOLD *The Deva's Song*

FOR SEVERAL LONG, tiring but uneventful days they made their way through the countryside, trusting to fate and what road signs remained standing. Prudence read out loud, hoping to discourage Marion by the vastness of Spain. Cordoba 150 kilometers, Madrid 580. Cordoba to Marienda 100 Kilometers, Marienda to Madrid 485. But something was wrong. No matter how far they walked there was no mention of Cadiz and the distance to Madrid not only failed to shrink, it grew. After several days and several small villages, they stood looking up at another sign: Madrid 580 Kilometers. Prudence had to admit that, though she didn't want to get to Madrid, they didn't appear to be getting anyplace else either. They made a wrong turn somewhere, strayed off Dordo's map into uncharted territory. They had simply gone around in circles. Her mother was so focused on finding her husband that all she saw was the name Madrid and turned in the direction of that arrow even if it made no sense.

At first Prudence tried to get her mother to study the map with her, but when neither of them recognized any of the names, her mother lost interest. Then it dawned on Prudence that some-one, perhaps to fool the enemy, had turned the signs around.

One night, while Marion slept, Prudence slipped the map out of her mother's purse to study it. The next morning when they came to a sign Prudence pretended to recognize a village name and pointed in that direction. Her mother followed. A few more days, a few more signs and Prudence once more began to recognize some names.

Whenever they passed one of those roadside shrines, they stopped to rest. Prudence thought her mother might be praying, she didn't say, Prudence didn't ask. She was through with prayer. The smell of death had dealt the final blow. If dead people went there and dead people smelled like that, heaven was not for her.

From the occasional peasant they encountered, at least those not too scared to talk, they learned that many of the local uprisings had turned into orgies of revenge as Dordo warned. Neighbor turned against neighbor, family against family. At times the sin, the offense that killed appeared no more than some slight, some insult from long before the war. People shied away from strangers. What stories they did hear were mostly just that—stories. It surprised Prudence that they saw few signs of the war, a few burned shacks, nothing that looked too impor-tant. She began to relax a little. They might make it to Cadiz all right if only they could spot a road sign telling them where it was.

One day they met a woman willing enough to talk of grudges that had smoldered for years. Her face appeared so distorted with wrinkles that, at first, Prudence mistook her grimace for a smile. "How little, *Señoras*, how little it takes to ignite them"—a radio broadcast, a rumor brought by a stranger, men recruiting

in the village and the ransacking of the houses would begin—
"only those of the rich," the woman said, raising her eyes piously
heavenward, "we no bother the houses of the poor." Slyly she
gestured toward some bits and pieces of furniture she had pre-
sumably acquired in this fashion. But how poor was poor? That
pitiful pile of furniture could hardly have belonged to the rich.
Her mother would never have had anything like that in the
house. And they were rich, she knew they were because one
day, when her father wasn't within hearing, the village teacher
chided them. "It is a sin to be rich; and you Whitleys have much
to confess."

By that standard this woman with her battered chairs and
tables would have no trouble gaining heaven. "Our men, they
have left to fight, our young women have gone to the larger
towns in search of the men. Bah! Such foolishness. They listen
to the speeches, Agrarian Reform, I spit on Agrarian Reform.
Why should we till the fields of some *hacendado*, they say. Soon
we will have our own. And so, what comes of their reforms?
Los hacendados have disappeared, the fields are deserted. Food is
scarce."

She and her mother might have learned more had they gone
into the larger towns but Marion insisted on avoiding them.
"I'm not ready yet, I'm still practicing my speech." They were
careful to only brush the outskirts, unsure of what faction, what
army, might hold sway.

Late that afternoon they heard voices, smelled a camp-
fire. They could almost hear the crackle of food cooking. They
ducked behind a group of trees and spent the whole night
watching and listening. They heard little but laughter. In the
morning, they decided to risk going in to ask for directions. "We
are reporters, not politicos," her mother reassured them. The
men seemed glad enough to see them. They even offered food.

At first, the men viewed their queries as to where they were with suspicion; but before long Prudence and her mother found themselves overwhelmed by a gaggle of differing directions and dire warnings of what lay between here and there.

"Lucky for you, perhaps; but for us, *Señora* it matters little that we care nothing of the politics. We must do as we are told even if it takes time from *sus trabajos*. For years now, each group of initials that pass this way promises protection, freedom, whatever—they all promise something—but we get nothing, always nothing and now they tell us we must have papers, the proper papers; yet with each group, what is proper changes. Red papers, blue ones, white or gold seals, it is all the same—" the speaker stopped, gave Marion a sharp look, "And I think perhaps, you two, you no have papers."

Marion looked at Prudence, Prudence looked at Marion. The time had come to move on. That morning, her mother had made her dress up a bit for the encounter and now as they hurried away, Prudence found the rocky ground hard on her ankles. After what they thought to be a safe distance they sat down by the side of the road and rummaged around in their overnighters. At least her mother had the foresight to include walking shoes for the both of them. After a turn at massaging each other's feet, they set off again. A few yards down the road a stake-truck stopped offered them a ride. The two looked in the back—the truck carried produce and chickens—they let their feet speak for them.

The driver, a farmer, had little to say for the first few miles but eventually he started talking. *"Los Americanos?"* They said their piece, about the reporting, the war and then her mother— later she said her women's intuition made her chance it—added a new line about telling the poor man's side of things.

"Ah *Señoras*, I can tell you a story for *los periodicos*. I am old they no come to get me for to fight but one day they comman-deered my truck, Franco's men." He told them how they ordered him to sit in his truck, not to turn around." An hour, maybe more, he sat there and waited. Every now and then something heavy landed in the back of his truck. Thump, bump. Thump, bump. A soldier hopped up into the truck, "Drive on, old man."

The old man was quiet for awhile. Prudence heard only the clanking of the trucks wooden slats against the metal bars, it sounded like the clang of shovels, almost as if the truck tried to warn her about what was to come.

"Right about here," he coughed, cleared his throat, "right here they tell me to stop." They opened a jug of wine and told him to unload. He figured they forgot the need to keep all this a secret from him and when they realized it, they would shoot him.

"I pulled about twenty of them from the back of the truck."

"Twenty of what," Prudence asked. Her mother hushed her.

"Bodies, Señorita, twenty bodies. Men, all men. He raised his arm, his tattered sleeve flapping like the wings of a crow. "There, right over there where the earth is raw from the digging. His hand fell back on the wheel, the truck rolled on. Prudence turned around to see through the smudge back window, she didn't want to lose sight of the spot.

"Is he there, mother? Do you think he's buried over there?"

"Shut up," her mother hissed. "Just shut up."

A little further down the road, the driver let them out. Prudence abandoned any pretense of counting kilometers, put-ting one foot in front of the other took all her effort. At last Marion sat down on a small outcropping of rock.

After what they had learned that day, they could hardly doubt that her father had made a mistake bringing them here. For years this country had wallowed in misery and conflict. He must have known. He should have known.

"Damn that bastard, damn him to hell."

"Mother, perhaps Mrs. Lupinek was right. Maybe we should just go to Cadiz."

"But what if he needs us?"

He. He. He. Right now Prudence cared more about *me* than *he. Me* was tired, hungry, *me's* feet, *me's* legs, *me's* ankles, every part of *me* hurt. When had *he* ever had need of them before? Her mother wasn't fooling her. Her mother needed *he.*

That night they slept in the open. Far away on the distant horizon they saw flashes of light. Guns. Big ones. In the morning a breeze blew across the plain carrying a half-familiar odor. Prudence stood up, her nose wrinkling up in protest, she began walking, following the smell. She hadn't gone far when she heard Marion's footsteps come up behind her. Just ahead she saw a bundle of filthy rags lying on the ground. Some animal was at it, shaking it about—a dog. As she approached she could see it gnawed at something, a bone, some meat appeared left on it.

"*Hola* pooch, what have you there?" Without dropping his bundle, the animal pulled his lips back, snarled. "It's all right, I'm not going to steal—" Prudence stopped, backed up a step. Part of a hand dangled from the bone. Bile set fire to her throat. She turned to warn her mother. Marion had doubled over. She started toward her, Marion waved her off. Unsure of where to look, Prudence turned back and let her gaze drift beyond the dog to another bundle, a gray shirt stretched taut across a bloated torso, a trail of tiny brown spots wandered over and around it. Rubio had pointed out such a trail running over the carcass of a rabbit. "It's dung," he'd said. "Beetle dung."

A black writhing omen rose into the air, a swarm of flies flew past her. She looked down at the head of a dead man, a dark splotch spread out around it, as if his suffering had leaked from him, staining the earth.

She felt a touch on her shoulder. "Come away," Marion's hand sought hers, "please." The two started back for the road.

Prudence took a few steps, hesitated, "Don't look back," her mother cautioned; but as water runs down hill, some things can't be stopped. She turned. The dog had moved a ways off from the bone; it nosed about her mother's vomit.

That evening as they settled down, their backs to the hayracks, Marion broke off a piece of bread. "Chew slowly, make it last." The bread came from a farmhouse they had passed a bit ago. After giving a wide berth to a young boy working in the fields, they had headed for the house hoping to find a woman. Some sympathetic bond, a shared acquaintance with trouble, made it easier to talk to women—old women had the most to say and the nerve to say it. "I've read a lot of scripts," her mother told her, "I know how we women are." So far Marion had been successful at reading people, spotting who was safe to talk to, who wasn't. Prudence thought the two of them were beginning to form a pretty good team. This time, though they had hoped for a bed in the house, the owner offered bread and her haystacks instead.

"*Estoy solo, Señoras.* I no know who may come." Grateful enough for the food, they said nothing about having seen the boy in the field. The woman looked off in the distance, waved her hand vaguely towards her fields; and in an off-hand manner, as if passing the time of day, mentioned that straw made a very good blanket. Reluctantly they followed her directions until they found a hayrick large enough to afford protection from the wind, Prudence sent the woman a silent *gracias*, the heat given off by the hay worked its way into her tired muscles. Anxious to put the horror of the day behind them, Marion pulled off armfuls of straw and spread them over and around them.

"Close your eyes," Marion said, "sweet dreams." She wished her mother hadn't said that. Lately her dreams seemed to have more to do with bitter almonds than sugar.

Prudence leaned back and looked across the field at an old gnarled tree, so stripped of leaves and bark that there was no telling from what seed it had sprung. The way it stood out against the darkening sky, took her back to the eerie groves they passed on that first drive to Rodicio. Somehow this one, lone tree managed to give off even stronger feelings of foreboding than the entire grove of twisted olive trees. It didn't help that a trio of large black birds claimed its topmost branches, yellow eyes glowing sardonically against the sepulchral black of their feathers.

Marion broke the stillness. "A clutch."

"What?"

"That's what they're called isn't it? A group of ravens." Prudence didn't know, but she liked the sound of it. Clutch. She looked at her mother, hoping she would see the humor in it; she didn't.

They settled back into a silence that needed filling somehow. The longer it lasted, the worse she itched to fill it. Something about the sickly yellow of those eyes, the way they stared at her made her want to drive the birds off. "It's one of those words isn't it? Those words that make the sounds of what they mean?"

"What?"

"That's what they're doing, isn't it? Clutching?" She looked down at her hands, her mother's. Their arms cradled their knees, one hand held tight to the other. Marion followed her gaze and looked away, embarrassed. When she turned back, her face showed no fear, no embarrassment. How did she do it? Put off her feelings like that?

"Don't let them spook you."

"Aren't you scared?"

"Yes, but—"

"But what?"

"Remember what I've told you. Chin up, look over the heads of the crowd and never let them know they've got you bamboozled."

"Bamboozled?" There was a silly sounding word.

"See, you can laugh. If you can do that, you can fool them."

Prudence wasn't so sure. She didn't see how keeping her chin up would make the memory of that day go away. So much about the world she didn't know; so much she needed to understand.

"Mother, I mean, Marion. What happens when you die?"

"Shh, Prudence. Not now."

Once she asked Nanny that very question. She remembered the puzzled look Nanny gave her, and the length of time it took her to come up with an answer. Prudence thought she might have forgotten the question. At last Nanny cleared her throat: "Well child, what did it feel like before you were born?"

"Nothing, I didn't feel anything at all."

"Well, there's your answer." The answer saddened Prudence but Nanny had smiled. Maybe with the life she led, taking care of other people's lives, "nothing" could seem like some kind of something. But for her, her life's juices still un-tasted, untried, the very idea of "nothing" seemed intolerable. She needed a better answer, she wasn't going to let her mother shush her.

"Dying, does it hurt? Or is it like a light going out?"

"What a strange thing you are. Besides, how would I know, I'm here aren't I? I'm not dead."

"Do you think Nanny thought about me, I mean just before?"

"Before what?"

"Before she died."

"I'm sure she did, Nanny loved you very much. And as for her hurting, you saw her. She looked peaceful enough."

"What if she thought I just went off and left her? She wouldn't have done that to me. We should have been with her."

"No dear, she just went to sleep. That's all."

"And she wasn't scared?"

"No. I promise, she wasn't scared a bit."

One more promise not to be relied on. Prudence felt no better than she had after seeing her brother pale and still in his bassinet. She knew what she had to do. She'd get out her diary, write a letter to Nanny and tell her that she loved her, she'd never forget her and she was sorry that she'd left her all alone.

Prudence meant to stay awake until she heard her mother's little snores. She wouldn't bring out the diary until then. Though that elusive moment that bothered her so: that little blip in time when she was on the brink—on one side awake; the other, asleep—slipped right by her. Tired as she was, she fell asleep.

TWENTY-SIX

To Bear Witness

> *"...one thing I know, that,*
> *whereas I was blind, now I see.."*

—JOHN IX, 4

PRUDENCE SQUIRMED and squiggled as the sharp pebbles, clumps of earth and prickly bits of straw chafed her skin. Down in the place where dreams take shape they became the roughness of the bark of a tree: *she straddled a limb, her back pressed against the clouds and tried to ignore the crowd of people below, tried not to see the hatred yellowing their eyes, not to fear the dark depressing folds of cloth that cloaked their identity. The tree trembled, the crowd pushed against the trunk, trying to get at her, pull her down.*

She woke. In the chill light of early morning she saw the tree. The sun put one eyebrow over the hill and set fire to the dewdrops that skittered up and down its naked branches. The ravens were gone. She ran her tongue around the inside of her mouth, it felt dry.

A little way off her mother picked the straw from her clothes. "Come over here, Prudence. Let's see what I can do to make you look presentable."

293

"Why do birds wings creak when they fly?"

"Oh, for heaven's sake, Prudence, how would I know?"

Father would have. To even think such thoughts made her feel disloyal. She struggled to her feet and tried to shake the cramps from her legs as she hopped from one foot to the other until she reached her mother.

"You missed our visitor." Marion punctuated her speech with brusque pulls of the hairbrush until satisfied that she had dispatched the last of the tangles—the large ones anyway. She picked up her coat, gave it a shake and spread it out on a bare patch of ground.

"Ready for breakfast? The woman from the farmhouse brought us some cheese. I tried to give her money. She wouldn't take it, can you imagine?"

That bright voice, the forced smile and busy hands fussing with the brown paper package, dividing up the hard yellow cheese—her mother appeared cheerful, far too cheerful, had something happened during the night? Was it possible? Could she have come to her senses, given up on Madrid and decided to stick to Dordo's plan?

"It would have amused you, Prudence, to see how different the woman was this morning, so much friendlier; she acted as if the two of us shared some unspoken conspiracy. She told me that all I had to do was follow the river and eventually it would make its way *a la ciudad grande.* She meant Madrid, don't you think?"

Marion hadn't given up. She wasn't going to. "I don't see a river—"

"Over there, that clump of trees on the horizon."

"They look so small."

"Well, it is a bit of a distance but that's the direction she pointed, '*un brazo del río, un brazo del río,*' she said."

"Arm of the river?"

"Yes and if we follow it, we would be certain to reach the *cuerpo del río*, which I hope means body not corpse." Another bad choice of words on her mother's part. It made Prudence feel queasy. Her mother didn't notice.

"She said we must avoid the village, I think she called it *Reposo*, something like that, anyway it ended in an 'o'." That wasn't much help, half the towns in Spain ended in an 'o,' the other half ended in 'a.' If only her mother were more, well more . . .. That wasn't fair either, her mother was doing the best she could.

"A band of anarchists controlled it. She told me 'to deal only with *los comunistas*.' I didn't want to tell her that I would if I could but I can't tell them apart. They all have guns, and they all think they will save *la españa*. Ha." Prudence could see her mother turning into her father right in front of her eyes.

Late the next afternoon they reached the river and without saying a word to each other they stripped off their outer clothing, joined hands and plunged into the water. When the shaking stopped, they took off their underclothes and in some sort of an effort to wash them, flailed them about in the water. Prudence let out a shriek, "A fish! There's a fish tangled up in Nanny's brassiere! Get it out!"

"No, no. Hang on! Wrap it up in your slip or something, then toss it up on to the land." Prudence ignored the part about the slip and hurled the whole thing as far up the bank as she could. Marion flew out of the water after it, laughing the whole way.

They put on their outer clothes and hung the rest on the branches to dry. Marion sent Prudence off to gather twigs. With the help of some leaves and her cigarette lighter, she touched them off. The fish took a bit of chewing to get down; it tasted more like rubber boots than trout. Prudence felt warm and full as she fought hard not to think of *Aura Oreo, Jaspeadora* and *Dorodo Rojo.*

Marion buried the bones a little way off. "Poor thing, it must have been pretty old and tired to swim right into you like that."

"Maybe he's had this river to himself for so long a time, he forgot how wicked people can be."

"Your father was . . . is right, you do have an active imagination. Anyway, there was enough fish to fill us up. We must make the bread and cheese last as long as we can. Let's see what we can do about making up the beds. You get the sheets, I'll fluff up the pillows."

If her mother could make jokes they just might make it. Like a scary movie it would all come right in the end. Prudence went off in search of a good spot to bed down. They had to stay hidden and yet she wanted enough of a clearing so she could see a bit of sky. From her room she had seen the villages, the mountains, even last night in the field she watched the stars but here in the trees and brush she felt trapped. Who knew what, or who, might sneak up on them. She shouldn't think that way.

She pushed and prodded the soft earth until she formed a mound just about her length, covered it over with a blanket of leaves. About the time she had it right, her tiredness cut loose and all the starch ran out of her. She lay down, closed her eyes and came wide-awake. She thought she should write the day up in her diary, but her mother's breathing didn't sound quite right.

Instead, her jacket rolled up and stuffed behind her head, she looked across the rather flat expanse of her chest and willed her breasts to grow, to fill up the tiny cups of Nanny's brassiere and hearing no loud explosions, no crackling fires, only the uneven inhale, exhale of her mother's breath, she turned her attention to the stars. They took her back to the house in India—the nights she and her father braved the snakes and other creepy things to lie on their backs just off the porch and study the stars. When the rains came and she sighed because they could no longer see the sky, he had pasted little paper stars all over her bedroom ceiling, arranging and rearranging them until he had the positions, the relationships just right. For the planets, he dulled the points a bit. The closest stars, he left large; the distant ones he trimmed to size. Two whole days, celestial chart in hand, he painted and pasted. That night, after the lights went out, he sat beside her as her ceiling came alive. Her bed became the earth as he pointed out the soft glow of the dippers, Orion's belt and the illusive Betelgeuse.

How could a man with the patience to make a universe for his daughter one year, go off and leave her the next? That time seemed so far away and yet the sky didn't look all that different from her ceiling. He might have gotten some things skewed off to the side somewhat and others she couldn't see at all, but she didn't care. He had made that magic for her, just for her. Sometimes she thought maybe she shouldn't hate him quite so much. She could love him just a little bit, couldn't she?

For the next few days, keeping pretty much to the river bank, Marion and Prudence had the world to themselves, joined only by the occasional rabbit, the scurrying quail or up above, the soaring hawks and circling kestrels. No people, no roads; but all the clean water they could drink and safe enough places to sleep. There was one problem. Though it seemed all the fish in the river were curious and nibbled at their legs, they found no other dull-witted enough to be lured into the folds of a brassiere. "Too bad we didn't bring along some of your father's fishing gear. But we didn't. There's nothing to be done for it, the next town we come to we'll have to go in."

"As long as it isn't Reposo."

"Reposo? Oh yes, I don't know what that woman meant, down here by the river there are no sign posts. I've looked the map over and I don't see a town named that anywhere." Prudence watched her mother running her fingers along the line of the river, following it northeast toward Madrid. Didn't her mother ever look at the sun? Prudence knew they were headed westward. She said nothing.

"It looks as if the next one is Castoso, it's near close to the river and probably got its name from the water. I think the word means pure. Maybe we'll find a road—"

"But the woman in the farm house said to stick to the river, didn't she?"

"I'm tired of walking along the bank, tripping over roots and getting slapped in the face by branches."

They spent one more night in the brush. Just before dark they gathered more branches and dried leaves for a little fire and what was left over they made into their beds. Long before dawn they woke to the sound of rifle fire. Prudence sat up

"Stay down," Marion cautioned. "I don't think it's close but—" Just then a great flash of light, lit up the world. A huge thump shook the ground. "That was closer."

Prudence scooched her way through the grass toward her mother. "I saw some rocks not too far over there." Marion pointed off to her left. "When I was gathering brush."

They crawled on to where they thought the rocks might be. "It seems a long way, mother, are you sure?"

"Yes up a head, that big shadow. It must be the rocks." When they reached the base they pressed their backs against the cold stone. "We should be safe here." After forever the thumps stopped and the flashes moved off into the distance. Though near by, in the bushes they heard rustling noises.

"Little animals, Prudence. The guns must have frightened

them."

At last everything quieted down and Prudence saw that the sky had purpled up a bit. "Mother—"

"Marion, you're supposed to call me Marion."

"Marion, it will be light soon."

"How do you know that, Miss-You-Haven't-Got-a-Watch?"

"Rubio taught me a lot of things."

"Don't be silly. You hardly spent any time with him, child.

"Prudence, you're supposed to call me Prudence."

"All right, Miss Sass. We'll get going. But stay down." Her mother motioned for her to follow. They crawled on their hands and knees through grass and brambles for what seemed a long way. The brush got thicker, branches slapped at their cheeks.

"It's a good thing we rolled up our stockings and stuck them in our pockets."

"But my knees hurt. Can't we stand up yet?"

"Don't whine, Prudence."

The sky got lost, it grew all dark again and then they felt pebbles press into their knees.

"Water, Mother, I hear water."

"Damn, we're back at the river." Her mother stood up, took a few steps and then she stumbled and fell. Prudence heard a moaning sound.

"Mother, what's wrong?"

"Nothing, I tripped on something—

"But you moaned, I heard you."

"That wasn't me."

Prudence felt her spine go all tingly and cold. And then it got light enough to see. There on the ground around them lay three men, their bodies all twisted in strange shapes. One man had his mouth open. The guttural moans appeared to be coming from him.

"What should we do?" For the longest while her mother said nothing. The light of dawn grew stronger and stronger. The moaning stopped.

"Mother?"

"Shh! Not so loud? They'll hear us?"

"They're dead, Mother. They can't hear." It was light enough now to see the puddles of blood. One body was missing an arm, another one a leg, the third appeared to have no stomach.

"Let's get out of here, as far away from this damn river as we can. I don't care what the old woman said."

Late the next day, over the hungry growls of their stomachs, they heard the crowing of roosters and the tinkling of little bells that could only mean flocks of sheep or goats. And flocks meant sheepherders. People. A town. Despite their hunger they decided to spend one more night in the open and enter the town the next morning. "People are apt to be less excitable, less leery of strangers in the early morning hours," Marion said.

In most small towns, the villagers gather at the fountain. No matter the time of day, you can find old men playing chess, women exchanging goods or gossip and at the very least children being children and generally getting in the way. Marion and Prudence tried to walk purposefully through the twisted streets as if they knew what they were about while they listened for the telltale splash of water. Along the way they spotted only one goat munching away at a window box of geraniums and a mutt who ran past them, his tail between his legs. One last turn and they came to a plaza. The fountain was hidden behind a group of men who lounged against their rifles. Their uniforms of brown shirts, black pants and berets, held no clues as to where their loyalties lay. Someone once told her that the different colors meant different sides. She couldn't remember which was which. To Prudence berets just meant trouble. True there were plenty of patches sewn on the shirts but no emblems that either one of them recognized.

Bored and listless, the men appeared not to notice the two women. They kept their eyes on a man seated at a card table, his paper shuffling being offered up as a clue to his importance. Her mother took the hint and marched right up to him.

"Sergeant Major—"

"You flatter me, Señora. I am but a lowly corporal." Even seated he appeared to bow in mock humility.

"Corporal it is. I wish to take *los fotografías de su jefe, por favor.*"

"*¿Porqué?*"

"For the American paper, so we may tell them that—" Prudence held her breath. What would her mother say? Which side were the men fighting for? Her mother barely paused before plunging on "—that Spain will be saved by such brave men as you." She pointed slowly around the plaza, making sure to include the entire band. As quietly as she could, Prudence let her breath leak out and fall on the stones of the plaza.

There she was again, that brave woman. Why had Prudence never pictured her mother this way before? Courageous? Smart? Why was it that in all the pictures in her mind, as well as the ones in the family album, her mother took up less space than her father? He stood out in strong contrasts of black and white, her mother muddled along in shades of gray. Prudence looked down at her father's camera, hanging from its worn strap, she wanted to rip it from around her neck, throw it away for all the half-truths or even outright lies it told. People counted on photographs to show things the way they were, really were. But how could they? The universe stretched away in all directions, its edges impossible to conceive. Photographs compressed the world into tiny rectangles closed in by fluted borders. All that motion frozen in a gesture—an open mouth, a step not quite completed. While the air vibrated with the light of a million colors a photograph took all that, flattened it, distilled it into scraps of black and gray and hid it in albums—bits of life tucked out of harm's way into little gummed corners. False images: her mother sitting across from her husband in this room, in that room, out walking, riding in the roadster, surrounded by guests. Never in all those pictures did her mother hold the foreground. He dominated everything, his very presence pressed everyone else aside. Her eyes always drawn to his, she had rarely noticed her mother. But now . . ..

"Follow me, *Señoras? Señoritas?*"

"*Señoras* will do just fine. Now about your headman?"

"This way *por favor.*" The corporal led then into a building just off the square, right through it and out again into a walled courtyard where another man sat at yet another table, shuffling still more papers.

"Wouldn't it be nice," Marion whispered, "if in this part of the country, they fought their war with bits of paper instead of bullets? Prudence nodded.

The man ignored the corporal's salute, barely looked up at Marion or Prudence before waving them off like flies.

"What do they want? Have they come to plead—?"

"No, they are—"

"I don't like foreigners interfering with my work." The sunlight glinted menacingly off his glasses.

"We aren't foreigners, we're foreign correspondents."

The corporal rushed into the conversation, interrupting as if to justify the impertinence of bothering so important a man. "The women, they wish to take the pictures, they wish to show the world—"

302

Her mother refused to be intimidated. "The American papers need to know the great work you are doing here. *Señor,* we have come to tell your story."

"Why didn't you say so? Sit."

They looked around. Where? Her mother cleared her throat, this time the man raised his head, "Corporal, where are your manners? Chairs for the ladies."

The chastened soldier rushed off, Prudence and her mother tried to look businesslike. Marion produced a notebook and began asking for names, "The spellings please, I must have the correct spellings." Prudence made a show of taking the camera from its case and adjusting the lens. She took aim at the seated man. Click. He stopped his shuffling, gave her his full attention. Click. Click. He smiled. She tried not to flinch at the sight of his chipped and blackened teeth.

Two wooden chairs were produced and only after they were seated did Prudence look around, across the yard on the far side a man stood against a small wall. Self-conscious, unsure of himself as if he thought something was expected of him, his eyes darted this way and that, he appeared to be seeking answers. She didn't think he was getting any. Just then the headman clapped his hands. Several men appeared, carrying tables.

The chief settled himself behind one of the newer ones and began selecting men to sit behind the others. The corporal placed a sheaf of papers before each one. When the chief appeared satisfied with the arrangements he called out, "The witnesses, *por favor.*"

The door opened again, two women half stumbled into the yard rubbing their eyes as if unaccustomed to the light. "Is this the man you saw?"

"*Sí, Señor.* He is the one." They spoke without looking at the man, one woman had tears in her eyes, the other tried to conceal a smirk.

"Good." He turned to Prudence. "Did you get that?"

She nodded. She hadn't actually snapped but he appeared not to have noticed. At least she had the camera pointed in the right direction. She'd have to be more alert.

"And you, *Señora,* you make the notes of what they say?" Marion smiled.

"Bring in the next batch." Three men in leg chains entered the enclosure. Though Prudence wasn't sure just what was happening she turned the camera on them.

"No! *Uno momento, Señorita,* the faces, only the faces. We no wish peoples to have the misunderstanding." Prudence raised the camera, pretended to adjust the lens. Sometimes moving through a country where you barely know the language can be like pushing your way through a fog, she thought. You're only certain of the ground you stand on. You must concentrate on that, everything else is guesswork.

Once more the headman pointed at the man against the wall, repeating the same question and once more his pleasure at receiving the same answer was obvious.

A wave of his hand and the three were taken away. "You did get—"

"*Sí, señor.*"

"Good." He turned to the men at the other tables, "Now it's up to you, take your time." He consulted his watch, perhaps a minute passed, maybe two. "Now?" he said a bit testily. The men at the other tables chorused their agreement. Prudence watched the man make a large X on yet another piece of paper and sign it with a flourish. She was about to learn just how much damage a piece of paper could do.

He clapped yet again and a larger group, perhaps the men from the plaza, trotted in, their rifles held in front of them.

A whistle sounded, Prudence wheeled toward it. The men fell into line, *el jefe* stood up, raised his arm, pointed at the man against the wall, dropped his arm. The noise burst cruelly against her ears. Something told her to turn toward the man at the wall. She caught his look of surprise, incredulity— a but-you-couldn't-have-meant-me, a Laurel and Hardy sort of look. Then he slid down until he was sitting on the ground, his legs stretched out in front of him, his hands folded neatly over his stomach. The surprise melted from his face, a little puddle of blood dotted the corner of his mouth. Minutes passed, minutes that seemed like days, months. Prudence became aware of the smell of garlic, rosemary, the savory aroma of cooking. Somewhere, someplace ordinary life went on, people cooked, people talked. Time passed.

At last, the man's hands slipped to his sides. She saw the seepage, the bloody thing oozing from his shirt. Through blurry eyes she thought she saw the bulls, the horses, the flashing of the cape.

"*Señora,*" the Captain shouted, "did you get the pictures? We must have them. One of the trial, one of the jury, the reading of the sentence"—apparently she'd missed that part—"and then of course, the best of all, the execution. The world may call us *Los anarquistas, los renegados,* but your pictures will tell them we believe in law and order? *Viva la españa.*" He held out his hand. "Give them to me. I must have them. Now."

Prudence trembled. She looked toward Marion, her mother appeared unruffled. "Of course, *Señor,* but, as you well know, these things take time. We must take them to the States for developing. For the world to know, the papers must print them. We will send you copies of *los periódicos.* A man as informed as you knows the mails are not to be trusted, either in or out. Anyone, everyone intercepts them. The American papers have many sources, your copies will arrive by special messenger. No need to worry."

Even before her mother finished, Prudence stopped shaking. Her mother may not have stood up to her husband, might have looked off in the distance during the bullfights, thrown up at the sight of . . . it didn't matter. When it counted, she came through. A few days earlier, an accident, a dropped camera, an open case, a roll of film disappeared down the side of an embankment. There was no film. Her mother hadn't flinched. Right there, with the harsh sunlight bouncing off the headman's glasses, it came to Prudence who her mother was—an actress, a *real* one like the one she must have been on Broadway before everything went all wrong in Hollywood.

And here in this barren courtyard with the volley of rifle fire still ringing in her ears, Marion—with the charm and grace of a hostess reassuring her guest that the luggage has not been lost, all would be well—smiled at the chief. "And now, *Señor*, if you could be so kind, we have not, as yet, had our lunch, perhaps. . .?"

TWENTY-SEVEN

The Battle for Cadiz
"Sweet the memory to me of a land beyond the sea. . ."

—LONGFELLOW, *From Collections. Amalfi*

"TO PROTECT YOU from *el diablo*," the man shook his fist toward the sky as he ordered the tarp stretched taut over the bed of a large truck. The day had gone pretty well, though not well enough for Prudence to chance a quip about the name settling more comfortably on him than it did the sun. She kept her joke to herself even as the man leered at her mother. Just then a little breeze came up, something lodged in her eye. As she squinched and rubbed, she thought she saw horns pop out of his head, a mustache sprout across his lip, she watched and waited for him to give it a Simon Legree twirl, but of course nothing of the kind happened. She stopped rubbing.

Now, six hours later, lying in a ditch, she knew that the tarp had done nothing to protect them and the Devil was not the sun.

The tarp had only trapped what little air the cramped space allowed, heating and re-heating it until each flap of the canvas sent oppressive waves slamming up against her skin, leaving it raw and chapped. Afraid to touch herself anywhere—surely her skin would peel away—Prudence kept a tight hold on the edge of her seat. Not that it helped all that much. With every bump, she and the wooden slats parted company, only to come together again with a whack ferocious enough to set every tooth in her head to aching. After the last jolt her tongue made a quick test run around her mouth to check for chipped teeth. She caught her mother's eye and rolled her own heavenwards hoping for a little sympathy, a pat or two like Nanny might have done.

"I don't want to hear one word out of you, Missy. Not one." Marion unclenched her fingers from the boards just long enough to proffer a handful of broken nails and bruised knuckles. "At least you can't say your feet hurt."

But they did. Everything hurt and had since shortly after they clambered up into the back of this truck, smiling their *gracias* at the Colonel—Marion graciously promoted *el jefe* with every "thank you."

"No worry, your journey she will be *sin accidente, Señoras*," one of the soldiers pointed to the tarp. The tarp? Why was everyone so concerned with the tarp? Prudence could think of more important things to worry about. Her mother, for one.

Prudence had a strong feeling, a hunch that though she knew in which direction they would be heading, her mother didn't. Maybe, Prudence thought, she might be developing that woman's intuition her mother took such pride in. She liked the feeling of being on an equal footing with her mother. At times she thought she might even be a step or two ahead.

While Marion had lingered over lunch, basking in the attention of the men, Prudence ogled the ogler. Nanny had often told her that knowledge was important but it was even more important to know where to find knowledge.

In between compliments and leers the Colonel (or whatever

he was by now) let his eyes gravitate to one particular chart tacked to the wall. Prudence made a great show of a restlessness she didn't feel and paced about, pausing to study first this map, then that, careful not to linger too long in front of any one. When she thought him preoccupied, she stopped in front of the one he had seemed so focused on and noted the colored tacks, the way he connected them with strings. A particularly colorful piece of twine stretched along a squiggly blue line, both the line and the string ended smack in the middle of an orange blob labeled Cadiz.

By now the headman had attained the rank of Lieutenant and all through lunch he took his eyes off her mother only long enough to throw puzzled glances her way. "*¿Está inquieto?* You have the restlessness, *Señorita?*" Prudence nodded. He turned back to the smiling Marion and in an off-hand way ordered the Corporal to give the restless one a tour of his garrison. The man was so transparent that whenever he got an idea she had the feeling she could see a light bulb come on in a balloon over his head. "And, please to make lots of the pictures as you go, lots of the notes, *sí?*"

Her "*sí,*" barely crossed the room to where her mother sat, it sounded so weak, so tentative. Something about Marion, the way she flattered this man, leaned into him and smiled up at him, made her wonder if her mother wanted to get rid of her as well. She hated thoughts like that, they came flying into her mind almost as if they belonged to someone else and had found her by accident like voices drifting across a room, a radio playing somewhere just out of sight.

When she returned, *el jefe* frowned. "Ah, finished so soon? You took *mucho?*" She nodded, not trusting her voice. "Good! The *campaña*, she is to begin soon. The others, the communists, they will snatch the credit from—" he stopped, afraid he had said too much. "The world must know of our loyalty, that we are ready to fight, *las photografias* they should . . .." The worry lines evaporated, another light bulb appeared. "I have the idea—we will make you the quick journey home."

His solution included the use of the truck and, while her mother prattled on about the glories of Madrid, Prudence became aware of what she did not hear. She heard no mention of the capital, no mention of any destination at all. He talked only of escaping the heat, the feel of cool sea breezes. He must want them on board ship and under sail as soon as possible and Cadiz lay close at hand. "We must keep you far from the fighting, nothing must happen—" He stopped but his worries had nothing to do with them, of that she was sure. Nothing must happen to his precious photographs. He looked so intense, so determined Prudence worked the camera closer to her side, afraid he could see through the leather case and into the camera with its empty spool.

He had promised them lots of things for the journey, comfort was not one of them. At first, they had the truck to themselves—other than the driver and the two soldiers who rode up front. Marion commandeered the blankets she found stacked in a corner and formed them into seat cushions and then, barely fifteen minutes underway, the truck braked to a stop, the back flap lifted and three heavily bandaged men squeezed in along either side of them. Before Marion and Prudence could do more than scooch to one side, another group, more heavily swathed in gauze took the seats across the way. Prudence looked at her mother, she seemed lost in thought and unaware of what these wounded men meant. She and her mother were the afterthought, the truck had been scheduled to take these men to a hospital. Her confidence in her hunch grew; Cadiz, a large city, would have just such a hospital.

She turned her attention to the men. Were they in pain? Badly hurt? The one who settled in directly across from her appeared worried and afraid. Though thick pads, secured by strips of bloody cloth, hid his eyes, something in the tightness of his mouth, the nervous way he kept putting his hand to his bandages, gave him away. Her mother reached out, touched his knee and murmured, "*Estará bien*, you will be fine."

The truck engine died, they sat for a long time. Then a hand pushed aside the tarp and two stretchers slid in along the floor. A man poked his head in and motioned for Prudence and Marion to surrender their blankets.

For a few miles no one spoke, only the groans of the men on the floor broke the silence. Prudence's discomfort shrank before their pain. She had the feeling that their moans had more to do with reassuring themselves they still lived, than it did with easing their pain.

Whenever they neared a village, the truck slowed, she could hear the barking of dogs, the mutts that chased along, nipping at the tires. When the truck came to a complete stop, someone would come and help one of the wounded men down. "*Buena suerte*," the others called after. She might catch a glimpse, a street sign, a market, a café bearing the name of the village. Though she had to discard the idea that they were headed to a hospital, still her confidence grew. Dordo's map unrolled in her mind; they were definitely on the road to Cadiz.

At one village, they all disembarked to stretch their legs and fill their lungs with fresh air. Across the way, a group of women sat on a bench placed at one side of a bright blue door. It opened and two nurses came out and the first motioned to one of the women who got up and followed them over to a table set up in the courtyard. The first nurse stood by the table holding a small glass bottle, a tube dangled from it. The second one motioned the woman to a seat, grabbed her arm, swabbed at it and, before Prudence could blink, plunged a needle into the woman's arm, while the other cranked a little pump. Prudence watched horrified as blood poured into the tube, pulsing and pushing its way up into the bottle. When the bottle, sparkling crimson in the sun, could hold no more, one nurse bandaged the woman's arm, the other pinned something onto her dress and motioned to the next woman in line.

"What are they doing to those poor woman, they're killing them?"

"No *muchachita*," the driver said. "This is something brand new for the wounds of the men. The blood goes from the women to the hospital and into the wounded. Some of the wounded anyway, it all depends . . . but then, so much depends on the luck, no? Come, we move on." Prudence took one look back as he helped her into the truck. It wasn't until later that she remembered what he had called her, *muchachita*. Her mind held only thoughts of the women, how brave they must be—as brave as the men. No way would she let someone steal her blood.

At the next village, small hands bearing loaves of bread, wheels of cheese, poked through the tarp. A babble of young voices called out, "*Trentecinco centavos, por favor. Dos pesos, tres pesos.*" The price escalated with each offer. The soldiers stared blankly at the food but made no move to take it. Her mother leaned forward as far as she could and held out some money. One of the soldiers took it, but instead of handing it over to the boys said, "*demasiado muchos, Señora.*"

"Never mind, just have them give us whatever it will buy," her mother replied, "we need all we can get. Something to drink too, ask him for that, *por favor.*" The little boys smiled and handed in long hard loaves of bread, at least five of them, and rolled in two giant wheels of cheese. Prudence helped pass the bread around, but drew back as one of the men pulled out his bayonet. He grinned, Marion laughed. Prudence felt foolish when he began to carve the cheese into manageable wedges. Marion took a piece, broke it into even smaller bits and put it to the lips of one of the men on the floor, he barely nibbled at it but when the goat skin bags of wine appeared everyone drank their fill. Prudence hesitated, put her hand to her head, remembering the way it ached that last time.

"I know, I know but take little sips, dear. You need to drink something."

The driver appeared at the back of the truck and handed Prudence a jug of water. "¡*Beba*! Big sips, it is all for you," he nodded toward Marion, "¿*Esta su mamá*? Her mother pretended not to have heard. Before returning to the cab, he tied back the flap, leaving a much larger opening. Once under way the air cooled a bit, but full stomachs and the warmth of the wine loosened tongues. Questions were asked, names and smiles exchanged. Even the two men on the floor revived enough to talk of their villages, their mothers. Eyes grew moist, eyelids heavy and though the tumbling one against another might have made it seem an impossibility, sleep overtook them all.

Prudence hadn't come fully awake when she found herself lifted from the truck and pushed face down in a shallow ditch at the side of the road.

"What—?"

The driver pointed at the sky. She lifted her head. "There, there he is, *El Diablo*." A small black dot in the sky circled overhead. Though the driver eyed the plane with loathing, somewhere mixed in there she sensed his admiration, even envy. She pictured herself up there, scudding over, under and around the clouds, so far from danger, everything clean, everything cool. With each pass the plane flew lower and lower until she could clearly make out the black crosses painted on its under-wings. From the talk around the table at the *Casa de Castillo* she thought the planes might be German, but for all the time spent crossing Spain, Prudence still hadn't learned to tell one side from another. Even el jefe's *"Viva la españa"* hadn't helped. They all said that. Even the farm wife.

"Keep your head down. Those devils, sometimes they no show the respect for *el cruz rojo*," he pointed to the top of the truck. Now she understood. The protection they had talked about: the giant cross stitched to the tarp. And the Devil? The devil was Franco.

She tried to get up, she had to find her mother. Across the road she saw the two men who had ridden up front with the driver, and just beyond them she saw a hand waving at her. A soldier next to her mother made a grab for her hand and pulled it down. Prudence managed to send back a tiny wiggle of her own. Glad enough to have her mother in sight, she couldn't help but feel angry that she wasn't here, right next to her. Nanny would have been.

Low enough now, the pilot must see the white field, the red cross, but he showed no signs of leaving. The soldiers grew more nervous as each moment stretched thin. One man grabbed his rifle, raised it. "Keep the damn thing out of sight, they'll shoot for sure if they see so much as a glint of barrel." The driver turned to Prudence. "Under the cross of red, we must go unarmed."

It was only then that she thought of the stretchers, the men lying on them. Were they still in —?

"Look," she shouted at the driver, "it's getting smaller."

"Stay still!" What was he afraid of? The plane was going away. Then, in the road, behind the truck little puffs of dirt rose into the air. Just before she heard the sound, she saw the top of the tarp rip open in a hundred little places. She started to scream. The driver put his hand gently across her mouth. "Shush, *muchachita*, they would not have made it anyway."

What did he mean? Who? He seemed to understand her confusion. "It no is *necessario* to make their going more difficult."

She looked across at the truck. The tarp hung in shreds. "I'm—I didn't think—" And then an explosion and a wall of air hit Prudence full in the face, as if some giant had reached down and slapped her. She raised her head up again. "Get down!" the driver screamed at her as he pulled on her coat. Prudence turned to stone, where could her mother be now? She caught one quick glimpse of her before the sky came alive with little bits of fire, like snowflakes painted in a thousand shades of red and yellow. The sky seemed to pull back, just a corner of it, and she thought she saw into the foreverness behind it, into the enormity of nothing. And then it was over. The world fell quiet. She heard a bird, a lone skylark hidden under its tuft of grass calling to its brothers, its sisters.

Another sound broke this new stillness, her teeth, they clicked and clacked against each other. She shook and shook; every part of her trembled. She feared she might wet herself, right here, right in front of the soldiers.

"Do not worry, *muchachita*," he put his arm around her. "A bomb. A small one only. It missed." That name, he had used it again. He knew she was no grown-up. She hadn't fooled him. It didn't seem to matter and though the plane had gone, she couldn't stop shaking.

Her mother came towards her, then she was there next to her, grabbing her, shaking her. "Stop it Prudence, stop right now." She couldn't.

"Don't you give up on me, not now. We're so close." Prudence couldn't find her tongue, it got all tangled up in her teeth some-how. "Prudence Maria Katrina Abigail, that son of a bitch did one good thing for you, he made you tough. Now get up!"

At last all her mother's anger found its way into her, she stopped shaking, looked up at her mother. "Why? Why would anyone shoot at us? What did we do, Mother? What did we do?"

"Not us, child. The trucks."

"But the wounded men—why would anyone shoot at wounded men?"

"Perhaps they thought the truck empty," the soldier's voice seemed hoarse as if some cheese lay caught in his throat. "Maybe they just wanted to warn us away." He stood up, brushed his clothes off and helped Prudence to her feet.

"Don't go over there, Prudence. Don't look."

"*Sí Señora*, I no let her. We will try to get the truck to run-ning but you must proceed now on you own." He saw the look of panic crumple Marion's face, the fierce anger wiped away by fear. "They have spotted us, from here on you will do better not to be seen with us. We must find some other way to get these last ones home," he gestured toward the truck. Right from the start there had been no intention of the truck going into Cadiz; they knew all along who controlled what. The new medicine, that blood, these men would get none of it. They weren't going to a hospital, just back to their villages.

"But how do we know where to—?"

"Keep to the road, *Señora*. To be safe, if you hear planes go into the ditch. Hide your film, you will be entering Nationalist territory." He walked over to the back of the truck and handed Prudence her suitcase. It was covered with blood.

TWENTY-EIGHT

Road to the Sea

> *"Melancholy and remorse . . . enables us*
> *to sail into the wind of reality"*
>
> —CYRIL CONNOLLY, *The Unquiet Grave*

"I NEED TO CATCH MY BREATH," Marion said. Prudence looked around for a spot to sit, but finding none she eyed her suitcase. Tired enough to ignore the dried brown stain, she turned it on end and sat.

They had only gone a couple of miles since the driver wished them *Buena suerte;* but with the drone of the plane still ringing in their ears, they had moved along quickly and tired easily. Fear and uncertainty were heavy loads to carry.

A breeze lifted the stray hairs falling down the back of her neck, Prudence became aware of a sensation she hadn't felt since: moist air. She jumped up, laughed and danced circles around her mother.

"Prudence stop, you're hysterical. I know you've been through a lot but soon we'll find—"

"Don't you smell it? The salt?" She ran her tongue over her lips; she could taste it. The driver was right, it hadn't been far.

She stopped long enough to notice the puzzled expression on Marion's face and her elation evaporated—her mother had listened to no one, not the driver, not her daughter. She had no idea where they were.

"How many miles to Madrid?" Marion had asked just before they set off on foot. The driver, brow poised quizzically over startled eyes, glanced towards Prudence. He would leave it to her to put the matter to rights.

"Mother, Madrid isn't near the sea. We haven't been going toward Madrid. As a matter of fact we've—"

"Don't be silly, the General told me—"

"I thought you knew, Mother," Prudence tried to make her voice steady, confident to cover her lie. "I thought you knew we were headed for Cadiz all along."

"I knew no such thing."

The look on her mother's face told Prudence she had spoken to the air. "Mother, you must smell it? The ocean? We're almost to Cadiz. I tried, the driver, he tried to tell you—we were never, no way—we aren't going to Madrid." She felt a scream creep up the back of her throat. "Remember? Back at the *Casa* what you promised? You said we were going home."

Marion stared uncomprehendingly. It scared Prudence. What was wrong? Anybody could have looked around, noticed the change in the country. The truck had crossed mountains, terraced olive groves. The dry badlands had given way to farms, and right now, this very moment a flock of birds flew over them so low she heard the creaking of their wings. Surely her mother recognized them as shore birds—those long legs, the pointed beaks, all that squawking and hollering.

"Come on, Mother, we must start looking for the road that will steer us around the salt flats and into the city. The driver said it would veer off to the left. We'll be at the port in no time,

Dordo promised a British ship, remember? Prudence wasn't strong enough to argue. She would have to keep up her pretenses a little longer. Dordo had only said there might be a ship.

Prudence was the first to spot the little waves, the way they peaked in delicious triangles of white. The ocean. Safety. Home. Tired as they were, even her mother started to run. At the dock they put their hand to their eyes to shade them from the glare and stared out to sea. No battleship. No destroyer. A few fishermen, some small boats, that was all.

"Oh God." Marion collapsed on the wharf. "After all that, nothing. What shall we do now?"

It seemed odd to Prudence but despite her mother's bravery, her acting skills—somehow choice had become hers. She was glad her mother thought of her as an adult but all that responsibility had exhausted her. Hadn't her father said almost the same thing that day by the fishpond? Was that why he went off? He was tired of her mother, tired of her? But Helen, he hadn't been tired—.

A man approached. "*Señora, Señora* Whitley?"

Prudence gave a start. Her heart started pounding, the air went cold all around her "Go away, leave us alone."

"Child what's wrong with you," Marion gave the man one of her special smiles. "*Señor,* perhaps you could—"

"Mother, he knows who we are."

"I've come to take you—"

"Where, take us where?" They were so close and now, they would be taken away, put in a stable or a warehouse. After awhile they would be shot, just like—

And then Prudence felt her breath come back into her body, her heart stilled. "Oh God, Mother, look—"

"Prudence, your language." But her mother had seen it too, one boat a little larger than the rest. Her voice changed. She sounded calm, almost happy. "That's not a ship, Prudence. It's a yacht." With that her mother reached in her bag and pulled out her compact and began applying fresh lipstick. Prudence turned back toward the boat and saw the tall slender figure standing on the deck, a silk scarf blowing out behind him the standard that proclaimed him "the good guy," a knight of Ivanhoe.

"Here, over here, I've been waiting forever," the shout traveled across the water, bouncing across the white caps.

Marion turned to the man who had addressed them. "Hurry, please hurry. Take us out."

Calm at last, Prudence could see that the man was a fisherman, not a soldier.

His small boat pitched and tossed, but at last they pulled alongside, Ivanhoe turned into Bazil. He let down the ladder.

Her mother stood up. "Careful, wait till we set an anchor," the fisherman warned. Bazil climbed down into their boat, took hold of Marion's hand and eased her way up the ladder, leaving Prudence to clamber up behind them, banging her little suitcase against the side of the yacht.

Once on deck, the words spilled out of Bazil too fast for her to understand them. Dordo had managed to get a cable out. Cadiz teamed with rumors, one concerned two strange American reporters—"women, one young, one very beautiful who were walking their way across Spain. I hoped, who else." Bazil said that out of all the rumors he heard, this was the one he chose to believe. "I wanted to sail for Málaga right away, but Dordo said that would be ill-advised. You had already left and my yacht would be confiscated and that would help no one."

Prudence, her legs still trembling, hardly listened. She couldn't take her eyes off her mother. Right there in front of her,

Marion began to shrink as if someone had let the bravado drain out of her like air from a birthday balloon. Prudence rushed to her, put out her arms to hold on to her, to keep that woman, the one who'd kept her safe, to make her stay forever. That woman loved her. But Marion slipped away. Her mother returned.

Prudence's suitcase slipped from her hand and her things spilled across the deck—the slips, the clothes, Nanny's brassiere, her diary. Marion grabbed Prudence by the arm, twisting her flesh.

"Where did that come from? Didn't I tell you to burn that damn diary?"

"I—"

"You could have gotten us killed." Her mother grabbed it.

"Give it to me, it's mine. You've no right—"

"You had no right to keep such a thing secret from me." It seemed like forever Prudence stood stretching as tall as she could, her arms, her fingers ached with the effort as her mother held the book just out of her reach. A moment, a second later, and the diary sailed out over the side. Part of Prudence went with it. Her mother hadn't paid any attention to what her husband wrote, and she hadn't paid any attention to what Prudence wrote. They were only things important to her, who else would care about how she felt, who she loved, who she didn't. Only a few pages mentioned anything that anyone's army would care about.

After the offending book sank beneath the waves, her mother's anger slide from her face, she turned a winsome smile on Bazil and Prudence knew that the helpless, needy Marion had returned. Prudence had not forgotten what she'd promised her father.

She had hoped things would be different. She felt cheated, mad and then she felt something odd, something completely unexpected—she realized she loved her mother and she hated her. She would never understand love, it was too complicated. She would do her best to avoid it in the future. But there was no denying she loved her mother more often than she hated her. She would do her best to keep her promise and take care of her.

BOOK THREE

SPAIN 1950

TWENTY-NINE

The Embassy

" Trust not him with your secrets."

—LAVATER, *Aphorisms on Man*

THE SUN STREAMED in the windows of the hotel. Down below horns honked, garbage cans clanked, men and women called companionably to one another. Too much food, too much wine and far too many lonely dreams, Pru reached across the bed for Henri. The pillow was empty. She opened her eyes. Henri was in Canada filming the final scenes of his latest movie. She was in Málaga. She shut her eyes again—last night…the note shoved under her door, she wasn't ready to think a bout that yet.

"This is something you must do for yourself," he had told her. "I'd only be in the way." He was right; still she missed him. Their marriage might be different than most, it didn't matter. It worked.

She could forgive Henri for not coming, not her mother. Marion took pains to remind Pru of her duties as a daughter, while forgetting her own. If she wasn't playing Hollywood star, she could always slip into the role of lonely wife-on-the-edge-of-a-nervous-breakdown, both parts seemingly easier to play than that of mother.

At a cocktail party on some Hollywood hill, Hedda Hopper had pulled Pru aside: "Tell me dear, is it true?"

"What?"

"That the lights of Broadway weren't quite bright enough for your clever mother and so she deigned to try our humble silver screen."

"I wouldn't know." Pru did know but she wouldn't give the columnist the satisfaction of an answer. Marion had wasted little time on her decision to leave live theater, "How hard can it be to do a few lines a day?" In a hushed and darkened house, slipping into the persona of another was easy, but on a sound stage crowded with busy disinterested people Marion had stumbled over her own self-consciousness, and stuttered and stammered her way into obscurity. Producers and directors rushed to lose her number. She sought refuge from the threat of poverty in a simple enough role—that of wife. Roland was rich, Roland was respectable and Roland was there.

Nevertheless Marion had that certain something; that tilt to her chin, the way she cocked her head as if your conversation was just what she had waited a lifetime to hear, and that soulful look she could put on—her special aura never left her. Even Hedda had to acknowledge it, though not in her column.

Hollywood was an out of sight, out of mind town. To miss a reading or a party would be a mistake. No way would Marion shake her equilibrium by leaving the country, and so it was Pru's equilibrium that got upset. All that food, all that wine, the music, the things she heard last night, the things she almost heard and . . . the note. Pru needed to clear her head. She threw back the covers and made for the shower.

Despite the General's assurance that the Hotel Alameda met American standards, the showerhead in her bathroom dripped more than it flowed. She lathered her body with the strong smelling soap and gave her mind over to the task of making decisions. What she should do next? What had Marion expected Pru to find? The sender of the telegram? Or must she actually produce her father or his——. She couldn't bring herself to use the word, not yet. Her irritation grew as the tepid water dribbled off to cold. She couldn't shake the thought that this trip was just a sop to Bazil. Her mother, not one given to ad-libbing, most probably already had a well thought out script in mind—one that would assure her a comeback. Truth was not so important to Marion that she couldn't overlook it when it suited her purposes. But would she write Roland out of the script and surrender the edge that being the suffering wife lent her?

Why are you so hard on your mother, so sure of her motives? Bazil's voice oozed from the showerhead. She answered him. "Why? Because, Bazil, we could have waited in New York with the rest of the émigrés." *What of your own motives?* Okay, so it still angered her that her mother had given no thought to the fact that her daughter lost her father, her Nanny and her footing. Marion took her to California and that big barren house far from anywhere, and then guaranteed her further isolation by sending her off as a day student at a school where most of the girls boarded. Pru never managed to break into the cliques of overconfident girls, sure in their belief that God was in his heaven and all was right with the world. They read the right books, spouted their parents' politics and everyday walked past a wall map that colored every country good or evil. Pru drove her teachers crazy with nothing but questions. Could a country even be called good, or evil? What about a whole people? It was even harder to tell about people. Could you hate someone and love them at the same time? Could you get so muddled up that you mistook one for the other? The teachers had no answers. Pru grew lonelier with each new class while her mother slipped further and further away from the role of motherhood, slipping more comfortably into portraying the more glamorous, larger than life Marion.

The water turned icy. Pru came back to her senses. She was far from a high school girl now. She cranked up the hot till the tap rattled and gave her body a quick rinse. It was time to get on with it. She stepped from the shower, shook out her wet hair and her indecision. She would go back over the rumors, the ones that were strong enough to reach California, the one thing they had in common: Rodicio and the *Casa Carrillo*. And then, last night in the café, with the General all that talk at the table: the war, bodies by the side of the roads and Americans. She would go to Rodicio. She had her own motives, maybe not as dramatic as Marion's. She had a feeling that if the answers she brought back didn't translate into a blockbuster movie, she'd never get free. Fed up with being a walk on in her mother's life, a mother married to Bazil would be a mother she wouldn't have to protect. Nobody could do a better job of protecting Marion than Bazil, if only her mother would let him. And Bazil had earned his prize. When, in the early days of World War II, the English abandoned the Balkans, so did Bazil. Either Hitler or Stalin would gobble up his barony. He walked out of Sophia taking his money, his mother and his sense of ethics with him. His riches—the Rubens, the Titians and the tapestries, he left behind. Part of Bazil's charm lay in the fact he was a romantic and with Roland in limbo, he had set out for California and the woman who made his "heart leap."

The girl who, despite her childhood bout of puppy love, made no effect on his heart, cleared the steam from the bathroom mirror and studied her body, the changes time made to it . . . not all that much, not enough for students to stop using her as their muse. As she toweled her hair her thoughts turned to Rubio, her other childhood crush. What changes could time have made to his body? The fact that she never expected to see him again left her free to emulate her mother and turn him into whatever she wanted; but now and then reality intruded and she realized that the changes might not all be good. What with the war, his rabbit-hunting rifle, his itch to fight the Moors *he might not even have survived*. Peacetime held hidden dangers for the losers. Could she find out what happened? Did she want to?

She never talked of Rubio with her mother; Marion only remembered people who remembered her. She knew nothing of the nights Prudence and Rubio wandered the ravines behind the *Casa de Carrillo*, "Hunting rabbits," Rubio had said. The hunt hadn't interested her as much as Rubio had.

She stepped into the bedroom, the air cooled off her skin as well as her memories. At least she could laugh at her own foolishness—no slouch in the imagination department, she could give Marion a run for her money in crafting romantic scenarios.

Over by the bed, she reached for her robe and saw her purse: the note. She could ignore it no longer. Time to take Bazil's advice and check in with what passed for the American Embassy. In other times, under other circumstances she would have considered the note a prank and ignored it; but who even knew she had come to Spain? And if by some chance they had found out, how had they known of her last minute change of hotels?

She wrapped herself as best she could in the rough stiffness of the towel and crossed the room to the telephone. She would call down to the *conserje*.

"*Un taxímetro, por favor.* I must go to the American Embassy."

"*¿Qué dijo?*"

"The American—"

"Ah, *si, señorita. La embaja de Estados Unidos es cerrado.*"

"Well yes, but—

"Your country, mine, *señorita,* they no like each other." The complacent shrug to the woman's shoulders, her indifference, made its way through the phone line.

"I'll need a cab, nevertheless."

"You do not wish to wait for *el general?*"

"Why would . . . never mind, just call the taxi. *Gracias.*"

Pru knew the embassies had not reopened, Bazil had told her about the unofficial legation—an *ad hoc consulate* he called it. Politics were politics, but business was business.

Out on the street, riding down the broad avenues, the driver assured her he was one of those in the know, after all he was a cabbie. He turned around and gave her a look that could only be called a leer, I can even find *la Señorita* a—"

"No thank you, *Señor,* the embassy please." She settled back, opened her purse and unfolded, folded, unfolded and folded the note again. By the time they pulled up to a rather rundown old building, no flags, no banners in sight, the notepaper looked as grubby and worn as the outside of the office.

Inside, secretaries, busy at their typewriters, made a show of not looking up. A smattering of minor officials drummed fingers on desks, some cluttered, some not. They ignored her. At the front desk Pru cleared her throat. The receptionist never bothered to look up, "There is no ambassador here, not even in Madrid, surely you know that?" Well yes, she did.

"A Chargé d' affaires, perhaps?"

"No."

"An assistant to the *Chargé d' affaires?*"

The woman shook her head, avoiding even the pretense of

helpfulness. Her mother had warned her that Bazil's advice was worth what she paid for it,—bureaucrats and their staff took extra pains to learn the art of not helping people. They made a specialty of looking busy while not doing anything.

Pru drew herself up, trying for a powerful performance, that of irate taxpayer—not that she'd earned enough with her paint-brush to pay much in taxes.

"Just what is it you do here, then?"

"We mind our own business, you would do well to do the same," the woman had perfected the art of the shrug. Uncharacteristically for Pru, she held her tongue and turned her attention to the rest of the room, searched out the largest desk, the one with the tallest stack of papers—if you need some-thing done, ask a busy man, Nanny said. Actually what she had said was a busy woman. Nanny had few illusions when it came to men.

Pru approached a desk hidden by clutter, stood there a moment and then cleared her throat, the young man looked up, boredom already clouding his eyes. Had he heard of her father? A Mr. Whitley? His possible whereabouts? He out-shrugged the woman. Sensing that she might lose him all together, she got down to the business of the note.

"Rubbish, utter rubbish. Why bother yourself with such horrors? A pretty thing like you would do better to stick to the usual tourist attractions."

Just as she began to doubt that this place had any stand-ing at all, a door at the back of the room opened and an older man stuck his head out. "Miss, this way please." He ushered her inside to a small leather chair across the desk from his and held out his hand, "Mr. Arthur here," he said. "I'm what passes for the assistant to the Assistant *Charges d' affaires,* all unofficial of course. It should all be official soon. America needs Spain.

Anyway, I couldn't help overhearing. Perhaps I can clear a few things up for you." Pru sat down, handed him the note.

He took a moment to study it. "Ossuary is a mysterious word to be sure, but in reality the ossuaries are a practical if outdated solution."

"Ossuaries?" She must have looked puzzled, it hadn't occurred to her there could be more than one. He thought she hadn't understood.

"Let me start over. As in the States, we have paupers' graves. It's handled a bit differently though. Out of deference to the church, unclaimed bodies get a temporary resting place. After five years, if no one appears with the necessary fees to insure proper burial, to make more permanent arrangements—" he paused, searching for the right word and gave up with a shrug, "—the corpse is dug up and placed in the 'bone pit.'"

The room went dark, she felt herself tipping over, falling. Her father in a pit? It couldn't be. Surely someone would have told her—the room stilled, the light returned. Someone had. Last night. The note:

"Señorita, *if you wish the truth,* la verdad sobre
el señor, *you must take the journey into the bowels
of the boneyard.*"

Mr. Arthur talked on but his words settled in the air just out of reach. She shook her head, trying to pay attention.

"Your father, how well do you know him? I mean, who did he favor?"

"I don't know. All I know is he wrote. Of his life, I know nothing, where he was born, not even how old he is—was—is. Of his politics I know even less." Her father had told her how to live her life. About his own he had little to say and what he did do contradicted what he said. "The facts of his life changed as often as the weather."

Mr. Arthur laughed. "Well, you know writers, so creative it stands to reason they'd get creative with their own biographies."

How could she explain the she had only known her father as a man who was away more than he was home; though the fact that he ran away from a button factory didn't seem important enough to tell Mr. Arthur. She could tell him he was a risk taker—a man who took trips and risks with equal abandon. He always wore pinstriped suits, derby hats, and smoked big cigars. He welcomed those who admired his writing. And it wasn't much of a secret that he wanted his wife to dote, his child to obey. In the end, none of that proved enough?

She wasn't about to admit that to Mr. Arthur. There was a lot she could have, should have, told her mother. Pru still woke at night to the smell of tobacco, the murmur of voices, the rhythmic creak of tired leather on an old couch and doubted her mother knew.

"God knows I loved that man," Marion would say, "that sense of duty of his. It's that damn civil war that took him off. He couldn't have meant to leave me —us." Pru knew her father had other senses he favored more, yet she said nothing.

"Well," she managed a weak smile for Mr. Arthur, "I never looked at it quite your way before. I guess you could say he was creative. Anyway none of that really matters, I'm here because I need to know the facts of his death, I mean if he's dead."

"Ah," he said as he came from behind the desk, "so many come here for the same reason."

"Perhaps I should go to the English Cemetery, I would have if not for this note."

He laid an arm across her shoulder meant to comfort. "No need to search the English Cemetery, I am familiar with it— have you thought that perhaps he didn't want you to know, thought it best this way?" His remark brought her up short.

How many times had he heard this story? How many fathers had escaped fatherhood this way?

"No, no. Not him," she protested.

His sigh told her more than she was willing to admit out loud. How had he divined the very thing she feared?

"The pits," his arm dropped from her shoulder, "the bone pits, may seem crude but at one time they had proved useful." She shuddered. "The young man," he nodded his head toward the outer door, "has much to learn about tact and diplomacy before we open officially but his advice is sound. I too would advise you to stick to tourist centers."

"But here is something I must find—"

"That might not be wise." Though she found his voice kind, his tone sympathetic, the words were not. "Americans are not all that popular today —your Lincoln Brigade, your United Nations and their need to isolate *La España*, leave her out in the cold—"

"My?"

"Sorry, 'our.' "

"But the Lincoln Brigade, the U.N, what has that to do with me?"

"You are an American, that is enough. I've been here so long I forget that I am not a citizen."

"You were here then? You knew him?" Of course he did, everyone else had. "You—" Someone rapped on the door. Pru turned. General Lemona poked his head around the corner.

"I interrupt?"

"No, no." Mr. Arthur's voice went flat. His face had lost all expression, his shoulders tool on the bureaucratic shrug. "I am advising the young lady what to do, the botanical gardens in *Park Calle Alameda*, the *Alcazaba*.

"Good work. I myself will escort her—"

"Thank you, General, but I leave this morning, I wish to—"

"Then I shall arrange a car for you, one of my men will chauffeur you wherever you wish."

Damn.

THIRTY

Out Maneuvering the General
> *"Things are seldom what they seem,*
> *Skim milk masquerades as cream"*
>
> —GILBERT, *H.M.S. Pinafore*

THE LIMOUSINE DROVE slowly on the way back to the hotel. Pru couldn't stop staring at the huge portraits of Franco that glowered from every wall and then she found her attention drawn to the man sitting beside her—the two were not that unalike. Despite the fact that Lemona had slipped back into his tour guide persona, he managed to look as threatening as the omnipresent portraits

"The coast, Torremolines, very gay; the night life so cosmopolitan, every bit as satisfying as New York. You'll like it" No she wouldn't. She couldn't even think with all his prattle. She had to get rid of him; either he was oblivious to her discomfort or he had plans of his own. He never skipped a beat.

"Why don't I take you there, or perhaps" he steered the conversation eastward, "to Valencia, the city of flowers. The blue and white domes, the green hills and the red roofs, it is the city of painters . . . you paint, Señora." There it was again, his questions that weren't really questions. His voice lacked the upward lilt of a question, he hadn't asked if she painted, he knew; at least he finally got the name right.

What else did he know? Enough to make her uncomfortable. And that patronizing smirk on his face, she'd like to wipe it off his face with one her paint rags. She knew the type, like so many men he thought of her as painting pretty little pictures on tidy little canvases, propped up on oilcloth covered kitchen tables. She managed a smirk of her own as she imagined him tip-toeing his beribboned self through the muck of stacked canvases dripping globs of paint. She might have trouble in the love department but paint, color were things she responded to—their sheer physicality. Red, so sexual; black, luscious, funereal; a little yellow for a searing sun and —damn—why had she never thought of it before—the colors she used the most in her work were the colors of Spain.

He might be a general but he was a man after all; and one who seemed bent on seducing her. All right…if he was trying, however badly, to seduce her, why not turn the tables on him? There were some pluses in having an actress for a mother. She turned to Lemona and bathed him in a smile, radiant in its deceit. "Valencia? Paintings, you say? In the churches? Icons, I have a burning interest in icons."

Now it was her turn to babble, at least enough to keep him from asking questions, the ones she had no answers for. "And flowers, how charming." She mustn't overdo it. Underplay, underplay, Marion's voice whispered in her ear, but it was working. Reassured, his smile, slipped dangerously close to a leer and he proceeded to sketch out her trip's itinerary. They would leave at two, stay over at Cartegna, he knew a place. In the morning he could do a little business. She shuddered to think what that might be. "Our navy, the ships, I'll take you on board. Then on to Valencia." He would book rooms at the best hotel. On and on he went, about the university, the library, the churches and all those domes until he had her entire two weeks in Spain booked.

She managed to block him out enough to form a plan. She would ask the *conserje* where she could get a car. Mr. Arthur, using expansive gestures of his arms to create a picture of a countryside bleached white with bones, had spoken of bone yards in the plural. How would she know which ossuary? Why would someone write such a note and then leave everything so vague? She needed a car and not one that had ever felt the weight of Lemona's backside.

"Thanks," she cooed as he helped her from his limo. "Till two then." She gave him a wish-I-were-Mona Lisa smile, intriguing but not too blatant.

"You'll not be sorry, Señora Brancusi, we will do the sights."

She'd heard that phrase before. Did she walk around with a sign on her: Show me a cathedral or a tall building and you can show me your bed? It had worked with van Dulken but she hadn't minded. She had several days lay over in New York— papers must be procured, letters of credit. Those things took time and Bazil had arranged an introduction to van Dulken to smooth her way. "This chap is part of the German delegation to the U.N. He'll take care of you." Van Dulken had done more than that. He'd met her plane at La Guardia, made arrange- ment for her flight to Lisbon, mixed up her departure dates, changed her hotel reservations, held her hand as they climbed the stairs inside the Statue of Liberty, and brushed her cheeks with his lips as they trotted around Central Park. On the deck of the Staten Island Ferry, huddled together against the wind, he nibbled her neck. In Birdland over scotch on the rocks they listened to Miles Davis. His thigh pressed hers. At the Peter Cooper he took her to bed.

Bazil had handed her to van Dulken, who passed her on to the mysterious *el señor*, who apparently had done the same for the general. She was beginning to feel like a set of mismatched luggage passed from hand to hand, a little too good to throw out, yet its usefulness still an unknown. Anyway, what did it matter? She had her plan.

She hurried up to her room, changed into flats and a pair of slacks and picked up her phone to call down to the desk. Something about the instrument, its ominous black, stopped her. She dropped it back in its cradle. *The* conserje, *of course.* She told the General everything, every move she made. Someone else had filled him in on the rest—van Dulken a likely suspect. Perhaps he could have known someone who knew the General and dropped her name casually? She hoped it was only her name he dropped. Yet somehow the General knew more about her than how easy it would be to seduce her. He had plans all right, but they were more along the lines of keeping her from having time to nose about burial pits. She might be a bit paranoid, her assumption could be wrong, but either way her solution would work.

She had to get out of the hotel, away from eyes that pried, ears that listened. She would sneak down the back way, go out for a walk, ask around where she might find a car for hire. Left in the dark as to her plans, the *conserjé* could do no harm.

Out in the streets, her paranoia evaporated in the perfume of the acacia trees, the beauty of the oleander. Smelted by the intense light of day, the general, his medals, separated out, leaving behind the dross of mere man—an element easily dealt with, vanquished through aroused expectations, salted with flattery.

Pru walked a few blocks towards the business district, slowing down to look at the goods in the windows. Wooden furniture, nicely carved. Flowers, cheeses. She dawdled in the sunshine, interpreted signs, oiling her rusty Spanish. In one window, she saw a shawl, black lace with golden filaments threaded through—a nice gift for her mother. She cupped her hands to her eyes, peered in the window, looking for a price tag. Marion's adage, "If you have to ask, you can't afford it," barely cleared her mind when she spotted the necklace. This was no paranoia—this was real. That design, her father had sketched it out on the back of one of her school exercise books, the little blue ones. He'd even taken her with him to the jeweler. Specially made for her mother, she wouldn't have parted with it. But how could she prove it now? The copybook had disappeared even sooner than the necklace. The particular day it happened was as muddied up in her memory as everything else. Could it have been the day she caught sight of the woman retreating down the darkened backstairs, hunched over from the weight of a bulging pillowcase that clacked and rattled its way down. More probable would be the fateful day she and her mother found the door to the *Casa de Carillo* wide open, and stumbled into the overturned fury of their belongings, emptied drawers, jumbled furniture. During the war a piece of jewelry like that would have changed hands many times and Málaga was the closest city of any size to Rodicio.

Times were better, so why had no one purchased it now? And then she spotted the price tag, even Marion couldn't afford it. She turned away, hot tears scalding her vision. A young man took her arm, "*Señora,* may I be of some help?" She looked up into steely-blue eyes and saw something familiar about them. *No! No! It couldn't be.* She shook herself—a trick, her memory, her imagination overworked by the necklace and all this fussing with the past. She would get nowhere in this country if she tripped over imaginary siblings at every turn in the road.

She shook her head, turned and walked quickly away. She

wouldn't look back, she wouldn't. She did. The young man stared after her. She gave him an apologetic shrug and moved off. He didn't look anything like her. Nothing at all.

A few blocks more and she passed a garage where a group of men huddled around a sedan, heads buried under its hood. Off in a corner, parked under a calendar—back home it would be Rita Hayworth in a black lace nightgown, here Manolete twirled a blood-red cape—she spotted a limousine, a little dusty, a little worse for wear but still, more comfortable looking than the cabs that careened around. How she wished she had the time to ride elegantly about the city in the bright yellow and black horse-cabs.

"*¿Quiero alquilar un automóvil a ir en campo?*" she hoped the men could overlook the flat accent and understand she wanted a car.

A few snickers, a few winks followed by some comments, *una mujer desgastado los pantalones*—something about a woman in pants and then someone volunteered to drive her, she hesitated. She told them she wanted to go far out in the country, to Rodicio.

"Ah, Rodicio!" exclaimed the oldest. Another pulled his head out of the engine, "Our uncle, he know the country," he snickered. As if to make amends, they all spoke at once, the one on top of the other. "The car, she is American. *Una Cadillac.* You will like her, they almost leered at that. She tried to look business-like and informed them she would be in the country perhaps, "*una semana.*" They assured her a week in the country would be a joy for the uncle. This appeared to amuse them all over again.

"Then the uncle it will be. Please have him at my hotel, at the back door, in one hour, *por favor.*"

"*¿Porqué?*" Only a rude peasant would call for a lady in such a way.

"The back door or he needn't come at all!"

"*Sí, sí, señorita.*"

"*Señora.*" She smiled. "*Señora* Brancusi." She emphasized the *Señora* and the men became respectful, all signs of flirtation banished. Another plus for having married Brancusi, traveling through Spain as a single woman, a *Señorita*, would be a liability.

"*Perdón por favor*, it will be as you wish." The men disappeared back under the hood, the sound of their amused laughter followed her out the door. She didn't care. She had beaten Lemona at his game, whatever it might be.

"*¿Los americanos, están más allá de comprensión, no?*" one called to another.

"You are quite right," she told the disinterested streets, "but that's the problem isn't it? We all find each other a bit beyond comprehension." A few people stared at *del ángulo loca*, but if she dealt with her fears, kept her emotions in check, she would have her answers. She could go home, to Henri, to her studio, to her life.

THIRTY-ONE

Tio

"...nor uncle me no uncle"

—SHAKESPEARE, *King Richard II*

"JOSE, ANTONIA, RUIS DE AMADEO, *a servicio.*" He had almost as many names as she did. "But everyone call me *Tio.*"

"Prudence Maria Katarina Abigail Brancusi nee Whitley, everyone calls me Pru."

He smiled, a beautiful smile, "Si, *Señora.*"

"As you wish, but I will call you Tio." She found it reassuring for a man called Uncle to be driving her around. She sat back in her seat prepared to relax.

As they threaded their way to the outskirts of the city, he chatted away in a mixture of languages, a mixture of idioms: a little English here, some Spanish there and over it all the salt of French, the pepper of German. "*Me gusta a manejar* Madame to Rodicio." He would be happy to take her there. He knew the way. He passed through Rodicio many times driving *Herr* Schiller."

Herr Schiller? Later Pru would worry about the German and why his name sounded familiar—most probably a bit more of her paranoia. Right now she needed to find out why Tio, an educated man played the role of rustic and knew about Rodicio. "You grew up around here then?"

"No, No. I am from far away. *Soy de Asturias.*" The way he said it—I am an Asturian—she could hear the drums and bugles of pride, what could she do but believe him, and yet—

"I thought men from Asturias were blond." He gave her an odd look, took off his cap and ran his fingers through his coal black hair.

"I thought all Americans were gangsters."

She laughed. "Why did you leave?"

"I am no longer among the young. The mines, it is too much. And other work is out of the question for one with my—" She knew what he meant, his "past."

"Anyway you look at it, work he is no easy to find. I come south to my nephews. They get me jobs." They talked pleasantly for a while, she told him she had lived here a while ago herself, that she and her mother had lost track of her father. Not quite sure if she could trust him, she deliberately left things vague. He knew nothing of a *Señor* Whitley, but she mustn't worry, he knew his way around. "Not another one," she muttered.

"*¿Qué?*"

"*Está nada.*"

"Poor *liebchen*, you no can find your *pápa*? You are not alone, many in Spain cannot. I hope for you *el suerto*, that you find him. " The caring in his voice, the gentleness, disarmed her. Her skepticism, her Lemona induced wariness of men, slipped away. She could learn to like this one.

With the seriousness and purpose of a man on a mission, Tio guided the Cadillac expertly through shapeless clouds of dust. Horse-drawn wagons mounded heavenward with hay kept to the center of the road, making passing a challenge. To the pig-headed drivers, Tio offered gentle reminders of their ancestry, saving his more colorful curses for the vendors who pushed and pulled hand-drawn carts, vegetables spilling to the ground. Only the donkeys, overburdened with the loads no one else would carry, were spared his wrath, even though, along with all the rest, they competed for what little road the dawdling herds of sheep left open to them. Pretty, in a bucolic sort of way if Pru didn't look too far off to the sides of the road where every now and could be spotted a rusting tank or burnt-out lorry.

She drifted in and around her past until, without thinking, she spoke up and asked Tio if he'd ever been afraid. She caught his startled look in the mirror and realized her mistake. How could she have asked a man, a Spaniard at that, to admit to fear? But once started she couldn't stop. "The war, I mean. Did it frighten you as much as it did me?"

"You were here then, in *España*, during—"

"We came just before, in February."

"A terrible time."

"We were here for the beginning."

"The beginning? I think not, *Señora*, only God knows the beginnings of things. We mortals stumble along and then find ourselves right in the middle of a trouble. We went in just a wink of time from the Monarchy, to a dictator, to a Republic and God alone knows how many prime ministers and then back to a dic—well never mind."

She pretended not to notice his gaffe. She learned enough from the refugees that made it to California that it was best to call Franco *El Caudillo de España, por la gracia de Dios* as they looked cautiously over their shoulders.

"It's the endings," she said, "that I have trouble spotting, the knowing that a thing is over, that it's time to move on."

"No, beginnings, they are harder. In '31 we had the elections, the demonstrations, one might have thought ..." He gave a disparaging laugh. "But it could just as easily been the strikes of 1917, the riots of 1875. The idea of government does not rest easily on our shoulders. You know the story of St. Teresa?"

"Of Avilla?"

"*Si!* She is the Patron Saint of *España*. They say she asked God to give our people greater blessings. 'Give them, Oh Lord, a beautiful country, rich in the products of its soil.'"

"And did he?"

"Oh yes. The good Saint thanked him. It had gone so well she decided to try for more. 'And may this land enjoy the blessing of a good climate.' Once more the Lord complied. The dice appeared to be favoring her so she kept going, 'May it be peopled with beautiful women, may their children be well-behaved.' God found this, too, agreeable, but then—oh, then, she went too far. 'Oh Lord, grant them good government.' The heavens rumbled and God spoke, 'Ah, my dear Saint,' he replied, 'you have gone too far. Even I, the all mighty God, cannot do that.' You see, *Señora*, we love our elections, but they are too light a meal, the results never satisfy. War chases elections like a sneeze she chase the dust. But *mon amie*, you must have been *l'enfant*. And yet your papa—?"

"He didn't know."

His dismissive shrug, told her he didn't believe her. "The war, she come to my family, I no bring them to her."

"I wasn't all that young, almost twelve, we . . .." Why the need to convince this man of contradictions, this miner who spoke four languages, yet tripped over pronouns, who pretended to have trouble with English while he spoke it with more eloquence than she.

"Tio, all those languages, where did you learn them?

Some time passed before Tio answered. At last he said, "The

internationals, they come to the war, it was necessary for the survival to learn. Why is it you foreigners, your need to come to my country, to interfere in our war? Your Papa—"

"The troubles maybe, but not the war . . . he couldn't have known that." Even to herself, her words had the hopeful sound of an amateur's bluff. As to her father's need, maybe a curiosity, his craving for adventure brought him. He'd had enough of stories on the depression, he needed to write about something with more life. She hadn't understood his needs anymore than she understood her own. She told Tio about Bazil, how he said that the two of them, father and daughter, feared the quiet not for its stillness, but for the fact that in stillness, their thoughts, their emotions, might catch up with them. They might accidentally feel something.

Back then, she took it for granted that their trip to Spain would be like the others: grist for his books, his profiles of a country. He claimed to chart the soul of a land. He preferred scholarly tomes on esoteric subjects—the paintings, the culture, with a bit of politics, a philosophical musing or two thrown in for good measure. Dry heavy things; but on that trip *The Times* wanted an American's viewpoint—he told her mother. But had he known war was imminent and still brought them?

"A reporter? For *The London Times*—" A glance at Tio's face in the rear-view mirror told her his opinion of reporters. How could she justify returning to a country she felt lucky to have escaped, to look for a man she pretended not to care about? But whether or not she loved that man, needed him or just wanted it settled—none of it was Tio's business. She was here. She might as well get on with it.

She could hardly tell Tio about the few clues she did have about his disappearing act, clues she hadn't even shared with Marion. Several times she'd come close but then if she were in her mother's place, would she want to know? She and Roland must have been happy at first, Roland anyway—she remembered that look of pride that crossed his face when he walked into a room with Marion on his arm and people crowded around. But, after awhile, the gossips claimed his ego found it trying that no one sought his autograph and he itched to be off on some new curiosity, adventure, to shirk off old responsibilities and old wives. No she wouldn't tell Tio all that but perhaps she could tell him the good things, the interesting things about her father. How famous he was, everyone knew him, how all the important politicians and generals came to his table at the *Casa de Carrillo*. At the mention of the politicians, the generals, Tio jerked the car to a stop at the side of the road and turned to glare back at her.

"Who, *Señora*? Tell me their names."

She'd been uneasy with the general, but now this man frightened her. "I don't remember names." It was true, she was a child and memory plays tricks on children, "mustaches, pot bellies, whether or not they made loud noises at the table. How much wine they drank, how it dribbled down the mayor's chin when he was scared." What did he want from her? "That's the sort of thing I remember," she tried to explain.

"You must remember some names, tell me."

"Rubio, I remember that name."

"Who this Rubio?"

"A donkey driver, just a boy. He was my friend, he told me things." She did her best to control the stammer in her voice, "I remember, the Moors, he tried to warn me about the Moors." At the mention of the Moors the fight went out of Tio. "The rest, she do me the good," he said. He turned the car back onto the road as if that had been the purpose of the stop after all.

For minutes that seemed like hours they drove on. Tio chatted on amiably about the passing scene but Pru's mind was so preoccupied with her dilemma — did she love her father? Was he a good man? A petty tyrant? Whose side *did* he favor?— she almost missed the small shrine by the roadside. "Señor *Amadeo, pare, por favor.* I must see this." Like those they had seen years before, this too held a statue of the Virgin. Our Lady of Sorrows—*Nuestra Dama de Dolores*, the sign said. Taller than any Pru remembered, this one must be special. Her brown eyes flecked with a patient sadness, her robe a deeper blue, more richly trimmed than most roadside Virgins, the Blessed Mother had no need to brave the elements, a little roof sheltered her. Fresh flowers and candles ringed her feet.

Pru got out, walked over to the shrine. *Tio Amadeo* came round the cab to stand beside her. He removed his cap, dipped one knee and made the sign of the cross.

"Ah, *Señora*, she is in remembrance of the priests, the nuns, they die here." Pru shuddered.

Someone had propped a picture of Franco against the stonewall that ran along for a short distance behind the statue. The wall, peppered with little holes, drew Pru over to it. She settled her fingers into first one and then another of the hollows. Sister Agatha? Mother Mary Thaddeus? She remembered Sister Sabatini, how sad, how scared, she had looked that day kneeling on the crude cellar floor, praying. Had God heard them, or had they too—

"The war, she is over, *Señora*, it does little good to think too much on things."

"Yes, but—"

"The sky is blue. The air clean. We alive. Do not ask too much." But she did, she always did.

"*¿Tengo un fósforo?*" Tio Amadeo searched his pockets and

handed her a match. She dropped some coins into the little metal box and lit one of the candles.

"We go now," he took her arm and led her back to the car. The tenderness in his gesture terrified her, it might unstop her tears. She hadn't cried then. She wouldn't cry now. How often had she said that? Once, on the crossing from London in the early days of the war, World War, World War II—hard to know where one war ended and another began—everyone topside on the lookout for torpedoes, the talk was of London, how the bombs didn't care who they hit. She had tried not to, but under every wave she saw danger. A sailor, perhaps a refugee, had come up behind her, just like Tio, and put his arm around her. "We'll make it, child, the Germans wouldn't dare. This is a Portuguese freighter." She'd had to choke back sobs then too.

"Let go," Tio said. "Cry, it's better than letting sorrow eat you." But she hadn't heard him. All this dipping back into the past made her miss the obvious: the land, the road; now she saw it clearly. "I've stopped here before, this very spot. I'm sure of it. And that village we went through, I've been there too." No wonder she hadn't recognized it with all the children, the dogs and burros crowding the streets. The stencils of Franco's face sprayed on the walls left little room for the initials that once shouted there.

"You are mistaken, the shrine, she is since the war, *Señora*."

"Yes, I know, I didn't mean the shrine." She looked around at the olive groves, the almond trees, the oak studded hillsides. Then she heard a gentle cooing sound . . . and she remembered it all—the parade, the shouts, the rocks.

"Turtledoves," Tio said.

"I know, Tio, I know."

"We must go on, *Señora* Brancusi, we should arrive before dark. A few miles more and we will see the church tower of Rodicio."

Why before dark? Tio's anger, even if it had passed, rankled a bit. The passing scenery didn't help her apprehension. The passion for rebuilding had not penetrated the dryness, the dust to make its way to the small towns. Huge craters interrupted the even patterns of the fields; stone fences badly in need of mending meandered on mile after mile. Detours and downed bridges made the road more perilous than before. The eerie look to ruins where villages might once have been, their houses with walls half gone, made her anxious; but she could wait no longer. She had to see, to know.

"Tio, there is a back road, it bypasses Rodicio, do you know it? I want to go by *La Casa de Carrillo* first."

"*Señora*, I take you through town, we need the food. I know you want to start looking for your Papa but the back road, she is too dangerous."

"No, no. It's not him, it's—"

"These last few miles, you have looked so worried. No need, *Señora*. I know the roads. I take care of you."

Why had he turned so stubborn? "It's not that, it's just—" But just what she didn't know. That house had not been home, safety, or any of those things to her. She remembered telling herself back before, that when they reached their destination she must be careful, no matter where they landed, not to grow too fond of it. She knew, even then, that eventually someone, something would come along and pull her away. Prudence grew into Pru without ever finding something to hang on to.

"Where are you staying the night, *Señora*?" Tio's voice pulled her back. She looked blankly at him. "You have not obtained the rooms? They're few to be had. Not many people stop in Rodicio anymore. Too many old communists."

"Still?" She had planned to stay at the *Casa de Carrillo*. Someone at the dinner table last night had made some reference to it's being an Inn.

"Franco's men are everywhere, but out here in the country there are still places to hide." The words raised her spirits; if places existed for communists to hide, there might be room for her father to hide.

"You are not the only one with secrets, *Señora.*" Not above his own sense of drama, Tio paused to look around, as if danger lurked under seat cushions, "we are far from the ears, *Señora Brancusi.* I tell you now . . . I too—"

"A communist? But, back there, at the shrine. You crossed yourself—"

"Asturians, we believe what we believe. I no follow all they say. Why should I? Communists, they can't agree, not even among themselves. Why, without their ideological squabbles we might even have won." His voice climbed the scale in anger until it cracked. She held her breath, at least Tio trusted her again, maybe now she would learn something.

"Back then I was young, with much bravery. So much matters to the young, right?"

"Yes, but tell me—"

"Ah, *Señora,* I was handsome then, *trés distingué.*" Again, that shift of language.

"You still are." Perhaps she shouldn't have said that; but fortunately he was so wrapped up in his past he hadn't appeared to noticed.

"Ah, you should have known me then, I went down to Ría Pravia to help unload the guns. Our blood boiled—the excitement, the tenseness of the bullfight the moment before the bull enters the ring! And then *Los Policía, La Guardia Civil,* the Trotskyites, they were all over us."

"Trotskyites, but they were on your side—"

"With intellectuals who can tell? They throw out the priest,

take over the pulpits and then they talk, talk, talk. That's all
they were good for. Me, I'd rather be killed for a goat, than a
lamb; but most of them, they sat on their . . . they did nothing
but preach."

"Why?"

"Not the time for the asking of questions, *Señora*."

"Call me Pru."

"A strange name this Pru." His lips pursed around the alien
syllable. "Is it for a boy? Your mama, she wanted a son?"

"No. My papa."

"All papas, they want sons."

"And then they send them out to die." Her father hadn't
meant for her to die, still what had he thought would happen to
them?

"In our country fathers die along side the sons."

She felt his anger, though this time not at her. Her troubles shrank, became unimportant next to the magnitude of
his. They had entered the last stretch of flat country before the
climb to Rodixio. They drove in silence through fields dotted
with the rotting hulks of cannon, more abandoned tanks. Tio
surely must know more than he let on, she wanted to hear it all.

"The strike, the anarchists did they help you then?"

"No, the anarchists were young hooligans, they no help in
the mines. They worked only at the stirring up of trouble. We
miners we were pretty much on our own."

"And?"

He gulped in a huge breath of air. "And I looted. I burned."

"Is that so different from the anarchists?" She had gone too
far, asked too much. "I'm sorry, I didn't mean that. You don't
have to tell me."

He was not to be stopped. "Then the killing started. They
told us to line the priests up along the wall." Tio pulled the car

to the side of the road, once more he turned to face her. She felt a passing twinge of fear, but his voice softened. "I am a good communist. I want what is good for the worker, but I no kill *los padres*. I am a Spaniard. Ask us to defend the door of the church, we will be there; but ask us to cross over it, we will refuse. Particularly on Sunday." He smiled. Time to let it drop. She smiled back.

Tio fell silent, apparently the question of where she would stay forgotten in his need to concentrate on the road. Pru had slept through this that first time and hadn't realized how steep, how dangerous the approach was; but she knew the village ran out along a vast escarpment, the *Casa Carrillo* stood on the highest point at the far end of the village, the houses of the villagers turned their backs to the precipice. The convent took up most of the largest open area on the side near the main road. At the very end stood the plaza, acacia trees lining three sides, the open side skirted the cliff. All the flat, arable land lay below, far below, a healthy hike for the villagers.

At the edge of the town, they passed a group of men with their donkeys. They called out, "*¿Qué ta, Tio. Qué tal?*" She stared at them. Rubio? No. He wouldn't be that old, that wrinkled. That beautiful topaz skin of his couldn't have faded to the color of stale chocolate.

"They know you here, quite well—"

"I told you," he shrugged. "I drive *Herr Schiller.*"

That name again. Who? When? Something told her she'd have to remember it, and remember it soon.

THIRTY-TWO

The Dance

> *"For I dance*
> *And drink, and sing,*
> *Till some blind hand*
> *Shall brush my wing."*

—BLAKE, *Songs of Experience.*

PRU MANAGED to persuade Tio to at least drive by the *Casa*, just a look, a quick one she had said—the matter of where her lodging was still unsettled—but when the car stopped in front of *La Casa de Carrillo* and Tio jumped out and hurried around to help her, Pru could hardly muster the courage to take his hand. His knowing, slightly ironic smile steeled her resolve. The rundown facade of the *Casa*—the pockmarks, the missing chunks of masonry, chipped tiles, broken and rusted grille work—didn't really welcome her.

The part of her that still remembered the things she saw as a child—the people, the ones who disappeared, the damage done those that lived, their houses, their things—that part of her felt no surprise at finding the *Casa de Carrillo* battered, scarred. The untroubled part of her, the California one where wars didn't happen and the sun warmed a morning, that part of her couldn't conceive of all this.

If she were to get through this she better learn to control her memories—to allow this one, to shut that one out. But faced with all this damage, the childhood side of her loomed larger, took on more importance and the adult side found her bombarded by memories.

Tio Amadeo cleared his throat. "The horror, the ugliness of it all, she is hard to take. The government no waste the cement on the villages, the cities, the monuments they get built." Pru gave a start, she hadn't spoken, not out loud. Had he read her mind? "Your face, she tell the story. Why you no tell me this house she was your home?

"House, not home."

"Still...."

She tried to form her mouth into a smile, it refused to cooperate, she saw him watching her with concern, "Civil war, she is worse," he said, "the memory hemorrhages with pain. You have the look of one who walks with ghosts."

"Tio, why is 'war' a feminine noun?"

"Enough of the past, each day is for the living of that day only." His grin returned, "I take you to the café. We drink *vino, tinta de rojo*," his cheerful voice propelled her into the present. "Until the rose, she come back to your cheeks and then we see about the place for you to stay."

It might be easier to cope, to absorb the changes on a full stomach. "And food, Tio, I could use a little—"

"*A su servicio*." Tio Amadeo drove down the hill toward Rodicio, every part of her strained to take his advice, to let go of the past, but images of Marion pushed in—Marion walking down dirt roads, chin high, lugging a suitcase, calling for Prudence to catch up. How could it be that from time to time

Pru let all that slip away in her irritation with the everyday Marion, the clingy Marion? *All those broken promises. Guilt—how does one let go of that?* There it was again, the feeling that she might never be free of the past, never be able to pay off her debt. Even when she and Henri moved back into the *Casa de la Paloma* in an attempt to assuage one of Marion's God-knows-I-loved-that-man black moods, it hadn't been enough. She'd made her promise. She would stick to it. But she made another promise, this one to herself—in the unlikely event she ever had a child she would extract no promises from them.

In the café, Tio led her to a table by the window. *"Uno momento, por favor."* He disappeared up a staircase at the back. Someone placed a glass of wine in front of her. Pru peered into the waters of Lethe, the sweet red liquid of forgetfulness tickled the back of her throat on its way to warm her soul.

One sip, two. She felt better already, good enough to turn her attention to the room. Its simplicity calmed her ghosts. The high-back cane chair pressed against her spine, anchored her to the here and now, nailed her to a room where candles leaned crazily in old wine bottles and plain white-washed walls multiplied their light. She ran her fingers across the scarred wooden table etched by lovers in times gone by. *"Sanchez ama Mercedes,"* overwritten by *"Ruis y Isabelle."* If only that paint that had oozed down those old walls had used the word love and drawn hearts around the initials. *Amor* might be the one thing strong enough to undo the past. But love is so elusive; a blink, a moment's inattention and you've missed it. She drew in a deep breath, the smoky sweetness of the air—a blend of fine cigars, thick coffee, burnt chocolate. It felt good to forget, to let the moment be the moment.

Outside, darkness slid quietly over the streets, cloaking the town in a gauze of twilight. Her fellow drinkers looked her over with the idle speculation given to tourists, those who were among them for the short term, no one they would have to deal with. Here and there a tentative smile came her way. It felt right to smile back.

"*¿El norte americano?*"

"*Sí, un canadiense,*" Tio had returned. Pru looked up at him, his eyes locked on hers, trust me they said. "*Señora* Brancusi is on her way to Madrid. She is here to taste your wines, sample your foods." He mentioned nothing about who she was or that she had lived here before. The name Whitley meant nothing to Tio but someone here might remember it. She would not contradict him on the Canadian mention. He had been right about the wine; she would listen to him again. On a warm night like this, good wine, good company—who would want to be reminded of ugly times?

Nor would she inquire about the change in his appearance, how this supposed stranger, this passerby, had managed a fresh shirt and enough pomade slicked over his hair to lubricate the Queen Mary. Like most Spaniards, he was not tall, but from his posture—so straight, so proud—he appeared to be. His bushy mustache tamed and waxed to a point, gave his face a look of amused tolerance. Was it because of the lesser mortals that surrounded him? Did he count the silly American who didn't know much about herself, her family among them? But no, he smiled benevolently at everyone and beamed at Pru as if she were a member of his family, a favorite niece. He turned to the proprietor, "*La Señora,* she needs a room, your best."

"You must speak with *mi esposa,* she does the renting of the beds." His attentive wife appeared in the doorway to the kitchen. "*Pardone me,* my rooms, they are filled with cousins in for the fiesta."

"There will be a fiesta *mañana?*"

"*Sí, Tio,* the feast of St. Joseph. If we saw you more in the Church you would know this." Tio? More in church? Pru cautioned herself not to make too much of her suspicions. Intuition told her that these people knew Tio, knew him well. But then, maybe she had misunderstood. Perhaps he hadn't said he didn't know anyone here, just that he didn't stop here often. And then again, maybe he could read her mind, probe its honeycomb of secrets, since he possessed so many of his own.

The trembling light of the candles erased the years from his face, exposed traces of the handsome man his past laid claim to. Though his hands, their gnarled fingers twisted like lumps of tallow, betrayed his age, they added to his intrigue—the hands of one who struggled. And then his eyes, the way the brown blurred into the black of his pupils like those of a deer, drew her to him. She'd like to paint those eyes, the browness of them. You could trust a man with those eyes. Rubio had eyes like that. Anyway, Tio had kept her secrets. She would keep his.

The doors of the café opened to a parade of men carrying scarred and battered guitars, tambourines, and castanets. Without her quite noticing the room had filled with grandmothers, babies, young men escorting young women and those advanced enough in age to have fought in the war brought their wives. The wine bottles never emptied, the dancers never tired.

The lead guitarist, his face as sad as a Picasso painting, bent over his instrument. The strings, in their soulful soundings, spoke of all the emotions, from elation to anguish, he spared none. She looked at the dancers, at the couples sitting close together in darkened corners, the children running in and out, around and under the tables. With each new song, the enormity of her nostalgia choked her, a hunger for things she never had—for love, for friends, for someone who would always be there to banish this separateness, this aloneness that gnawed at the pit of her stomach. Right now the only thing at hand to assuage her hunger was food.

"Tio, *por favor*, I am very hungry."

"Food, plates of it for the *Señora*. You have the love of *los ajos, no*?" Scarcely had the plate of lamb cleared the kitchen than her mouth began to water from the rich aroma of the garlic.

"You bring my guest the lamb? Why you no serve her the shrimp?"

"Please, Tio, the lamb is fine. Besides we are far from the coast."

"Not so far as all that. In Andalucía one is never far from the spirit of the sea, the bravery of the bulls, the beauty of the women." He raised his glass as a chorus of *oles* rocked the room. He bent down close to her, whispered in her ear, "May you dine, *en salud buena*. Later we do the dance." The debonair, continental Tio vanished, Tio the Spaniard wolfed down his food and hurried off to join the dancers. Pru ate slowly, savoring every bite while the proprietor paced back and forth in front of her, nodding approvingly. From time to time Pru would put her fork down, rest her taste buds, look around the room and speculate on the lives of the people. Rubio—could he be one of them, would she know him if she saw him? That is if he'd—? Some things she didn't want to think about, not yet. She concentrated on the food until she couldn't manage another bite. Yet somehow her full stomach only served to accentuate the emptiness of her heart. Hers was the only face to stare back at her from the watery rings her glass left on the table. She was alone. The young women that danced by had their arms possessively draped across their partners' shoulders to make sure she stayed that way. *Hands off* their glances told her. The young men with their slim hips, their muscular chests pressed against the rough cloth of their shirts, and the graceful curve of their thighs left her warmer than the wine.

"Ah *Señora*," the proprietress came to clear Pru's plate, "the night, it is made for the young, and the young they are made for the love. Our time, she is over."

"But not for—" Pru stopped. She had started to say but not for me when she saw the woman staring at her wedding ring. A ring that said, sit on the sidelines like us. For a moment she felt she understood the old women, their immersion in huge plates of food, each other's company. How else could they bear the sexuality all around them? Their plump bodies, clothed in black, arrayed around the outer edges of the room, told of lives now lived for others—she wasn't ready to give up herself. "The only person who can stand in your way, slow you down, is yourself," Pru's head filled with the comforting sound of Nanny's voice, "other people can't, not unless you let them." She wasn't about to let that happen. Not even Marion's neediness could hold her fast forever, could it?

She looked across the room to where Tio sat a crowd around him, everyone talked at once. He laughed at the men, their jokes. They laughed at his. She felt a little twinge at the way he flashed his smile at the women. She could tell a lot from the way they leaned in close to him, hurried to fill his glass, the way they tugged at his arms, teased him onto the dance floor.

He saw her watching him and twirled and stomped his way across the floor toward her. She held her breath, waited. He reached her side and held out his hand.

"But, I don't know how—"

"To dance takes only the heart. And you have *mucho corazón*." She smiled. She took his hand, he led her into the circle of dancers, whirled her around the floor till her legs ached, her arms felt heavy. When the guitarist struck the first chords of the flamenco, she shook her head regretfully and fell back into her seat. On the sidelines, watching the dancers, her heart thumped and bumped about in a dance of its own, her feet tapped out pale imitations of the intricate steps.

Now and then, the music slowed and Tio came for her. She gave herself over to his careful embrace—glad to be led somewhere she wanted to go by someone she was willing to follow.

Around eleven, a tired Pru begged off the next dance. An elderly woman made her way across the floor to where she sat.

"*Señora*," she asked, "at the Casa de Carillo, can I rent a room?"

"Si, *Señora. Mi hermana*, she is the caretaker. She will rent to you the bed. *La Casa*, she has many rooms. She is owned by the German."

A German? The music was loud, but Rubio's voice came from inside her head, she heard it clearly: "*Don Carrillo, el bastardo rico,* he own your house and all the land you see, every last hectare of it." Nothing German about the name *Carrillo*.

"*Un Alemán*, he no like it here, he seldom come."

So many guests had come from so many countries—she had told Tio the truth—it was hard to keep track after all this time. Pru forced her attention back to the old woman. "My sister, she no get paid, still she tend the house, what else is there for an old woman to do. It gives her the roof and when *el jefe* is away he lets her rent out some rooms—her wages for the keeping up of the *Casa*."

"This German, do you know when he bought it?" Pru shouted to be heard, but the music stopped, the woman looked startled. "Forgive me, I didn't mean . . . .." The woman melted back into the crowd. The lead tambourine rapped his knuckles on the taut parchment, a call to battle. The music resumed.

Could the men in Málaga have confused the German with an American? Not likely, not in a country that had known so many Germans. Besides the woman said the landowner was scarcely ever there. Had it been just last night in Málaga, that conversation about the American living in Rodicio? Odd that no one there mentioned him, even if they did think her Canadian. They might have at least mentioned the one English speaker to the other.

She made her way to where Tio Amadeo sat. He smiled a smile so welcoming, she wanted to fall into it; she struggled to keep her balance and asked, "Can you drive me back to the *Casa de Carillo*? The caretaker there rents out rooms."

"That place, she is too gloomy for a pretty one like you, why you still want to go there? Come, another dance."

"All right, Tio. One more, but then we go." An excellent dancer, his steps firm and sure, his arms strong and steady he guided her through the unknown. As she whirled around the room, she studied the women sitting at the fringes of life and realized that Spain was not a country she wished to grow old in; but it surprised her to find she liked the feel of his arm pulling her closer, the way his hand nestled her head against his shoulder, his breath, warm, welcoming to her ear. She should have felt secure. She didn't. She felt restless, confused. But oddly enough, almost happy.

One dance became two; two, three. For the second night in a row it would be almost dawn before she found a bed.

Back at the *Casa de Carrillo*, a metal bell mounted on the wall to the left of the big double doors, gave her pause. She didn't remember a bell. But then why would she? No one ever locked that heavy door back then—not until that day anyway. Now, like a penitent seeking admittance, she gave a tug to the cord. The door opened, it happened so quickly, the woman who motioned her in must have waited, knowing all along Pru would ring.

"It is late. How you get here, *Señora*?" She inspected Pru closely, a bit like Marion, after one of Pru's infrequent dates.

"They told me at the café. Your sister, she said—"

"Who bring you here?"

"My chauffeur." Why hadn't she said Tio? Was it that awkward silence that wedged itself between them as they started for the *Casa*? She had wanted to ride up front, next to him, to talk about the night but Tio sounded nervous, oddly unsure of himself. He had told her it wasn't proper. Hurt, she retreated to the back seat.

"My room, *por favor.*" She adopted Marion's haughty manner, it was none of the woman's business how she got here. The woman continued up the stairs, candle held high over her head. As Pru reached the first landing, she spotted someone below watching her from the shadows by the library door. She leaned out over the rail.

"Who is—?"

"Nothing, no one."

"But I saw—"

"You saw *nada, Señora. Nada.*"

Pru wanted to ask if around here *nada* meant none of your business; she thought better of it. "One more thing," Pru asked, her voice more conciliatory, "the room in the back, on the right, may I stay there?"

"The *Señora*, she know this place." Like the General, the woman appeared to have little need to ask questions. Pru did. Who was this woman, and why was it everyone seemed to know more about her than she did? Rodicio was a small village; it was possible the woman had worked here for years. But her sister knew only the name Brancusi, this one could know no different. If only she would turn around, the light was dim and Pru needed a better look at that impassive face.

"*Uno momento, Señora?* I wish to ask you—" but the woman continued up the stairs as if in a hurry to get this task over and done with. As they passed Nanny's old room, Pru felt that lump rising in her throat. Would it never go away.

She went on down the hall to her old room and a night filled with dreams of her childhood.

It would be morning before she realized that she forgot to ask Tio why he called her a Canadian.

THIRTY-THREE

Locked Drawers – 1950
> *"Secret guilt by silence is betrayed."*
>
> —JOHN DRYDEN, *The Hind and the Panther*

PRU SLEPT TRUSSED in a web of unfinished dreams. Bits and pieces—Spain and its crucifixes, soldiers, bayonets, her mother's scream, her father's treachery, execution squads and diaries floating out to sea. Toward morning her dreams filled with images of Tio, a Canadian flag, the mystery woman of the staircase and the shadowy figure in the hall. She whirled and spun and fought to come awake. But the air, its weight, left her languid, bereft of the willpower to push against it.

A voice drifted up from the patio below, and penetrated her reveries. The woman from last night? The keeper of *La Casa de Castillo*? Somewhere beneath those padded hips, stocky thighs, arms plumped up by good cooking and goat's milk, there existed a woman Pru felt she knew. Last night, when the door opened, something familiar peered out at her from between tight, little folds of skin, those wrinkles that lent gravity, dignity to a face that made such an effort not to smile.

From the patio below, the one voice separated into two—a

quarrel. She must get up. She opened her eyes. Three large nail holes high on the wall across from the bed, the place where the crucifix once hung, caught her attention. She was here, in Spain, back where it all started, back where it almost ended.

"Why you bring her?" Definitely a woman's voice.

"I no know."

And then the words *Americana* and *bastardo* wormed their way into her consciousness. She came fully awake.

"*Calma abajo.*" Tio's voice?

"That pampered little girl," the woman shrieked, "why you bring her here?" It had to be the onen from last night talking. "The nose of her, she is too long?"

The laugh that followed definitely belonged to Tio. Her nose did run on a bit, but not enough to cause this woman's hysteria. Maybe the woman's talk wasn't of her? She certainly wasn't a girl.

"She asks *muchas preguntas*? And, last night, she saw him. I know this. There will be trouble."

Pru sat up. If she is the *she*, could the *him*—last night's shadow in the hall—be her father? Her hopes soared but along with them came the image of that figure—too slim, too youthful. But then, who?

"If she sees him, what harm?"

"She'll try to take him—"

"*Ridículo*, you know who it is she comes for. Stop worrying, she'll not stay long. Why would any *Americano* stay in this village? The *Guardi Civil* will see to it. Even here buried in the backcountry we have our pride, and the spurning by so important a country hurts." So that's why Tio called her a Canadian.

"Oh, Tio, like all of them, you talk *mucho grande* but most would drop everything and go to America if they got the chance." The snap of fingers ricocheted in Pru's ears.

"And that one she like her *Papa*, I see it in her eyes. She take what she wants."

"*Mujer* stop your foolishness. Why would she want to? Even if she did, he no leave you. He's a good boy."

A boy? The figure slouched like a youth. The woman should listen to Tio. If the shadow didn't belong to her father, why would she be interested? Time to get up, get on with her day. Still she made no move; things change, she mustn't expect too much.

"That one, she no better than the boy, yet she have every thing . . . he has nothing."

"He has you."

"Bah. You think I not want more for him?"

The anger in the woman's voice shocked Pru. Why? What did it have to do with her? More importantly last night, in the café, Tio told her about an ossuary that lay but fifty or sixty kilometers to the north.

"It's an old one," he had said, "very small, not many important people, your *Papa*—"

"Maybe they didn't know who he was. If they'd known he was important, they wouldn't have shot him, would they?"

"You A*mericanos*." Tio's sigh had flickered the little candle on the table. How little she knew of war, of Spain and its ways.

Enough remembering of last night, of Tio's mysterious ways, enough of the woman's anger. Pru forced herself to go over to the window, make sure who the voices belonged to—she wasn't quick enough, the patio stood empty and not just of people. The pond. She knew it wouldn't—couldn't be there, not the same anyway; still she blanched at the bareness of it all. Its flat surface, ugly and gray, stretched from one side of the house to the other, interrupted only by the occasional tub of roses, red ones, yellow ones. Pale imitations of her goldfish, *Ora Aureo*, *Jaspeadora* and *Dorado Rojo*.

Pru tried to shake the memories. She needed time,

untroubled moments free of sadness; but what she needed most was to find her father, go home and get on with her own life. Hurriedly she dressed and headed down the stairs, hoping to catch Tio, set up the trip to the ossuary.

But the walls of the *casa* were not about to let her off. Though bare of paintings, the crucifixes gone, still the past shoved its way up through layers where her memories lay imprisoned. The teas, the dinners, the trips, the people that passed in and out of her life circled the rooms, vying for her attention. So many people that she once loved had disappeared. Love had become a complication Pru wasn't equipped to handle. To love someone invited the gods to step in, defy your hubris and take delight in seeing to it that what you loved vanished.

So little time, so much to absorb, so hard to understand. That's how she'd felt as a child. That's how she felt now.

Her memory disintegrated into the rubble of the convent, the bullet-pocked wall and thoughts of what might have happened to the sisters. She used to believe that those who were gone, the ones she had loved, would go on existing if she thought about them hard enough. At night, prayers done, she would spend time picturing her brother, what he might have done, his toy drums, his balls, his bats, the two of them on bicycles out in some park, circling round the flowers, even fishing. And then Nanny's name appeared on the list and it had become too painful to contemplate. The list had grown too long.

As she wandered through the *Casa*, she noticed that some of the furniture hadn't changed, even though a lot of important things had. The war over, the dead were dead, so it was with the pond, with her fish. For all her remembering, all her prayers, she had given no one back their life. Not Nanny, not the nuns, not even her father. She paused at the door of the dining room . . . had she, did she, ever pray for him?

She heard footsteps behind her and turned to see a sullen-faced young man—the one from last night? He motioned her into the main dining room, hurried into the pantry and drew the door closed behind him. Alone, except for a stray ghost or two that crouched in the corner—a whiff of tobacco, a hint of perfume—she saw the huge carved sideboard, now battered, scarred and barren of candle sticks, linens or silver. The elegance, the beauty that once belonged to the room had vanished, some of it while she and her mother were still there. She had her suspicions as to who took the silver, but the large pieces, the urn, the decorated platters, the sconces, the things that belonged to the *Casa* must have vanished later. Most probably pawned or commandeered during the war.

The young man returned carrying a pottery mug filled with steaming coffee and set it down in front of her. She smiled, *"Gracias."* He neither looked at her nor answered. Hurt and a little puzzled —she had done nothing to him, nothing to his mother—she didn't hear the woman come in, but her spirits rose at the aroma, the smell, the rich heavy spices. *Huevas a la Butifarra*—eggs and Catalan sausage, gently spiced with paprika and remembrances of the mornings she woke to the sweet smell of peppers and, still in her nightclothes, she would steal into the huge kitchen, duck under the hanging kettles and beg Cook for that spicy treat.

"No, no, Prudencia," Cook would tease, "you must eat like the Spaniard. I do the pastries and thick chocolate drinks for the morning. Only *esos locos, los americanos* ask for the broken eggs. No taste there. Nothing to wake the tongue." Despite Cook's protestations, at breakfast her plate appeared filled with fluffy eggs, liberally sprinkled with enough peppers to "wake the dead," Nanny would chide.

A coincidence? A twist of fate? Pru no longer believed in

the vagaries of fate. This must be someone's idea of a joke to serve that dish after all these years yet the woman didn't appear blessed with a sense of humor. Who put her up to this? Pru looked up at her, the same woman who showed her to her room last night. A pair of shrouded eyes set in a face studied in its blankness looked back. Perhaps a trick of shadow, a cloud passing over, the room dimmed. Hardly long enough for Pru to notice; but as the accusatory light of morning returned, the face bent over her gave up its secrets. Stripped of fourteen years, the weight of countless sweets and endless lonely nights, the pentimento of *Señora* Itturaldi lay exposed. Pru remembered the woman summoned from the village to replace the hastily banished English cook. Though it hadn't seemed that way at the time, the new cook was still young. The kitchen overheated with talk of her marriage to *un hombre sin valor*, a worthless man who followed the bulls and never sent money home to his wife. Young then and therefore invisible, Pru became privy to the back-hall gossip and knew the loves and sorrows of most of the locals: the first maid's husband headed a field crew for Don Carrillo, the butler played the guitar at the local café and the boy who delivered the cheeses washed his face on Sunday and helped serve mass. Cook, the stories went, was forced to marry a much older *Señor* Itturaldi, something about a debt her father owed, but *Señor* Itturaldi got stuck with a less than innocent bride, one who definitely knew a thing or two. She "*ha leido el libro.*" She remembered asking her father what they meant that she had "read the book," he had laughed and told her not to worry, he would not be assigning that volume to her.

Even without war, life in the backcountry of *Andalucía* came hard. Every hour, every day of the last fourteen years set their mark on *Señora* Itturaldi, making it difficult to believe that this woman with flesh that rumpled and dimpled into the carelessness of the aged, was only thirty-six or seven. Without the aroma of the sausages, Pru would never have recognized her.

But why the charade? Why pretend she didn't know Pru? Surely Tio already told her what he knew. Could she be waiting for Pru to speak first? Without the slightest glimmer of recognition, *Señora* Itturaldi set the platter down and retreated to the pantry, her look as sullen as that of the young man. Apparently everyone in Spain had their secrets, their reasons for remaining silent. Pru could wait. The eggs couldn't. It would be a sin to let them grow cold.

The door to the pantry remained shut, yet Tio hadn't left. The voices may have softened, the arguments stilled, but she could separate the cadences of Tio, his multi-lingual approach to things, from the *Señora's* terse answers. Finished with her eggs and the two of them occupied with each other, Pru thought it would be a good time to go into the library, begin her search.

At the door, she stopped as if confronted by some barrier, some barbed wire of the mind. She never entered the library— her father's domain, the pulse of any house he occupied—without his permission unless he happened to be somewhere else. Sometimes she couldn't resist the pull of his collection of forbidden volumes: *Medical Marvels*, with its diagrams of distorted bodies, two-headed babies, and the woman with a sling under her giant belly as she awaited the birth of her twenty-two babies— perhaps partially responsible for her not wanting children. The photos of the burning Hindenburg in *The Disasters of the World*, or the drawing of the collapse of an earthen dam in India. Her hand on the doorknob, she couldn't shake the sense of herself shrinking. Expecting to feel her Mary-Jane's pinch as they squeezed her toes, she looked towards her feet but saw only her sturdy walking shoes. Stiffening her resolve, she pushed her way in.

Though badly scarred and worn in places, the chairs, the

tables, the throw rugs were as she remembered. Dark and massive, the desk squatted on the tile floor, an impenetrable fortress of locked drawers and secret cubbyholes. She thought of the night it gave away its secrets. But now, as she pulled on the drawer—the center drawer—it wouldn't budge.

"As is," the lease had stated when they rented the house. Don Carrillo, a man of great pride, Rubio said, surrounded himself with the furnishings that had served his family for years. He had made a half-hearted offer, he would move his things if the Whitleys insisted. "But, *Señor*, the house, the furnishing, one is nothing without the other." As they had no time to buy new, her father agreed. The upstairs sitting room with its stately-homes-of-England overstuffed pieces had been a sop to her mother's comfort.

After all the changes, the destruction of people and places, it seemed odd that here in this room so little had changed. The new owner, this mysterious German, had not done much. He plastered over a few holes, repaved the patio, but no one had bothered to repair or replace the crucifixes she last saw lying splintered on the floor, covered with excrement. If Don Carrillo had sold his beloved *Casa* to this man, he wouldn't have left the family's heirlooms, portraits and rugs behind.

That couch. That damn couch—it's still here. Another trick of light and she thought she could still see the imprint of their bodies in the crushed and torn leather. She stretched out her hand to touch the cushions, put her fingers in the cracks, rip out the stuffing. She drew back as if some unexploded shell, some invisible fire still burned within.

Pru turned away, walked over to the desk, not a little chagrined at the deliberate way she struck her heels against the tiles to drive the past from its hiding place. Despite the clicking and clacking, her bravado drained away like a tidal basin after a quake. Slowly she reached out, ran her hands across its marred surface. What violence, what turmoil had it taken to scar such things, such symbols of indestructibility? Without plan or conscious thought her fingers sought out the latch on the middle drawer. She remembered the day her mother broke it.

So much in this house had fallen into disrepair—every room, every piece of furniture or bric-a-brac carried the onus of war, the scars of neglect. The detail of a broken lock seemed such a minor matter—the desk didn't really look as if anyone used it. And yet here in this house, abandoned by its master, disintegrating under the present owner's sins of omission, it came as a shock to discover that someone had taken the time, the trouble to fix this one thing. The drawer would not open. She tugged and tugged. She looked around to find something to pry it open, all the anger she felt at the couch, her mother, at Helen, her father, came rushing up at her. She took it out on that desk. It didn't matter that she pummeled it with her fist, kicked at its legs—the drawer stayed shut, as if to tell her that some secrets were meant to remain secret.

The door to the library opened. "Will the *Señora* be taking lunch with us?"

It took Pru a moment, she stared right through the woman. Cook cleared her throat, repeated her question.

Pru found her voice. "Thank you, no. I have made plans. I will be going—" She stopped. Perhaps she should keep her plans to herself for now. But Cook had talked to her. She must keep the door open, somehow. "Thank you for the eggs. As always, they were delicious."

Isabelle smiled. *"De nada."*

But Pru knew was learning about *de nada*. In this country nothing ever turned out to be *nothing*.

Pru found herself caught between Isabella's stoicism and her mother's craziness. What happened to the defiant child that asked all the questions, demanded the answers. How many times had Henri come home and found her disgusted with her complicity in her mother's schemes, the way she avoided reality? And yet wasn't she playing the same game now with Isabelle?

So what to do about it? "Nothing, absolutely nothing," Henri's solution was to take her dancing. While they waited for their margaritas to arrive, he would remind her that the love of a child for a parent is both irrational and uncontrollable. "It's all bound up in guilt, in need—good fodder for a movie, but hard to live with."

"So what's to be done about it?"

"Absolutely nothing," he would say as he led her out to the dance floor.

"That's exactly what Nanny would say." The two were a lot alike, though Henri was the better dancer. If only he were here now; she needed his common sense even more than his dancing. She had let the past get the better of her. She would get away from the *Casa*, the dusty curtains, the noisy ghosts. Nanny would say she needed exercise, fresh air and a colonic. She would skip the latter but she could at least get out and explore the village. Perhaps she might learn why so much of life was *nada*.

THIRTY-FOUR

Oregano, Rosemary and other Spells
"Secret guilt by silence is betrayed."

—JOHN DRYDEN, *The Hind and the Panther*

IT HADN'T CHANGED all that much—this village already
so old that fourteen years became but a mere hiccup in time.
The war had left a mark, but far less than her memories would
have led her to believe. A few buildings showed the effects of
bullets and shells, here and there a wall appeared missing; but
the savvy villagers knew better than to foul their own nest. They
fired their anger at the church, the large landholders, places
like the *Casa de Carrillo*. In the village, the butcher still hung his
carcasses in the window, the baker baked his breads in the same
oven and the goat boy roamed the streets hawking his milk—
not the same boy, he would be grown by now —and the goat
most likely eaten during hard times. Rubio too would be grown
and his donkey—would anyone eat a donkey?

The smell of rosemary and oregano led her to the town
square, its herb garden, its fountain dappled with a few inept
patches and the occasional new tile; but the water looked as
clear and inviting as she remembered. Plumbing had yet to find

its way down into the village.

The women waiting to fill their jugs welcomed her. They had no need for such a divisive invention. "Sinks, faucets, so *poco amistoso*, the devil's design for separating friends." You couldn't count on a man to carry home the news of village. Men's talk left out so much of what really mattered: *Señora* Garcia's new baby, the late hour Carmelita's husband returned home, the marriage of Lumina to Pablo and the size of Lumina's belly under the white gown. Pru heard the music of the fountain in the cadence of their vowels, the way their laughter tumbled from their lips; but when she answered no, no and no to their queries about her life, they looked at her so sympathetically, she felt a hollow place open up, one she hadn't known she possessed.

They handed her a water jug and motioned for her to drink. She tilted it onto her shoulder and sipped. The women laughed conspiratorially when she spilled a little, but it was a friendly laugh. They told her that the priests were back, saying their masses, baptizing the babies, but when she asked about the nuns, the women grew quiet, peering at her suspiciously. No one answered.

The camaraderie broken, she said her goodbyes, thanked them for the cool drink and moved on to investigate the row of shops, the huge banner-draped portraits of Franco that effaced outdated slogans. As unwelcome as Tio had told her the portraits might be, no one dared deface them these days.

She moved off into the country, away from the church so as not to see its crumbling façade. She walked to the edge of the escarpment. The fields that lay in the valley below looked like patches for a homemade quilt. She followed a trail here and there but by late afternoon hunger overcame her.

She walked back into town, to the *tapas* bars, the cafés. In the largest one, she ran into Tio. He appeared pleased to see her. "*Señora*, the sights, you see them, no?"

"I see them, yes."

"Ah good, now I will show you the real Rodicio." And for the next few days, he did. She welcomed Tio's distractions where she had feared Lemona's. He introduced her to the shop-keepers, the local schoolteacher. On Sunday he even took her to mass where they received more than their share of stares. The bleached lace of the altar cloths, the bundles of flowers heaped at the foot of the statues, banished signs of the war. Even the baby Jesus had found his way back to Mary's lap.

Some days they did their sightseeing in nearby villages, on others they wandered the countryside, watched the goats and sheep graze, fished the streams. Tio made tackle from a willow branch and string. They spent their evenings at a table in the café. Some times, the proprietress cooked their catch. Last night a steaming casserole greeted them; rabbit, braised in its own thyme-drenched juices. Tio speared little morsels onto her plate, covering them with bits of onion, cloves of garlic that glistened like pearls in their bath of wine. "Food fit for the saints," he had said, "prepared by the faithful."

On this, the fifth night, the two of them ate their din-ner companionably as they listened to the wings of a lunar moth beating its way through the night. Something inside her responded to the tireless but futile throb of the small creature and she began to talk of her father, the night of the man in the beret, the knock at the door.

How to explain her father, his constant need for the new, the rare, the things most people only read about. Men had warned him that with the war to end all wars over, a gentleman of the civilized West might live his whole life and never experience such horrors. Tio nodded in apparent understanding, even sympathy, with her father's need to take advantage of any small outbreak or sporadic revolution, to accept it as reasonable that a man might love his wife, his child and still feel the need to take such risks.

How could he? She must make Tio see the wrong her father had done. She told of the night in the library, the little animal cries at the back of the room. How she had blamed her mother, resented her, but he would never have done such a thing without Helen's scheming.

"A good wife, she knows men's needs—"

"My God, you Spanish, your *machismo*. Men! You men,—" she stopped. Who was she to chastise Tio? Hadn't she blamed her mother, Helen, herself—everyone? She hated her father for going, but had she blamed him?

"And you," he teased, "did you understand him? Did you love him without the need to understand, the way a woman should?"

"Should! Should," she tried not to shout. How could she love him unconditionally? "Didn't all children defy their fathers? Test them?" He certainly had his conditions: that she be good, that she be smart, that she be everything he wanted her to be.

Tio seemed puzzled. How could she be so sure? The swiftness of her answer startled even her. As much as she found her father lacking in love for her, just that much she knew she had come up short of his expectations. Why else would he have pushed and prodded her to be better, to work harder? She had shamed him and so he shamed her for the amusement of his friends.

Tio's eyes filled with disbelief. "But he did," she insisted, "he did." The poetry, the way he made her recite for his guests. He selected poems no child of eight, maybe nine, voice pitched high, tense with anxiety, should even try. "Forward the Light Brigade Charge for the Guns," she had squeaked. The laughter started before she reached the second line. She had stopped, wheeled about and screamed in his face, "I hate you, I hate you."

Tio tried to hold back his own laughter. He couldn't. "I am

sorry, *pequeña;* but how is a father to love such a child?"

"Okay, okay. It's funny. But still, a father . . .."

"You are right, of course."

Such a silly, unimportant thing. How absurd that she had let it hurt her all these years. Had she but known the horrors gestating in the belly of a continent: the burning churches, synagogues, firing squads, open pit graves and gas chambers, things might have gone differently. But how could she foresee that, with the crash of a sudden summer storm, bombs would rain down on cities, washing away everything—houses, children?

"Oh, *Señora,* you must not take the blame, you are right, there is no way to know what life holds. Who would want to?"

Despite his reassurances, the sense of liberation she felt the past few days vanished. The weight of childhood, its powerlessness, settled back down on her. Would she always be plagued with her seeming inability to take control of her own life? How much longer would she just let things happen to her?

"All children suffer that indignity," Tio shrugged. "They get over it. The girl turns around and suddenly, the first child is born and she is a woman. For the man it comes when he is tested by war, his first battle."

"Which hurts more," she asked.

He laughed. "Why you no have babies?"

She had other things to do, she said. Despite her pleasure at the chatter of the village women, she didn't want children. She tried to explain about painting, how important it was to her. Her future lay in there somewhere. "But I can't seem to go forward until . . .." It wasn't a matter of age, or babies. She had lost herself, swimming in a lake of swaying reeds, flotsam obscuring the way, a veil of consciousness that kept her from seeing herself, her future clearly. The details yes, what she would do tomorrow, that sort of thing she could see well enough, but the big picture, the meaning of things, eluded her. She seemed mired in the worries of a daughter—that her father might not love her mother enough, that he might not want a silly child who spent her vomit on a dying bull. She could forgive her childish doubts, but not the fact that they still bothered her. What is normal for a child, is irrational in the adult. That all that might still be part of her, important to her, that's what she couldn't forgive. "That's why I've come," she explained. Why else would she agree to undertake this journey, to ignore the mystery of Cook, the warnings of the envoy, the machinations of General Lemona? About her guilt, her broken promises, Pru said nothing.

"You are like your Papa, then. No?"

Had she any of that bravado, determination left? "Yes. No. Oh." She tried to shake an image of her father on the couch, his pants around his ankles, of Marion, dependent on her husband, on Bazil and the glass in her hand.

Tio listened as she rambled on about the time after her father left. That's where her real story started. "You mean the story, she is not about to end?"

"Don't I wish," she said. As Tio laughed and poured more wine, a little ache crept down her arm, as if she held a weight too heavy to bear. She looked at her arm, outstretched, reaching for something to hold on to—perhaps a hand, the soft, plump hand of Nanny.

Like a swarm of unwelcome flies, an uncomfortable stillness smothered the café. Guitars rested in their stands, glasses deposited tired rings on tables, and even the candles steadied their flame. The room waited, silently, politely—hushed by a story she hadn't meant to tell, to a people who had no need to hear it. She flushed with shame. How could she inflict her pain on a people who had already endured so much?

Tio took her hand, wrapped it in his, brushing it lightly against his lips. "*Mi pequeño*, I am so sorry. *Sus heridas*, your hurts they are many." Candles sputtered. Glasses were raised. Life went on. With the abruptness of a moth veering to avoid a flame, his smile disappeared. He glanced around the room, the drinkers once more absorbed in their own lives.

"Everyone carries their own cross." She wanted to tell him she knew, but he left her no space. His voice tangled with his emotions, "No one escapes *los dolores de vida*. You are young yet, why you wallow in sorrows? Life she doesn't go on that long, not long enough to waste time wresting secrets from crumbling walls. *Tu Niñera*"—Pru took comforted in his use of *Tu*—"your Nanny, your Papa they are gone. Poof, that is it. We are here, you and I. Soon enough we go. There is this saying in the cafés of *mi Andalucía*—to wander down the line of time, is to walk a path leading to sorrow. If you wish to avoid the pain, the dance, she will be gone."

"The dance?"

"The pleasures, the joys, one cannot have those without *Los Dolores*."

"But why not? I am tired of the pain, my mother's pain—it's just too much."

"Why you carry *su Madre's*? In this country, it is the mother who carries the child's. *Usted norteamericanos, usted confunde cosas.*

"You don't understand—"

"*Es no necessario*. Your glass, she needs the filling." He filled it. He filled it again. And again. She stopped worrying about her *dolores*, his changeable English, his *machismo* and even his use of *mi Andalucía*, his poetic sayings, his philosophy. Had he said such things in clipped English, they would sound pompous, overbearing but the very earthiness of his Spanish, his little grammatical glitches ground his thoughts and gave his words the ring of truth, of peasant wisdom. Wrapped in a glow of wine, she would let Tio be as Spanish as he wanted.

They left the café and made their way up the hill. The walk helped to clear her head. She must tell him about tomorrow, what she wanted to do. She hadn't missed the point of his adage, but she would have no peace until she knew. She must go to the cemetery.

As they walked up the hill towards the *Casa* the night air settled lightly against her skin like the blessings of a priest, the anointing of the oils of forgiveness, and a quiver, a slight flutter—contentment? Happiness? Something more exhilarating, silenced her. Tio sensed her uneasiness.

"You have it once more, *Señora*—your serious face. Your papa, he is the ghost, *el espiritu se preocupa.* He burrows into your soul. Forget the past."

"I want to, Tio, I want to. I'm so tired of wasting time with the detritus of my past."

"I no know this detritus, but look to the stars, *Señora* and tell me your fancy. I will pluck it down for you."

In one of those moments she would later wish could have lasted forever. She pointed high in the sky to a star off a bit, all on its own. "That one, *por favor.*"

THIRTY-FIVE

The Ossuary

> "*. . is come to lay his weary bones among ye*"
>
> —SHAKESPEARE, *King Henry VIII, Act III*

PRU WOKE TO A HEAD ON FIRE. Nowhere near ready for
an assault mounted by the clear unfiltered light of a Spanish
morning, she kept her eyes shut. The roughness of the stone-
washed sheets against her skin carried her back to last night, the
touch of Tio's hands, so strong, so stable ... and yet she felt sad,
as if she had lost something. Last night she had hoped that Tio
had felt something too. "I will fix your sadness," he had said and
she felt a rush, heard the noise of a thousand trains on a thousand tracks. She had looked up at him expectantly, but his face
hadn't softened like it should have, like hers had. And when he
spoke the magic shattered: "Tomorrow we go and look for word
of him." He hadn't understood at all. Her ache had nothing to
do with her father.

Now in the harsh light of morning, the kind that rarely
allows one to indulge in self-delusion, she decided to on a little
bout of self-pity, a no-one-understands-me pout. She wouldn't
get up, she'd stay there forever and nurse her hurt; but the rich

386

smell of coffee pried open her eyes. The boy stood in the doorway, holding out a cup. His shoulders hunched, drawn up into
himself, he studied her carefully as if he thought she held the key
to what prevented his shoulders from straightening. With her
head pounding from the *Amantillados*, she just wanted him gone.

She motioned for him to leave the coffee on the bureau. He
set the cup down but made no move to go. She shut her eyes,
opened them again. He hadn't budged. Once more she waved
him off. He stood his ground. "What is it like *Señora?*"

"What is what like?"

"Your country?"

"Like everything, like nothing. But the coffee, *por favor.*" A
look of comprehension, some sort of animation lit up his face.
He gave her a tentative smile, his diffidence gone, replaced with
a touch of haughtiness, the way people who are a touch unsure
of themselves cover it up.

She would say no more. He left. She drank the coffee then
got up. At the pitcher on her dresser, she poured the water into
the porcelain basin. Hand-painted clusters of butterwort flowed
around its rim, the pale yellow of the petals, the delicate green
of their slender stems lifted her spirits. Nanny and Tio were both
right. There were pleasures to be had if one focused on the present. She gave herself over to the cold of the water, the roughness
of the towel. Over at her mirror, hairbrush in hand, she admitted that perhaps it was better this way, better that she and Tio
kept it all business. Would she never be ready for something
more than a temporary pleasure, an itch scratched, a pain banished? Was it her fault? She shouldn't have talked so much. If
only she had listened she might have asked his real name. The
Tio thing, the uncle, maybe that's what got in the way.

She laughed. The mirror threw the boy's smile back at her
and something more—the image of Marion, standing by her

desk, locking those letters out of sight. *No, no, not now. Not yet.* She pushed the image away.

She dressed, started for the stairs and heard voices down below. The front door slammed. A moment later, the gate squeaked. She went to the window in time to see Tio hurrying back towards town, the hunched figure of Cook at his side. What now?

Downstairs in the dining room, a place was set for her. She ate her breakfast, cold pastries and endless cups of coffee carried in by the boy who now appeared melancholy. Once or twice she tried to draw him out. How much did he know? What had the *Señora* told him? Obviously something, why else would he have looked her over so carefully? And yet, it couldn't be true—there was nothing to tell. Wouldn't she have felt something? Surely there would be more than this dull numbness, the way she felt when confronted—but he hadn't confronted her. She had to get hold of herself, quiet that inherited sense of the dramatic that left her so open to suspicions. There was nothing to this, nothing for Isabelle to tell, for him to know. *Nada. Nada. Nada.*

Her coffee grew cold, was Tio ever going to come for her? What were those two up to? Tired of all the mystery, the intrigue, she wouldn't wait around to find out. She'd find someone else, some other way to get there, not that she knows exactly where the cemetery was. Perhaps the boy knew. Through the window she watched him chopping and hacking away at the bougainvillea with an angry sort of vigor. Maybe it was only the extra work her rooming at the *Casa* caused that fueled his anger.

Later she heard voices in the kitchen, and went to the door, pushed it open. Cook had returned. That secretive slope to her shoulders reminded Pru of the day of the pillowcase. Perhaps she thought Pru had come for the silver as well as the boy? She had no interest in the silver, she even hoped the money had somehow made *Señora* Itturaldi's life a little easier during the war, the hard times that followed. Better it bought food, she thought, than that it purchased rifles, killed women, children. Maybe even the Mayor. She decided to say nothing. She would ask about the Ossuary instead.

"Someone told me of the burial ground near here—" not exactly the truth, she'd overheard it, but still—"I have need—"

"No."

"But they said not too far from the village, somewhere between Rodicio and Galatea I would find—"

"You will find nothing, *Señora*. There is nothing to see between Rodicio and Galatea, only barren land. The small hectares left to the peasants are too sewn with mines for the farming."

"But at the embassy—"

"You and your embassies, your passports, your America! Go away, *Señora*." Startled by the outburst, Pru hadn't time to avoid the finger waggled in her face. "Leave us in peace. You come here and upset everyone with your stories, your questions." Pru stepped back..

"Who? Who have I upset?" And then she looked beyond the tears in the woman's eyes and saw the boy, his fists clenched, his face botched. A little dot of red smeared across his lip where his teeth chewed on his lip.

"What is it, Cook? What is wrong?

"I am not your cook."

"I am sorry, I meant *Señora* Itturaldi.

"Ah, so you do know my name?"

"The eggs, the way you fixed the eggs." For just a moment Pru thought the *Señora* might smile.

"Do not concern yourself with me," she scowled. "Finish your business and be gone. Why you want to unbury the dead, anyway?"

"The dead? Then you know, you know about my father?" Pru almost choked on her words. Of course Cook would know about her father, probably more than she did. "You know what happened to him?"

"How could I? You saw me here in the house that night, remember?"

It took Pru a moment to remember, so many were there. "Oh, yes. The money, you were worried about the money." The look of contempt on the woman's face, her anger, all probably justified. "I was little, *Señora* I don't remember much."

Pru thought things might go better if she could reassure the *Señora* the she had no interest in taking the boy—why would she even want to? And furthermore she didn't care about the silver or whatever else was missing. The two stood there staring at each other for a minute, two; and then Pru thought of a way she to get through to the woman.

"The *Casa*, you keep it up very nicely. It's good that you have such a strong son to help you, it's good that he stays with his mother." *Señora* Itturaldi hesitated a moment and then walked towards Pru, the tight little lines around her mouth relaxed a bit, her eyes softened. She looked almost younger, almost her age, which wasn't all that much older than Pru's. War, an illegitimate child in a Catholic country, to say nothing of poverty, didn't help a woman's looks.

"Perhaps, *Señora* Brancusi, you will find what you seek if you don't look so hard for it."

Pru sensed a truce. She would try, she said; in the meantime she must walk down to the village, find Tio, she had hired him after all. She had only to tell him where she wanted to go.

"I will go and find Tio, *hasta luego*." *Señora* Itturaldi gave a little chuckle. "All right so my Spanish is still awful." She started for the door with no idea of how to find him. He was there, leaning against the car, waiting for her.

They hadn't traveled more than an hour when he pulled the car to the side of the road. "Here, this is it, this is where . . ." She sensed his disappointment in her. They hardly spoke on the drive out. She let her hand rest on the skirt pocket where she had placed her father's picture. She wasn't sure why she put it there but it helped to give her the courage to go through with this.

When the dust on the road settled bit, she stepped from the car and there, spread before her she saw acres and acres of graves. She hadn't counted on so many. "How will I find—"

"Do you wish for me to go with you, *Señora?*" Tempted as she might be to accept his offer, the scowl on his face told her what he thought of her plan.

"No, this is something I must do alone."

"As you wish."

"Perhaps though, *Señor,* you would be good enough to tell me where to start?"

"Up there on the hill, do you see that shed?" He pointed to an area enclosed by a rather haphazard fence made up of wooden slats so old, so dried out, they tilted with the crazy angles of drunken sentinels. In some places they appeared to have collapsed and lay almost touching the ground.

She started up the hill toward the gatehouse. The sun warmed her, a small breeze carried the sweet smell of rabbit brush. The sky, the earth had entered into a conspiracy to keep her mind off the secrets buried beneath her feet. It wasn't enough.

Hundreds of small mausoleums climbed the hill. In ragged

rows they told their stories, oozed their sorrows. Family burial plots, three or four bodies encased in stone-walls one on top of the other, some with extra room, waiting for others to come and join them in their obliteration. Between each layer she noticed little ledges crowded with crucifixes, religious medals and, on the newer graves, silver candlesticks. It took awhile to realize what was missing from all this show of piety: epitaphs. No here-lies-a-noble-father, a-selfless-mother; no exhortations to rest-in-peace-beloved-daughter-of. None of those telling clues that exposed the lives of the dead, the lives of the ones left behind.

Beyond the mausoleums, those less possessed of this world's goods were consigned to the damp. Elaborate statues, the Virgin, St. Anne and small angels made up for the inconvenience. As if competing for God's attention, each monument stretched higher, shouted louder than the one before: hear me, bless me, I am the more deserving. How like the cities of the living, the land of the dead.

As she reached even humbler graves, she thought she could almost hear the whispers, the smothered pleas for help—the dead in their grief for the loss of ones to mourn them, the nothingness of it all. Their pitifully small headstones jostled each other for space. She looked around for a place to sit.

As she neared the fenced-off area she saw a man leaning against the door, his face like old leather left too long in the sun. He looked at her with indifference, his eyes dulled by a film impenetrable as a widow's veil.

"*Buenos dias.*" He ignored her feeble attempt at pleasantries. His face had forgotten it once knew how to smile; the muscles it took to form such an expression, so long unused, lay flaccid beneath his skin.

"I am looking for the grave of one Roland P. Whitley?"

"There is no such a one here."

"But there are many, how would you know?"

"*Señora*, I have watched over them for many years, we have become friends, the dead and I."

"But I was told—" She had to make herself understood. "I was told that sometimes, that at . . . that I might find the . . ." She didn't think it would be this hard. Maybe if she tried a little Spanish; the words might seem less hurtful in a foreign tongue. She took a deep breath. "*Quiero encontrar los huesos de* . . . the bones of Roland P. Whitley." There, she'd done it, she had spoken of her father not as a person, but as a loose connection of ossified remains. She felt sick.

"Ah that, she is different." He seemed pleased. "*La Señora* has come then to pay for a proper burial?"

It's true, then. He is dead after all. She felt deflated. How odd. She hadn't realized she still held out hope that he lived, nor how much she cared. The answer came so easily she resisted it. Some part of her refused to accept his death, just as she and her mother refused to believe the man in the beret. She couldn't leave now. "I wish, that is I must see for myself where —"

"*¿Dónde qué es?*"

"I told you, the grave."

"I know of no such grave." She realized her mistake. "I mean the temporary burial place, I wish to see where the bones of Roland P. Whitley are."

"I do not know that name."

"But you said they were your friends—"

"I remember them when they receive proper burial. For a modest price I even arrange for the Sacraments. Until then, they are no one. This *Señor* Whitley, when he die? In the war?"

"Yes."

"Ah, with you foreigners it is always the war. Like the bad tooth, you no let her go."

"Well I think . . . that is I think so. I am not sure. Somewhere surely you have the names of those—" She pointed back toward the enclosure.

"We are not savages. We keep records."

"And may I see them?"

"They are not here, *Señora*."

"Then where?"

"You must go to the office."

There would be more delays, more forms to decipher, and another bureaucrat to appease. Angered, irritated and deflated, she turned to go and only then did she notice the spectacular view in front of her. Looking past the seemingly endless jumble of graves, across the road, beyond Tio and the car, she saw a plain so vast it extended to the horizon. Across its length and breadth olive trees retreated in neat, evenly spaced rows and the rows multiplied into groves, each grove butting up against its neighbor at precise right angles. The whole pattern made a mockery of the graves, their disorganization. How could Cook, the gossip of Rodicio, not know of this vast a landholding? Men from the village most probably found work here. Why had she told her the land was sewn with mines? But landmines came in all different kinds. Did Isabelle hate her father that much? And then a thought caught up with her, it wasn't all that new, it had whirled its way around in her mind since morning —could Isabelle have loved her father? Her father, a romantic figure? Daughters had trouble contemplating such things. But then her mother loved him, Helen loved him, why not *Señora* Itturaldi?

The old man cleared his throat. She turned back in time to see a huge glob of spittle wet the ground as he motioned her towards the door. "*La oficina*, she is here."

Once her eyes adjusted to the dim light, she saw a room furnished with one chair, its leather cracked, the floor littered with its stuffing and a wood-burning stove. "It gets cold up here on the hill, cold and lonely. Not many come any more." His eyes directed her towards a door at the rear of the room. "In there." She tried the handle, the door wouldn't open. A little push and it gave way. Pru stumbled into a room no bigger than her mother's shoe closet, the air inside older than the gatekeeper. She tried not to gag.

"Here it is written, everything, the deaths, the executions. All done with papers, writs." The books closest to her were bound in leather, their gold dates hard to decipher. The first one said 1820. Two volumes down she saw 1920 but as the years went on the volumes grew in number and size, leather gave way to cardboard bindings. The first one was dated May 1931. Sometime in 1939 the numbers tapered off.

Her eyes traveled across the shelf until she came to 1936. She would begin with the July entries. She took down the book, two cardboard covers with loose papers tied inside, and looked for a place to put it down so she could sort through it. The old man pointed to the stove.

Pru walked back and forth between the two rooms, each time checking a different volume. Her back ached from bending over the cold stove. Her eyes burned from trying to decipher various spidery handwritings in the half-light of the shed. After an hour or so, she found July 23rd— Foreign Newsman—*nombre no sabe.*

"Ah yes, the one without a name, we move him to the pit not too long ago."

"But how? The date, so recent."

"True this one he die many years ago. But a lady, no two ladies they come, each alone, but they come and pay and pay. But still she not enough monies for the proper burial. Then the first one she no come anymore, then the other. We dig him up."

Pru could almost smell Helen. Did one have red hair, red, red hair? But she couldn't ask the question; the words wouldn't come, not in English, not in Spanish. Could the other be Isabelle? But Isabelle had no money. She turned to the gatekeeper, tears of frustration in her eyes. How little she knew about the man who fathered her.

"Come, we will check the body. Perhaps the *Señora* remembers a coat, a cap, some article of clothing?" A clear sharp picture of her father blocked out the old man —his tan jodhpurs, his boots, his fact-finding, getting-down-to-business clothes as he called them. Nanny had it right when she said he wore them because they made him feel like a *working stiff.*

The old man coughed as if to get her attention back, "If they weren't requisitioned or stolen you might be able to identify them."

"Where?" She spun around the room.

"Outside, *Señora,* in *el osario.*"

He led her around in back of the shed and opened a small gate into the fenced in area. At first she saw only mounds of earth, each mound stabbed by a wooden stake with numbers etched across it. "This is where they wait, hoping their families will come." He pointed to yet another fence, a tall one kept in good repair, "This is where the luckless ones wind up." He led her over there. As they neared the smaller gate, she gagged. A heavy dank smell, not the freshness of the rabbit brush, but the stench of something gone bad, the underbelly of hell turned over by a pitchfork. He opened the gate and she stepped into an area where bags of bones dotted the field like refuse dropped carelessly from the back of a truck. She shuddered at the piles of old rags, bones jutting out from a sleeve, a pant leg, torn and molding fragments of cloth.

Time had a way of burning everything the color of charcoal. A button, a belt buckle, but that was about all she could see in the rubbish. "What your Papa he wear the last day you see him?" The caretaker hovered over her, trying to be helpful. She wanted him to go away, leave her alone. Did he think she would steal the bones? That he wouldn't be able to collect his burial fee? "The rules," he said, "they do not permit the unattended visitor."

"Jodhpurs, boots. High ones."

"What is this jodhpurs?" He didn't wait for an answer. "The newsman, he is over here." He led her to the edge. She looked down. Her legs buckled, she knelt at the edge of a pit. Her mind wouldn't take in what it saw. A hole, filled three-quarters full, some dirt, some skulls, some bits of bone. She saw things that could be a whole body more or less intact, held together by clothing so encrusted with dirt it was hard to tell what they were. Pants? Coats?

"It's not much, our pit. Twelve meters long, seven meters across, the smallest onion in the bunch. Now in the bigger towns, Madrid—"

"Stop, I don't want to know anymore."

"As *la Señora* wishes." The old man hunched his shoulders with indifference. "That's him, that gray coat." Her father's riding pants were khaki but the sun might have bleached them as it did the bones. Who knows? She had come this far, she forced herself to lean over, take a closer look. No lip, no edge to the pit, she could see herself toppling, her body plunging through an ocean of dusty bones into Dante's inferno. She shook her head to clear it and saw the heap of rags he pointed to. A pair of tattered pant legs jutted out from the lump of cloth that might once have been gray, she really couldn't tell. After a moment, tears of relief dripped little rivulets of mascara down her cheeks. There, where the pant legs ended, an ordinary pair of shoes, cheap leather oxfords, nothing her father would have worn. No jodhpurs. No boots.

397

She scrambled up, stepped back from the pit and let out an involuntary gulp. Air, she needed air, lots of it.

"How can you—?"

"I'm used to it, *Señora*. It is only the damp, the clothes, the dead they no smell after all this time. Your nose she will get used to it. She took another breath, the second, better than the first. He was right. Already the smell seemed no worse than the corner of some old attic, open to the ravages of sun and rain.

"Do not upset yourself, *Señora*. War, she is like that, a bad smell. But, no need for the worry, sometimes after the harvest the villagers come and help me with the burials."

"And the killing, did you get used to that too?"

The old man began to cough. For a few minutes he sputtered and choked. Should she help? Should she pat him on the back? She didn't think she could bring herself to touch him. The coughing stopped. "Would the *Señora* like to see the wall—"

"Here? They shot them here? I thought—"

"Some, they brought them in trucks, less dead weight to carry." His face almost, but not quite, escaped his grim demeanor. Clearly he had used his little joke before. "The men, they jumped or were pushed from the trucks, all roped together. A lot of them fell, I could hear bones breaking. They marched them over there." He pointed in the direction of a low stone wall, chipped away in a thousand places. From a thousand bullets.

"Only a few they try to run. By the time they got here, they were so tired, so long without hope."

"In the back?"

"Oh no, I told you, we are not savages. Their backs were to the wall."

"Then the last thing they saw . . . this, this . . . pit?"

"Sí, *Señora,* it could not be avoided." Her anger and her pain must have shown. "It was night, the stars, the moon, they not come that often. Most were young. The young have so much more to lose. They could hardly see through their tears."

My God, why hadn't she thought of it before? "You were here then, during the executions?" He didn't answer. She reached into the pocket of her slacks.

"This man, do you remember—?"

He looked at the picture carefully, turned it upside down, as one might view a body. "Ah no *Señora, No lo sé.* I told you, it was night, always night when the trucks they come. There were so many."

She forced her mind away from the sound of his voice. Tio, Cook, their argument. What if it was about not letting her get too close to whatever they wanted to keep hidden— her father, alive somewhere and living with Helen? It must be that, if he were shot, what would they have to hide? They hadn't done it. In Madrid, it would be the Fascists; nearer to Rodicio, if what General Lemona's men said rang true, it would be the Communists. And Cook, at the Casa that night, she couldn't have done the shooting. Tio could have played no part. He hadn't come south until after the war—and yet, she heard echoes of the *mi* of Tio's *mi Andalucía* from the night before. She shook off her ridiculous suspicions. The activists, the ideologues, the anarchists—very few escaped. The death books told the stories. March 1937 filled one volume by itself. Another for April. One more for May.

"*Los exaltados*," the old man spoke gently, she hadn't realized it but she must have given voice to her thoughts, "No matter of what stripe, what color their beret, *Los exaltados*, the extremists, they rarely survive."

She had to get away or she wouldn't survive. She started back down the hill, then turned back and took out several bills and handed them to the keeper. Her eyes were so clouded over with tears that she couldn't tell what they were but it must have been enough, he touched his cap, "*Gracias, Señora,* may you find what you seek and may what you find be worth the seeking." Were all Spaniards poets? Perhaps so much death made poets, or at least philosophers of them all.

She made her way down the slope, past the graves of the rich, the well known, the loved. When she got to the car the driver's seat was empty. She opened the rear door and saw Tio sprawled across the back seat. His snores eased her way back to the land of the living.

She opened the door to the front, started to climb in, then stopped. The rocking of the car woke him.

"*Señora,* did you—?"

"No, nothing."

He seemed almost relieved. "I did not think so. Not here."

"Then why didn't you say something?" She walked around to the far side of the car, to face the olive grove. The trees appeared to be freshly planted; perhaps Cook didn't know about the place after all. She must get over feeling that everyone wanted to harm her. The real pain wasn't coming from outside. Memories hurt more, far more.

Tio came up behind her. "You wouldn't have believed me. And you were right—there are things one must do for oneself."

"The records didn't tell much."

"Our records, we were not as careful as the Germans. We had our trials, not like your Nuremberg. We dealt with ours quickly. It goes differently when the world is not watching. This is a small ossuary, not so important, a forgotten wayside of the war. Madrid, we go there. The records are more complete. And it's larger, much larger."

"Another ossuary?"

"*Sí*"

"I don't think I could, the pit . . . there must be a better way—"

"¿Madre de Dios, Prudencita, the gatekeeper he no take you in there?" She could only nod. "Come, I take you home."

Pru settled back in the seat of the car, hot, tired and discouraged, feeling as used up and thrown away as the heaps of rags and bones that piled up behind her eyes. Tio studied her through the rear view mirror. The olive trees flashing by the window made her dizzy. Suddenly Tio pulled the car to the side of the road and stopped. He got out, came around to the back seat and climbed in.

"Sometimes, she is necessary to choose life over death." He kissed her hand, he kissed her cheek, her left one.

"Why you no tell me about this?" he said as his fingers chased the scar on her cheek. "Don't tell me your Papa he duel with you?" He was smiling.

"No. I'm a lover, not a fighter."

"I thought perhaps this was so—"

They made love slowly, carefully, as if each thought the other might break. And then they made love again. This time Tio banished the pose of the gentle man and Pru forgot her fears. She let go, let herself feel. Her passion rose with enough force to drive away the piles of old clothes, the bleached bones. The stink of bodies.

It was not a forever kind of lovemaking. She wished it were. But she knew enough about herself to know she wouldn't take the easy way out. She wouldn't run away like her father, or chase nirvana like her mother—neither path held any appeal for her. Long ago she had tired of the battles their dueling beliefs waged across the field of her soul. But the ossuary had overwhelmed

her and she had needed to rejoin the land of the living. Tio took
her there.

Tio was warm, Tio was wonderful. Tio was not the answer. She
would settle for a warm bath, cold wine, and dinner.

THIRTY-SIX

The Tell Tale Glove

> *"Still as they run they look behind,*
> *They hear a voice in every wind."*

—THOMAS GRAY, *On a Distant Prospect of Eton*

PRU WALKED the last quarter-mile or so to the *Casa de Carrillo*. They had driven back to Rodicio in silence, a comfortable one. No need for talk. She asked Tio to drop her off at the bottom of the hill. She walked slowly; she needed time to collect her thoughts. Some sixth sense—a little of her mother's woman's intuition—told her she didn't want to confront Isabelle, not yet.

She opened the door quietly and slipped upstairs. Despite her contentment she needed to get her mind back on why she had come all this way. Upstairs she ran a bath.

The water in the tub grew tepid as she wondered how she could work up the courage to talk about her father with Isabelle when she couldn't even do it with her own mother. She added more hot water, tried to soak up her confusion, gave up and wrapped a towel around herself for the run back down the hall to her room. Isabelle stood in the doorway, cup of tea in hand.

"Drink this, you feel better. I have some cold supper for you downstairs."

Pru tried not to sound surprised at this puzzling bit of kindness. She managed a simple *"Gracias"* before dragging a chair over to the rear window where she sipped her tea and waited for the view to sooth her.

The mountains appeared as magical as ever, the setting sun played across their contours. Years before, she watched this palette of colors run the same spectrum as familiar shapes melted away into the dying light. She thought of Marion back in California, curious as to what news she would bring back. But no, at this time of day, Marion would be struggling to come out from under the anesthesia offered by Bazil's cocktails from the night before—martinis dry enough to challenge the arid plains of Spain.

Her cup slammed into her saucer, she jumped up. How could she tell her mother about the ugliness of the Ossuary? She wouldn't believe her. She tried to resist her next thought—would Marion care even if she did? All her laments of "God knows I loved that man," long ago rang hollow to Pru's ears. Marion worked hard to forget Spain, except where it helped her image. Maybe she had succeeded. A dry martini could do that.

"Why," Pru would ask Bazil, "why the drinks? Why not help her to face her life instead of —"

"Leave her be, you're too hard on her. It takes time."

Time and time enough, Pru thought, even if she wasn't sure when the drinking started. Pru hadn't thought of it as a problem until Marion began to pace. "Waiting," she would say, "for the sun to cross the yardarm." And when the sun defied both the heavens and Galileo and shook itself free of its orbit to cross earlier with each passing day, Pru blamed her father. His disappearance had caused her mother to retreat into a life of too little to do, seasoned only by gin. She blamed her mother for not shaking it off and marrying Bazil and she blamed herself for not protecting her mother. But if she could come up with the right answers, all that blame might melt away. If only she knew what they were.

She should have gotten out years ago, she knew that and yet Marion appeared so vulnerable, blood red nails clutching the fragile stem of a glass. How could a daughter desert a mother who hadn't deserted her, who hadn't blamed her that time she watched? That time she did nothing.

Stop! Who cares? Not her mother across the ocean, Bazil in attendance. Not Brancusi busy with his movies, not Tio. "Elfsay, itypay," she laughed at herself and thought of Isabelle, the supper she had for her.

Crossing the hall to the dining room, she saw it: the glove, just one, a man's—black leather, soft and expensive looking, lying on the floor in front of the hall table. Something about the smoky sheen of it, the way it curled into a semblance of a fist, robbed it of any chance at innocence, any look of something left heedlessly behind.

Pru bent down to retrieve the glove—there was no need for her to ask. Lemona. She doubted the General was given to acts of carelessness. If he left the glove, he left it because he wanted her to know he had been there, or worse. She stormed through the dining room and into the pantry. Who was this man to follow her everywhere? She was an American tourist. She had a right to travel unmolested around Spain.

In the kitchen *Señora* Itturaldi stood at her chopping block, pounding a piece of beef into submission. Unmindful of the mallet, Pru shoved the glove under Isabelle's nose. "This, what is this—?"

"*Un guante*, the glove of a gentleman."

"There is nothing gentle about the General. Why did you let him in?" She could hear her own voice, its high-pitched screech skirting the borders of hysteria. The day had gone badly enough.

She didn't need this. Lemona might still be in the house. How had he known she would come to Rodicio? The customs manifest? Wasn't there a blank for why she was here, where she was visiting? And then again it could be nothing more mysterious than she was a woman and he was a man with connections. And Americans since the war were a rare sight. To a general, Americans might bring back thought of the Lincoln Brigade. She was a challenge. That's all.

Then she remembered something she'd noticed as she dashed through the pantry. Too distracted at the time, it hadn't registered—that table set for one. Who? Lemona? But why would Isabelle help him? He was definitely one of Franco's. Isabelle's sympathies lay elsewhere. She forced her voice down a notch or two. "What did you think you were doing?"

Señora Itturaldi seemed not at all surprised that Pru knew the owner of the glove. "Who are you, that you should tell me these things?" She poked the mallet in Pru's direction as if to punctuate her sentences. "This house," poke, poke, "she no longer belong to your Pápa, she belong to Herr Schiller." With a look of triumphant finality, the mallet came down on the block. Meat juices spattered the two of them. Pru jumped back.

"Yes but he came here looking for me, didn't he?"

"Once again the *Señora* presumes," triumph gave way to slyness. "He has come to see Herr Schiller."

"Schiller?" That name, where had she heard it before? The man Tio drove. A bit too much of a coincidence. Every muscle tensed inside her. She felt the familiar creep of paranoia. *Think!* When she hired the car she said she wanted to go to Rodicio, that's what made the men think of their uncle. That's all. She couldn't worry about that now, besides the name Schiller went back further than meeting Tio, much further.

"*Sí. Frau* Schiller *El General es un amigo bueno de Frau* Schiller."

The German, of course. The one who wanted the house all those years ago. So he finally got it and a wife to boot. Why this awful feeling in the pit of her stomach? She only rented a room in his house, their house, why should *Frau* Schiller care? Yet, *Señora* Itturaldi's smug expression, the pounding of the mallet, told Pru the illusive *Frau* Schiller might be someone she should care about. If the family were here they would be use the dining room and, family or no family, General Lemona would not eat in the pantry. That table was set for her.

"Where is she, Isabelle?" Pru tried a conciliatory tone.

"*¿Quién?*" The tone of voice told Pru that once more Isabelle felt testy.

"I wish to thank my hostess, for her courtesy in letting me the room."

"*No está necesario, Señora,* they leave that sort of thing to me." That told her nothing of the woman, whether Pru ever knew of her, heard of her. It didn't even tell her the woman's whereabouts. Never mind. The name Schiller was more common in Germany than Hasenpfeffer. She better concentrate on Lemona. She didn't want him to pop up, no telling what damage he wanted to do. Tio! Good heavens, that must be it—he learned where she had gone and had come to send Tio back to Málaga so he could drive her. That was all.

Never mind what he wanted, she must find Tio first. Without him she would be dependent on the General. She started to ask where he might be but caught herself. Isabelle, her loyalties, where they lay, or if she even had any—Pru hadn't the time to figure it out. She would go to the village and search the cafés herself. She started for the door with every intention of leaving, but a bit of wickedness came over her. She couldn't stop herself. She walked over to the chopping block, dropped the glove dead center in the middle of the juices. The thumb came to rest on a piece of suet.

She looked to Isabelle, instead of the expected scowl, she saw a smile. The Isabelle of her childhood returned, "You must listen to me, *Señora*," she said.

Could this mercurial change be a trick to stop Pru from reaching Tio before Lemona? As if she had read her mind, *Señora* Itturaldi's ample chest heaved with a sigh large enough to drive the last of the air out of her animosity.

"Tio, he is no dumb. He no wish to see the General, he no wish the General to see him."

"So what is it, Cook, what are you trying to tell me?" Pru kept her voice level. Could she trust this change in Isabelle? It seemed unearned, to have come too soon, too quickly. She must be careful.

"Cook! Bah, such a name. You want I should call you tourist? Meddler?" This time her laughter sounded genuine. "You, your *máma*, you no care what happened to us. Why, you never even ask about that young boy, the one you walked out with at night?"

"Rubio, you knew about Rubio?"

"Yes, *Señora*, I know. He care for you and you—you come here you ask about your *Pápa*, *Pápa* this, *Pápa* that, but you ask nothing of the boy."

"What about Rubio? Do you know what happened to him?"

"*Sí*, I know."

"And?"

"He no longer here."

"Where—?"

"For awhile he was our hero. He shot the mayor."

"Oh, God. He was just a boy."

"Then the fascists come, they no care he just a boy, they shoot him and nail his body to the courthouse door in." Isabelle picked up the glove and carried it over to the sink. "But you, your *máma,* a few houses burn, you run away."

"Not from him, not from you. We didn't know, we couldn't know." No wonder Isabelle was angry. "I thought about him a lot, those soft eyes of his, he was my first—damn." Pru clutched her stomach, she thought she might retch.

A gentleness replaced the scorn in the *Señora's* eyes. Pru recognized the woman of the good times when she listened to the kitchen gossip, the warm bread, the little tastes of soups and stews, the extra whipping cream on her *tortas.* "It wasn't you, it wasn't Rubio we ran away from—" A door slammed, heavy footsteps startled them both.

"This way, *mi Prudencita.* Hurry." Isabelle pointed to the kitchen door. Pru didn't hesitate, she ran down the back steps and around to the street, the familiar name, the *Prudencita* that escaped Isabelle galvanized her into action. Once more she ran.

Isabelle was right, she had done a lot of running. Half the time she never knew from what, from who? W*hom,* Nanny's voice brushed against her ear.

Once out in the road, Pru hesitated. Where should she go? If the footsteps belonged to Lemona, she'd be safe at a café; and yet no car was parked out front. Rodicio had no trains and Lemona hardly seemed the type for the bus and those footsteps sounded too heavy, too masculine for *Frau* Schiller. If they belonged to *Herr* Schiller that would leave the General heavens knows where. She better get a move on, anywhere but here. She started to laugh—she was at it again: running from trouble, at least this time she had Isabelle's blessing.

She would go around to the patio and look through the dining room windows, see who—too late, the beam of car headlights swept across the front of the Casa. No place to hide. She crouched below the white wall, the only cover at hand. The engine died right out in front. Not wanting Lemona to find her cringing in the bushes, she tried to force herself to stand. Her legs wouldn't obey; and then she heard the crunch of gravel—a woman's footstep. She stood up prepared to face *Frau* Schiller.

"*Gut Abend, Frau*—Dordo, Mrs. Lupinek! What are you doing here?"

"Pru, is that you? You startled me. I'm looking for you, that's what I'm doing. I heard you left Málaga almost before I heard you were there. I couldn't help but wonder why you hadn't come—"

"I didn't know—" A chagrined Pru realized she hadn't even thought to look up Dordo. She could tell the truth and say that she hadn't really thought this trip through. Her anger at her mother for not coming, at herself for not putting up more of a fight, left her feeling so preoccupied and put upon she hadn't given thought to anyone else's feelings. She should have made inquiries.

"We learned you'd gone back to Holland; I never thought— but never mind, I'm really glad to see you. I had to leave sooner than expected." Should she tell Mrs. Lupinek why she was here?

Dordo must have sensed her hesitation, "May I ask why you are hiding out here? That is what you are doing, isn't it? Hiding?"

"Well, yes. I—that is—" Pru offered up hasty apologies to Hereclitus, as she prepared to step twice into the same river. Mrs. Lupinek had rescued her once, perhaps she could do it again.

THIRTY-SEVEN

A Little Knowledge
> *"To know that which before us lies...*
> *Is the prime wisdom."*

—JOHN MILTON, *Paradise Lost*

DORDO PUT A COMFORTING ARM around Pru, "Look at you, crouched in the bushes, shivering." She opened the gate, gave Pru a little push. "Come along with you, into the car. You seem sort of—"

"I have to find Tio."

"Your uncle?"

"No, no. My driver. That's just what . . . everyone calls him that."

"Ah, the Uncle to Everyman. Is this the Spanish version of your Uncle Sam?"

Mrs. Lupinek's infectious laugh brought Pru to her senses and she returned a tentative smile, climbed into the car and waited for Mrs. Lupinek to go round to the driver's side before she asked, "What are you doing here?"

"I told you, looking for you."

"But how did you know—?"

"At a dinner party I was seated next to a diplomat, one of your shipboard acquaintances, he mentioned your name. Of course, the Brancusi part meant nothing, but when he bragged of dancing with the daughter of—"

"I didn't tell—"

"You didn't have to. Your mother is still "a somebody" in the gossip columns. Your life is not as anonymous as you would like to think."

"Certainly not in this country, here everybody seems to know all about me."

"This man you speak of, am I to take it that he might be more than a kindly old uncle, I mean at least to some?"

"Um. Er . . . I—" Pru's tongue tripped over her thoughts. She fell silent. What was it about the air in Spain? Either it turned everyone into a poet or a mind reader. In some cases both.

Mrs. Lupinek started the car, slipped it into gear and took off, tires squealing. "Seems to me that one of the last times I saw you, you were making moon eyes at the Count. Did you and your mother ever meet up with him? I tried to cable him."

"He got your cable. He and mother . . . well, I mean—"

"Ah, I thought perhaps they might. Your mother deserved so much more than . . . never mind. We'll save all that for later. Could you use a spot of wine?"

The car rounded a curve, from Pru's vantage it appeared as if they would sail out over the side and drop to the village below. She clutched at the armrest and wished she already had some wine.

"The road, Mrs. Lupinek, watch the road."

"Hang on, I'll get you there. Then you can tell me all about this uncle of yours."

The word uncle grated. Why had he told her to call him Tio? She would ask his name if she ever saw him again. If you

412

don't learn to think in Spanish, he told her, you will never learn to speak it. If she had, surely the word Tio would have bothered her long ago. Now she owed Mrs. Lupinek some explanation of her crouching, as well as a good reason not to have looked her up. One eye on the road, she sketched a quick picture—her return to Spain, her run from Lemona.

They pulled up in front of the first café, the one she and Tio frequented. The air inside seemed stale, overused. Old men sat morosely over their wine, the smell of apathy drove out the tang of garlic sauce and pickled fish. No one gave any sign of recognition or greeting. Content to return their neglect, Pru scanned the room. At a back table, partially blocked by the proprietress pouring wine, she spotted a large fist wrapped lovingly around a glass, a brown sleeve dotted with gold buttons rested on the table. She held her breath, waited for the woman to step to one side. There he sat, back straight, defiant jaw cutting the smoke-laden air, enthroned in the best chair the humble café had to offer. Lemona's concentration on the woman's neckline and the aroma of the wine gave Pru time to flee. Out in the night, doubled over, head well below the level of the windows of the café, she cursed Tio, "Damn it all, whatever your name is, where are you?" At least it didn't seem as if Lemona had gotten hold of him as yet.

"This crouching thing, you seem to make a habit of it." Pru jumped at the sound of Mrs. Lupinek's voice, yet again she'd let Mrs. Lupinek slip her mind. "Am I to assume that gentleman in the dark corner is the nefarious General Lemona?"

"Who else?"

"You hardly gave me time to check."

"Shh! He'll hear you."

"Oh Prudence, you can handle him. Now your father—there was a man to fear."

"My father didn't have his own army."

"Pish-posh. Of course he did. What would you call that band of followers, hangers-on that clung to his every word? Any of them ever disobey his marching orders? Take your side in anything? Like that day at the bullfights—"

"But you weren't there."

"Of course not, what a barbaric ritual. But I heard all about it before dinner that night. I was still there when you came downstairs and gave him what for. Now there's a girl who won't easily be stopped, I said to my seat mate, I think it was the German—".

"Herr Schiller?"

"I think that's who, it doesn't matter; anyway I told him you'd be as formidable an opponent as your father and you would go far. And for heaven's sake call me Dordo."

"All right, I hate to disappoint you Dordo, but I can't say I've done—"

"You will, you will. Now, as to the General—I've never met him, we move in different circles, thank God. I've heard of him, everyone has, he is a toady. A hired gun. A man who would do anything for anybody who paid him."

"That doesn't sound all that reassuring. Why is he interested in me?"

"You are a foreigner which in today's Spain turns you into a suspicious character, you don't even have to lift a finger. Mrs. Lupinek gave her a searching look, "Further more you've grown into an attractive woman—"

"Thanks, but—"

"Never mind, Lemona is usually too preoccupied for much of that sort of thing."

"You seem to know him far better than I—"

"He is famous, infamous."

"Either way, he certainly loves his wine, his food and the

bolero. In whatever time those pursuits leave him, he's not above a bit of flirtation."

"Flirtation to a Spaniard is a life-jacket to a drowning man, necessary if one is to survive. As for a serious romance, as I understand it, Lemona has a wealthy wife and prefers to pay for his dalliances. No reprisals, no complications that way. But, as he met you at the dock, I suspect it involves more than your good looks. It might be that someone has hired him to keep track of you, that is all."

"That's all? That's quite a bit as far as I'm concerned. Besides, you saw back there in the cafè, the silent drinkers, their mournful looks? They weren't that way the other night when I was here with—"

"The elusive uncle? Anyway, the uniform of *El Cuadillo* is still not popular out here in the country. And a General at that…they have more to fear than you do."

"Well it was popular enough with the men that night in Málaga. Why would all those men, captains, lieutenants, dance attendance on a mere toady?"

"You must have been in the *Café de Olvido*—"

"How did you know?"

"His aunt runs it. And even a toady can have his band of merry men. It's strange, Pru, I know that, but after every war there are those who cannot put it aside."

"Half of Spain, it seems to me."

"I don't mean those who cannot forget. No one touched by civil war ever forgets. Look at your South, at you, your mother. It's more than that. I'm talking about those who cannot let go of the violence; men for whom war is the most intense, the most alive they've ever felt. It is these Lemona gathers around him. He'll have their loyalty as long as he provides them with the intrigue, the adventure they crave. Happily they follow as he tracks down one man's enemy, or protects someone else's friend or even—"

"I still don't see how this is supposed to make me feel better. It hardly makes him any less dangerous."

"Lemona and his ilk are useful for some purposes, and I won't say the government doesn't avail themselves of their services now and then, but if they really wanted to silence you they would have done it by now and with someone far less flamboyant and conspicuous. As for Lemona, we don't have to go into all his bad habits."

"But why me?"

"It's possible someone just wants to look after you, a beautiful young woman, an American wandering unescorted around Spain—"

"I do have my chauffeur."

"Ah, yes, the uncle. All the more reason for you to have a chaperone. How old is this uncle, anyway?"

Pru hadn't thought about it, forty? forty-five? But then, the war, it aged everyone; besides she didn't care. She wished Dordo wouldn't look at her that way. A man's age wasn't important, so she liked them a bit on the mature side. So what?

"Perhaps Bazil or Marion asked him to look after you."

"I thought of that, but it appears as if Lemona tries more to distract me from something than to protect me."

"Who might want you watched, perhaps discouraged from visiting certain places, certain people?"

There it was, that feeling at the back of Pru's neck, the fingernail that slid down the blackboard of her past. "My father? He might, I mean if he were alive." The full impact percolated slowly, dripped its way through obscuring layers of time. A part of that child remained buried, not all that deeply, inside. It didn't take much to make those uncertainties, anxieties surface. If her father were alive, if he had gone so far as to hire someone to keep her away, it could only mean he didn't want—

"To hell with him, I'll find him if I want to."

"Listen, dear," Pru felt a hug, a comforting arm around her. "I left Spain not long after you. Hans and I went back to Holland. The German invasion trapped us there."

"I'm sorry."

"We didn't fare too badly, not as bad as some."

"Couldn't you have left?"

"I didn't take my own advice. We waited too long." Pru smiled, remembering how Dordo had hurried them out of Spain.

As the two walked arm and arm down the street, Dordo stopped. She appeared to be studying something hanging in a darkened shop window. Pru said nothing. She remembered that the refugees who came to California wore that same numbed look when brought face to face with their pasts.

"Dordo, are you all right?"

"What? Oh, where was I? Oh yes. I didn't forget you or your mother. When I got back to Spain I made inquiries. I would have gotten in touch with you had I heard anything. Rumors, yes. Real news, no."

"We didn't miss a rumor. Marion still gets letters almost every week; they all claim to know something. Mostly they want money, but still it keeps mother from settling down. That's why I'm here." Pru tried to keep her voice from sounding accusatory. "And then the other night, in Málaga I heard talk of an American reporter living around here."

"Oh my, you are going to need that wine. Let's try the café around the corner."

They settled at a table, the atmosphere far more congenial than at the last place. A warm burgundy quickly filed the edges off the night. Dordo signaled the waiter to bring a plate of anchovies.

"The salty flavor really whets the appetite." But for all that, Pru still had a tight knot in her stomach, a lump of foreboding. She nudged the conversation back to Dordo's last words.

"You meant more than the cold when you said I needed wine, what—?"

"You don't know, do you?"

Even as Pru shook her head she realized it was more in protest than denial. "It's about Mrs. Schiller, isn't it?"

"Yes." For a moment no one said anything, and then Dordo drained her glass, motioned for more. The two of them watched the red liquid splash against the glass. "Her accent has dulled a bit with time. She is the one they call the American reporter. Every now and then, or so I have heard, she writes for the papers."

"In German?"

"No, dear. She isn't German." Dordo spoke quietly, for Pru her voice had the roar of a thunderstorm.

"It's Helen isn't it?" Somehow, locked up in some empty little cranny of her mind, she had always known it was Helen she would find. Back there, back in the stable, despite the tortured looks, the torn clothes, she never quite believed Helen. Not her whole story. Pru knew the real reason the two took off for Madrid—the war only provided the excuse. Her father had packed everything, everything but that one damn camera and at that he probably just overlooked it. He never meant to come back.

"But if Helene's alive then. . . ?"

"Then what?"

"If they shot my father, why wouldn't they have killed Helen too, to cover it up?"

"In the early days of the war there was still some civility, a Spaniard does not easily kill a woman."

"No, but they don't mind. . . ." Pru heard her mother's voice:

say nothing, tell no one. She had no right to betray her. How hard this journey backward in time. It held as many twists and turns—as much ugliness as the path they had followed to Cadiz.

THIRTY-EIGHT

Loss of Faith

> *"Little by little we subtract*
> *Faith and Fallacy from Fact . . ."*
>
> —SAMUEL HOFFENSTEIN, *Rag-Bag*

PRU'S HEAD ACHED, her stomach brewed up a minor rebellion over the combination of anchovies and wine. Even the floor of the café refused to stay put. The stomp of dancers, the twang of guitars made it pulsate and sway beneath her feet. A scrim of smoke floated over the room, thick enough that the misty silhouette at the next table might well be Lemona and she would have no way to know. Most of the villagers appeared to be here, men with their wives, their girlfriends, a few children and one or two dogs slept under the tables—an air of companionship fast distilling into bacchanalia.

As the last of the *pajarete* lay far away at the bottom of her glass, the warmth and solace of the wine collapsed into befuddlement. Pru solemnly studied the dregs as though they disguised her fortune. Dordo raised her glass, tipped it towards Pru, "Here's to us, now let's go home." With a determined ring, two tumblers hit the wooden table. The night was over.

"Tomorrow we can finish our talk."

"Sure." Pru answered even as she realized she wasn't sure of anything. She had no idea what they had talked about, or what could be left to say. In some way Dordo had helped. Not that she'd solved Pru's problems, but she had made her forget most of them. Pru tried to stand. Her legs refused to honor her signals. Sit down, they said, there's something ... what? Eyes shut she tried to blot out the music and concentrate.

"Tio, I haven't found Tio yet."

Dordo sat there a minute, maybe two, almost as if she had abandoned the decision to go, then she gathered up her things along with her dignity and rose from the table. "I don't know how you did it. You monopolized the conversation the entire evening, and somehow you managed not to tell me one damn thing about him." Pru opened her mouth to speak, Dordo held up her hand. "Guess what?"

"What?"

"I don't care." By the time their laughter died so had the strains of a raucous *malagueña*. The dancers stood motionless, the men tuned their instruments to reflect the oriental strains of a *pequeño* and the music worked its way through the smoke and into the hearts of the listeners. The room hissed them into silence.

"Come on, then," Dordo whispered. "I'll drive you back to the *Casa*."

Pru hadn't forgotten Dordo's driving. "Thanks no, I'll walk." It would take more sherry than she could stomach to blot out that earlier drive.

Dordo appeared miffed. "Don't be silly, I can still—"

"It's all right, the moon is full. I'll hail a passing donkey."

"This Tio, he must be some man, you're off for another look see, aren't you?" Dordo tossed some coins on the table and left.

Pru stepped into the street and blinked to rid her eyes of darkness, the smokiness of the café. Moonlight bounced from one whitewashed wall to another. The buildings crowded in on the twisted streets, making it hard to get her bearings; but as the noise of Dordo's motor faded into the night, she saw a dark shadow looming off to her right. The hill that rose behind the village? She set off in that direction, wrapped in a blanket of thoughts she hardly noticed the chill. If she hadn't blathered on about Tio, then what? Who? A little breeze came up and carried with it a name. Rubio? Had she talked of him? Why? The romantic music? The sweet wine? Wine can do that. You relax your guard, down it comes and wham, you get a good clear look all the way into the center of your heart and there it is, the thing you have resisted knowing. Maybe consciously, maybe not. It doesn't matter. This whole trip, even though she wouldn't barely own up to it, she saw Rubio everywhere—those eyes, brown and soft and slow like the eyes of deer, she saw those eyes on a lot of men, Tio most of all. The memory of them, locked away in her memory bank, made their way across the ocean to a new life. You don't forget your first love. There in the woods behind the house in California, she had faced a constant bombardment of reminders. To look into the eyes of a deer was to see Rubio.

Pockets stuffed with teenage angst and acorns, she would wander the woods in back of her mother's house, book in hand intending to spend the afternoon reading. But a few paragraphs into *"Farewell to Arms,"* or slogging through *"As I lay Dying,"* she would hear the faint stir of leaves, the snap of a twig, some little indication she was not alone. Hesitant at first, the deer stayed hidden until she remembered what Rubio told her.

"Sway slowly back and forth, like a bush, a small tree caught up by the wind. The deer won't have the fear, just the curiosity."

She would sway ever so slowly and the deer would come up almost to her and she would lose herself in those wet and dewy eyes, those seeds of sadness. As they approached, she felt it again, that flutter, the same weakness to her legs she'd felt the nights his hand touched hers. The years wore away, her feelings didn't. She still harbored romantic fantasies, as unreal as her mother's scripts. They had met at that precise pinpoint of time when a young girl is most vulnerable. She took Rubio and fashioned him into the chalice for her longings and daydreams. Kind, handsome and, most important of all for a first love, unattainable.

Unattainable. The word exploded in her mind. It had taken all this time, but finally she understood—she'd never out grown the safety that lay in the unattainable. First she had courted her father's elusive approval, then her fantasies fixed on Rubio, next her crush on Bazil, then her flings as she called them—New York, van Dulken—just one among many. She needed things, where was the harm? She wasn't van Dulken's first infidelity—he must have had a wife hidden somewhere—she wouldn't be his last. There was always the comfort of that adage—there's safety in numbers. And wasn't Brancusi, in his own way, just as unattainable as all the rest?

The unattainable required so little. But a tiny spark with Rubio's name on it, clean and bright in its innocence, still glowed—even now she thought she heard the clip-clop of donkey hooves striking the stones behind her. She wheeled around to confront a ghost and saw instead the large figure of a man, half leading, half pulling a well-laden donkey.

"*Señora*—"

"Tio, you startled me." Rubio went crashing to earth. And weren't they somehow the same—Tio and Rubio, both elusive, both mixed up in her emotions. But the flatness of Tio's s voice lacked any sign of pleasure at having met up with her.

"*Señora*, what are you doing here on the roads at this—?"

"Looking for you." She winced at her exaggeration, she had forgotten him.

"I had things to do."

"The general is here. I thought—" the other night, they'd been so close, she'd told him about Lemona.

"I'm not afraid of your bogey man."

"Perhaps you should be." Her reply sounded petulant, unreasonable even to her. He didn't owe her an accounting of his time.

"Once, *Señora*, I had that fear, but time passes, the tiger's teeth dull. I have only the hatred. You need not be concerned for me. But you, it's late. Where are you off to?"

What an odd thing to say. It wasn't as if the road went anywhere else. Why was he so caught off guard at her appearance? She tried to keep the annoyance out of her voice. "To the *Casa*." She couldn't resist teasing him, "And you?"

"To see you safely home, Cook is worried."

"You mean Isabelle."

"You know then."

"Yes."

"All?" How much he had asked with that one small word.

"All." How much she accepted with her answer.

"It is good then, no more secrets."

The wine, the late hour, left her confused. She nodded, it took a few beats more before she wondered how he knew Isabelle was worried—Isabelle had made no mention of having seen him. Maybe there just hadn't been time, the way Pru ran out to avoid Lemona. To cover her concern she chattered aimlessly on and on about Dordo, the drive and her hitchhiking on a donkey, until, out of breath and things to say, she asked, "Who's your friend?" She hoped he might explain the donkey, the load it carried. Its

424

destination could only be the same as hers, why would Tio, a supposed casual visitor to the town, be carrying provisions to the *Casa*? She knew why, somewhere inside of her she knew.

As if aware of her scrutiny, the donkey stopped. Tio adjusted the load, prodding here, pushing there; then he gave the rope a tug, the beast a swat across its flanks. The donkey laid his ears back but started on up the hill. Tio looked across at Pru.

"The full moon, she is a thief, no?"

"What?" She was tired, confused and definitely not in the mood for Tio's peasant wisdom. She didn't even try to hide her puzzlement.

"The moon," his patient sigh annoyed her. "Everyone knows, she robs the sky of stars."

Was he trying to tell her that too much light obscures things? Idle conversation and feelings get obliterated? Is that what he meant? Silenced, she walked on. He left her at the front gate, she listened to the clip-clop of hooves as they continued on around the side of the house to the kitchen. Aware of the cold, she approached the door, reached up to give the bell a tug—it was late. She tried the handle, it gave way.

Inside, the only light came from a small candle on the hall table. It had burned for quite some time, its flame about to drown in a puddle of melted wax. Quietly she crossed the hall, pinched the flame into nothingness and headed for the stairs. It took all her willpower to avoid the kitchen. She would not spy on them. For a man who, supposedly, only passed through this village, he seemed well acquainted with Isabelle. What was it everyone wanted to keep her from finding out? Where did she figure in all this? If at all. Early on in the evening Dordo had chided her for possessing the usual American conceit of assuming that everything that happened had something to do with them. Dordo was right. All this mucking around in

the past had produced no answers about her father, only suspicions. She didn't like being suspicious, it took up too much
time. But something about Spain, it's aura such that she found
herself suspecting everybody and everything—the woman in
the hotel, Lemona, the gatekeeper at the ossuary, the whole
Spanish government, Isabelle and now Tio, a man who only
last night she thought she might love.

An hour later she woke, the roof of her mouth sticky with wine,
her tongue swollen from the salty fish. As she searched for her
robe, she could almost taste the solution, goat's milk. Those
nights, those interminable dinners, sitting up straight, minding
her manners, nibbling on who knows what food while she concentrated on the being seen and not heard—Cook would knock
gently on her bedroom door, hand Nanny a cup of warmed
goat's milk. "To see la *señorita* off to *"tierra de hadas."* It would
work; she sailed off into the land of dreams and woke in the
morning with no trace of the night to torment her.

She started down the stairs. A faint light filtered in through
the windows. At the pantry door she paused when she heard
voices—not Nanny's, but real ones. Isabelle? Tio? Quietly she
crossed the room, and stopped at the threshold to the kitchen.
A well-banked fire in the open stove gave an intimate warmth
to the center of the room, while a pot steamed with the aroma
of fish stew. A table, covered with dishes, bread crusts, saucers
of oil, tumblers of wine, half empty jars of olives and marinated
artichoke hearts bumped up against dishes of *Azucada*. Little circles of sprinkled sugar dusted the table around the remains of the
paper-thin pancakes. Tio had not arrived unannounced.

Isabelle sat at the table, her back to Pru, Tio paced like a
caged bear. "We owe it to her. She was brave enough to come

here, she has a right to know," he said.

To know what? She needed to know; but, as she stepped back into the shadows, she heard a noise behind her. She turned to see the boy. He stood so close their shoulders almost touched. Had he come in without her hearing, or had she passed him by and not even noticed? He didn't acknowledge her nod, instead he leaned forward, intent on what his mother had to say.

"Not again, Tio. We've been over this, we have agreed."

"I didn't agree, Isabelle, I think—"

A voice, a raspy Scottish burr issued from the far corner of the room, just out of reach of the fire's light. "No. Absolutely not, the nosy little twit. Doesn't she know enough to let the whole thing drop?" Pru's eyes took a moment to adjust, then she saw a man, a woman. The woman—shorter than Pru remembered, a little more spread out, even a little dowdy, the fire in her hair faded to ash.

Pru pressed herself back even further into the shadows and right back into her childhood. It was all so familiar, this standing in a doorway, half hidden, while she watched, listening to other people live out their lives.

She looked at Helen and saw not the red-headed predator she remembered, not the reason for the secret she had tried to keep from her mother, but the young woman—Helen couldn't have been as old as Pru was now—the one whose vacant eyes stared at Prudence from beneath the soldier with his pants around his boots, his buttocks heaving up and down.

Stop it. What need have you to feel sorry for her? If it hadn't been for Helen she wouldn't be here. Her father might not have gone off. How did one separate truth from lies? All those nights listening to her mother cry, trying to come up with what really happened, not what she imagined. Could her truth be someone else's lie? And what if, like Marion, you didn't talk about it, pretended it never happened? Where was the truth in that?

"Why has she come to Spain now?" Helen appeared to be asking the man next to her, she sounded annoyed. "Why not years ago? What does she want from all of us?"

"Well, my dear wife, that telegram didn't send itself. Someone sent it. It certainly wasn't me. If it wasn't for my connections at the U.N. we might not have learned any of this. But don't worry I set Lemona to keep track of her. She will learn nothing I don't want her to. Even now, say the word and I can make her disappear; poof, just like that." He snapped his fingers. Shocked, Pru recognized the German, the businessman in the dark suit, the one whose neck disappeared between his hunched shoulders, a man who gained confidence from the fear his ugliness inspired in others. "Don't worry," he had said to the Mayor that night all those years ago, "Franco will put those communists in their place before they can take care of all the land owners. For some of course," he nodded toward Don Carlos, "help may come too late."

Don Carlos had jumped up from the table, "Get out of my house, you damn foreigners, all of you, you'll be the ruin of Spain. We don't need your war, your rebellions. What we need is Alfonso returned to his throne, the priests to their church."

Pru remembered Schiller, leaning half out of his seat, so far across the table, she thought his mustache might catch fire. He had snapped his fingers under Don Carlos's nose, "Your house? Ha? For how long? To hang on to your head will give you trouble enough."

"Now, now, *Herr* Schiller," her father disliked scenes he wasn't in charge of. "Calm yourself, for now the house is mine and Don Carlos is my guest."

Pru remembered what *Herr* Schiller said next. He had said it under his breath but she heard it: "Not for long, *Señor*, not for long."

Had her father heard it too? Had he decided to ignore him?

428

She was never sure, he had merely turned to the maid, "A bit of wine for *Herr* Schiller. He needs a restorative for his nerves."

"*Gehen sie verdammt*," Schiller had barked. "Better for you, Roland, if you stand with me."

She remembered the way she felt, cold all over. This man had threatened her father. The heavens should have opened, thunder and lightning descended. Instead the room grew quiet as it held its collective breath. Her father seemed unconcerned. "Strange isn't it." he said, "All of you are so sure that somewhere there exists the one man who can perform miracles, who can save Spain. And yet—" he looked directly at Schiller, "for every one of you, he wears a different hat." Prudence remembered picturing a clown hopping in and out of a little car, changing costumes as he went. She had giggled. Her father had only to point at her and the maid came round and pulled out her chair.

She had started up the stairs to the sounds of yet more shouts, more curses. She and the maid, guarding the coats and hats in the hall, exchanged glances. The door to the dining room opened, someone ran out. She flattened herself against the wall in time to see the German cross the hall and yank his hat and cloak from the outstretched hands of the now terrified maid, shouting over his shoulder, "You Americans, so sure of yourselves, you will pay. I'll see to it."

A man of his word, here he was, snapping his fingers again. "Lemona will do what I ask. For a price, of course. Thank goodness for my friend, his connections at the U.N." This time it was her grave the rabbit ran across. She should have known. Spain wanted in the U.N.; van Dulken worked for the U.N. and the German delegation would not want an American to stir up old sins.

"You will not harm the girl." Tio spoke up. "There is no

point to it. The property was never hers, never even *Señor* Whitley's. Even then, you needn't have—"

"Needn't have what?" The coldness in that voice froze Pru where she stood. Even Tio fell silent.

"So that is what you thought all these years? You thought I had him—"

"But Don Carlos—?"

"He was different, Isabelle. Don Carlos got in my way."

"And the child's father? He no in your way?" Pru caught Isabelle's glance toward Helen, though her soft voice barely made it across the room. *Herr* Schiller, too, looked at his wife; but no question darkened his eyes. His voice dropped to an ominous growl and he turned his attention back to Isabelle.

"There are plenty around here who think it was you who turned the father in."

"I—?"

"Everyone knows you hated him," Schiller shrugged, "what does it matter? Didn't I give you safe haven and kept you and your bastard fed ever since?

"As for the cable," *Herr* Schiller spread his anger around the room, "why is it no one owns up to who sent it? If it hadn't caused trouble enough, whoever you are, you followed it up with that ridiculous note about the bowels of the earth." The tips of Pru's fingers turned to ice: how could he know what the note said, the very words? "When she didn't appear to be coming to Rodicio quick enough, one of you shoved it under her door—a little dramatic but apparently effective, eh Isabelle? "

Tio spoke up. "Leave Isabelle alone. Why would she have sent it? The boy, she doesn't wish to lose him."

"And you?" Now it was Tio's turn. Herr Schiller seemed determined to lacerate everyone in the room. He leaned in toward Tio, "Did I denounce you?"

"You couldn't be everywhere at once," Isabelle said as she shot Tio a better to say-nothing, do-nothing look.

Herr Schiller glared at them both. "You think that I don't know about the things you did in the north, the reason you had to leave your hometown? Have you forgotten so soon that it's thanks to me you have a job, a car and Isabelle?"

Tio had Isabelle? Before Pru could think about what that meant she became aware of the emptiness behind her—the boy had gone. She learned more by his absence than his presence. Why hadn't she figured it out before? The boy sent the telegram, he left the note. She even knew why and yet she felt nothing. What was wrong with her?

Tio pulled himself up straight. "*Herr* Schiller, I have spent some time with the girl." Tio couldn't have feelings for her, anyway not the ones she wanted him to have if he persisted in calling her a girl. "She means no harm. If you know nothing of Mr. Whitley, why not tell her? Why send people to watch her, to scare her?"

Though Helen played nervously with the glass in her hand, her voice had an odd calm to it. "Ruis is right, Frederick. There is no need for any of these histrionics." So Tio had a name and it wasn't Rubio. Of course she knew that all along, it was only that the other night, the softness of his arms, his kiss.

Herr Schiller turned toward Helen. "And, *mein liebling*, as for you—"

"I know," now Helen's voice sounded weary, like someone who had heard all this before, "I know what you did for me. I'm just not sure what you did *to* others. It was all so unnecessary, so—"

"Well, I can lay the blame for this present mess at your doorstep, my love. If you hadn't convinced me to send them that damn manuscript—"

"So? Tell her about the boxes in the basement, how you found it there and sent it on to California, an act of kindness on your part."

"Did you know, my sweet wife, that I knew you had thrown in a few chapters on your own."

"Yes, I know you keep close tabs on me and they did publish it after all. She'll see it that way, I'm sure. Besides, it wasn't the manuscript that brought her. You saw that telegram in her luggage, the date, it came long after the manuscript." Now Pru understood about Lemona, the hotel in Málaga. While she was at the embassy, *Herr* Schiller had the General, maybe the *consejere* search her things. Still he knew what the note said. How? She had it with her. The Ambassador—Lemona was with him when she left. Was there no one she could trust?

"And shall I tell her about you and her father—?"

"Don't be a fool, Schiller, it hardly matters. Her mother knew, her mother knew about all of them, the other secretaries, the maids, wives of friends, the—" Isabelle started to protest. Helen glared at her. "Don't be so naïve, she knew about you too. He made sure of that."

Pru shook her head. Had she heard right? Marion knew all along. She hadn't trusted Marion for a long time, but she always though Marion's sins were more of omission—her inability to face up to things. And now? Perhaps Marion was more devious, more deliberate than Pru had ever given her credit for. All the times Pru struggled with her conscience, to tell or not to tell, the times she wanted to force her mother into letting go, moving on, but held her peace. All that anger at her mother, her clinging, her demands; even those times she had wanted to shout it out just to hurt her, and now it seemed that the secret she choked on all these years was no secret at all. So what were all Marion's tears about, why would her mother have tried so hard to find him? What was it Marion wanted from Pru? Damn it all—who had used her more? Her mother? Her father?

Pru felt a rush. It would be later before she recognized the feeling for what it was—fresh air, a release, the smell of freedom—but at the time, her anger blinded her to its possibilities. Was everyone flawed? She was no better. Nothing had changed. She had come half way round the world only to repeat her mistakes. Here she stood, legs filled with lead, feet nailed to the floor. Her whole life spent in the shadows, forever reacting, never acting. She watched. She listened. She excused herself—*that's the way I learned*—but had she learned nothing? This time it was her father's voice she heard, the reins he had said. It was time to pick up them up. She stepped from the shadows.

"Is he dead?"

Later when she replayed this scene in her mind, she remembered that no one had the grace to even act surprised, it seemed more as if they had staged the whole performance for her benefit. The tenseness left their faces. Cheeks sagged, jaws slackened, lips went flaccid in a slow slide into indifference.

"I asked you a question, Helen. Is he dead?"

"What a tiresome child you were, all that mooning faith in the great one. Your father was a bastard, a real bastard. My ticket to a better life carried me to hell and back instead. And what did you or your mother..." Helen shrugged. "What does it matter? You were a pest then, you're a pest now."

"Just what should we have done to help you? I may be a pest but you're a—"

"And you, little Fraulein Whitley?"

"*Señora* Brancusi."

"Ah yes," *Herr* Schiller broke in, his grin malicious, "The great director. I know about your so-called marriage." It was Pru's turn to be the recipient of Herr Schiller acid tongue. "But you, what do you know of his father? The films he made in Germany? Did you know he deserted the Fatherland because his son, your esteemed husband, appeared on Hitler's list of degenerates? But then, by now, even you must know that."

In her anger, Pru rushed at Herr Schiller. Helen rose out of her chair but not to defend him. In her haste to find the back door, she tripped, caught herself with her hand on the doorknob. Isabelle put out her arm and made a grab for Pru. The two made good their ignominious escape. The door closed behind them.

For a long time no one moved, no one spoke. Then Isabelle filled a glass with wine and handed it to Pru.

"Why all this secrecy? Why won't you tell me what happened to my father? I learn one little piece, then another. Then someone takes it all away and gives me nothing in return but a glass of wine. Will you never let go of the past?"

Isabelle motioned Pru to a chair, offered her a slice of onion, a piece of anchovy. "Chew on this, my proud, Americano: you too have one foot mired in the past, like a crane stuck in the river you wave the other futilely about in search of a future."

"Enough! I'm tired of your homilies. "At least I look for one." That was unkind, why had she said that, it wasn't even true. She'd paid little attention to her own future, living the life her mother wanted. Her mother had chosen the man she married—no matter that she loved him in her own way. He was an unattainable male who would never insist on an intimacy, an intimacy she feared more than anything. She had played it safe. Twenty-seven years old and she had never taken a risk, never done a damn thing. As a child she daydreamed about making her name; now, as an adult her dreams were still filled with unpainted masterpieces. "I'm sorry, it's just that—"

"You feel a betrayal, *Señora*?"

"I—I think the betrayal is mine, I have betrayed myself."

Tio spoke, softly at first. "It comes to everyone eventually, this loss of faith."

"I never had a faith, not one of my own." Answers came to her faster than she could ask the questions. Her mother's passivity? Probably long before Pru was born, something—perhaps Roland, perhaps Hollywood—had destroyed Marion's faith in herself and she had failed to find a replacement. Bazil kept auditioning for the job; but like Marion appeared afraid of the role.

"We all put our faith in something," Isabelle sounded wistful, nostalgic. "For some it's religion, for some it's people." Pru winced. "For us it was the politics."

"Well not me, I won't waste my time anymore. Particularly with people, they aren't worth it."

"Ah, but your memory is short. Like all lucky little American children, you had two parents." Pru saw a malevolent gleam, a little yellow fleck enter Isabelle's eye, a smile quiver the corners of her mouth. "Well, perhaps in your case you didn't have parents you could put your faith in, but what did it matter, you had everything else, books, toys, plenty of food, and you, you had your precious Nanny."

Pru felt her skin burn. Almost cruelly, resentfully, Isabelle added, "But your mother was foolish, your father went away, and your Nanny died."

"How do you know, you had gone by then?"

"Hiding, I was only hiding."

"Along with the silver?" Isabelle looked stricken, Pru hadn't meant to say that, the words just slipped out, she wanted them back. They wouldn't come. She wanted a lot of things back, a lot of things that weren't going to come. In her mind she saw a flash, a flash of red, a flash of gold: *Ora Aureo*, *Jaspeadora*, and *Dorado Rojo*. The endless variety of colors that matched the *ists*, the endless duplicity of people.

"Isabelle, tell me what you do know about him, was he red?"

"What do you mean, child? A Communist?"

"Was he gold—?" Why were they looking at her like that? What had she said? "I mean—"

"You are upset." Tio pulled out the chair next to her. "Isabelle knows nothing. Mostly people disappeared just like your father and you knew nothing. But now and then, one side or the other would post lists, if only to scare the rest of the people. Three neat little columns of whom they had beaten, whom they jailed and whom they shot. The Communists posted them on the church door, the Fascists tacked them up in the town square."

"Your father's name was never there." Isabelle's eyes pleaded for understanding. "I looked, believe me child, I wanted to find it. I never did."

"But the talk in the village, someone must have known whom he supported."

"A lot of people shifted with the wind. It was only if you were shot that people knew for sure which side you were on."

"How, Tio? How?"

"If you were shot by the Fascists you were a Republican. If the republic loaded the gun, you were a Fascist. Of course, mistakes were made, but what did it matter?"

"And what if it was an anarchist?"

"Ah, if the anarchists shot you, you were unlucky."

"Unlucky?"

"Yes, some rival in love, someone who wanted you gone—" Isabel looked up quickly, her finger flew to her lips as if she would silence him. Tio paused. Helen's name hung in the air. Pru choked up, a suspicion growing inside her, a thought as dark as the old cracked leather of the library couch.

"*Herr* Schiller then, he loved Helen back then, even before?"

"Loved? Wanted? Who's to know."

436

"I don't believe you Isabelle. I remember . . . back then, everyone gathered in the kitchen, all the gossip, you would know."

"One does not always want to know what one thinks one wants to know. Your father, he had many interests, many wom—"

"Go on, Isabelle, many what?"

"I only meant that politics was not—"

"No more of your damn riddles." Pru stared at Isabelle, she wouldn't blink, she wouldn't turn away. "I want an answer."

Isabelle cleared her throat. "*Herr* Schiller, he coveted this house. Don Carlos refused to sell. It happens a lot in war. It is so easy to get rid of someone in your way—you just denounce them to the authorities. It is most probable that to make certain he would get the house—"

"Get a man shot! For a house? Who did he get to do it?"

"With Don Carlos it would have been the communists. Don Carlos was a landowner. Landowners didn't last long around here."

"And Helen, what did he do to get Helen?"

"He did what you and your mother did not, he rescued her from the stables."

"And my father—"

"With your father it would not be so easy . . . he was an American. Most probably it had nothing to do with Helen, most probably just a mistake, a simple mistake. Who would be so rash as to *atribuirse el mérito* for such a killing?"

A mistake? Roland P. Whitley, a mistake? No! Isabelle must be wrong. "Is the truth that hard to tell?"

"Stop it, leave her alone. If Isabelle knew, Prudencita, she would tell. She doesn't know, perhaps no one knows. In war the truth becomes whatever those in power say it is."

Damn the two of them, their peasant wisdom. For a long time they sat there. Outside the window, the sky was turning. Pru felt a drop of moisture on her cheek, it ran down, and settled into a little puddle in the corner of her mouth. Tio leaned across the table, wiped it away.

"He is most probably dead. After all this time what does it matter who shot him? No one would do anything about it anyway. And as for whose side he was on, whose side he had helped, maybe he hadn't meant to help any side, maybe he just searched for his own truth. A dangerous thing to do in time of war."

"Maybe you are right, but I can't help it, he betrayed all of us. If he hadn't gone off . . . if it wasn't the war, if there were so many . . . my mother, why would she put up with it?"

Tio had no answer. Isabelle did. "There is a place in the soul of a man, any man, a certain hardness that will keep him forever apart from a woman. It is this separateness that keeps a woman from ever knowing a man, really knowing him. A closed-offness that keeps *ellas* from ever knowing *ellos.*

"It is so with woman too, but there is something in her nature, a softness to her flesh, that makes a woman give this place away if a man asks for it."

"But why, Isabelle, why do women do it?"

"Because in the night, in the emptiness, the uncertainty of the dark—man comes back needing the secret place of the woman. And we women, we live to be needed."

"Not me. I want no part of that, I—"

"Who knows, you might be different." Isabelle glanced from Pru to Tio. "But I think not. You see, *Señora de el listo,* you do not have the smartness you think you have. There is something after all, to this woman's peasant wisdom."

"I'm sorry, Isabelle, that was rude of me."

"De nada."

Tio got up, went around to where Isabelle sat, knelt down beside her and put his arm around her shoulder. She leaned into his chest, and looked at Pru—she couldn't be sure but she thought she saw a little smirk, a little smile of triumph and she remembered something she had seen that first night, the initials carved in the table at the café—she'd sensed it then, just another one of those things she didn't want to know. Pru felt a dull ache form just below her heart. Tio was as unattainable as any of the men she knew.

Pru headed for the door. She turned back but she wouldn't look directly at them, she looked just above the top of their heads, just past them at the back door.

"Tio, I'll need the car in the morning. Early, very early."

THIRTY-NINE

Going Home

"Melancholy and remorse . . . enables us
to sail into the wind of reality"

—CYRIL CONNOLLY, *The Unquiet Grave.*

TIO GAVE A CURT bow and closed the car door. Pru ignored him and turned to take her last look at the *Casa de Castillo*. She would not have him think she noticed, that she caught the significance of his insult, his subtle signal that their relationship had altered. A slight movement to the curtain in the dining room window told her that Isabelle had. Pru imagined her smile, the tinge of triumph at its corners, a look not unlike that of the calico cat stretched out along the whitewashed wall—content, pleased with its place in the sun. She envied the beast its simplicity, no troublesome memories, no painful emotions to contend with. Neither she, Isabelle or Tio—Ruis—possessed that luxury.

The drive to Madrid would be long, with the window separating driver and passenger shut, it left little room to bridge any misunderstanding. Some of the fault lay with him, most with her. Tio had greeted last night's announcement that she would leave with a dismissive nod. Her voice cool and controlled, she had

440

issued a few more commands before she turned to leave. Out of the corner of her eye she saw Tio lean over, take Isabelle's hand, bend toward her and drop a small kiss on her forehead. A wall of coldness slapped against her back as she walked from the room. Isabelle's thoughts chased her through the pantry—the American was going home, back to a place that even wars failed to scar.

So who cared what Isabelle thought? This land wasn't Pru's, its troubles were buried too deep for bandages. The chance of any information, any solace she might have hoped to extract lay smoldering under old sorrows, old slights, old quarrels. Helen and *Herr* Schiller locked in an uneasy truce; Tio and Isabelle with their own pasts to live down; she expected nothing from them and could do nothing for them. As for Isabelle's son— would she always think of him that way? Perhaps at another time she might have admired his cunning. But for now her brother—his telegrams and notes—had caused enough trouble. He would have to wait further for someone to come and take him to America. She would not be her brother's keeper. Could her mother know about Isabelle's son too?

She understood the reasons for the boy's deception. He could not help who his father was, nor could she. His mother needed him. He should stay, take care of her. Pru left him a note, ordering her words carefully, she would let no trace of feeling seep through. She didn't know his name. She didn't want to.

Though the sin wasn't hers, guilt recognized no distinction. She would speak to Bazil. Between the two of them they could set up a fund for the boy, perhaps a scholarship for the University at Madrid.

Now it was time to turn her thoughts homeward. She would carry home neither the promise of widow's weeds, nor sensational grounds for divorce—she had nothing but rumor and innuendo. Neither seemed worth packing.

Besides, Marion seemed to know far more than Pru would ever find out—the whole charade may have been little more than a fishing expedition, a chance at a dynamic ending for the script—a script for which Marion had probably already hired a ghost writer. Pru had wearied of the whole mess.

She felt like opening the window and tossing out her illusions with each mile they traversed. The back of Tio's head, his strong, unbending neck put an end to her foolishness, those hopes kindled that first day when he had walked up, taken the suitcase from her hand. The light in his eye, the compassion in his demeanor reminded her so of her first love. Somewhere inside her she must have hoped he would turn out to be Rubio. She was enough of a realist to not expect it, but maybe she had hoped for a touch of romance, enough to carry her out of herself, to offer her an excuse to stay in Spain out of reach of her mother's cannibalistic neediness for awhile.

She had fooled herself into thinking Tio might want something similar, Ruis—she must think of him as Ruis— had put his arm around Isabelle, showing Pru there was no chance of that. He wanted only a break in his routine, a chance to earn a few more *pesatas*, an excuse to drive to Rodicio and see Isabelle, that's all.

After she packed, she had stretched out on her bed hoping for sleep, for something to ease the hard lump of loneliness. She could almost wish the old crucifix still on the wall for a little company, a little distraction from her dreams.

The night seemed to go on forever. Towards morning her dreams grew sluggish and lazy, but eventually the dawn arrived. She rose, dressed and went downstairs to say her good-byes to Isabelle. She had ordered Tio to bring the car around at eight, which would give her time for one last conversation with Isabelle.

She pushed open the door and found the kitchen empty, the

fire cold, neither Isabelle nor the boy anywhere in sight. Just as well. Anger had Pru wound so tight, she probably would have said things that would hurt both and help neither.

Settled down in the back of the limousine, her feet on her luggage, she watched the car devour countryside that had taken her and her mother days to cross, roadside signposts putting her ever closer to Madrid. Right after they passed the first marker that mentioned Cadiz, she noticed something odd—though the traffic was light, almost non-existent, Tio's eyes focused more on the rearview mirror than on the road. She turned in her seat and saw the car following them, large, black and official looking, little flags flapping from its fenders.

Shouldn't the general have had enough of this game by now? Surely Herr Schiller had no further reason to pay him. Something in her perverse nature made her want to roll down the window, lean out and shout, I'm going. I'm going. Maybe they should turn down the road to Cadiz, just to throw a little scare into Lemona for a change.

Tio's straight, stiff back told her he was angry; but the rear view mirror reflected back something more—he wasn't angry with her, he was angry with himself. She leaned forward and rolled the window down.

"You lied, Tio—Ruis. You could have told me you knew the Schillers had my house. "

"No *Señora*, I didn't lie. At first I didn't know why you came here, and then, well then . . . I don't know. But I didn't lie, I just didn't tell you the whole truth. War teaches you to say as little as possible, you never know when it will come back to haunt you. Besides, I know even less of your father."

She noticed a flatness to his voice, all trace of accents, idioms gone. "And that's my fault? Is it my fault that my father . . . my father foisted himself on Isabelle?"

"No *Señora*, nor is it your fault that I did not know the boy was his son. She never said. I never asked. She was young, the child was hungry and I was running from my fellow country-men. One night in a café in Málaga I was drinking with my nephews, a man—a little, no a lot on the drunken side— asked me to drive him to Rodicio and I found a way to earn some money. It no your fault," the Spaniard in him surfaced again, "that I found Isabelle. I was lonely, she needed help. We worked to bury the past; but somehow by coming here, you dug it all up, made us all think that things might have been different, things we didn't want to know."

"And for that you are angry with me?"

"*Si, Señora*, for that and for being—"

"Being what?"

"It no matter."

"Everything matters, everything or nothing. Kindness mat-ters, people's feelings. Love, matters a lot; but in there some-where, the truth matters. It matters most of all."

"You ask too much, you can't have all that."

"Why not?"

"The truth is all together a different thing. Truth shifts, it changes. There are those who say truth depends on who does the telling, I tell you, *Señora*, it depends more on who does the listening."

"The truth can't shift. A thing is either true or it's not."

"Your Papa, he tell you that?"

"Well, yes."

"He was wrong, *Señora*. Like the earth we stand on, the truth shifts constantly and what a man does with his life is search for it. Like dogs, we all dig at it until we find our own."

"And then?"

"By then it's time to pull the dirt in over us."

The car rolled on, the heat increased, but still she felt a chill. She had no answer, no argument. Maybe she hadn't learned the truth of her father. She had learned some truths about her mother. By the time they approached the turn off to Cadiz, she'd had enough, enough of her parents, enough of Spain. She let the turnoff slip away to the right, taking her past with it. Pru rolled down a window and the fresh air cleared her anger away. She thought about the look on Bazil's face that day as he reached out to her mother—would Henri look like that when she landed? *There, again, that emptiness.*

She looked up. In the rearview mirror, Tio smiled at her.

"Perhaps you no find what you came for because it *no es possible* to find people when you look for them as you think them to be."

"Please, no more riddles."

"You say you look for your *Papa*, the powerful man, the man of the bulls, of the star-filled ceilings, the loving father. Perhaps he never existed. You tried *Señora*. You must not blame yourself."

Tio—Ruis had done it again, stolen into her head, read her thoughts.

"Don't keep chewing that bone. It's not just you, *Señora*, it's all of us. We were all so easily duped."

"That's it isn't it? Duping people—that's what causes all the trouble. Without the flags, the speeches would there be no war? What good is it? When a war is over and the killing done, what has anyone accomplished? One tyrant's backside just warms the newly-vacated chair of the other."

"*Señora*, you are too young to become the cynic, and you are a woman."

"More of your riddles, Tio?" She just couldn't seem to call

him Ruis. Ruis belonged to Isabelle. Tio would always be hers. "I don't understand what being a wo—"

"Isabelle, she like to say that men dream big dreams, dreams that fail, women pick up the pieces and move on."

At the airport the attendant looked at her quizzically as she handed him her one small valise. She nodded. As to the rest of her things, Isabelle could either mail them to her or not. She really didn't care. She wanted only to get away to someplace where the sun did more than burn the sky—where it lit the shadows, exposed the truth. She had left so much behind in this country where everything lay hidden. Including hope— hope was for people who believed all things were possible. Her father lied, her mother lied, she had only her art left to believe in and—it would take too much effort not to be cynical.

She moved over to customs. "The picture, she does not do you the flattery, *Señora*." With a smile that could almost pass for friendly, the starched official handed her back her passport. "*Bueno suerte.*"

She glanced out the window toward the plane. It looked a bit bedraggled as it leaned a little to the left—in this country, not such a good thing to do—and there he was in the shadow of the wing. She hoped Dordo was right about him. Dordo! She had completely forgotten the woman, where had she spent the night? Where was she now? She would write her when she got back, thank her, apologize.

The customs inspector held out her luggage tag. "*Señora?*"

"Sorry." She thanked him but it was his turn to be distracted, he too saw the figure in the shadow.

Tio, having found a place to park the car, followed her out onto the tarmac. This man who had seemed so handsome, so intriguing, now looked old, his shoulders slumped, his hands hung useless at his side. She couldn't help but feel a petty leap of joy, perhaps his dejection just might be at her leaving.

But how could she leave and go back to Marion and peer into those baleful eyes? She would see nothing but reflections of her own failure. She never found her father. She would never find Rubio. Perhaps it was as Isabele had said—she was looking for the wrong people—a noble man and an innocent boy. Who is ever what you thought they were? For that matter, what cause, what fight was ever about what you thought it was?

"I failed, Tio. I—"

"Your Papa should not have left you here, your Mama should not have sent you back. Go home, *mi querida*."

"Home." Damn that word anyway. It meant nothing, yet the showy figure under the wing was there to make sure she did just that. In the harsh light bouncing off the tarmac even Lemona looked a bit wilted.

She turned back to Tio. "Can you, can Isabelle?"

"Do not worry. This stubborn country will heal," he peered at her closely, "perhaps with more of the speed than you. The sons will prosper, they will forget the ghosts of the fathers. Well, maybe not the sons," Pru thought she detected a small smile, "but the grandsons."

The man of many languages, philosophical thoughts, the coal miner, the communist, the believer, Isabelle's lover—the man of contradictions—leaned over, brushed her cheeks with his lips and opened his arms. Her tears soaked into the rough wool of his suit.

"Forget Lemona, Prudencita, his time is passing. Go, but remember to forgive, to forget."

Should she forget Isabelle, her son? Would she ever be ready to accept the word 'brother?' She knew she should be grateful to Tio for caring for the boy. But gratitude was not the emotion she felt. She turned and walked toward the plane, her unwilling feet stumbling a bit over the tarmac.

"But me," he called after her, "don't forget me." She heard it over the whine of the engine, the thump of the propeller. She had heard that, hadn't she? She wanted to turn, to make sure, to tell him she wouldn't, couldn't forget him. She wanted to run back and tell him he was wrong about forgetting the other. There were parts of the past that stick forever, stamped perhaps on that ephemeral thing—the thing whose existence she had come to deny—the soul. She envied Tio his belief, if only she could—but then she heard it again, that voice, the one that had haunted her through this whole trip, Nanny's voice: *if wishes were horses beggars could ride.*

The propellers increased their pitch, the noise ripped apart the quiet of the sky and she didn't turn, didn't tell him. She kept walking, gave a little wave as she passed Lemona. He stepped forward, caught her hand and kissed it. She was so astonished she didn't have time to pull away.

"*Buena Suerte,* Señora Brancusi, my apologies. Your country, mine, it won't be long, we will be friends again, no?"

As usual he didn't wait for her no. He saluted her smartly, then stepped back for her to pass.

She said nothing, suppressing a smile she gave him only a curt nod. Nanny's voice could still be heard over the roar of the propeller—*good riddance to bad rubbish. Go home, Prudence Maria Katarina Abigail Brancusi, nee Whitley. Go home.*

She climbed the short flight of steps to the plane and the last sound of Spain she heard was the click of Lemona's heels. An hour or so later, somewhere out over the Atlantic she came face to face with her own flaws. Too close to her mother's flame to find her footing and sapped with guilt, she had allowed herself to grow too weak to break away. She resolved to end this nonsense. For all her vows, her work, her worry, all she had done was waste a great deal of her energy keeping secrets from a woman who knew them already. She would talk to Brancusi about moving out, getting a home of their own. If she didn't, she would suffocate.

The plane circled low over New York. Pru could see the tidy little back yards, a woman hanging up her wash. No signs of war, just the real everyday things that made up life. She had only a short layover until she would fly out to Los Angeles and her new life. The plane taxied to a stop, she gathered her things and headed for the exit. The stewardess handed Prudence her coat, she started down the stairs, that's when she saw Marion. Her heart gave a little leap, her mother had come all this way to meet her. Odd though, she wasn't waving. She didn't look happy, she should have, Pru saw a few reporters in the background. One man stood quite close to her mother, it wasn't Bazil. Though he didn't wear a uniform something about him made her think of Lemona. The dark glasses, the scowl on his face said government man. As Pru came down the stairs, the man stopped Marion from approaching. Instead he walked up to Pru and slapped something into her hand: a summons to appear before the House Un-American Activities Committee.

"The what committee?" She had no time to ask questions, reporters pushed forward, snapped pictures and yelled out their questions.

By the time they were free to return to California the publicity had turned on Marion. In enough trouble already, Hollywood wanted no part of a politically questionable has-been. Pru lost both the heart and the nerve to leave her mother in the middle of all that. She could always leave when things settled; but one thing led to another and—

BOOK FOUR

CALIFORNIA 1950

FORTY

The Station

"Till the sun grows cold,
And the stars are old,
And the leaves of the Judgment Book unfold."

—TAYLOR *Bedouin Song*

THE NIGHT WAS COLD for June. The fog hung in for most of the day, things never got a chance to warm up, but outside it was clear now. Pru put on her camel's hair coat, the silk lining cooled her skin. Ever since the cablegram, her skin had felt dry, feverish, like a day under too bright a sky, too searing a sun.

She'd dressed with care, more care than usual, kicking her paint-stained jeans and denim shirt to the back of her closet. She sent the hangers scooting back and forth, in an impatient search for the sheath. It was Henri's favorite, a rich black, no collar, no do-dads, just simple classic lines—the way he liked to construct his films.

The sheath slid over her head and settled a little too loosely on her hips. Henri told her he thought she had lost some weight. "I've just been busy lately that's all."

"It's more like you haven't done anything but worry since

455

the cable came."

The day the cable arrived she had asked Bazil if he thought it was the real thing this time or just one more lie in a seemingly endless stream of them.

"That's what you are going to find out," he said.

"But why me, why is it always me? Not Marion."

"She needs you, Pru. She needs you."

Marion wasn't the only one with needs. Pru treasured her relationship with Henri, but somehow after Tio, friendship hadn't seemed enough.

She fastened a small string of pearls around her neck. Her mother bought the dress for her two years ago. Though she hadn't put it quite that way, she hadn't wanted Pru to embarrass her in front of the entire U.S. Senate in some arty get up. Though she had told the senate "the truth" as she knew it, she never confessed to her mother that she actually liked the dress. Apparently the senators were not all that impressed by either her dress or the fact that she knew little or nothing of the activities or beliefs of one Roland P. Whitley.

Bazil gave her the pearls. "You stuck by your mother through that ugly HUAC affair." Not that Pru had that much choice. Someone had to and she always seemed to be that someone. Though none of them had heard from him in sixteen years that tiresome adage—out of sight, out of mind—held no truth for them. Her father hadn't been out of anyone's mind, not for a minute and his presence was all over a house he'd never set foot in.

She needed the confidence boost the dress would give her. She had learned a thing or two from her mother, "Get the clothes right for the role and you can ace the part." But the coat was her own touch, the cut of it, the weight of its cloth formed a shield for her to hide behind. She headed for the stairs.

"That won't do, not at all, Pru. You need this one." Pru

looked over the rail and saw Marion holding up her full length mink, an offering, an apology.

The mink had entered their lives years ago, right after her father's manuscript—done up in plain brown paper, no return address—arrived. Marion tore at the wrapper, surely this would tell what happened to Roland. But the manuscript, an impersonal chronicle gave nothing away. Not even Helen's hand written annotations helped. Marion lost interest. It was Bazil who made the rounds, found a publisher. He presented Marion with the fur to make up for the shameful meagerness of the advance. Apparently the publisher had a better grasp of the market than either of them. The book dropped like a stone into the well of history—tales of corrupt officials, military debacles and the horrors of a civil war in the 1930's couldn't compete with the Holocaust.

Pru had wondered how it was that she was the only one to notice that if her father had written all those folios, he had lived beyond the day the soldier pounded on the door. But the many annotations sprinkled through the manuscript, didn't appear to be her father's style. They read more like the last few folios. True, Marion had only given it a cursory glance and Bazil had too much at stake.

But that was earlier and now the latest telegram had started the daisy game all over again. Was he? Wasn't he? Once more, Marion refused to make the trip even thought this one consisted of only ten miles. Though Marion wouldn't go, she was not about to give up on the coat.

"You'll want to make a good impression," she insisted.

"On who, Mother?"

"Whom, dear, on whom."

"Whom whom…w-h-o-m. Now answer me."

"Reporters—*The Times, The Examiner,* they'll be there. We're still somebody, you know Pru, we count."

"No, Mother, we don't. We haven't for a long time."

Bazil come up behind her mother, his rage betrayed by his in his voice, "Pru, you have no right—"

Everyone's nerves were raw and all because yet another cablegram had made its way across the Atlantic, this time this yellow strip of pasted words read more like fact than fiction. The sender claimed to be the Attaché to the American Ambassador of the recently opened embassy in Spain.

In her mother's house at the foot of the Sierra Madre's Fate, Kismet and Karma were everyday guests; and whenever Pru checked the attic of her mind where the past lay done up in tissue . . . *voilà*, there it was, that touch of Kismet: that certainty that this day would come eventually, if for no other reason than that her mother's life was one long movie and, her movies always had proper endings; sometimes happy. Sometimes not.

And Pru, only a bit player in these scripts, found herself on the way to meet her father's train. The depot lay just ahead. She almost missed her turn.

"Keep your mind on the job at hand. The here, the now is more than enough," Nanny would have said. "After all, Luv, who knows?" It turned out no one had. In one terrible night, Nanny's here and now had come and gone. Pru's *here* was this Lincoln coupe and the ever-present ka-thump of tires; her *now* was whatever fate the cable had proscribed. Nothing eased the thud in her chest, the whir in her ears. Her pulse outraced the car. There it was, her destination: the clock tower on the depot, the windshield framing it with the deceptive prettiness of travel brochures. A quick yank to the wheel and she skidded into the parking lot. Behind her, tires squealed in protest.

"Nice signal, lady!" She turned. A man leaned half out of his car—his face the color of her leather seats. "You lose an arm or something?" She ignored his anger as she was about to retrieve the final piece to the puzzle that was her life. A piece that long ago fell through the cracks, dropped into the chasm created by her mother's weakness as it slammed against her father's strength. *What was that biblical phrase that kept running through her mind? Oh yes, the weak shall inherit the earth.*

Pru slid the coupe between two fender-heavy Cadillacs, the chrome-studded kind her mother hired for public appearances. "One cannot be overlooked stepping out of such a vehicle," was one of those lessons in morals and manners that tumbled effortlessly from Marion's Revlon Red lips, notes from a descending scale that left irritating echoes in their wake. Marion had no answer for Pru's constant query, "How can the studios consider you for ingénue roles if they don't know you're around?" The studios knew full well her mother existed, but Marion failed to acknowledge that such roles eluded her with a cruel consistency.

As Pru got out of the coupe, it came to her that maybe now her mother could marry Bazil. She and Henri could look for a place of their own. She locked the door, a concession to her mother's mink in the back seat—she might have weakened enough to take the coat, that didn't mean she'd wear it. She heard the train before she saw it.

The ground shook, the palm trees that lined the track rattled their fronds, starlings took to the sky. People straggled out to the platform, women with feathers that curled about their hats; men with fedoras, tweeds and broad ties, moved forward expectantly. All but one, the owner of the noisy tires, lounged casually against the adobe front of the station. *Damn, Marion is vindicated— a reporter.* Pru recognized and distrusted the nonchalant disinterest of the breed. Instinctively she closed her eyes the way Bazil taught her that time in Washington. "Don't flinch. Look over their heads," he had said.

A single headlight pierced her reverie, lit up the track and cast the bystanders into silhouettes. Her stomach knotted. She'd drive off, leave her father. *Tit for Tat* Nanny would have said. The thunder of the wheels cut to the bone, the noise pinned her in place. With a screech, a whoosh, the train stopped, a man kicked open the door, lowered the stairs and set out a stool. People pushed past, Pru was in no hurry. The crowd gathered at the door, faces lifted in expectation. She moved on down the line to the far end of the train to the baggage car. Over the click of her heels on the tile apron, over the murmured greetings, she heard the rattle of the luggage cart. She didn't turn. She knew it would be the big one with the iron wheels, the high wooden sides. The doors of the car slid open. Her eyes tried to shut, her head wanted to turn away, her legs told her to run, not to look back; but she willed her body still. She'd be damned if she'd flinch now. Two burly men pushed and shoved the heavy box toward the door. Grunting and swearing under their breath, they slide the coffin onto the cart.

Almost dark, streetlights filled out the forms of trees and on the horizon the first harbinger of night struggled to announce its arrival. *"Star light, star bright, first star I see tonight. I wish I may, I wish I might . . ."*

The cart moved off, an old film unreeled in Pru's mind, stark in its blacks and whites. She'd seen it before: *La Casa de Carrillo, Roland P. Whitley in jodhpurs and boots, camera slung over his shoulder, luggage piled by the door, she runs up the stairs, slams her fist against the wall. She won't cry, she won't. A door shuts. The music swells.* Flash.

Before the flash could cut the gloom, Pru sensed the reporter angling around her. At the entrance to the office the parade halted, she bumped into the cart. Another flash! She turned, pushed the reporter away.

"Surely you've better things to do than photograph a box."

"How's about getting out of my way."

"Me? I'm in your—?"

"Look lady, I got a story to get. My boss says get it, I get it. Know whose coffin, excuse me," he sent a mock bow her direction, "whose *box* this is supposed to be?"

"Supposed? What do you mean, supposed to be? Who else—?"

"Don't you read the papers? The *Daily Mirror* calls him John Doe. My editor ain't buying. He did some digging—say you're not a reporter, are you?"

"No, I'm—"

"Then what do you care? A lothario or a politico, anybody could have shot him. Maybe a communist shot him, maybe a fascist. If you ask me, my vote goes to a jealous husband, if even half of what I've read about him is true"

"Well, I didn't ask you."

"So you didn't. Anyway, most likely it isn't even him, not after all this time. If it wasn't for the wife, who'd care? That's who we're interested in. Sort of hoped she'd be here, claim the body and all. A real beaut, an old film star—bet by this time she hopes it's him . . . sure you're not a reporter?" She shook her head. He leaned in close, studied her. "Hey, didn't I see your photo in screen rags awhile back, a year maybe two? Some sort of hearings? You can't be the old guy's wife, you're not—"

"Not glamorous enough?"

"Old, I was going to say, old enough. She's a has been you're a—

"Says who?" She might criticize her mother. No way she'd let just anybody.

"Hey, that's it, you're his—" Flash!

The stationmaster intervened, "Leave the little lady alone."

With as much flourish as his old body allowed, he bowed and ushered Pru into his office.

"Now don't you bother your pretty head about him, Missy—"

"Mrs., it's *Mrs.*" Pru could do without such gallantries. They were her mother's stock in trade. "Pleasantries may cushion one's way" her mother liked to say; but, for Pru they had a way of concealing poisonous barbs that pinned her down, a butterfly to velvet, a creature robbed of flight, a thing to be looked at, appraised.

The tiny office reeked of cheap cigars and neglect. A clutter of dented file cabinets and torn calendars put Pru on edge. "They're not going to bring *it* in here, are they?"

"Quigley and Sons, they'll see to it, Mrs. Whitley."

"Brancusi, Mrs. Henri Brancusi." Her words floated right past him.

"Your mother, lovely woman, I've seen her movies, all of them." This adulation never ceased to stun Pru. She could hardly sit still through any of her films. Up at the house, Bazil screened them any chance he could.

The stationmaster nodded toward a man tucked into the shadows. "The coroner here, he'll take you, an identification must be made."

"All in good time." The coroner emerged, lips curled in a watery smile, his voice worn from speaking things no one wanted to hear. "I'm sure you're anxious to know if it's . . . of course, who else could it—?" He hesitated, unsure if he'd gone too far.

"But the cable . . ." Pru didn't like the way this was turning out. She felt more superstitious than confident. "For sure" or "of course" were more of those words one shouldn't apply to her father. Better to expect the unexpected, she knew that. Besides, after all these years it shouldn't matter to her who this was. But it did. Her hands itched for the grainy feel of salt, a pinch to toss over her shoulder.

Through the window she saw the coffin. The reporter leaned against it, ashes from his cigarette drifted down onto twisted saints and whip-tailed devils locked in an eternal dance around the placid sheen of wood. Even that quintessential bit of Spain nailed to the lid, that tortured crucifix, received its share of desecration. Pru couldn't help but smile—obviously the reporter never suffered the wrath of a nun, the penance of an angry priest. Her smile faded. The coroner looked at her expectantly. She opened her mouth, "take it away," she shouted. That dark and terrible ebony box could have nothing to do with him, it was too small, too narrow to hold her father. Not *her* father.

The room closed in on her, beads of perspiration broke out across her forehead. She shut her eyes. Opened them. The reporter, the coffin, nothing had moved. The stationmaster pointed to an old swivel chair. "Make yourself to home, Missy." It seemed she hadn't shouted, hadn't screamed, apparently she had said nothing at all.

"The circumstances . . ." The coroner cleared his throat to get her attention, his crooked teeth and pitted skin took her back to the bone-yard outside Rodicio, her horror of the graveyard, of the old caretaker. What does it matter he had told her, that his teeth were stained and cracked, "the dead, they no care."

"Odd, don't you think? A body turning up after all this time," the coroner smirked. "But then it might be fresh—"

Pru blanched.

"I mean recently deceased." She wouldn't acknowledge his questioning look. Her own doubts were enough.

"The room, is it necessary—? I don't have to be in there with . . . it. Do I?" "I'm sorry, little lady, but we don't know yet, do we? We need an identification."

The stationmaster, annoyed with the coroner for stealing the limelight, pushed a clipboard toward Pru. "The police and all, they'll have to be there. Meanwhile, I need these here papers signed. Cartage, you know. A fee for the coffin sitter, that sort of thing. Don't worry, Quigley and Sons will have the body—er, the coffin at the house in time for tomorrow's wake." The old man looked to the coroner, "Right?" He received a curt nod, then turned back to Pru. "If you don't mind my asking, Mrs. Whitley—"

"Brancusi, Mrs. Brancusi."

"Why the coffin now, after all this time?" He shrugged. "Well, never mind. 'Taint rightly my business."

"You're right, 'taint."

A faint smile lit the coroner's face. Her rudeness amused him. "I guess a wake is a wake no matter how late," the smile grew. "Anyway, we'll do our part. The casket will be there, that is if it's—" Pru gave him a withering glance. He ignored her and chattered on, form after form found its way under her pen. She signed on this line, on that, a half-dozen times or more. She made out a check. Her hands shook, she smeared the ink. He frowned. She wrote another. At last, it was over. The coroner offered her a ride.

"In the—?"

"Oh, no Missy," he laughed, "I have use of a city car, a Cadillac."

"Thank you, no." She'd follow.

"As you wish. No rush, he's not going anywhere." The stationmaster frowned at the coroner's little joke and opened the door for her.

"God speed, Miss Whitley."

"Brancusi, Mrs. Brancusi."

At the door of her coupe, she looked up, saw Venus. "How many times must I tell you Prudence, that's not a star? The light of the stars is deceptive," her father had warned, "it comes from things that no longer exist." Maybe the light should have died along with its star. It hadn't. Back then Prudence hadn't yet begun her search for the illusive light in a canvas, but still, for her, it was people who disappeared.

Yet a day, maybe two before he disappeared, he took her face between his hands. His look had frightened her and she struggled free. "That's right, Prudence, run," he had said. "Never look back." At what? The war? Her mother? How was a child to know? But she wasn't a child now, why hadn't she run? Why come to the station at all? As the daughter of a man who detested illusions and a mother who dwelt in them, she had spent her life trapped by the best, the worst of both.

The crowd had gone, the parking lot was empty, she took one final look back and saw the hearse squatting at the freight dock, two men struggled to slide the coffin in between the heavy curtains that leaned in toward each other, like hands poised in prayer. She climbed into her coupe, turned the key and cranked the little motor to lower the top. She felt nauseous. She needed the air, the wind.

She pulled out of the parking lot and a car fell in behind her, headlights like flash bulbs. What more can that reporter want—pictures of the corpse? Would sixteen years dead leave much of a man? Bones? Hair? Enough to ferret out its secrets? Enough to let Bazil marry, to set Pru free.

The fresh air hadn't helped. She should turn back, find a rest room, but then she realized she wasn't sick. She was hungry, maybe not for food, but for something and the coroner's office wouldn't have it, her studio would—a place to think.

The wake wasn't until the next day. Marion, diverted by napkins and menus, wouldn't even miss her and the coroner was right—her father would wait. She turned right instead of left and headed for her studio. The bottle of Chardonnay she had in her little fridge might help build up her courage to look at . . . to make the identification. How formal the word identification made it sound remote, something easier to face than the fact that once again she would look into the face of the dead.

"Get out your notepad," she shouted, "I'll give you something to write about, something to pop your bulbs over." If the reporter decided to follow he'd be chagrined to find himself in front of a grubby studio and not the grand mansion of a Hollywood star.

She pulled up in front of the little bungalow and without a backward glance she went inside. Over at her closet, she pulled out a pair of jeans, ran her fingers back and forth across a dried lump of Cad Red and scraped at a streak of Lemon Yellow clogging the zipper.

Once into the jeans—at the studio she only kept comfortable clothes, ones she could paint in—she drifted over to her canvas and let her work take her over until she felt a pang of hunger and looked at the clock. The day had disappeared, the night with it—eleven, eleven am. She had painted the night through. Would she still have time to make the identification?

She put down her brush and studied her work. Her eye focused on a little blob of carefully knifed-up gold paint. She rather liked the way it glinted in the morning sun. Despite the fact that such a bright spot in corner was against the Rules of the Gallery Gods, it worked. She'd worry about what it meant latter, for now she'd leave it.

So much of her life was lived by others' rules, in her paintings she felt free to ignore them. So many minor irritants, little reminders that her life was not her own, *Call me Marion, mother is so aging"* Big ones to knock you off balance, *While I'm gone take care of your mother.*

Damn it anyway—what does a daughter owe a father? Peace? A final resting place? And this daughter, that father? A spider that spun a web so strong, she had yet to escape—did she owe such a father anything? As for her mother, despite the animus that hung over them more troublesome than a cloud of insects on a summer's night, she knew what she owed; but how much, and for how long? She would play the daisy game once more and then this night should end it.

Pru headed for the door. Through the window she saw the reporter leaning against her car. She went out, intending to send him on his way. Odd. Her car appeared to be leaning too.

"Damn, you think of everything."

"That's what I'm paid to do."

FORTY-ONE

"Fini"

> *"One thing at least is certain, this life flies;*
> *One thing is certain and the rest is lies."*
>
> —EDWARD FITZGERALD *Rubáiyát of Omar Khayyámo*

THE CAR TURNED into the long, steep drive and twisted its way to the top through a line of cypress that guarded the *Casa de Paloma*—yet one more house that failed to become a home.

A gap in the trees exposed the hearse, it looked awkward, out of place as it squatted among the sleek limousines. She hadn't expected it to arrive quite so soon, she wasn't ready to face the consequences of her decision. Making it was hard enough. Owning up to it would be harder.

"Weird," the reporter said. "Spooky."

Pru looked across the front seat at him. "What kind of a reporter are you? The sight of a hearse shouldn't—"

"Not the hearse," he pointed at the cypress, "those. You'd think with the money they must spend on this place they'd keep `em trimmed up better. And for your information, I'm a damn good one."

"Sorry, It's just that I'm—"

"Apology accepted," he gave her a nice slow smile.

"It's been a long time since I really looked at what goes on here—"

"Isn't this your home?

"I live here, there's a difference. But, you're right, things are a bit of a mess."

She studied the dark and twisted shapes, the way they leaned away one from another, as if unwilling to admit to kinship, a fitting epigraph for the house they announced.

"And thanks—for back there at the coroner's. Say, what's your name, anyway?"

"I thought you'd never ask. It's Jim, Jim Crawford and no, no relation to Joan."

It was her turn to smile, but before she had time to put her all into it, the reporter slammed on the brakes, she pitched forward—"What's he doing there?" He gestured toward the policeman checking credentials at the door.

"Don't worry, Jim, I'll get you in. It's Marion's way of making sure no other leading lady shows up to steal her lines. Anyway, drive on round to the back, we'll go in through the kitchen."

It was the bargain she made—if he got her inside the *casa* unnoticed, she would guarantee him a chance for some pictures—as long as they weren't of her. The one he'd taken of her at the station had made the morning paper. He'd showed it to her with pride. Not exactly how she felt about it—her mouth gaping open, her eyes squinched up. "Daughter of famous beauty—" She had read no further. Her mother would be furious.

Even her mother's friends knew her Lincoln, and she hoped that by arriving in the reporter's car, her lateness would escape notice. Besides, the two flat tires on her coupe left her with little choice. As it was she'd done enough to keep Marion in a state of nerves, and now the news of her tardiness would be providing titillating tidbits for the early mourners to munch on while they awaited Marion's grand entrance. Still, Pru needed to get to the back stairs unnoticed. The sight of a daughter attending a father's wake in paint-encrusted jeans would send Marion into one of her dramatic toots. She might even stage one of her faints. Pru didn't think she could stand another scene. She couldn't believe how tired she was. It wasn't just that she had stayed up all night— it was more the feeling that Marion's sorrows and messes were somehow her doing, that it was her responsibility to fix them.

In the kitchen the maids, the cooks paid no attention to the pair, they had enough to do to lay out bowls of iced caviar, trays of watercress sandwiches—their crusts skillfully excised—all the while mounding up platters of plump shrimp and carefully bring-ing into balance pyramids of strange cheeses and grapes. In front of her, rose petals surrounded a huge, grotesque block of ice, its craggy edges and translucent chips defined a chilling image of her father. *Someone's gruesome idea of a substitute for an open coffin?*

She caught the reporter's eye, "Now that *is* weird" they cho-rused. That smile of his, it was the kind that made one feel good all over—nice, natural, not a Hollywood smile. *Another time, another place…who knew?* But for now she hurried him through the pantry and out to the hall before their laughter could draw attention.

As she started up the backstairs, she gave him a little push towards the front of the house. He threw her a look of panic, "You gave me your word. Won't they—?"

"Not this crowd," Pru laughed, glad to see him ill at ease for a change, "they'll welcome you with open arms and turn their best profile, just make sure you have plenty of film left for Marion when the real show begins."

"You act like you hate your Mother."

"I don't hate her. I love—"

"You have a weird way of showing it. She's a star, you should—"

"Et tu Brute?" That the reporter was taken in by Marion's dazzle shouldn't surprise her, nearly everyone was. She'd even succumbed to Marion's charm now and then, besides did any of it matter now? Yet, somehow, Marion's irritating poses, her delicateness, her helplessness, had whittled away most of Pru's sympathy. And lately her own needs kept getting in her way. Ever since she'd left Spain and Tio, she'd found it hard to concentrate on her work. Despite all that, she was getting known. A few good shows, some favorable reviews and she appeared to be on her way. She did, however, find it hard to keep the momentum going after the latest spate of telegrams.

She started up the stairs, stopped and turned around, "Jim?" He looked back at her. Not that she owed him an explanation, she just felt like giving it. "I don't hate my mother; but my mother—Marion … sometimes all this razzle-dazzle wears me out."

"That can happen with families sometimes, I guess," but Pru could tell that something else was bothering him. "I'll see you later, won't I, he asked."

"Well yes, I'll need a ride back to my car—and by the way, those flat tires—?"

"Okay, will do." That smile again, nice.

At the top of the stairs, Pru tiptoed past her mother's room and pushed open the door to her own. Bazil stood at the window.

"Well?" he said. He didn't turn to face her.

The sight of that rigid back waiting for her made her feel as if he already knew she would lie. She stalled. "Bazil, for God's sake, have you seen that thing down in the kitchen—?"

Still he didn't turn. "Where have you been? The police called hours ago, they found your car at your studio—"

"I was a little late, that's all." His back rebuked her. "I got a ride."

471

"With whom?"

"A reporter." Pru watched Bazil flinch. "Don't worry, Marion's counted on one or two slipping through."

"But why was your car at your studio?"

"I'd gone there to think, I got to painting, and you know me. Time just got away."

"And—?"

"And what?"

"The identification. You must have gone there, the hearse—?"

She said nothing. Time slipped by, still she said nothing. The last few hours were still whirling around in her head. And she hadn't decided what she would tell Bazil. Everything? Something? Nothing? Maybe she should start by telling him how cold she'd felt as she made her way down the stairs into that barren room with its ugly green tiles? Should she tell him how her heart sank when she saw the empty coffin. How she wanted to scream at somebody, everybody, *no, not again, this can't be happening again?* But the coroner had steered her towards a gurney in the center of the room. When he jerked back the wrinkled, dirty-gray sheet he said, "Take your time, Missy, take a good look."

"I'm sorry—I thought I could, but I can't." The flecks of dirt, the little balls of dust, she hadn't been prepared for any of that.

"Yes, you can." The reporter placed a steadying arm around her as he rebuked the coroner, "Couldn't you have cleaned it up a bit?"

Would she repeat what the coroner had said? "That costs extra, you know." He'd gone on and on about the papers the Spanish government sent along claiming that work crews found the body when they were widening a road.

Would Bazil ask as she had, "Where? Which road?"

"They didn't rightly say, probably somewhere in the coun-tryside near your old villa."

She had turned to go, but the detective grabbed hold of her, "We've waited long enough lady, let's get on with it."

"You don't have to," the reporter had said. "I can bring you back later ... maybe some breakfast might help?"

"No, I might as well get this over, but thanks."

The voices in her head finally quieted and she knew what she would do. She wouldn't tell Bazil any of that. She'd wait, make him ask, it might be easier to just tell him what he wanted to know.

"Well, is it . . . is it him?"

For just a second her room grew dark, a bird perhaps, a tree branch something blew across the window. In the background she heard the string quartet tuning up; and the loudest the most intrusive noise of all ... the ticking of her bedside clock.

"It's—" The lie caught in her throat.

"Is it—?"

"Yes." The second time, the lie came easier. With a lot of tell-ing she might someday come to believe it herself. Why shouldn't she? She didn't know it was him, but then again she didn't know it wasn't. *It could have been. It should have been.*

It had to be.

Pru walked up to him, put her arms on his shoulders and gently turned him around to face her. "The clothes, his build— I'm sure."

"Pru?"

"What?" What did he want from her now? Hadn't she done enough?

"Are you sure, really sure?"

"I signed the papers."

Her legs buckled. Bazil reached for her, she waved him off. Somewhere along the way she had stopped searching for the truth. She remembered the elation, the feeling of freedom that had come over her back at the *Casa de Carrillo* on the night Helen confessed, the night she learned her mother knew everything. But freedom had turned out to be a hard thing to hang on to, and family a hard thing to let go of. It all slipped away after she landed in New York and got swept up in the maelstrom of the HUAC, the speeches, the senators. And when the press turned against Marion, her mother collapsed. It frightened Pru. A few weeks wouldn't hurt, she'd told herself, just until Marion could get hold of herself. Time enough then to would break away. But anger and loyalty had a way of intertwining. It had held her fast.

"Was that all?" Bazil's voice brought her back.

"Well, one of the detectives asked me if I wanted the bullet."

"Wouldn't they need that for evidence?"

"Evidence of what, he was shot in Spain, they don't care who did it."

Bazil's face betrayed his relief. It was over. "I must go help your mother."

She wanted to tell Bazil that Marion didn't need their help. She was stronger than either one of them. All these years, how could she have been so mistaken? There was nothing weak about her mother. That was just a game, a role she'd taken on. Her mother had faced down soldiers—fascists, communist, who knew how many *ists* she'd stood up to—and never flinched, not once. It was time for Pru to face down her own demons.

Bazil embraced her, dropped a kiss on her forehead. "Now get out of those clothes before your mother sees you. We'll go downstairs and say our good byes to this whole damn mess."

His step had that old spring in it as he started from the room, but before he closed the door, she said, "An odd thing, Bazil—I don't know what to make of it. There was a medallion, a gold one. The coroner found it stuffed in a pocket."

"Should he have gone through his pockets? Shouldn't you be the one—" But Pru didn't answer him, her mind was on her painting, the one on her easel, whether she should tell him about the gold spot, the one she kept putting in all her paintings? No, he wouldn't understand. Henri would—the medallion, the man on the dock, the villagers in the parade, her fears—all those feelings hadn't disappeared. It had taken all those years for them to work their way out of her head, down her arm and into her work. She had one more question.

"Bazil, what do you know about who he fought for, died for or if he died for anything at all?"

But the door had closed. The sound of someone's laughter startled her. It was her own. She may not have known all the symbols, not even all the *ists*— the Loyalists, Royalists, Communists and anarchists and one more *ist*, the adulter*ist*. This last one had had caused her more trouble than all the others. She thought to protect her mother. She kept what she knew, or thought she knew, to herself. And all along it hadn't mattered.

Her mother was her mother; her father was her father. The truth was the truth. For all that it was time for Prudence Maria Katarina Abigail Brancusi, nee Whitley, to become herself. She walked across the room, dropped the medallion into the wastebasket.

She went to the window, a wind had come up. A few clouds heavy with humidity moved in from the southwest, presaging one of those summer storms Mexico sent to the Sierra Madres, those little nudges to Californians, those little reminders of their origins. Had she paid no attention to her current surroundings?

Had she let herself become stuck in the Spanish countryside? Now these colors all seemed new to her, fresh— the black-green of the trees pressing against the silvery-grey of the sky, colors she hadn't used in years. Surely she could do something exciting with these colors.

Pru looked down on the long line of cars, the chauffer-driven limos elbowing their passengers nearer the door. Others having given up trying to get through the crush, had pulled over and parked halfway up the driveway. The women in crepe and floppy hats struggled up the hill, one hand to their heads, the other desperate to untangle skirts that clung to their legs. Two men moved in the opposite direction, one turned, looked up at the house and saw Pru at the window. He blew a kiss and mouthed the word "later." He made a glass raising motion with his hand. Pru smiled, waved back. Henri was leaving. The man with him, she knew him too, she even liked him. But Henri was special, very special to her. No matter who she found to love, she would never have another friend as loyal as Henri. But it was time she started looking

This was Marion's show. The two of them had come, offered their condolences and were leaving the field to Marion.

Pru changed her clothes; a sheath again, this time a red one. Henri had bought it for her, to cheer her up the time Betsy Palmer turned her down for a one woman show.

"She'll soon realize her mistake," Henri had said, "and you can wear it to your opening, I don't doubt you'll get it yet." *And wasn't this just like an opening, a beginning?*

At the top of the stairs she peered over the balcony at the hall below crowded with people. The quartet played quietly, the doors to the living room stood open and there, at the far end of the room, as far from reality and the casket as she could get, a dry-eyed Marion held court—chin at just enough tilt to leave the neckline smooth, youthful. Her elegant hands carved sentences out of the air.

How pleased Marion was with herself, the role she had created. Hollywood had no idea what a good actress Marion really was. They'd soon find out and it probably wouldn't take them as long as it took Pru. Marion didn't need her, never did, all along Pru was the one who needed to be needed.

The guests milled about as unsure of their role as she had been of hers. The uncertainty and dry throats of the mourners, the extras in Marion's little scenario, inclined them toward the left and the bar. Their training, their sense of theater inched them over to the right toward her mother, the receiving line and the pop of flash bulbs. The only things missing were the dollies, the overhead cameras, the klieg lights.

If she could materialize as a mouse and make her way down that line she would hear stories— her father as the hero, her father as the goat. The dastardly villain, the misunderstood, the persecuted. The stories would all be true, they would all be false. She can accept it now. He was not a hero, not a goat. He was only a man, maybe a dead one, maybe not. What mattered was that she had known the good of him, known the bad—she had loved him, she had loved him not, she loved him. Perhaps there never were any winners at the Daisy Game.

She made her way downstairs through the crowd, ignoring the startled looks her red dress produced. She even ignored the proffered hands, the whispered condolences. What do they have to do with her, who she was now? She fixed her gaze on the front door.

She would take nothing with her, what she needed wasn't here, never had been. She had lost nothing, found everything. As she passed the tables piled high with hors d'oeuvres, she soaked up the aromas—the oregano, the sausage, the garlic— and remembered the women of Rodicio, the sights and smells of the village and she knew what mattered, what really mattered.

. . .as one more old movie unreels in her mind—the widow stands by an open grave. It's raining, it's a Hollywood film after all. Only the widow's umbrella weeps as the minister's voice moans like the wind, "in life there is death." He is wrong.

She'll go back to her studio, and get on with her work. Later when Henri comes by, she'll introduce him to the reporter. He'll have a good bottle of wine with him, something with a pricey French label, she'll put out the glasses and they'll talk. She'll ask him about the director, the way he had the minister play the scene.

"Doesn't he know he's got it all wrong?" She'll say.

"How's that?" Henri will ask.

"It's not that there is death in the midst of life, it's that in the midst of life there is oregano, sausage, and garlic." And that, she'll tell him, that's what really counts.

NOTES

NOTES